Emyr Humphreys was born at Trelawnyd in Flintshire, and attended the University of Wales, Aberystwyth, before registering as a conscientious objector at the outbreak of the Second World War. After the war he worked as a teacher, a drama lecturer at Bangor, and as a BBC producer. During his long bilingual writing career, he has published over twenty novels, which include such classics as *A Toy Epic* (1958), *Outside the House of Baal* (1965), and *The Land of the Living*, an epic sequence of seven novels charting the political and cultural history of twentieth-century Wales: *Flesh and Blood*; *The Best of Friends*; *Salt of the Earth*; *An Absolute Hero*; *Open Secrets*; *National Winner*, and *Bonds of Attachment*. He has also written plays for stage and television, short stories, *The Taliesin Tradition* (a cultural history of Wales), and published his *Collected Poems* in 1999. Among many honours, he has been awarded The Somerset Maugham Prize, The Hawthornden Prize, and the Welsh Book of the Year Award.

A MAN'S ESTATE

EMYR HUMPHREYS

Parthian
The Old Surgery
Napier Street
Cardigan
SA43 1ED
www.parthianbooks.co.uk

The Library of Wales is a Welsh Assembly Government initiative which highlights and celebrates Wales' literary heritage in the English language.

Published with the financial support of the Welsh Books Council.

The Library of Wales publishing project is based at Trinity College, Carmarthen, SA31 3EP.
www.libraryofwales.org

Series Editor: Dai Smith

First published in 1955

Library of Wales edition published 2006

ISBN 1-902638-86-7
978-1-902638-86-7

Cover design by Lucy Llewellyn
Cover image *Cholera Cemetery* by Brian Gaylor
Printed and bound by Gwasg Gomer, Llandysul, Wales
Typeset by Lucy Llewellyn

British Library Cataloguing in Publication Data

A cataloguing record for this book is available from the British Library.

LIBRARY OF WALES

FOREWORD

I first encountered the full riches of Emyr Humphreys' fiction in the boot of a car. It happened in the car park of the arts centre in Ferryside, after a conference in the early eighties at which Emyr had topped the bill and I had been a supporting performer. We immediately struck up a friendship, and as we made our cordial goodbyes he took me out to his car. I was lucky: in the boot were some of his books. He generously presented them to me, including a copy of *Outside the House of Baal,* the definitive epic of twentieth-century Wales.

But it wasn't the first time I'd seen a novel of his. When I was in my early teens, my parents bought me a copy of *A Toy Epic*, the short semi-autobiographical work that, originating as a BBC radio drama, had won for Emyr in the late 1950s the Hawthornden Prize, then one of the United Kingdom's most prestigious awards for fiction. All that had lingered in adult memory was a feverish adolescent interest in the maladroit sexual fumblings of Albie and Frida. The Ferryside experience was altogether different, more like a cultural conversion, as the car boot indeed provided booty – it was a veritable Aladdin's cave, packed with treasure. In these remarkable books I found 'my' Wales – bilingual, bi-cultural, multi-regional, and self-maimed by being culturally self-repressed.

At my Welsh university, in the early sixties, English-language literature from Wales was taboo, a subject as embarrassing in educated company as sex, best kept hidden so as not to reveal to the sophisticated English the supposed poverty of Welsh culture.

How appropriate, then, that *A Man's Estate*, published a bare decade earlier, when Emyr Humphreys was in his mid-thirties, should be a darkly atmospheric Welsh family saga about the shameful secret of origin – the gargoyle root of national, as well as personal, identity. The sinister shades of Gothic fiction seem to haunt parts of the narrative, as does the style of ancient classical tragedy (and with the same mythopoeic resonances). This is a novel that isn't deceived by the obsessive surface respectability of a residual and stagnant Nonconformist society but insists, in the name of subterranean truth, on entering the grim catacombs of cultural, emotional and sexual repression. The result is a fiction which is part ghost story, part murder mystery, and part quest for redemption – with a quizzical look at Wales' ancient habit of looking to England for salvation. As Hannah, one of the main characters, says, the many voices of the multi-layered narrative lead us 'back through the labyrinthine wood of incidents behind whose apparently solid trunks sinister outlines seem to move in the dark'.

Silhouetted against the broodingly omnipresent past, the ordinary sensuous details of the present seem repeatedly to stand out in stark relief:

> A young lad sat on the red frame of a roller drawn by a large black horse... The roller drew the surface of flattened brown earth after it like a smooth carpet... There were many peewits about. Their plumes trembled as they stepped daintily on the crushed earth. We crossed a narrow lane and passed through a rusty wicket into a field of young hay where the sunlight gleamed metallically on the surface of the clean untrodden grass.

Sunlight is a rare presence in this sombre, compelling novel, and its occasional visitations seem at best rather bleak and wintry. The text is dense with the compression of feelings. To open the novel is to step into a sauna of overheated sensibilities.

Why, then, is *A Man's Estate* so unremittingly intense? It is, in a way, a novel about 'the last things', to adopt the millenarian religious terminology of the Welsh Nonconformist tradition which lies at the work's dark heart. A way of life is ending, in an agonising implosion of values and relationships, and what is to succeed it is altogether unclear. In this respect, it is very much a novel about the Wales of the immediate post-war period, a Wales already (if unknowingly) headed into post-industrial dereliction, and a Wales still (and knowingly) experiencing the final stages of the long death of the Welsh-speaking rural society that had, for more than a century, sustained a most remarkable Nonconformist 'civilization'. Although he himself had actually bucked the trend by unfashionably 'converting' from the Church in Wales to the Welsh Independents (Annibynwyr), Emyr Humphreys still brooded in this work of 1955 on whether anything could be saved from what had become a doomed and deformed religious tradition.

A novel about Wales, and about the Wales of a particular and by now peculiarly distant period *A Man's Estate* undeniably is. So does that somehow make it merely 'local' in its appeal – a 'provincial' novel? I do not think so. 'Soak the smallest thought in time,' notes Hannah, 'and it soon swells to the size of a world. Therefore when you set out to explore the smallest thought you need to be prepared for the longest journey.'

It did not surprise me to learn that the novel was conceived, and partly executed, some distance from the Wales that is its subject. It was begun when, thanks to winning the Somerset Maugham Award, Emyr Humphreys was briefly resident in Austria: obliquely mirrored in its concerns there may be the historical exorcist's question of how post-war Europe was to lay the ghosts of its guilty past. In *A Man's Estate* these concerns are localised: Emyr Humphreys' Wales, like William Faulkner's American South, becomes a society oppressively burdened by the uneasy phantoms of its past.

There may well have been a strong personal animus behind this interest in socio-cultural transition, because the period of writing *A Man's Estate* was a watershed period in Humphreys' own life. Although his debut novel in 1946 was about the Wales of the 1930s, his next three works of fiction were London-centred, reflecting his own period of residence in Chelsea, during which he established a substantial reputation as one of the most promising young talents on the British fiction scene. With his growing family, he returned to Wales permanently in 1951, and *A Man's Estate* was therefore the product of a life choice that also involved a radical reorientation of his whole career. With his departure from London he effectively turned his back on the international reputation he was beginning to build and committed himself to the unfashionable, and frequently unrewarding, service of his native culture. While the large body of work that he has produced over the last fifty years, including some twenty works of fiction, has secured his reputation as the greatest novelist of twentieth-century Wales, he has been steadily overlooked by English critics. In other words, he has himself fallen victim to a kind of cultural repression.

Among the exceptional novels Emyr Humphreys has written, *A Man's Estate* is currently much the least well known, in part because, although it was originally reprinted five times (and with a Welsh-language translation in 1980), it has not been available for almost twenty years. Its appearance as a volume in The Library of Wales is therefore a historic event. A notable added feature of this edition is its final paragraph, based not on the original English version but on the Welsh-language script Emyr Humphreys prepared for the televised version of the story in 1992. It is the author's present opinion that this provides the novel with 'a more "rounded" conclusion'.

In stating his credo as a writer, Emyr Humphreys uncompromisingly asserted: 'the main function of the novelist remains to celebrate and by one means or another to perpetuate the language of the tribe.' But he also noted that 'just as a poet today needs a mother to resent and recoil against, the... novelist needs a society to embrace with love and criticism'. It is the very essence of *A Man's Estate* that it does indeed celebrate its Wales by embracing it with at least as much criticism as love. That is surely the secret of its enduring power to arrest and to disturb.

M. Wynn Thomas

A MAN'S ESTATE

'Plant ydym eto dan ein hoed
Yn disgwyl am ystad...'

'We are all still children waiting
for an inheritance...'

Dafydd Jones o Gaio

ELIS FAMILY

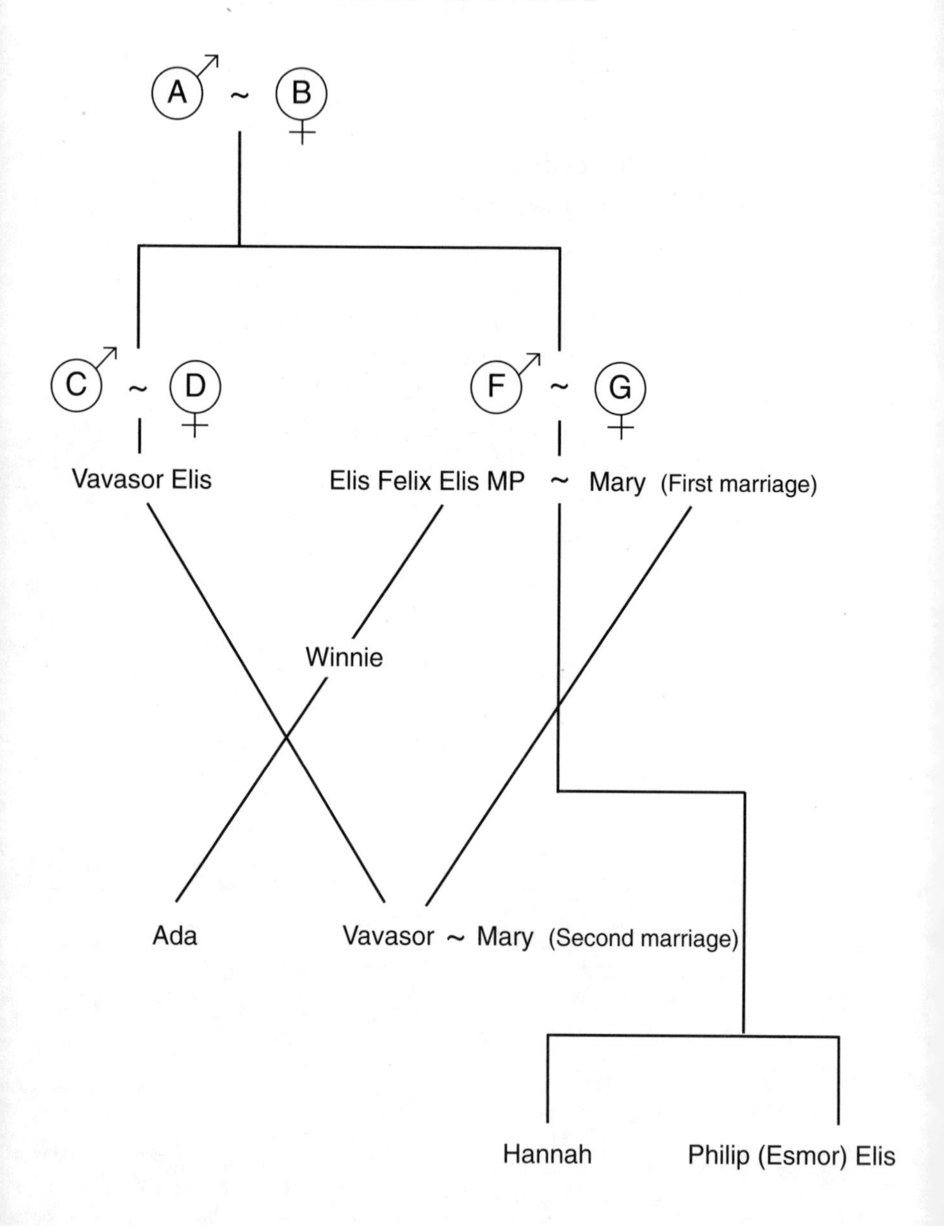
A
B
C
D
F
G
Vavasor Elis
Elis Felix Elis MP ~ Mary (First marriage)
Winnie
Ada
Vavasor ~ Mary (Second marriage)
Hannah
Philip (Esmor) Elis

PHILIP ESMOR-ELIS

CHAPTER ONE

I

'My dear Philip,' he said, 'you mustn't get bitter,' he said. He was all right. These were his rooms, oak-panelling, books, sherry and all the time in the world.

'Bitter,' I said. 'You'd be bitter if you were me.'

'Let's get the thing straight,' he said. Ten years older than I he sounded and the bow-tie underlining his little face. Smug strokes under a signature. Gondola under a balloon. I didn't want his advice I wanted his support. But he was more ready to give advice. What's wrong with me to have this kind of friend? 'What does your aunt say?' he said.

'I'll tell you what she said: "*Dear Philip, I'm sorry to hear you've been passed over. But you're young enough, dear, aren't you still? Perhaps you should have stuck at the D.C.P. as I said at the time, instead of rushing into research. As for the three hundred, I wish I could help you. But as you know the cost of your education has sadly depleted my narrow purse, and for the time being I'm afraid I can't help you any more. Now you have chosen your path there is a sense in which you have to fight alone. Your father was a solitary fighter and I can only commend his courage to you, Philip, as I have done so often in the past.*

I must confess I see Sir Christopher's objections to your marrying Margaret now, very clearly. You still have to work your way up and prove your worth, in a sense. You say you are getting too old. Thirty is the greenest youth in all the more serious professions, dear boy! You and Margaret must just be patient a little while longer, unless you feel inclined to go and claim your Welsh inheritance as we call it. (But among that litigious and prevaricating race that would hardly be a short cut!)

I believe you have it in you to reach the top, Philip, but you must realise it's a long struggle, with many setbacks. But it's at the top your dear father would want you to be and his spirit shows you the way.

Ever your affectionate aunt,

Gwendoline Esmor."'

'You see what I've got to put up with,' I said. 'The old bitch. She never wanted me to do protozoology. Never wanted me to touch science really.'

'What did she want you to do?' John said, smiling as if everything to do with me was absurd and funny. I wish to God he'd take me as seriously as he takes himself.

'Politics,' I said. 'That muck. Just because my father was an MP.'

'But you stuck out for pathology,' John said. 'Good for you, Philip!'

'Yes. But where's it getting me,' I said. 'Bloody Swades has got that Fellowship. Where do I go from here? Switzerland, you say. Take it, you say. All right, three years in Switzerland. Three years in Greenland. I don't give a damn where. But I want Margaret with me. I don't give a damn what her old man says.'

John lit his pipe and began to look wise above his bow-tie.

'I agree, old man,' he said, waving the match dead as if it were a magic wand. 'I entirely agree. But there are obstacles and we may as well face them. One, shortage of cash. (Wish I could help you there) and Two, The Master.'

'The old Bastard himself,' I said and John looked pained. I was doing my best to be uncultured. And why did he say 'we'? Did he think he was coming? He was too damned fond of tacking himself on to Margaret and me. Talking about her poems. Which he was going to print and which he wasn't going to print. Happened rather too often. And of course he could always justify himself by paying. God! Why haven't I got more money?

II

Margaret's poetry. I like her typewriter better. I like to sit beside her as she types on that neat little portable. I like her hesitations as her fine fingers poise over the keys.

'Do you like that, Philip?' she says. Big eyes gazing at me, loving me I hope asking for approval.

'I'm no judge, darling,' I said. 'I just love you that's all.' I put my arm around her neat waist. Think of bright remark about her being a beautifully designed job and pressing my hand down her thigh, but decide not to. That sort of humour doesn't appeal to her. Trouble with me is I don't understand women.

'You must learn, Philip,' she said, 'discrimination.'

'Discrimination,' I said. 'Nobody can say I haven't got discrimination!'

'Read it,' she said, 'and stop trying to kiss me. Daddy might come in.'

I think that Time the Chancellor of Death
Will worry and wear out the thunder in this Love....

'Unscientific,' I said. 'How can you wear out thunder?'

She got up from the desk.

'You're doing it now, Philip,' she said.

'Don't be cross, darling,' I said. 'I told you that I don't understand this stuff. I like it because it's a part of you, because I love you.'

'Your hands are so cold,' she said. 'Put your hand on my forehead. Hot isn't it?'

'No hotter than it should be, darling,' I said. 'Let's have a look at your throat. Stand here. Under the light. Say "ah".'

'Ah,' she said.

'Hum. Slight infection,' I said. 'I'll write you a prescription!'

She put her head on my chest.

'Your pulse is too slow,' she said. She put her arms around my waist.

'Hard old chest,' she said. 'Scientific. Very scientific.'

III

'I could be happy in the lab,' I wanted to tell Margaret only I'd told her before. I keep on apprehending the same things as if they took on a new meaning by each repetition. That means an idée fixe. God! I could be happy in the lab except for those damn careerists. So busy wanting to get on haven't got time to learn their job.

'What's that?' Swades stuck his nose over my shoulder.

'You can't do it that way,' Swades said, challengingly.

'Can't I?' I said. 'Just think, Swades...' And then I told him. How many times have I told the lazy incompetent swine. He's picked my brains for two years, and crept up the Prof's sleeve simultaneously. And beaten me to it, damn his eyes.

The Prof's just as bad. Worse, the old swine.

'Very nice work, Esmor,' he said. 'Very nice indeed. Been thinking along those lines myself. Suppose we prepare a paper for the B.M.J. Sign it together. What do you think?'

And his name first if you please. Professor A. J. de Veina Grooves, P. E. Elis. My name there as small as a punctuation mark.

'Very nice bit of apparatus you've got there, Esmor,' he said. 'Simple and effective. What's this for?'

I told him. Damn fool should have known.

'Of course. I see. I see,' he said. 'Thing has commercial possibilities, you know. Like me to mention it to Files at B.H.?'

I thanked him. God how naïve I am.

'Um. Yes. Definite possibilities. Bit rough here and there. Perhaps we could go over it together one evening, eh Esmor? Behind locked doors eh?' Sniggering old fool. 'Beware of plagiarists, eh Esmor?'

'You don't think...' Swades said, off on his old tack.

'No I don't,' I said. I'd been waiting for this. 'From now on I don't think for anybody except myself.'

'All right! All right!' Swades backed away as if he expected me to hit him. I don't always remember how easily my anger shows on my face. 'If that's your attitude...!'

'That is my attitude,' I said. My pulse accelerated like a thermometer in hot water.

The old man pounced out of his room like a moulting tiger, his grey tufts ruffled and his face red in patches. Pressure but no chance of his dropping dead.

'Esmor,' he said, all professorly inch of him, Professor A. J. de Veina Grooves, a dash of noble blood. 'Esmor. You've been running down my work to the laboratory assistants! Isn't that so? Don't deny it. I've got corroborative evidence.'

'Depends, sir,' I said, 'What you mean by running down.'

'I can take legitimate criticism with the best,' he said, looking over his glasses, pointing a finger myopically at my left shoulder. 'But there...! After all I've done for you! You are proving what I have no alternative but to call a difficult colleague.'

'Is that why I didn't get the fellowship?' I said. 'And I thought it was because Swades knew so much more than I.'

'You've got to get rid of this arrogant attitude, Esmor,' he said. 'It's not doing you any good. You'll get a bad name. Bad name in the profession. There's no worse threat than that you know.'

'I know,' I said.

IV

I want to get on with people. Is it a secret I haven't got or am I making too much fuss about it, which is what Margaret says, or suggests. The world isn't a rational place. I know how tissues behave, alive or dead. I know all about the live things that are dead. I know where I am in the lab. I love my science. I'm good at it; very good. Why can't I get on with it in peace? I don't ask much. But as sure as I ask I get it slapped down my gullet and the door bangs in my face. The world is full of rogues and bitches and sluts. I can classify the damn lot but that doesn't seem to help. People don't like being classified.

'But this cold,' Aunt Gwen said. 'Can't you do anything about it? I've got to get up for Speech Day. Can't you help?'

'I was a house physician, Auntie,' I said, 'not a magician.'

'I have absolutely no faith in doctors,' she said, blowing her nose into another paper handkerchief. 'They haven't even conquered the common cold.'

Even in bed she was neat as a public figure should be. Used to being looked at, without necessarily being admired.

Writing letters of course. A great deal of correspondence to get through. No joke managing a large girls' secondary school. Fighting for it. Building a reputation for it. Reaching out towards an OBE. Ah Dame Gwendoline she addresses herself in her dreams which come in strips out of the Times Educational Supplement. A great deal of correspondence to get through in that dreaded squat hand.

Dear Philip, Mr. Hislop tells me that your French and Arithmetic, Dear Mr. Hislop, Philip tells me, Dear Philip, I shall be coming to see you next week. I think it is better if you moved to another school, Dear Mr. Gunstone, as I explained in the course of our last conversation, Dear Philip, yes I am glad you are in the cricket team. You mustn't misunderstand me. But I'm sure you will agree that it isn't satisfactory to be tenth in one's form, is it now? Dear Mrs. Gunstone, I'm sorry I was unable to get away and visit Philip when he was down with ... but school affairs here kept me tied to my post as it were, Dear Philip, I am so glad you are better, I hope you took the opportunity to put in some solid reading, as I've told you many times, reading is the basis of any kind of education, Dear Mr. Wolfranworth, I am very disappointed with Philip's report and I would be obliged, Dear Philip, you really must work harder. That School Certificate is a hurdle that must be jumped. Now what about giving up one of those teams you belong to? All play and no work makes Jack an even duller boy you know. I must tell you frankly, because you are old enough to understand now. I am rather worried about the financial side of your education. Dear Mr. Wolfranworth, I would suggest that you draw Philip's attention rather more frequently to his father's distinguished career, cut off, alas, in its first flowering I regard it as my sacred duty... Dear Philip, I am surprised that you have chosen medicine as your career. It is a noble profession, but as I have explained to you more than once the law is the best foundation for a political career and quite frankly, it was a political career I wanted for you. I, who knew your father better than anyone else, I know that would have been his dearest wish. But in the last resort, the choice is yours. And I must abide by it. I shall of course do everything to help you... Dear Philip, I am overjoyed by your success. Mrs. Herman asks me to send you her warmest. Now we really must have a confab about the future. I've been thinking a lot about it and I've all sorts of plans as the architects say I want to submit for your approval...

'Philip,' she said, 'ask Miss Lewis to come up, will you? Will you be in to supper?'

'I don't know,' I said. 'Stay in bed, Auntie,' I said. 'It's the only cure.'

'Try and let her know,' she said. 'Things are difficult enough to arrange as it is.'

How could I sit still in my so-called study. Wishing I hadn't come home. Wouldn't have come but for shortage of cash. This damned room. My father's enlarged photograph over the mantelpiece. How can a man relax in a shrine? Father's own basket chair, his Welsh water colours, enough to keep you out of the place for life, wax polish over everything, so tidy you couldn't sit down. Under father's roll top desk a tin trunk of father's papers which I was expected to take an interest in. Three line whips for God knows what musty debate and letters of long dead once famous always pompous politicians. Unreadable notes for a projected work on Welsh education, all wind and water. When I hear the word Welsh I feel uncomfortable. God knows what complexes I've got through having my late lamented illustrious pa, Elis Felix Elis, MP, thrust down my throat in my raw unprotected childhood and youth. It's scandalous the way I was brought up.

All my life I've been trying to forget what she wants me most to remember.

V

'Box Hill, Philip. Would you like Box Hill? It's such a wonderful day!'

Oh those interminable school holidays and Auntie driving the Austin Ten with dangerous gaiety down the Kingston by-pass.

'Glorious day, oh glorious day,' she sang, as the wind trickled through her neatly permed faded blonde. 'Tea on Box Hill, Philip. We'll have fun. Let's take a walk, Philip, shall we, down this lovely lane. I've got a story to tell you...'

'Once upon a time and he was tall and handsome, but he had a dark wicked wife. She was a witch. She made him unhappy, so jealous she was. So horrid, so nasty. So narrow. So West North Welsh. And there was an Auntie Fairy who loved tall great and handsome and did comfort him.'

'I loved him, Philip. I want you to understand that. He

was my cousin but I loved him more than a brother. A love that passeth even the love of woman. I know you're young and many people wouldn't approve my telling you. But I wanted you to understand. Do you understand, darling?'

'Who was my mother, Auntie?' I asked.

'It's natural for you to ask that. I'm your mother, Philip darling. I should have been your mother. I *am* your mother.'

'Why do I call you Auntie?' I said.

'Too difficult for you to understand. Let's go back for tea shall we. You mustn't worry about these things. Promise me you won't worry.'

No recollection of losing a moment's sleep over the whole damned business.

'And the wicked Welsh witch found a wicked Welsh man whom she loved. And together they plotted to do away with the tall great and handsome. But the fairy auntie the tears streaming down her fair cheeks flew on her magic wand into the darkness of Wales and snatched out of the wicked witches' clutches the tall great and handsome's baby, which lay in the cradle above the beloved's grave...'

Fairy tales of a neurotic spinster. Was interested in it once. Neuroses were interesting. But inconclusive. I want things conclusive, clear-cut, satisfying. To reason, and to reach a conclusion. To ponder, work out, worry and arrive at a concrete reward. We don't know much about the destiny of man, old Rockingham used to say, but we can find out all we want to know about his blood if we live long enough. Haematology. When I first heard the word my nostrils must have dilated like a hound's on the scent.

'I wish you showed more interest in your father's

career,' she said. 'He would have been in the Cabinet had he been alive today.'

'That is the difference,' I said; only to myself – 'between being a live politician and a dead one. A different kind of box.'

CHAPTER TWO

I

'The Dower,' John said. 'That means the widow's third of income from landed property.'

'That's a euphemism,' I said.

'What d'you mean?'

'Calling that miserable little farm Welsh landed property.'

'How do you know it's miserable and little?' John said. Wonderful the way he manages to be donnish and legal at the same time. A distinguished career splitting hairs. 'I'm only interested in impractical law,' he says with a smirk at sherry parties. A valuable fellow of the college, verdict of Croutts, our mathematical bursar. Very good on old law. On next month's agenda there's the question of installing indoor lavatories in Rumpleton Rectory. Now the deeds say...

'That's the impression aunt always gave me,' I said. 'Satisfy my childish curiosity in the way she wanted, I suppose.'

'Farms are valuable nowadays,' John said. 'Even small farms. Even small Welsh farms. And you've nothing to show how big or how small the place is. You've never seen it and you have only the vaguest idea of its geographical situation.'

'Is it worth five hundred?' I said, jokingly.

'Could be worth a great deal more,' John said. 'This interests me, Philip. Interesting points in the law of inheritance. It was changed, you see, in 1926. But you come under the old law. Under that law, if you are the eldest son as it appears you must be, that property is yours.'

'How do I prove who I am?' I said.

'There are times when we all have difficulty in doing that,' he said pompously. 'But the law has its own rules. It wouldn't be difficult to prove.'

'Even without a birth certificate?' I said.

'Plenty of ways of doing it, apart from the fact that your aunt says you closely resemble your father.'

'Oh God,' I said. 'Has she been telling you that?'

John laughed in a way that annoyed me.

'Why don't you go and spy out the land,' John said. 'Incognito and all that. You might find it flowing with milk and honey. It might mean a couple of thousand at least and the solution to all your troubles.'

'It would be such a bore,' I said. 'I'm fed up to the back teeth with everything to do with my father.'

'What about your mother?' John said. 'She may still be alive.'

'Let sleeping bitches lie,' I said.

He found that very funny.

'You said there was an older sister.'

'I seem to remember my aunt saying that, years ago. When I was curious and interested.'

'That wouldn't alter the inheritance,' John said. 'It's worth investigating, you know. Stranger things have happened.'

'There are two places on this earth,' I said, 'I haven't the slightest desire to visit. Wales and Assam.'

'Why Assam?' he said.

'Missionary College my aunt is interested in,' I said.

I don't know why I should always behave like this with John: it's as if he expected it of me and I was constrained to oblige. Or perhaps glad to conceal my inward seriousness with a friend whom I would not really like to trust with the sacred things of my heart.

II

'My dear Philip,' he said, 'shall we go? The Master won't like it if we're late.'

'Bah!' I said.

'Come, come,' he said, picking up his mortar-board. 'Finish your sherry. We must humour our father-in-law-to-be, mustn't we?'

'You can keep him,' I said, swallowing my sherry.

We marched down the gravel path, across the inner quad and up the chimney-black staircase, side by side and friendly. John walks stiffly erect always conscious of his shortage of inches alongside me.

'Come in, both of you,' the Master said in a good

humour, turning from the tray over which he was measuring out drinks. 'Out of the filthy night. Know everybody, I think? What'll you drink?'

I only wondered if it was possible for him to dislike me more than I disliked him. How is one to behave like a gentleman when one is cheated out of rightful dues? The old fake ambling heavily about the room with drinks, his stick on his arm. Then, sitting down again, the lion's head still on the lion's shoulders. Scribbled a series on popular etymology. Even writes in the Sunday newspapers. All sorts of tosh about back to the land. An imposing fake. And he gets a title for it.

And John was at it. Margaret had come in, and John had switched on his machine, in top gear. Wonderful gift of the gab. Everybody listening. Even the Master. Especially Margaret. Wish she'd come nearer. Everybody knew about us. What was the use of pretending? Pretence. Fakers and frauds were the swine who got on in a world of pretence. John Neade was a bit of a faker really. All this so-called brilliant conversation; just froth. Margaret said so too. She said put it on paper she said and it's nothing and worse than nothing. But she was listening now. Same as everybody else.

Even Margaret's mother was listening. Neurotic hen sat on the window-seat with the Bursar's wife. Couldn't blame the poor bitch being neurotic: married to this alcoholic megalomaniac. Always had to keep her distance from the swine or he'd be rude to her in public. And now he was trying to keep his hold on his daughter. Wouldn't let her go. Ought to be psycho-analysed. And I've said it to

Margaret. She knows exactly what I think. No point in concealing anything.

Wish I could observe the world with the scientific detachment I use in the lab. That's what I need to learn really. Detachment. Cool judgement. Rational criticism. If I had decent security and this Margaret business was settled I would achieve it fairly easily. Not that I would bother much, so long as I got peace and quiet to get on with my own work. I'm more useful in the lab than anywhere else. I can do things there not many other people can do. And it doesn't look as if I'm much good outside. This is where the rogues and fakes flourish. But you can't fake science and a rogue can't cheat in the lab to get results.

'Elis,' he said, 'before you go. Can I have a word with you?' He waved his stick at the Bursar's wife who was last to leave as usual and closed his study door.

'Sit down,' he said. 'Margaret tells me you two want to become engaged. Would it pain you to learn I had any objection?'

'No,' I said. I wished I could file my nails. It always kept my nerves steady, filing my nails. Keep cool I said to myself.

'Well, I have,' he said. 'Margaret tell you?'

'Yes, she told me,' I said. I wasn't going to let him get too much of a kick out of the occasion. Keep cool I said to myself.

'Would you be interested to learn the nature of my objections?' he said.

'Naturally,' I said.

'Don't you think Margaret is too good for you, by the way? Young men in love used to think that sort of thing in my day,' he said.

'No,' I said. There had been moments when I thought she wasn't good enough for me. When she chattered too long about poetry with John Neade and about literary tittle-tattle. Nothing on earth worse. Or when she wore corduroy slacks and talked knowingly about pigs and horses.

'Don't think I'm being old-fashioned now, will you, Elis,' he said, plumping his damned ivory stick across the desk and levering his lion head back with a damned sarcastic smile. 'Do you wish me to tell you what I find wrong with you?'

My mouth shut like a vice. Keep cool I said to myself, keep cool.

'Money,' I said. 'Money I suppose.'

'Only partly that, Elis,' he said. 'I know I'm worldly, but only partly that. It's good for young people to be reasonably poor. And I'm sure you'll do well eventually. This fellowship business Margaret tells me you're worrying about; it's only a temporary setback. Switzerland may be better for you, after all. It's nothing to do with money. My point is, Elis, who exactly are you?'

I still kept my mouth shut but it was a great effort.

'Where do you come from? What about your family?' he said.

'Margaret's met my aunt,' I said. 'Anyway, what the devil does it matter?'

'Where does your aunt live?' he said.

'Streatham,' I said.

'Streatham,' he said. 'Rather characterless place. You're Welsh aren't you? That's the important thing. A man's blood.'

'I've got very good blood,' I said. 'Group O. General

purpose! Margaret's blood is good too. I've tested both.'

'I'm not being snobbish, Elis,' he said. 'And for God's sake don't try to be witty. It doesn't suit you. My people were little more than peasants. But they had roots. And I've got roots. The same Dorset roots. And Margaret's got roots.'

I wanted to laugh in his silly old lion's face. He'd begun to swallow his own musical comedy propaganda. In a minute he'd stand up and wave his stick and shout 'Back to the land! Charge! Back to the land!'

'Family is important, Elis,' he said. 'Not sure that you realise how important. How would you raise my grand-children? What are your views on the subject? Now Margaret has, such as it is, a family. Where's yours?'

'In Wales,' I said. 'And as far as I'm concerned it can stay there.'

'That's exactly my point, young man,' he said. 'You just don't care. Typical outlook of an intellectual barbarian.'

I'd rather be a barbarian than a fake, I wanted to say but I didn't. I regret the wonderful things my mistaken sense of tact has prevented me from saying these last twenty years.

'You ought to find out about them,' the Master said. 'Every man ought to. It's his duty to the nation. To his wife. To his family-in-law. You've no sense of *pietas*, Elis. That's what I've got against you.'

'I'm sorry,' I said sarcastically.

'Margaret is inclined to agree with me over this,' he said, 'so you'd better take it seriously.'

'She's never mentioned it to me,' I said indignantly. And how long do I have to reason with you, you egotistical old buffer. 'All this *pietas* business. Sounds like unscientific neo-fascism to me, I must say.'

He came near to blushing. It was anger of course, not shame.

'Unscientific, Elis? Breeding isn't unscientific is it?' he said. 'Who was your mother?' he said. 'Have you ever seen her?'

'No,' I said. 'And I don't want to. She gave me away,' I said, 'which means she wanted to get rid of me. So why should I bother to look her up? She was a bit of a bitch anyway by all accounts. Gave my father a hell of a time.'

'Exactly,' he said, gazing at me with judicial triumph. 'You are proving my point, you see. Should I encourage my daughter to marry a man with such unfortunate origins. I shall want to hear a lot more about your family, Elis, a lot more, before I give my consent to Margaret's marrying you.'

III

'But, darling,' Margaret said, 'you must humour him. After all he's going to be your father-in-law.'

'He's a bloody old fascist,' I said or muttered into the empty bottom of my pint pot.

'Think of me, darling,' Margaret said. 'Just think of me. After all he's my father...'

'Margaret,' I said.

'Yes,' she said.

'All this crap of his about *pietas*,' I said. 'Do you believe it?'

'Well,' she said. 'In a way I do. He's extreme of course. Tends to use it for his own convenience. But there is truth in it.'

'Not a word,' I said. 'I know because I'm the living proof, Margaret. My mother's alive – so what? My father's dead – so what? They don't affect me and I don't affect them. We're dead to each other, as it were, and everybody's happy.'

'It's a most abnormal situation,' she said.

'You've seen my aunt,' I said. 'Isn't that bad enough? I'm not joking.'

'I'm not either,' Margaret said. 'But you can't deny what is part of yourself.'

'I only know what dear old Auntie told me,' I said. 'It took me all my time to slough off all the nonsense about my wicked mother and heroic distinguished father.'

'Haven't you any curiosity?' she said.

'I don't need to look any farther than my aunt,' I said. 'I gave up studying her neuroses years ago. I'm a proto-zoologist not a psycho-analyst. I've got work to do. Useful work. That's good enough for me. All I want is to be allowed to get on with it.'

'I've got it you know,' she said. I wish she hadn't said it with such absurd pride. I mean I like to respect the girl's intelligence. 'I'm conscious of my inheritance. My inherited guilt in a way.'

'Better put down that gin and orange then,' I said. 'You're more likely to inherit the old boy's alcoholism than his sins.'

'I'm sorry darling,' I said. 'I should know better than to joke with a woman when she's feeling tragic. But you must admit it's a bit steep. *Him* reproaching *me* about *my* family. It's me that ought to be worried.'

'Philip,' she said.

'Yes, darling,' I said.

'Try and humour Daddy. Find out something about your family to tell him. I mean to some extent you've got to learn to live with him haven't you. I mean what's it going to be like for me if you two just can't get on. We've got to think of that haven't we?'

'Now don't worry, darling,' I said. 'I'll do whatever you say. Have another drink?'

IV

Cucumber sandwiches and tin coffee cooling. Poor old Annie Lewis pushing in the trolley, white, pale, bent. Aunt Gwen's faithful servitor. 'Been with me for years,' she said to visitors after old Annie had closed the door slowly behind her. 'A dear old thing. Such a character. Very pious. Very prominent in her chapel, I believe. Welsh chapel you know.' Aunt Gwen speaks from her great enlightened Anglican heights.

'What, my boy?' said Annie. 'Wish you could do something about this right ear of mine.'

'Ever been to Pennant, Annie?' I said. 'Let's have a look at it.'

I take her old shaking head tenderly between my cold hands. I feel compassion for her, love for the old one who gave me some kind of love when I needed it.

'It's in the North, Philip bach. What would I be doing in the North? And my sciatica, Philip bach. Very painful you know.'

'Take a rest now, Annie,' I said. 'I want to talk to you.'

'Can't, my boy,' she said. 'Your aunt upstairs. What's wrong with her, Philip?'

'Nothing much,' I said, grinning. 'Just a cold.'

'I thought as much,' Annie said. 'It's me that ought to be in bed.'

'Remember you telling me once about my father speaking in your chapel,' I said.

'Yes, I remember,' Annie said, nodding wisely. 'Great speaker he was. Beautiful Welsh. Good as Lloyd George, Philip bach. Wonderful man your father was. A great Welshman.'

'Like me,' I said. 'What I was wondering was, was Aunt Gwen there?'

'Shouldn't think so, Philip bach,' she said. 'They kept it very dark you know, this Plato friendship, as she likes to call it. I wasn't with her then of course. We had our little dairy in Willoughby Road. Kittie and Alice were still alive. And she hadn't got her headship either. Wasn't as important as she is now.'

'"You can't turn back in life," she says,' I said. '"I'm more London than Welsh," she says. "My life work's here."'

'Expect she feels it still,' Annie said. 'She wasn't his wife you see. That was the trouble. Wouldn't be recognised as anybody in Wales. And there wasn't any hope she would ever be. Very sad in a way. You are a doctor, Philip bach,' she said. 'You ought to try and understand.'

'You take more rest, Annie,' I said. 'Make her get you a daily woman for the cleaning. I'll speak to her about it again.'

'No, don't Philip bach,' she said.

'She pays you little enough,' I said.

'Never mind that Philip bach,' she said. 'It's a home for me you see. That's all I really need. There's no place like home.'

HANNAH ELIS

CHAPTER THREE

I

I sit watching through my square bedroom window a man ploughing a field that slopes upwards. If I lean back this field fills all the window space except the top right which gives me a further horizon and a small view of the bay. The white gulls wheel perpetually around the tractor and the plough. Of course I cannot hear, but I know the narrow-faced young ploughman, Idwal, whistles as he leans back to admire his own work.

The last time this field was ploughed I was twenty and Richard Davies, grey then but fifteen years younger than he is now and free from rheumatism, Richard Davies, head carter as we still call him although the long stable is almost empty of horses, he ploughed it with his first team.

I took out food to him and a can of hot tea and he squatted in the shelter of the hedge; his earth-covered boots pressing into the fresh grass newer now than twenty springs ago. I watched him, a man eating and drinking without ceremony in the field in which he works, and marvelled at his solemn sacramental pleasure.

In those spring days this Idwal on the tractor a lad then, he cleaned the stable while Richard Davies mixed the feed for five great horses and the second carter laboured to and from the hay barn, carrying with bucolic dexterity great bundles of hay and straw with one length of old rope doubled. Now Idwal is the chief tractor driver and Richard Davies has only one or two horses in the lonely smelling stable – always those empty stalls – which he looks after himself.

There have been many great changes. But my situation has not changed. I am thirty-five and my situation is the same at this moment as it was the day I was born.

I am in this bedroom because it is still too cold for me to go out after my bout of bronchitis and asthma, in spite of the early April sunshine that makes the smooth underside of the furrow glitter as it is turned. The east wind that dries the moisture in the crannies of the ash trees' bare branches and helps the bright sunlight bleach the pale bark, would flay my thin chest however well I wrapped myself against it.

In the untidy elderberry tree under my window some small bird is singing. Its tiny chest is better equipped to withstand this wind than mine. Some of those hostile gusts of cold air it turns into song.

I must eliminate the undertone of self-pity. I must describe my situation as objectively as our Biology teacher used to anatomise a rabbit. I am a spinster of thirty-five confined to her bedroom, having more in common with the faded wallpaper and mean worn carpet than the inexhaustible soil and the sap-concealing branches, the world I can see outside waiting in a posture of expectation for the slow embrace of Spring. That also is a poor way of putting it, still self-conscious, still throbbing with self-pity. What is the use of achieving the age of thirty-five without achieving also some dispassionate attachment to truth for its own sake and its own loveliness?

A spinster of thirty-five. Name, Hannah Felix Elis. Daughter of the late Elis Felix Elis, Esquire, MP, and Mary Felix Elis. My late father and my ever-living mother. Resident these thirty or more years at Y Glyn, living with her ever-living mother and her step-father, Vavasor Elis, Esquire, first cousin to her late father, in this large stone farmhouse always at some point threatened by damp, at the hub of four hundred and fifty sacred fruitful acres – one of the best farms in the north of the county.

Situations do not change chiefly because we do not wish to change them. It is possible it would now be more economical to dismiss Richard Davies and sell the last two or three horses. But we do not like to change anything and it has been the war and agricultural committees and our own reading and our devotion to thrift that has forced us to most of the changes. I say 'we' in these matters because like Uncle Vavasor and my mother I belong to the old dispensation. The difference between us is merely that they are thirty years older and nearer the end of this order of things than I am, and therefore act as if our very old-fashioned routine of living was, like themselves, to continue forever in a state of breathing embalment. For Uncle Vavasor and my mother all crises are events of the past, of which the present and the future are politely muted resolutions; for me, the crisis is still to come, a revelation that will explain the present, bury the past, and redeem what is left of the future.

I am aware and I have always been aware of being imprisoned in this situation which I would like someone to try patiently to understand. I have wanted the minister to understand, but he is too young. So much younger than his years. I have wanted my own unknown brother to return and understand but I am too old now, older than my years, to dream as often as I used to of long-lost brother's golden singing return.

Understand for example how much I love these acres. And how much my mother and my Uncle Vavasor value them; but how much greater my love of every animal, bird, tree, wall, outhouse, ditch, and bush, is than theirs. Their affections and attentions are always divided. My step-father loves his shop and the chapel treasury. My mother had Dick, my half-brother, her youngest son, once, and she has always had her public life. Since Dick was killed I suppose for her the farm comes nearest to her heart. But her love is very different from mine. It is – how else could her love ever be? – possessive and domineering. The farm is something to control, something to feed her insatiable appetite for power. (You observe at once how I attempt to make her love inferior to mine, as if I were jealous. But our concern for the farm is the one bond between us.)

We are the most important family in the district, but our time is running out. By being what we are, we constitute the greatest bulwark in this small corner of Wales against the forces of change. I have always been conscious of this part also of my situation and this sense of responsibility binds me, often against my will, to these two ageing representatives of our tradition.

But they are unaware of this longing for renewal and redemption that possesses me. They are not concerned with renewal. In their absurd egotism they seem to believe it is sufficient for them to be merely themselves and to go on being themselves for ever, as if their corpses, with public co-operation, could go on performing (with adequate success) their perennial parts.

I, for a lifetime it seems, I wait for you. I expect you, coming to claim your inheritance, beautiful and dangerous, to destroy and restore. I fear your coming and yet I long for your coming. And when you come you must use all these words, wear like a magic cloak this roughly woven consideration of my self to direct your anger and strengthen your resolve, to eliminate your hesitations and purify your acts. And I, as I weave the cloak, must restrain my own passions, my pattern must be your needs and not my own frustrated desires. I think towards you in an effort to break the clock-faced thoughts towards myself. I think towards you since this minister disappointed me, with even greater expectation; although I am prematurely old, although I am worn and sick and ugly, I go on dreaming like a green girl.

II

Uncle Vavasor is not black-blind. He sees shapes moving in a thick mist. His other senses are abnormally keen and he is not easily deceived.

Often, when we are alone in the shop together, among pyramids of patent medicines and popular cosmetics, so boring to look at, he is the only living figure upon which my eyes, bright with tireless curiosity, can feed, and I fancy I understand him better than anyone else on earth, better than my mother even, although in many ways she is a shrewder woman than myself.

Because of his limited eyesight, Uncle Vavasor feels the need of a wider scope than most men to occupy his time with that pulse of busy-ness that makes it difficult for any untoward thoughts or events to occur. He is and therefore he does; he does and therefore he is. He fills his time with being what he long ago settled upon being and he appears gratified with being what he is. That is characteristic of each of us, my step-father, my mother and myself, who live in the same house and sit at the same table and rent the same pew: we have each of us, each in his or her own way, accepted the limitations of our existence so well that they have become our first defences against any threat of hurtful or disturbing intrusion. We despise restlessness and unreliability. We have the reputation of keeping ourselves to ourselves, which in our part of the world decks a faint garland of virtue about our name – or so we assume.

Uncle Vavasor is sixty-three. He is very thin, but the tweed suits he wears are so thick that you do not at first notice this, until you observe the loose skin of his neck is untouched by the stiff white wing-tipped collar that encircles it. His head is large and bald enough to appear flat along the top. The eyebrows above his deep-set staring blue eyes are thick and red, and seem to blink themselves when he exposes his old false teeth – beneath a broad moustache that my mother trims, after shaving him – in a constant nervous smile that is meant to disguise the hopeless intensity of his stare. I alone know just how little he sees. While he stands behind his counter and I stand behind mine, I have slowly bent my knees while he talked to me and while he stared firmly in my direction, until my whole short thin form must have been out of sight; or I have slowly lifted a hand and held up two or three fingers, bending and extending them, as he spoke. He saw nothing. I am convinced that by sight alone, especially when he is talking and his other senses are relaxed or given over to himself, he sees very little.

For thirty years Uncle Vavasor has been treasurer of Salem Chapel. (Once when the lights fused he was able to continue uninterruptedly with the annual statement of accounts he was presenting to the church meeting.) For thirty years he has been sole proprietor of Parry and Elis, Chemists and General Dealers, High Street, Pennant; for thirty years he has been married to my mother.

During this time, within my power of recall, nothing has altered. We are constant and unchanging; we are the Elises, the remaining fragment of a tapestry that for the last thirty years seems untouched by the moths of time. By the standards of our small community we are both wealthy and intelligent, but we live as quietly and as carefully as if the earth were fragile and the air about us inflammable if inhaled too rapidly or too roughly. We are unquestionably the busiest family in the district; but we are always busy in the same pursuits. Our routines fit so tightly upon our time that you might believe that the flux itself had at last been tamed and set to circulate automatically within the framework of some device that trapped part of the stream of time, using over and over again the same priceless seconds and successfully shutting out the great flood itself.

It would be far from correct to say that in these thirty years nothing has happened: many things happened, but nothing that could shake this architecture of time, in which each week was a known structure of seven rooms into which, one after the other, you could walk with your mind often set upon other things, while your hand never failed to grasp the handles of the doors.

Nothing fundamental has altered, even Uncle Vavasor's appearance has never changed in my remembering. Ill-health etched in its imprint in his early thirties, furrowed his freckled cheeks and thinned his hair, and supported by an unchanging wardrobe where one rusty tweed suit, one rusty tie and one winged collar unobtrusively replaced another, has maintained a likeness which sometimes seems as static as a death mask. (There is a grey tweed suit for Sundays and a slightly different collar; but the difference is mere varnish to preserve more firmly the original portrait.)

His three great interests, his shop, his farm and the chapel. It is useless to attempt to establish an order of precedence. Uncle Vavasor is a firm trinitarian and he has the biblical conception of the indivisibility of human endeavour.

I should add that he is an alderman and a governor of the Grammar School and that he has twice declined the mayoralty of our town. He attends meetings with punctilious regularity and he is an attentive listener; but only in the shop, in chapel, on the farm is he fully engaged and fully aware of his own being and able to wrap his identity about himself like a well-worn jacket with a quick gesture of practised comfort and affection.

We each of us, my step-father, my mother and myself, cherish our identities. We may be guilty of confusing our souls with our identities, but we each treasure this as the most precious substance of our being. And we do not really mind very much that our love for our own souls needs little support from outside. I cannot say that I like let alone love either my mother or my step-father and I do not expect them to love me. I do not even know whether they love each other. But I am certain that we are tacitly in accord that any untidy extreme of emotion in our situation, either love or hatred, would be inconvenient. To each other we are sufficiently bound by duty, and thus each is left in peace for the more intensive cultivation of the soul. That would be our version of the truth if any extremity compelled us to reveal it.

III

Public affairs interest my mother more immediately than they interest my step-father. There are Causes with which she identifies herself, mainly Nationalism, Temperance, Education, and, since my half-brother Dick was conscripted and killed in battle, Peace. In a solid but limited and local fashion she has carried on our family tradition of public service which was once so brilliantly represented by my own father, her first husband, the late Elis Felix Elis, MP. Even after thirty years my mother's prestige owes something to the fact that she is still known as Mrs. *Felix* Elis; although her point of view has moved very far away from my father's progressive Liberalism.

My mother takes religion and politics very seriously, but the farm is her abiding passion. She is the real farmer of Y Glyn. Uncle Vavasor's authority is real, but my mother farms in his name. Uncle Vavasor intervenes and directs only in matters of general principle or mental accountancy after supper around the parlour fire. He farms as it were not so much on paper as in the middle distance upon which his blue eyes seem eternally fixed. It is my mother who lovingly discharges the business of day to day administration and I never admire her more than when I see her tall bony figure, wearing a long brown coat and a scarf around her hat and knotted under her chin, striding purposefully across a field to examine the conditions of a muck heap or to consult with one of the men. Out in the open air somewhere on our land she will occasionally smile and even joke, whereas in the house, in the town, in the shop, in the county council chamber, her long face wears an habitually grim look which is somehow intensified by the hair that grows untidily across her upper lip.

I cannot believe she was ever beautiful in spite of her

having been married twice. They must have been marriage contracts, profitable agreements coldly arrived at and coldly entered upon. My mother was the only daughter of old parents, my grandparents who farmed Y Glyn. She was distantly related to both my father and Uncle Vavasor. I have reason to believe that it was my father who rescued my grandfather from a heavy mortgage, but I cannot say how much interest he took in farming – whether the farm became his, or how much credit is due to him for having re-established Y Glyn on its present firm profitable basis.

Although I myself, Hannah Felix Elis, am now in my thirty-sixth year, small, thin, asthmatic, always smelling faintly of asthma powders, when I reflect upon the handsome photograph of my father that hangs on the darkest wall of my bedroom, my heart is saddened and chilled by the knowledge that none of the conventional trappings of romance could have adorned my birth; it is unlikely that the warm impulse of love attended my conception. I cannot believe that my father at any time loved my mother and I cannot recall any time in the past when I have loved her myself.

We observe our duties towards each other: to the world outside we present an unbroken front. But the deep antipathy between us is a crucial part of this situation I am trying to set in order, and to explain it I must rummage through the discarded calendars of thirty-six years and polish off the dust on days and moments when this attitude, like primaeval motions and writhings during the formation of the earth's crust, was thrown up between us. Over those moments of volcanic upheaval the elements of thirty-six years have worked their smooth sculpture and stamped something of the permanence of art upon our appearance and attitudes. Myself, small, bird-like, grey-haired, watchful, asthmatic, thinner than a crow; my mother, tall, majestic, firm-mouthed, physically powerful still in her late fifties, her once black hair no greyer than mine, a masculine arrogance thrown like a fox fur across her broad shoulders.

IV

It is obvious that I take an absurd pride in my power of detachment. I even believe that if I reflect long enough upon past events that have constituted or elaborated this situation which I call mine – but which is in fact the vice which holds us all, and all those who depend on us, living or dead – if I meditate long enough in a worshipfully cool manner with an honesty that both suffers and acts, eventually some vision of living will be vouchsafed to me, that will give full meaning to much that still appears meaningless, and that will prepare me for some future crisis of illumination. I can see at once there is more than a touch of absurdity about a spinster who has so much inward solitude that she can devote so much of her thinking to trying to conjure a glowing picture out of a heap of dry dust. In moments of humility, I fail to see my own justification for being so interested in such a tattered self, but I excuse myself by saying I am preparing myself for some form of redemption or at least my brother's return. I am the poor frame upon which these memories hang like rags, twigs and straw on a scarecrow in the wind; I am the breakwater extending into the jaws of time that saves so many inches of the broken shore from the hungry tide.

There was a time in my youth when I was sufficiently obsessed with my origin to make the history of the entire world pivot upon the time and circumstances of my birth. In those days I was given to searching out facts, although I found out very little. Now I wait until the facts find me out. Now I prepare myself so that when the moment of revelation comes I shall know what to do, how to act. In those days, having struggled to find something out, I never knew what to do with my newly won knowledge.

I imagine that I am spending this early April evening in my room preparing not only for a visitor but also for a visitation: preparing myself, preparing my part, preparing even the sketch of an action that you, protagonist, may be persuaded in your great quandary and dismay, to follow, should you be compelled at last to come. Nothing happens. But it is when nothing happens we say anything might happen.

V

What memories does a child of less than five collect of the flitting figure of her famous father? Fame, of course, is relative, and he died at the politically unprofitable age of forty. I have no doubt he has long since been forgotten at Westminster. If a relative (we ourselves would not dream of such a lapse of taste) should throw out a hint that he was 'marked down for high office', there are few left interested enough to confirm or deny the notion. My mother is cool towards our present MP, a pleasant young man who carries the same flag as my father did and seemed to be more interested in my father's career than most people. At one time he seemed anxious to prepare a memoir but my mother was so discouraging he gave up the project. Myself I would have been glad to help him. I enjoyed his company and I cannot help blaming my mother for having deprived me of it. (She does not like anyone to take to me. When the minister first came to tea, 'I'm afraid Hannah gets bad attacks of asthma, Mr. Powell,' I heard her say. It was true of course. And she had a right to say it. It amazes me how little ill-will I bear her.) My mother's public attitude is that my father was not nationalist enough and she deplores the influence of 'Westminster' and 'Party Headquarters' and 'ambitious friends' upon his patriotic efforts for the 'mother-country' (mother-country is a phrase my mother always uses with conviction).

I have not seen my father's ghost. I did not even see him in his coffin. I have fancied that there was some little golden age near my beginning when I was small and plump and petted and free from asthma and I have always attributed the petting of my late father (who had the reputation of being 'amiable' and 'jolly', in contrast to his cousin Vavasor, who was known as 'cold' and 'dry') chiefly because there was not, believably, anyone else to attribute it to, even if it did occur.

I have a firm recollection of being in my small bedroom at night, 'held out' by my mother who was being shouted at by my father who stood on the dark stairs. That I can remember and the shadow of my mother's head on the wall and the candle balanced dangerously on the rocking chair, that might so easily have set the whole house on fire. I have always been terrified at the threat of fire.

I imagine that I can remember the tickle of his bright kissing moustache, a bunch of fair hair growing out of his left ear, his musical laugh unlike any laughter I have afterwards heard. More distinctly, a ride in the dark inside of a motor car that smelled of rexine and petrol, probably on an election night, and the great contrast between the affability and hearty greetings when the car stopped and the hostile silence when the car was in motion. I imagine the hatred with which they stared towards each other in that silent darkness.

The evidence is slight, a shout on the dark stairs, the bitter silence in the motor car, things heard, things put together, but I am convinced they hated each other. Perhaps all parents at one time or another shout bitterly at each other over their children's heads: perhaps hatred between parents, suppressed or expressed, is commoner than I suppose, since my isolation would easily blind me to a very general phenomenon. I have only my own limited experience to go on; yet I cling to it as my criterion. (I have a great horror of being carried away on a wave of gullibility, so that I prefer to think the worst of things first, and if I am proved wrong, it is a pleasant surprise.)

My step-father and my mother never speak of my father. As a child I realised his name evoked an unpleasant atmosphere and I soon learnt not to mention it and not to ask questions that they were not inclined to hear, let alone answer; and as an adolescent I kept my revived interest in my father to myself.

VI

In Y Glyn three of us sit down to meals in the little parlour; my step-father, my mother and myself. But there are among the dead some who are never far from our table. My father for example, whose name is never mentioned. My mother's father and mother whose dry portraits look down at us from the shadowy walls. And Dick, my half-brother Dick.

He was born when I was almost seven and already attending the village school. I liked school very much and I was sorry when the afternoon sun shone in the west windows to indicate the end of the afternoon and the sad collection of pencils, rubbers, beads, crayons, sheets of paper and clay and a worn key turning in the lock of the capacious cupboard. One day I arrived home hungry for my tea, but the kitchen was clean and empty and neither of the maids were to be seen about the place.

I found only my Uncle Vavasor warming his large hands before the little parlour fire.

'Hannah?' His nose lifted like a dog on the scent. 'Is that you?'

'Yes, Uncle.'

'Go up and see how things are getting on and then come down and tell me.'

'Yes, Uncle.'

I ran down the dim corridor and up the stairs. The door of my mother's room was closed. I hesitated outside. I was not awed by any sense of awful mystery, only a realistic little girl calculating my next move between parents who were not always so easy to comprehend. While I was standing there, the door opened and the tall figure of Miss Aster hovered above me in an attitude of surprised disapproval. Miss Aster, formerly matron of some institution in Lancashire, lived in one of our cottages and she was my mother's devoted friend and admirer. 'Well, my girl? What are you hanging about out there for? Curiosity killed the cat. You're a curious little miss. Well now, you've got a brand new little brother.'

High above me, Miss Aster turned her bonnetted head back into the room. (I have no recollection of her ever taking off her bonnet in our house.)

'Want to see a little visitor, my love?'

Miss Aster habitually addressed my mother as 'my love.' She never got as far as using her Christian name, which was her ambition.

My mother was leaning back against a mountain of pillows. Gwladys, the elder maid, threw a cloth over a pail, but not before I had caught a glimpse of the bloodstained contents. I studied my mother earnestly; she looked pale and exhausted and altogether a gentler person than I was used to. She even smiled at me, and lifted a hand to draw my attention to the cot at the side of the bed. I was enchanted to have her being so nice to me. I don't recall whatever it was I saw in the cot.

'Do you like your little brother, Hannah?'

'Are we going to keep him, Mother, or are we going to send him away like the other one?'

The smile faded. I realised that I had said something wrong but although I frowned hard could not work out what. I began to chatter about school, but my mother interrupted me.

'Miss Aster. Her tea. If you please. I feel a little tired.'

'Come along now, Hannah. Now don't you be getting on your mother's nerves.'

'My husband, Miss Aster. Please ask him to come up.'

'I'll see to everything, my love. Just you rest and don't you worry. Gertie Aster will take care of things.'

VII

Miss Aster had every reason to ingratiate herself with my mother. She occupied Ty Porth, a cottage on our land, near to the shore, for a nominal rent which she was never asked to pay. My mother got her in, and for years it was my uncle's barely concealed wish to get her out. He felt the cottage ought to go to one of the men. Often he would say: 'That woman is getting too much free milk,' or: 'That woman eats more than three men,' or: 'I hope you are keeping some account, Mary, of all the free food that woman is carrying away with her.' I never heard my mother attempt to defend Miss Aster; on the contrary she inclined to join in my step-father's criticisms and supplement them with her own. Nevertheless she took all Miss Aster's devotion, seeing to it herself that Miss Aster neither wanted for milk, eggs, vegetables and butter nor had too much. In the ante-room to the little parlour (called the breakfast room but never used for breakfast) many an afternoon I silently witnessed my mother coolly treading the narrow path dividing parsimony and generosity, picking out and wrapping up with her own capable rapid hands the smaller eggs, while Miss Aster leaned over her, her gluey eyes gleaming greedily, a cluster of loose teeth pushing out her dry lower lip, her lips parted to aerate the saliva already accumulating in her mouth and to utter the most effusive thanks. '*My love, you're so kind, bless you. You're kindness itself you are my little blossom. What would I do without my love taking pity on poor old Gertrude Aster. If there's anything I can do my love, just send word. Send somebody down. Any time of the day or night. You know you can rely on me, my love, I'm that anxious to repay...*'

We were a household that frequently needed nursing. Both my uncle and myself were asthmatic and delicate and at one time I suffered attacks which may have been obscure forms of epileptic fits. (Miss Aster was always anxious to make me out to be an epileptic. The idea caught on locally and probably still circulates. It originated from her.) Then there was the infant Dick to look after.

She was an immensely strong and healthy old woman. Bearing some burden, she would plod down the narrow lane to her cottage near the sea with the gait of a flat-footed cart-horse, her crooked bonnet nodding between the golden gorse blooms on the tall hedgerows as her long shanks rose and fell. She saw herself as my mother's intimate friend and companion, and in the baby, Dick, she saw her chance at once of clasping my mother more firmly to her. It was Miss Aster, I know, who invented the notion that I was jealous of the new baby and that I should not be left alone with it on any account. No doubt I had been eager to make my claim on the baby, to play with it and help look after it; but that did not suit Miss Aster, who easily persuaded my mother that only two people on earth were to be trusted with 'little precious, bless him' – herself and my mother.

Miss Aster did a great deal to make my path rough in those early years, but I have no recollection of ever hating her, as I might well have done. From the first I regarded her as an instrument of my mother. Her primary aim was so obviously to please my mother, and if by nagging at me she was able to express that aversion for me which my mother would never admit even in her own secret thoughts, the very obviousness of her anxiety to please usually directed my resentment against my mother, the unloving origin of my being; the mother who must have grudged the necessity of giving me life and birth.

There were limits to the persecutions I suffered from Miss Aster's clacking tongue, and self-pity must not be allowed to blur them. Uncle Vavasor took rather more pleasure in me than most people – he admired my quick intelligence – whereas Miss Aster got on his nerves. The sound of her penetrating voice would start him biting the ends of his faded ginger moustache, and if the weather was fine, groping along the shelf he had specially constructed at the top of his high-backed fireside chair for his thick outdoor cap which he would swiftly substitute for his thin indoor one. Some days he would rush out with his hands extended in front of him, muttering, as though pursued by a swarm of bees. Miss Aster and my mother would continue talking as if nothing unusual had happened.

Her visits other than 'professional' were subject to a

strict time limit. Uncle Vavasor, unable to read as he was, was passionately fond of listening to the wireless. Nothing was allowed to interrupt the numerous news bulletins, English and Welsh, that he listened to with religious intensity. Miss Aster speechless but still undaunted would depart blowing kisses to my mother, while Uncle Vavasor, his ear glued to the loud-speaker would wave with a gesture that resembled a dismissal far more than a valediction.

Miss Aster could not speak Welsh but Uncle Vavasor had a trick of assuming that she could, so that in the course of years she did acquire some knowledge of the language. Uncle Vavasor did not always remember this (again more by design than by accident) and he frequently passed impartial judgement on her behaviour and opinions in her hearing. These she always ignored with an almost visible elevation of the spirit.

Being nursed by Miss Aster when he was ill appeared to be the greatest trial of Uncle Vavasor's life. My mother must have persuaded him of the economy of such devoted free service, and as a family we are all very willing to enjoy any form of economy. He bore her ministrations with a spartan silence which I too was compelled to learn, although his meditations on medical bills saved was a consolation I was still too young to share. 'Now then, my girl...' the ex-matron would say in her firmest and deepest voice, striding towards my brass bedstead with a steaming bowl of some obnoxious brew.

Miss Aster was a part-time member of our household; 'a little lower than the angels', her spiritual position hovered in the long 'breakfast room' between the 'little parlour' and the servants' big kitchen, although nine times out of ten her material person would be found within the parlour precincts, on a sewing chair turned slightly towards the window to gain a better light for her needle. Often from such an angle her eyes would turn accusingly in my direction as if I had never given her a satisfactory explanation to account for the necessity of my existence.

VIII

Fighting my way alone from this drab bedroom in an unauspicious moment of an undistinguished year through the undergrowth of irrelevant past events towards the heart of my situation; or working desperately fast to hold all the fragments and loose ends of memory and to force them into some intelligible pattern, I must somehow, out of myself like an industrious silkworm produce the thread that will bind the fragments together, or lead me back through the labyrinthine wood of incidents behind whose apparently solid trunks sinister outlines seem to move in the dark.

Perhaps the ardour of the journey will make me something more than the poor thing I appear to be, this Hannah Felix Elis, the chemist's step-daughter, the skeleton of a narrow bird often found in the lanes of these parts, very faithful in chapel, loyal to my minister, legitimately pitied but hardly loved. And if I return with the secret, the power it will give will transform me into a personality able to radiate judgement and find some mercy.

IX

My birth was different from Dick's.

It took place in a tall terrace house in Pennant, across the road, as a matter of fact, from our shop. My father had been in Parliament then four or five years and it was important for him to live in the town. Everyone was given to understand that the two mile journey from Y Glyn, by dog-cart usually, did not help him to catch the early morning London train. It was customary to admire my parents' devotion to their native place; it was known that my mother disliked London and that my father cheerfully made the long journey every other week so as not to be exiled in Babylon. At that time my aged maternal grandparents were still alive. My mother, their only daughter, would have preferred to be with them on the farm and I cannot imagine she found much pleasure in living in a tall terrace house.

My mother at the time of my birth. Twenty-five, a highly-strung, sensitive creature. Married three years. Still the adoring young wife. Youthfulness like blossom on a twisted bough still concealed the angular severity with which I have always been familiar.

It was a notoriously difficult birth. Miss Aster was present and her repeated accounts seem to have registered every agonising second in my memory. My mother was in labour thirty-three hours. Doctors and nurses came and went. Miss Aster – newly arrived in Pennant, lodging on holiday a few doors away in the same terrace – stood faithfully by, laying also as it happened the foundations of a long friendship. She telegraphed to delay her return to her important post. She telegraphed also to my father in London.

In my imagination my father is always a very dramatic figure. I see him receive the telegram, rush from the House to catch the night train that rattles and trembles as he gazes anxiously into the darkness that leads towards Wales.

He appears in the door, still holding his top-hat and gloves, dressed it might have been, for a wedding. 'Send him away!' She sits up in bed screaming, her long hair hanging down over her face, the billowing sleeves of her white nightdress laced at the wrist, bishop-fashion. 'I don't want to see him. I never want to see him. He wants me to die!'

Her hysteria brings on a new bout of labour pains. Her father, the old man, putting his arm around my father's shoulder, leads him downstairs. The new morning sunlight streams through the red yellow and blue fanlights above the front door, into the narrow hall, illuminating the heavy coats weighing down the stand that seems to stoop. It is the morning of my birth and somewhere there must be poetry even in that moment.

There were severe haemorrhages. Miss Aster made dark hints about the inefficiency of the family doctor. There was another birth nearby in a poorer street. 'He came straight from one to the other without sterilising his instruments.' My mother was very ill, and according to Miss Aster, I was 'a horrid sight'. That was my role in her story, 'the horrid sight'...'a lump of raw beef'...'couldn't see your eyes, and it's a miracle you can see at all, if it isn't a greater miracle that you're alive at all to tell the tale...' (The sole purpose of my unexpected survival, to tell the tale.)

A specialist came down from London. The bedroom began to look more like a laboratory. 'Test tubes everywhere,' said Miss Aster. 'I felt quite at home.'

Still my mother will not speak to my father. More than once he lies on the bed alongside her, long and handsome as he is, stroking her hand, her cheek, but she will say nothing. She lies still and silent as if her whole personality were in the painful process of taking on a new shape. The adoring smile, whatever the unhappy reason, has gone for ever and will never return.

One afternoon during this illness, my uncle Vavasor, then a pale thin red-haired shy man in his late twenties, appeared in her room, and prayed at her bedside. Miss Aster was most embarrassed. She stood by the window, rubbing a piece of lace-curtain between her fingers, not knowing which way to look. He prayed aloud and my mother listened to him staring with wide eyes at his bent head. Each day he called she would say 'You are praying for me still, aren't you, Vavasor?'

I myself was given to a wet-nurse. But I was a difficult baby to rear and according to Miss Aster I owe my survival to my maternal grandmother's discovery that I took to a certain brand of tinned milk.

X

In my memory, my brother, the circumstances of your birth are obscured by my father's funeral which must have taken place at least four months earlier.

I attended the funeral, holding my grandmother's hand.

Of her I can remember nothing now except her ivory skin glowing like a discoloured piano key out of the folds of black lace that she wore. My mother was not present.

The silent procession encircled the churchyard wall like the children of Israel bearing the Ark around the walls of Jericho. The pitch-pine coffin with gleaming brass handles bobbed up and down in front of us, borne on four stalwart black shoulders. I was impressed by the silence of such a large gathering of black-clad people on a sunny afternoon and I wondered where the occasional sobs that mingled with the rustle of black dresses came from. Myself I was dry-eyed and puzzled, still not convinced that the box contained anything resembling my father who was in London and unable to get back in time for this rare event.

Hen Eglwys y Groes is an island in the centre of our largest field. The building is of sixth century origin. By today one service a year is held – a popular local event – in August. Otherwise the damp interior is used only for funerals. There was singing at the graveside, in the minor key, threaded with the cries of gulls that made me look upward and screw up my eyes against the bright sun. I must have been happy to be there, my favourite spot in the world, this great undulating field that manages to include a church, a graveyard defended by clumps of trees and an ivy-covered wall, a small stream, a footpath, and a wild frontier of gorse facing the low sandhills and long shelving foreshore.

It was when they were lowering the coffin that a woman rushed forward. She stumbled against the heap of soil at the grave-side and covered her black mourning costume with pale earth. There was earth even on her red cheeks. Sorrow screwed up her face like old age and seemed to lengthen the nose and make the eyes small that darted glances about like a frightened ferret ready to bite the first hand to touch her. Eventually she was led away, by Uncle Vavasor plucking relentlessly at her shoulder and another relative who seemed to me to have to guide them both. Her cries, hysterical and pleading, seemed to stifle the subdued sobbing, seemed to transform the whole scene. My grandmother's hand gripped my small hand more tightly.

Is it a super-imposed impression that shows the whole congregation turning away, hurrying away from the solitary open grave?

XI

After this dark event you were born. I wonder if our earliest shapes, the little girl and the baby, were ever allowed to meet? I do not think so. And I have no recollection of the supposedly wealthy London relatives or friend of our locally suspected father, who must one day have come down to carry you away. 'My father's cousin.' The female form of the noun. No doubt it was whispered that the late Member of Parliament had broken Mary'r Glyn's pious heart, and sympathy and support in chapel, in the neighbourhood, in the town, allowed my mother to make her own arrangements about the immediate past, to salvage as much of her late husband's reputation as was necessary for her own prestige and to commit his sins and indiscretions to the incinerator of polite oblivion. The day you went I expect I was taken for a walk by one of the maids, probably to one of the farthest outhouses to watch her young man stocking mangolds under seaweed and salt if that was the time and season.

Why have I never left this prison to set out in search of you? Did I find it more comfortable to feed and cherish a great illusion? Do I still fear the rough event and the possible storm of your intrusion? Afraid perhaps that you would not distinguish between me and these to whom I am not altogether unwillingly tied? Of your indifference, your contempt, your condemnation? If you are like my father, handsome, successful, impatient, sophisticated you would not want an ailing sister nursing her misfortunes and stroking them as if they were purring cats. If you are otherwise, perhaps I would not want you.

So neatly I put my situation in the balance. In my thirty-sixth year I wait and I am skilled in waiting. But it is dangerous. It is easy to confuse the coming of a knight errant with the coming of the Saviour, and I sometimes see myself among the idolators throwing palms before the short nervous steps of the frightened ass.

Perhaps my situation will not release its secret until the day you come, and perhaps your coming will release also my soul from its doubting solitude. Beyond the salt desert, I imagine, lie the dim foot-hills of the Promised Land.

CHAPTER FOUR

I

I never saw you. I was given instead as a brother, Dick.

He may have been a normal small boy, rough, self-centred, heartless, rude. Even now I cannot pretend that my view of him is unbiased. To me he seemed atrociously spoiled. My mother just sat and watched his absurd antics with folded hands and a faint smile. Miss Aster marvelled endlessly at his wit and infant wisdom, his 'old-fashionedness,' his droll behaviour and engaging naughtiness. I was never allowed to restrain him; in fact I was reprimanded often for elementary acts of self-preservation. When he bit my hand or kicked my very vulnerable brittle shins Miss Aster would say, 'Now leave him be, Hannah. Don't turn nasty. He's only playing,' or, 'He doesn't mean to hurt you. He's only a baby.'

Once when he was six and I was thirteen he was with me when I was paying a bill for my mother at the Newsagents in Pennant. These were people whom I did not like, but at that age, being so nervous and shy, I probably gushed for all I was worth in my effort to please. I knew even then that these people were no friends of my family and that their veiled hostility put an edge of delight on what they heard from my chattering little half-brother. He was pointing at me with a clowning gesture that they found very funny. 'She isn't my real sister. I wouldn't have her. She's a dry little stick. Everybody says she's a dry little stick.'

Pierced with hot arrows of shame I knew how many times the newsagent and his wife would repeat the story. And I knew too with blacker despair that there was truth in what Dick was saying. My little half-brother, whom I often wanted to take on my knee, to pet, to hug, to kiss, a pretty boy, he was the herald of my grotesque doom.

There could never be any danger of Uncle Vavasor spoiling anyone. Perhaps early in his life he had examined the gentler forms of emotion and like a savage who finds a coin give under the pressure of his teeth had thrown them away. Sentiment for him was not legal tender. I believe he has as much regard for me as he has for anyone but the nearest he has ever come to any expression of affection has been an occasional 'Yes, yes,' or 'very good' repeated in a tone of hurried approval. I can remember when I was a young girl, in his most expansive moments pushing back his indoor cap and stretching his long legs before the little parlour fire, he would make indirect references to the dangers of unguarded feelings that made me smile.

I never saw him take Dick on his knee. Only once did I see him when he imagined there was no one else in the room, catch hold of his small son – Dick was about four at the time – and hold him firmly with his arms pinned to his sides, while he fixed the small face with the intense blue stare of his eyes, only made more alarming by the occasional fierce relief of two or three great eyebrow blinks. For a few moments the child was petrified, and then suddenly began to struggle and howl all over the place. Miss Aster came rushing noisily downstairs, pushing one of the maids roughly out of her way. By the time she arrived, Dick had been released and stood, his chest still heaving with frightened sobs, wiping his running nose on his sleeve.

'What on earth's the matter then?' Miss Aster demanded.

Uncle Vavasor continued to warm his hands and to stare into the fire, ignoring her question.

'What did you do to him?' She turned her wrath against me. 'Now you just tell me what you've done, my girl!'

Suddenly Uncle Vavasor snapped out, 'Leave Hannah alone, Miss Aster. She did nothing at all. And while we are on the subject, kindly try and restrain yourself from spoiling that boy.'

With great injured dignity, the six foot creature, as ever crowned with her crooked hat, withdrew from the little parlour. I was a little afraid for her. (Perhaps even then I was influenced by the conservative principle that if things are bad, disturbing them will only make them worse.) I was not old enough to realise how easily the most dignified persons can swallow rebukes and even insults if the interests nearest to their hearts are at stake.

I must also remember how merry he was and how there were qualities of the bright morning about his shouts and laughter. That laughter and those shouts – more than a trivial ingredient of the noises about the farm-house at different times of the day. The muffled thud of cows' hooves and the swish of their tails; the clatter of cans and buckets and clogs and hob-nailed boots; the majestic flicking of carthorses' feet and the carter's whistle; the rattle of machines for slicing, milling, threshing, crushing, mixing; and the rumble of carts, loaded and unloaded; the undertones of wandering well-fed hens, and the other-worldly music of the birds; add to all these our urgent or passive human voices, but above all some childish laughter, and the world is different. Or so I fancy now. But perhaps the music is still there and the absence of Dick's voice makes little difference. I cannot hear it now because I am already on the further bank of middle-age and out of ear-shot of youth.

II

When Dick was about nine, one Thursday afternoon when the shop was closed and Uncle Vavasor was taking a nap in his chair before the little parlour fire, the boy screwed two rusty hooks into the frame of the door of the little parlour about a foot and a half from the ground, and then tied some binder string across the doorway. He then ran outside, opened a gate between the home field where some steers were grazing, and an adjoining hay meadow.

Back he rushed to the house, stopping in the doorway of the little parlour and shouting in an excited voice, 'Father! The young cattle are in Cae Dafydd!'

Uncle Vavasor woke with a start, switched his caps with astonishing dexterity and blundered out, his arms slightly extended as was his habit, only to fall with a sudden cry of rage as if already he knew he had been tricked. His head cracked against the stone floor of the ante-room and he lay still.

He was still lying on the floor when I came in and caught Dick busily unscrewing the rusty screws, with his back to the prostrate form of his father. It was I that ran to Uncle Vavasor and lifted his head and, before I had really taken notice of Dick's headshaking and finger to lips, it was I who was shouting accusations against my spoiled half-brother. I was remembering then how interested Dick had been the previous Sunday in the story of Isaac and Jacob and how on the way home he and Henry Thomas, also in his class, had a long boyish argument about whether Jacob really had deceived Isaac or not, and how Dick said excitedly he could prove it and Henry Thomas said no he couldn't.

Neither my mother nor Miss Aster were at hand. It was one of the maids who first appeared in answer to my accusing cries and she in turn became hysterical and ran out into the yard screaming 'The Mister's dead! The Mister's dead!' Dick suddenly took fright and bolted, and since I was holding Uncle Vavasor's head, I could not prevent him. Eventually the maid found Richard Davies, the head carter, who came lumbering up to the house after her. This was unfortunate for Dick, because Richard Davies was devoted to Uncle Vavasor and very hostile both to Miss Aster – whose cottage he felt should have been given to his daughter and son-in-law – and to Dick who had been her key to power.

Richard Davies picked up the long frail body of Uncle Vavasor. One spindle leg encased in thick woollen stocking was thrust out of the trouser at unusual length and the large brown well-polished boot dangling from it emphasised the fragility of the unconscious man. With Uncle Vavasor in his arms, Richard Davies wiped his boots several times with care before ascending the stairs and laying his master's body with great gentleness on the bed. The maid and I trembled in the doorway, wondering what to do next.

'Keep him warm,' said Richard Davies and then covered my step-father with a thick blanket and took off the stiff collar and starched front which concealed his heavy woollen shirt. 'Ought to take his teeth out too I expect, although I don't like to.' He glanced doubtfully at his dirty fingers. 'And send someone for the doctor.'

He strode over to the window, forced it open, put out his head and bellowed 'Griffith!' two or three times. He sent the third carter of that day (a small young man who has since died of tuberculosis) spinning off on his bike to fetch the doctor.

'Now I'll catch that little devil,' Richard Davies said slowly, looking towards Uncle Vavasor as though he were putting his point of view about a difficult piece of farming policy, 'and I'll give him a good hiding before anybody comes along to keep his part. Wicked little devil, that's what he is.'

He made unerringly for Dick's hiding place in the hay barn. I could imagine Dick crouching in the darkness near the corrugated iron roof listening to the steady tap of Richard Davies' boots on the rung of the ladder and the rustle of hay and laboured breathing of the heavy man advancing with his head bent forward and his eyes gleaming angrily in the darkness.

Uncle Vavasor was in bed for weeks. When Dick was sent to apologise and confess, my step-father was sitting up in bed, inhaling the fumes of a smouldering asthma powder, his turnip-shaped head loaded with a green woollen night cap. Dick stumbled on from one unfinished sentence to another, as a person who walks against a high wind turns his head to breathe in broken gulps. Uncle Vavasor did not appear to be listening. As Dick was about to leave, he was called back.

'Off to school!' Uncle Vavasor said sharply, catching his breath and lifting the tin-top of smouldering powder closer to his nose. 'Off to school you'll go, my boy. Do you good.'

This decision, to send Dick away to a boarding-school, was the beginning of a conflict of will between Uncle Vavasor and my mother that lasted until Dick's schooling days were over. Everything that happened during those years increased Uncle Vavasor's faith in his own remedy. My mother got her own way as a determined mother could not fail to do I suppose, against a father so handicapped. But the effect of the difference was to push them far apart. There was no explosion that I witnessed; but neither was there ever any easing of the tension.

They were never a very intimate pair. Apart from

always addressing each other in the second person plural with a formal politeness not, I found later, normally used between husband and wife, each pursued an independent existence so that one appeared to look upon the other not so much as a person but as a familiar institution.

But before the long unvoiced struggle over Dick's school I remember a much more cordial atmosphere in the little parlour. Little jokes flourished: about Uncle Vavasor's caps and his home-made spitoon, about my mother's black earrings ('boundary marks' Uncle Vavasor called them), about the need for a new wireless set, and about Miss Aster. But each one of the founts of humour dried up in turn. The new wireless and Miss Aster were the last to go.

The atmosphere of restraint in the little parlour was greatly resented and detested by Dick, who seemed quite unaware that he himself was responsible for it. He gulped down his meals and wanted to escape as soon as his hunger was satisfied; he had no conversation and any information had to be dragged out of him.

Between the boy and his father there existed a sporadic commerce of harsh-voiced orders, monosyllabic answers and stubborn silence. Dick knew his father would never see the insolent look he had learnt to wear without any trace of nervousness. He knew more perfectly than I did what exactly his father could and could not see. And he also knew that his mother – to apologise for her own silence, for not defending him, for appearing to acquiesce in his punishments – would demonstrate her affection by slipping sixpence, or even a shilling, into his pocket, which suited Dick very well and completely undermined Uncle

Vavasor's 'Well, if we don't send him away to school, we've got to see he's kept short of money and put under proper discipline.' When Dick entered Derwen Grammar School in Form One he was already getting as much money in one week as I, in Form Six, had ever received in a month. These facts are trivial in themselves, but they must be stated because they add up to something.

I have sometimes wondered whether Dick would have liked me a little if my mother had not shown him so clearly and so often that she did not consider me a worthy object of affection. I could have liked him so easily and forgiven him so much if only he had shown the faintest signals of real affection. But he never did. Miss Aster taught him how to look at me; but I knew only too well that it was to please my mother that this old woman whipped up her own fundamental indifference into an active hostility. One complication of my situation; since the day I was born the most implacable enemy of my happiness has been the mother who bore me, and who still sits opposite me at every meal, who yesterday evening into this room with an air of busy sanctity carried my supper-tray saying: *Is your chest easier, Hannah? Your uncle's chest has been very tight today.*

III

I remember a winter night in the great kitchen, and all the simple inquiring faces illuminated by the dancing firelight as they listened to Owen Owens' rasping voice. I choose to remember such a night and such a story when

Dick was a rough boy of twelve and I was a nervous studious eager self-conscious nineteen, and our maids then were Gwladys – the best we ever had, who still visits us and still helps out at harvest and shearing and threshing time – and Meinir, who married Silly Morus by whom by now she has had, I hear, five children, three living two still-born – and I sat there between them listening, my hands demurely folded in my lap. And Dick squatted on the end of the long scrubbed table, sometimes with his arm on Willie's shoulder. Willie the 'gwas bach', aged about fourteen, with his square head and flat pale face; a bed-wetter upon whom Uncle Vavasor tried many cures with a scientific coolness in strong contrast to Gwladys' urgent indignation as she dragged the damp straw mattress once more down the stone steps from the stable loft. But Willie was amiable and well liked and the men all enjoyed his surprising wit, and with Dick he was a great favourite.

Owen Owens' harsh arrogant voice fascinated each one of us. But for his gift of story-telling he would have been disliked by everyone except Uncle Vavasor who valued him highly both as a shepherd and as a fattener of bullocks, perfectly versed in the art of moving the stock around to catch the grazing to the best advantage. Owen Owens was a long-nosed, sour, sharp-tongued man whose bad feet made him use his long stick like an oar. Although he was married and the father of children he only visited his native village about once a month, and the other men, always resenting his highland arrogance, joked that Owen Owens couldn't bear to leave his sheep.

We knew most of his stories. They were always true

and they were always asked for in a tone of deferential politeness and they were always sad.

'When I was a "gwas bach",' he would begin, 'not more than thirteen I should say but a damned sight harder working than that young waster there...' Nodding towards Willie, so that we would all laugh and each man would throw in his ounce or two of wit, according to his ability and my brother Dick would punch Willie's shoulder and Willie would smile and not mind. Then all settled down to listen.

'This farm was high in the mountains near a lake. A hard place to work, a long high mountain and a few hay meadows, but a good place for sheep. And at this farm it was the mistress that was the master.' (Subdued laughter at this point and a few remarks to which Meinir squawked a brief token of opposition. The well-trained listeners knew exactly where interruptions were called for and in what degree.) 'This woman was wild and masterful and her husband a quiet honest shy man was quite unable to handle her. It wasn't that he was a fool or weak or afraid of her. He was a good-looking fellow, well thought of in the neighbourhood, an excellent judge of sheep, with a good bank account. The trouble was he loved his wife too much.'

(The wind rushed through the cobbled yard outside the long window and the flames of the wide fire stretched into the cavernous mouth of the chimney. The table was laid for tomorrow's breakfast, bread and milk bowls upside down in eight or nine places, except where Dick sat, the paraffin lamp on the wall above his head turned low so as not to smoke in the draught.)

'She was beautiful, this farmer's wife. She walked like a

queen. She was full of pride and imagined every man wanted her. She was very hard. But worst of all, she was common. And that was surprising because she came of a good family. But to everyone except those who were in love with her the fault was obvious. Even I, a mere boy, could see it. It was like a disfigurement; in the morning when her tired face wasn't made up, it was there like a second face visible beneath the first; when she was made up in the evening you had to look for the first face under the second.

'Something about her husband seemed to get on her nerves. I believe it was because his patient gentlemanly behaviour showed her up, even to herself, for what she was. There may have been other reasons, but they were all to do with the fact that he was so much better than her.

'That winter the wife began to flirt with the new cowman, a carefree decent enough young fellow from Anglesey, very strong, good-looking and hard-working. He meant no great harm but he had no sense, no upbringing. He was young and foolish and still green enough to think every invitation had to be accepted. It was a long, dark, hard winter.

'One afternoon the farmer came home early from the market. The house seemed very quiet. His boots were untidy so he took them off before going upstairs. He caught the cowman in bed with his wife. He stood there in the doorway as if he had been turned into stone, not saying a word. The wife began to cry and then, still without speaking, the farmer turned and rushed out of the house.

'I saw him going through the yard as I was coming out of the pigsties, with indoor shoes on his feet and his coat open flying out behind, hurrying along like a man late for an important appointment.

'He didn't come back that night, nor the next morning. Towards lunch time the woman in her hard common way began to recover her composure. She began to give orders, laugh, and pass coarse remarks.

'Every other day,' said Owen Owens, pausing perhaps to spit in the fire or glance at the bowl of his cold pipe, 'it was my job to go up to an outhouse about a mile away along the path to the mountain and refill the racks with hay from the hay loft, and spread straw over the mounting muck on the floor of the lean-to and see that the black steers were all right. The day after the master left in a hurry I wasn't able to do this job until late in the afternoon. I took a lamp with me because it would be dark in the hayloft and the darkness would fall long before I got back.

'The snow had melted and it was unpleasant walking in the slushy lane. To my surprise when I arrived the steers were all pulling contentedly at a half-filled hay-rack. But there was no fresh straw under their feet. I lit the lamp and mounted the heavy ladder thinking to throw down some straw.

'The first thing I saw was the long shadow of legs dangling together as still as the pendulum of a broken clock. Trembling and sweating I looked up and there hanging from the beam with his tongue bulging out and his cold eyes staring at me, I saw my master.

'I was hardly more than a boy and I wanted to run, run away, shouting, screaming. I stopped myself. It was too late to do anything. But I couldn't leave him there. I picked up the ladder he had kicked away and I climbed up it level with his body. Looking away from his face, I took out my clasp-knife which was always razor-sharp and with one stroke against the taut rope, cut him down. He dropped with a horrible thud on the hay I had kicked about on the floor beneath.'

Gwladys and Meinir, as if instructed, had already clapped their scrubbed hands to their rounded mouths, and had already gasped and screamed and begged not to be told the worst details. Someone would ask what happened afterwards, since the story ended officially when Owen Owens said that he had not forgotten to spread straw under the bullocks before rushing back with the lamp in his trembling hand, the unwilling herald of evil news.

Sometimes when pressed enough he told, more impersonally, and with less interest than we felt – I particularly – the sequel. How in ten months' time to the general horror of the district the widow married the unwilling cowman, and how after a time, tired of living isolated in a sea of disapproval and unable to keep good labour, they sold the farm, and how wildly they quarrelled in public the day of the auction and how most people thought that one day the cowman would lose his temper completely and beat the intolerable woman to death. But all that actually happened was that they bought a smallholding in another county, where as far as Owen Owens knew or cared they were still hard at it nagging at each other like two devil goats tethered in hell.

My mind would dwell on this sequel long after the rest of the company had exhausted the subject. Was there in life I wondered some inexorable law at work that saw to the fit punishment of every evil-doer? Could this small story be taken like a smear of blood on a slide and put through certain tests and processes in my mind so that I, eventually, if I worked hard enough and thought long enough, I could see the Law of the Universe itself, catch a glimpse of the constellations trembling in their settings like bracelets on God's implacable arm?

One evening when Owen Owens was concluding this same story my mother and Miss Aster entered the kitchen and the men became respectfully silent while my mother asked me to accompany Miss Aster home to her cottage in order to bring back some mending needed for the next day. Two white overalls for the shop. It was a calm mild night, there was a moon, and my mother said that if I wrapped myself up well the walk would do me good.

I had no desire to go but I was trained to obey, so I went. Miss Aster's wide feet plonked along (her shoes always listed to starboard) and she stared ahead of her, silent, like a pilot intent upon his navigation. I had nothing to do except continue my endless meditation on Owen Owens' story. I did not stay at Ty Porth. Miss Aster and I had so little to say to each other.

When her door was closed I ran quietly down through the low dunes to the pebbly water's edge to admire the moonlight spinning on the surface of the incoming tide and to listen to the weak waves lapping softly at the shore. The smell of seaweed made me feel hungry.

Pleased with myself for not being nervous I was enjoying the walk back when I heard feet running to meet me. Willie came panting up. He grabbed my sleeve, pointing and gesticulating, dragging me after him towards the Middle Barn, fifty yards away. I could see a light in the barn loft. Willie scrambled up the ladder as fast as he could.

In the lamplight I saw what I first took to be Dick's body hanging with his back to us dangling from a rope. I screamed and screamed in my horror. It seemed the last and most outrageous escapade, the trouble and tribulation all my life had been a preparation for, more terrible than ordinary death. Either I fainted or I had a fit. If it was fainting, it did not last long; if it was a fit I did not – I can hardly bear to say it – bite through my tongue. When I came to, both Dick and Willie were bending over me. At once Dick began to laugh.

'All right, Hann?' No real concern in his voice, as if it were my duty to be all right in order not to spoil his brilliant joke. 'None the worse, Hann?'

In a spasm of extraordinary rage I turned, stiffening my fingers into claws, and drew my nails across his face as hard as I could. Anything to wipe away that smug and heartless grin. He screamed with pain, and surprise, dancing about the floor both hands over his cheek. 'Did you see that, Willie bach? That's my sister for you. My big nasty bitch of a sister. Did you see that, Willie bach?' He was still repeating the chant when I left them both and hurried home.

CHAPTER FIVE

I

Dick's closest friend was Frankie Cwm. I wonder now whether Dick knew – whenever it was between the age of six and ten that their friendship began – that Uncle Vavasor and my mother considered Frankie's family an unpleasant blot on the landscape to be ignored out of existence. Characteristically, when they wished something did not exist they eventually began to act as if it didn't. Dick, on the other hand, if he had taken a fancy to Frankie would not be put off by any deference to his parents' wishes. He had none of my trembling respect for parental disapproval or approval. He may not have chosen to know what I had always known so well. With such complete unintended co-operation the most impossible situations are easily brought into being.

I knew that 'the Seth Cwm brood' were condemned outcasts and their small cottage near the river in the village of Sarn, two miles from our farm, seemed to me a dark gateway to the underworld.

It was I who caught a glimpse of Dick entering the cottage, one bright afternoon when I stood on the bridge watching the low water wriggle through the dry-topped stones that most times of the year it tumbled over. My heart beat to see him so light-heartedly commit such wickedness. And I saw him cross the river with Frankie and they were followed by Frankie's sister, Ada, two or three years older, but a lonely girl I expect and glad to play with the two boys. And it was I who told my uncle in Miss Aster's hearing when he asked, 'Where on earth have you been, boy?'

II

Dick learnt to be very secretive. To most people, except his father, Richard Davies and perhaps myself, he seemed a gay, frank, open-hearted, good-looking boy. His broad face could carry a most winning smile and his bright dark eyes could search out yours and coax your sympathy and affection even against your will.

I am convinced that all through Dick's schooldays, Miss Aster knew well enough that Frankie Cwm was Dick's closest friend. More than anyone she must have been aware that the association could bring Dick little but harm; but she allowed herself to be persuaded by Dick. Beneath her hospital hardness she was a weak lonely woman. I can almost hear her now talking aloud to herself during her hours of exile in her own small parlour at Ty Porth, surrounded by the mementos of her irretrievable past – the photographs of a Royal visit to the Infirmary, postcards of Cannes in the nineteen hundreds, a testimonial from a titled private patient also yellowing in its frame, medals, souvenirs, coronation jugs and trays, these cherished articles which she had chosen to take with her to the nether world of her retirement – hear her saying, '*A healthy boy needs his little share of mischief and he needs a special pal, so what harm can it do him, I'd like to know? And say what you like about Frankie if say you must but he is loyal. That boy's loyal as a sheep dog that he is. And that's a very great quality when all's said and done.*' Clad in her asbestos opinions Miss Aster strode always unscathed through the burning lakes.

Ty Porth is a long, low narrow cottage presenting a white-washed back with only one tiny window to the rough road that follows the outline of the estuary. The front door and two bigger windows face south across our fields, and the generous garden is protected by a high stone wall. From the doorway of the cottage the only building in sight is the tall Middle Barn, where Willie bach and Dick played me their cruel trick.

Miss Aster no longer holds the twentieth century at bay in Ty Porth. For the past seven years it has been occupied by Richard Davies' nephew and his wife who had to wait so long to take up their tenancy. But when I was young it seemed to me that Miss Aster's cottage and the landscape about it including the Middle Barn, belonged wholly to the nineteenth century. This was the land of stabilized melancholy, this was the barn where the owl brooded, where the afternoons were long and sweet and gloomy; this was the crowded parlour where the twilight lingered, slowly extinguishing the last highlight on the last lustre jug, and the paraffin lamp being lit evoked indoors its own shadows, while through the tiny back window the last red bar of sunset, behind the black lighthouse, gave way to the violet night. All through my youth I had a special love of this part of the foreshore, and if I needed solitude would often shelter somewhere near. During my last years at school I brought my books and even revised for exams, either near the old church or somewhere around Ty Porth or the Middle Barn. And when I decided, because of my uncertain health, I would qualify as a chemist and work in Uncle Vavasor's shop, abandoning my earlier and more ambitious plans to become a doctor, and when my free time seemed to shrink to half-day holidays and become very precious, around the Middle Barn was a favourite place to day-dream.

These outbuildings were little used in summer except during the harvest. There was a threshing floor with dusty flails still hanging on the cobwebbed walls, and a stable where discarded harness hung with the dusty melancholy of tattered flags from the rafters of an old church. Even the straw piled up in the last bay was only the pale survivor of the last harvest but one, in the year and the time of the year I now remember. (Of the fruits of the earth nothing is older than the survivor of the last harvest but one, older even than those fallen oak-leaves that stick in the cleft at the base of the tree in the middle of Cae Llwyn and rot through the early summer of each succeeding year.)

It was in July. A Thursday afternoon when the shop was closed. The tide was out. For some reason Miss Aster was not at home. Clouds were threatening the sun, the air was hot and close, and the black seaweed smelled strongly in the brooding silence. The air about the gorse bushes on the edge of the foreshore seemed to find the dark green scent too heavy to hold. I saw there was a storm coming. I decided to move nearer the Middle Barn buildings.

Some obscure desire to hide drove me, restless and nervous as I was, and afraid of thunder, up a ladder leaning against the newly settled hay that filled the first bay. At the top I saw the figure of a youth sleeping. I must have made very little noise for he did not wake. My heart began to beat with excitement and shame. The youth lay on his back, his arms thrown out carelessly, and he wore only an open shirt. It was Frankie Cwm.

He was trespassing of course, this enemy to whom I had never spoken. He was up to some mischief or other, probably in league with my brother, this insolent outsider who had no respect for our family or our property. But I said nothing and I did not move. I was lost in an agonising trance because he was so beautiful. My hands began to tremble on the ladder. I wanted to touch him. A touch upon his smooth thighs that would not wake him or disturb him, a touch that would break the spell in which I was cruelly caught and give me a new power.

When I had almost gathered strength to move, suddenly I glanced at his face and I saw with a shock of cold horror that his narrow eyes were open and that he was watching me, like an animal, only with complete calm. Now his eyes were open I remembered who he was. A person whose face I had always considered sly.

'Hello!' he said softly. I did not know how long he had watched me staring at his nakedness. Was it my harsh breathing that had awakened him?

'Hot isn't it.' He was enjoying the situation. His voice was low, adult, persuasive. 'Want to touch me? You can if you like.'

He knew how much I wanted to, he could see it all in my thin unprepossessing face.

'You can if you want to.' He made a slight movement of offering with his legs that stiffened me with fright, and I looked at his face. He was grinning too much. Young as he was, fifteen perhaps, very little more, he wanted power, over me. To my fevered imagination his beauty became the beauty of a snake.

Still I did not move, until he seemed to weary of my stillness, and made an obscene gesture and began laughing. He had a long mouth and his eyes seemed to close into slits. Even as he was laughing the storm broke and the rain hissed on the roof and when the thunderclap came it seemed to me like the wrath of God. I stumbled blindly down the ladder dropping the book I was carrying in my clumsy haste, and I ran blindly out into the rain.

III

When I reached the kitchen door I was in a state of collapse. I spent the rest of that July in bed. It seemed to me then that no one had much sympathy for me. I was left alone for most of the day. In three weeks Dick only came to see me once. We had nothing to say to each other. He stood at the foot of my bed, already the tallest man in the house and likely to grow again. Because I so much wanted to talk to him about Frankie, to warn him, I could say nothing. Not one word. He was uncomfortable – an unusual condition for him, so gay and easy, already at sixteen equipped with a practised charm – as if he believed I disliked him, and he could not bear not to be liked. His broad smile seemed to say 'Look, I am making an effort to be pleasant, to make life more interesting, so kindly make some token payment of affection in return.' My unconsciously troubled and searching glance disturbed him I think. He could not guess that I was wondering how to help him. I wanted to save him even then but how could I do it? He would never listen to me.

IV

In my twenty-fourth year I walked alone in a warm world devoted to the endlessly various communion of living. The birds sang in the sun, the animals cropped the sweet grasses, but there seemed more communication between Owen Owens and his sheep, or the carter and the great lumbering horse he managed both to lead and ignore than between me and any other living thing. I wanted to be friendly with Dick, to help him, to be his ally, but he treated me like an interfering stranger best kept at a long arm's length. I knew for example of his friendship with Frankie's sister, Ada, a girl two years older than himself and I realised that it was this measure of success that gave him his gay self-possessed confidence. But he never seemed to need my help.

I was a person born out of hate and therefore specially equipped to stare into the shadows and discern the muted forms that writhed there while others walked in the sun. Or so I dramatised myself even on early summer days when the lark sang above the meadows and the south wind ruffled the tender sycamore leaves in the trees planted to protect the church from the prevailing winds, and sighed through the two stiff yew trees on either side of the lych gate. My place was inside the low church, where a hurried service was held only once a year and the plastered walls were damp, the tall-backed cob-webbed pews discoloured, the bare stone altar dusty, and where, even on the brightest June day, when the long dog's foot sheds its seeds in vain on the horizontal tombs, there was always a hard core of ancient cold.

Imagine me about this time on one of my pious romantic visits to my father's grave. I saw a girl's bicycle leaning against the crumbling west wall of the graveyard, near the trees. It was unusual for anyone to bring a bicycle so far, although of course, the parish had right of access across our land to the church. Peering over part of the fallen wall, between the trees I saw Dick with Ada, Frankie Cwm's sister.

Ada lay on Dick. She was kissing the tip of his nose and they were both smiling. The smiling fascinated me. They smiled with some kind of inward knowledge and inward satisfaction that I knew as I watched I would never understand and never share. She was wearing her school uniform and between her skirt and long black stockings I could see exposed part of the white young strength of her thighs.

I caught only a glimpse of them together, but the details of the scene have remained vivid in my mind and strangely static. I cannot imagine them moving, coming together or parting, these two still figures, one lying on the other, smiling as if for eternity into each other's eyes. I could have thought of it as a painting of the Garden of Eden, except that I myself was the third person in the bottom left-hand corner of the picture.

V

Soak the smallest thought in time and it soon swells to the size of a world. Therefore when you set out to explore the smallest thought you need to be prepared for the longest journey. I am tired now, after travelling such a short distance. The bed is so near and so inviting. This evening we shall be entertaining the minister and if I am to be at my best as I wish to be, I must rest. It is part of the folly of my sex and the dumb solitude of my situation that I should continue to hope, continue to expect him to rescue me long after I have realised with my reason that he does not consider me in need of any help. Because I believe in his goodness I would still thrust myself where I am unwanted, still certain that if I could only make the young minister see my extreme necessity he would create out of nothing the affection I need and demand. I rest for the sake of my mind, so that I shall be quick to turn any word or act to my advantage. I want to be clever enough to win happiness like passing a stiff exam.

IDRIS POWELL

CHAPTER SIX

I

If Vavasor Elis could see me clearly, would he greet me with so much respect, listen to me so carefully, welcome me so warmly? In my position I owe much to his respect. Behind him stands his straight-backed wife, trying to make me uncomfortable with her indifferent stare. To her, my youthfulness and eagerness to please, my too frequent smile, my fluttering uncertain hands are all signs of weakness. Her only direct feeling towards me is an irritation, a nagging desire to brush down my unruly curly hair. I often notice her staring at it.

They are not being rude leaving me alone in the middle parlour, or slighting. It is my fault for calling too early. (I could not make the absurd confession that my watch was half an hour fast. Not to Mr. and Mrs. Elis. Or to whom indeed among my congregation? Here in Pennant it is not my business to be myself. It is my job to be 'the minister'. People do not like to hear things that suggest their minister does not know what to do with all the time he has on his hands.)

This room is gloomy because the only window faces the enclosed garden; the leaves of a fig tree that never ripens lean over and block out part of the light. It appears to be used only for entertaining ministers. Here all my solemn predecessors since Bethania was founded have sat in the bottle-green gloom. And listened as I am listening to the grandfather clock in the darkest corner cancelling used time with an unwearying tick. (Not that they would be left alone so long.)

A dark room in a dark house. If I laughed aloud as I am always willing to do even now when I know there is little to laugh about, my laughter here would be more startling than in church. My friend, Emrys Wynne, our schoolmaster, has fanciful ideas about this house. He talks about an atmosphere of doom. Not being a poet myself I do not feel it. Waiting, I only take a hopeful glance in the mirror and at thirty with adolescent vanity, absurdly pleased with the dim image, I run my comb with guilty speed through my wavy hair. In immediate reaction I think there is nothing about me that carries authority, the authority that men and children recognise. Women like me better. With certain women I can say I am a success. They like my large brown eyes, my engaging clean but slightly crooked smile, my soft nose, like a dog's or a baby's. They don't mind my long thinness, or my feet that are too big and can't kick footballs. With sympathetic women even my liabilities are assets.

If I wish to strain my eyes in this poor light two great leather bound books lie on the red plush cover of the mahogany table by the window: the Bible and Fox's Book of Martyrs. The tokens of unalterable law. It is strange to be minister to people like these who belong to the orthodoxy that the liberalism that we have revolted from, first revolted against. I am so inappropriate.

Easy-going and harmless. Idris Powell who used to cheer the college side to victory or defeat and sing as loudly as he could, sitting or standing, on the journey home. Anxious to please God and his grandmother who had lovingly brought him up, giving himself to the church that did not particularly want him. An ambitious student, lacking in application and staying power. Preliminary MA. Unfinished research. Abandoned BD. Look at my friend Lambert. How can I help envying his degrees? Doctor Lambert Owen. The hammer of authority in his very name. The ideal of a minister. As I am the distortion.

II

This room seems sound-proof. What are they doing in this great dark house? Discussing me? Planning how to improve me? Or ignoring my existence, which is worse. I am compelled to admit that Vavasor Elis, Elis the Chemist, is the backbone of my church, or rather my backbone. People give me some respect when they see Vavasor respect me. His constant support saves me from being trodden underfoot by the other deacons. Sometimes in Mannie Elis Jones' swollen pale eyes I catch an intense desire to bully me; and the same longing in Parry Castle Stores' sanctimonious bleat that issues like an endless toilet roll from his letter-box mouth. If they could get together they both know how soon I would become their victim. Only the still blinking corner figure, listening with folded arms and lowered head to my sermons, that they would love to pull to bits, bars the way.

Elis the Chemist isn't an easy man to like. But I admire and respect him. During these three years of my pastorate he has done more to help me than anyone else. We must find our friends as we need them. When he prays there is a yearning in his heart that gives his rapid harsh voice the sharp edge of honesty. When he mentions sin, I know it is his own faults he has in mind and not someone else's. How much better than Mannie's syrupy wooing of the Eternal's attention: Look O Lord, what a fine job you've made of Emmanuel Elis Jones. I cannot prevent myself thinking these unchristian thoughts, even when I force myself to act as if I loved with special grace those who disapprove of my existence.

III

I wish Lambert would think more highly of Vavasor Elis. (I am one of those eager souls who expects all his friends to be each other's friends as well as his own.) But Lambert doesn't approve of anything in Pennant. '*Not the right kind of place for you, Idris,'* he murmurs, walking majestically at my side down High Street. Aware or not of the curious glances that follow his progress, he bears himself in a kingly way. Tall, broad, fair-haired, my best friend (although I cannot claim to be his. He has so many friends). A man with all the qualities I wished I had myself; authority, boldness, courage, eloquence that excites men, popularity. A Professor at thirty-two, already on the verge of being a national figure, his broad shoulders ready for the descent of the prophetic mantle. Everything I have always wished to be, I am afraid, with the hopeless ambition that is more painful than hopeless love. Obscure ambition brought me to my calling, love that I could neither give nor accept thrust me into this church.

Lambert glances about him, nodding perhaps at Mr. Parry wrapped in his white apron in the doorway of Castle Stores. '*I don't like the place,*' he murmurs, lifting his hand in regal salutation. '*Stagnant. Absolutely stagnant. A corpse in the drains. Can't understand why you came here, Idris. Really can't. I feel guilty too. Feel this is the kind of church I ought to be compelled to handle. And it's the Elises who keep it stagnant. They're the core of the problem; and I don't know how I could handle them, quite honestly. Can't think how you can stand it. Why on earth did you come here?*'

IV

I couldn't tell him I came because of his wife. And if I felt a flicker of triumph that Enid should find me something worth loving, it was soon drowned in a sweat of embarrassment and disgust with myself. Not that we behaved badly. Loving in itself is no sin. We were so careful and he was so preoccupied it would have been easy for us to commit adultery. It is especially easy to deceive a dedicated man. Nothing troubled him. We never needed to use the excuses we had prepared. He knew we must have been mostly alone for three days in a Lakeland hotel. But Enid was his wife. I was his friend. Why should he trouble? His silence was the challenge we could not ignore.

Even now as I am about to depart one further stage away from her so far away, I am troubled by the happiness we could have created and shared, by the certainty that the world would never see a more joyful pair of lovers. The wild Lakeland weather externalised the storm that raged in our hearts. The details of other people's passions may sound sordid and absurd but we can only use the cadenzaed vocabulary of high romance about our own. A sudden stillness at the heart of the pine plantation and the fitful sunlight pointing pale rays at us, our heads bent, trembling with sorrow and desire. The perfect understanding, the communion of two souls that can make an eternity out of a moment, established in the stale quiet of a hotel lounge, when hands have to be disengaged because of a passing porter. Late at night her hands pressed together, she leans forward towards the fire, her head slightly lowered and her short dark hair hanging forward. Then she lifts her large enquiring eyes, her expressive mouth, her determined dimpled chin; she smiles and I am absurdly happy. That evening a blue sweater, a black pleated skirt, a necklace and bracelet made of the same metal. So young. Twenty not twenty-eight. It was difficult to think of her as Lambert's wife.

When did it begin? Was it inevitable? What did it mean? We could say anything we wished and the other would not judge. That was the nature of the love we were giving up even as we created it, a love to heal, not to hurt. Like legendary lovers, woven on the edge of a medieval wood, too poor to trouble about time or place, we walked in the garden of the hotel at night as if it were a rich man's castle that would admit only our most innocent dreams. And often we laughed. How light we made our sacrifice, knowing we would have the rest of our lives to take it heavily. We wanted to exploit to the full the brief hour of revelation before we were swept apart by the tide of Time that would sweep us back to our appointed places. And what faith we had that our love which we could not use on each other, would do others good. Not for each other, but for others we said.

Even now after three years, here and now in this green gloom, or at any especially lonely moment, I feel as if God has hammered me into this place like a rawlplug into a wall.

V

'My dear brothers and sisters in Christ, I am not the untidy, simple-minded fool you take me for. While I fidget behind the bowl of flowers kindly given by Mrs. Aston Jones, Pretoria Villa, over and above the church notices and expressions of sympathy with ailing members I have things on my mind that would interest you to know. Do not underestimate me; do not dismiss me as a smiling nodding weak nobody who will smile and nod until the unruly hair becomes white and evokes after thirty years the so long delayed first fruits of wonder and respect, the consolation prize of the man who stuck it out. I, Idris Powell, minister of the gospel, pastor of this church Bethania – this church we are justly proud of – I loved the wife of my best friend; whom you have heard and admired preaching from this pulpit and hearing no doubt wondered what he could see in me – and she – I cannot expect you to believe it – she loved me. She found me worth loving. We declared our love and renounced it. In three days I think we pulled down and rebuilt our whole lives so that nothing could ever be the same again.

You understand that a Christian has no alternative but to renounce the love of his brother's wife. That is obvious, but it is not easy. Even now this love can glow bright or bitter. It is the source of my power to love and my power to hate.

Dear brothers and sisters in Christ, I came here as though she had sent me, determined to love you, longing to serve you. I had all this love to give you, coming fresh from the head waters of love itself. You will recall Our Lord's words on the woman taken in Adultery. You have of course always helped me to see where my duty lies. You have prompted my visiting: you have improved on my sermons: you have told me where I was most needed (always the next person, never yourself), what to approve of what to condemn. You have indicated in great detail how you expect me to behave. Many of you have shown an interest in my personal life. You have said quite frankly for example

(Mr. and Mrs. Emmanuel Elis Jones, Mr. and Mrs. Parry, Castle Stores, Mr. and Mrs. Emrys Wynne, and many other kind friends) – what a pity it is I am single. And that it is a pity I live in the Manse by myself. And that a church with long traditions to uphold like Bethania, needs a distinguished minister aided by a charming wife. In myself, such as I am, you have given me to understand, I am hardly worth the effort of influencing and as a monument to the fallibility of your powers of choice, I do not soothe you with an increased sense of certainty and security.

You have never given me a chance to use this store of love I brought here with me. You have kept me at a distance; not a respectful distance, but like a housewife who turns against an ornament that she bought in a moment of folly and paid too much for, you want me to stand in the most shadowed corner of the room. And because of this, dear brothers and sisters in Christ, I, your minister, an apostle of the gospel of love, I am the foremost authority in the world on all the unloveliest details of your characters.

By now she may have forgotten me, have nothing of me left, having lost me or shed me as I have gradually lost and shed the vision I brought here with me. I have no right to blame you, dear brothers and sisters, I am only allowed to blame myself. I shall ask you to help me. I shall ask you to accept as my wife a woman whom you long ago rejected; a local girl. Don't look the other way in your embarrassment and anger. Don't move away, talking politely to other families about the weather and your state of health. At least stay and look at me with curiosity, however cold.'

The freakish gibbering of an indecent exhibitionist, bringing dishonour upon his calling and the church. What right have I to impose my word-stimulated agony upon people who could never understand? One address like that and they would be right to throw me out; and I myself would be unlikely to deliver it outside the wilderness of my dreams.

CHAPTER SEVEN

I

I shall stay to supper. Naturally they will want to give me advice, and I admit their advice has been the only advice I have had worth listening to in Pennant. The chemist will speak as he always does in general terms about general principles. His wife will indicate the effects of my behaviour upon public opinion, upon the moral fibre of the community. And the daughter will hold – how can she help it – roughly the same point of view, less patiently perhaps, because I always feel that I have disappointed her in some special sense. I used to think I should offer myself to someone like Hannah Elis, so obviously in need of loving; an absurd enough idea, especially since I know to make her such an offer would be taken at once as a mortal offence. I over-rate my success with women perhaps because Enid, the wisest and most gentle woman I ever knew, admitted that she loved me. The truth is I irritate many women and for Hannah and her mother it must be more than irritation when they think of me in connection with Ada Evans.

II

I was working in the garden, not very effectively, but I have to make a show of working so as not to disgust the manual workers in my congregation. The leaves of my old apple tree had begun to fall and Miss Morris' cat lay sleeping at the foot of the wall warmed by the October sun. The damp steamed out of the matted chunks of earth I turned over with my spade. Hearing someone knock at my back door I was glad to straighten my back and see who was there. I waved my hand in the friendly manner I have tried to make my second nature.

A fair-haired young man in garage overalls walked slowly up the garden path. He was smoking, the smouldering cigarette concealed inside his cupped hand. I knew him only by sight, Frankie Evans, more generally known as Frankie Cwm. A family, as far as I knew then, traditionally not on speaking terms with the Elises and therefore difficult for me to speak to. When they saw my embarrassed restrained friendliness they made no attempt to put me at my ease. His father-in-law, Wally Francis, the Garage, grinned openly whenever I passed, as if I were a public joke.

Frankie nodded, awkward and shy, conscious of having to meet me on my own ground.

'Nice day, Mr. Powell.'

'Very nice.' If I were as weak as he imagined me to be we would follow that line for twenty minutes before he got round to stating his business.

'It's the wife that sent me here.' He screwed his cigarette stump under the steel shod heel of his oil-blackened boot. 'Asking if you would call, Mr. Powell, as a favour like. Her father's very bad like. Don't think he'll get better.'

I knew Wally Francis was seriously ill. I hadn't grieved over missing his fat red-faced figure in a young man's blazer and grey flannels, bright tie and beautifully laundered shirt, outside his garage or in the small town square on market days. Pushing sixty, but his trousers always pressed and his dark hair shining and in place. Loud Wally, whose laughter was a feature of the town, who was the enemy of Elis the Chemist and Mrs. Felix Elis, who had bought the vacant mansion of Bronllwyn outside the town and wanted to turn it into a drinking club, Loud Wally was lying in his neat bungalow unnaturally quiet and still as if trying to avoid Death's notice.

Parry Castle Stores as usual dangling in white on his own front step watched us wonderingly and resentfully (that I should be off somewhere not merely without his permission but without his knowing where) as we passed down High Street together. Housewives wondered to see Frankie's turned out steps alongside my untidy strides, their myth-making minds having more to make of so untoward an alliance.

Wally Francis' garage – 'Britannia Garage' was printed in tall black letters on a white board above the main entrance – stood on the brow of the small hill where the small town ended along the main road east. Next to it was 'Britannia Cafe', a long wooden shack dignified with a painted verandah. And next to the cafe Wally's new bungalow at the end of a length of tidy garden.

The cafe was empty. We walked through the billiard room to the over-crowded kitchen where Frankie's wife, Sylvia May, was polishing cutlery. When she saw me she lifted a fistful of knives and wiped her eye with the back of her hand. Outside the window there was a baby sitting up in its pram, and I couldn't remember whether she had three children or four. She was young, but shapeless: her hair clustered about her small face in tightly permed curls. She put down the knives with a clatter.

'My father's dying, Mr. Powell.' Her lower lip trembled as she spoke.

'What does the doctor say? Who is your doctor?'

'Dr. Pritchard. He's been very good. Every day he's called twice. Three times sometimes.'

'What does Dr. Pritchard say?'

'He's done his best for my father, Mr. Powell. I'll say that for him. Old friends they are, as you know. He's done everything he can hasn't he Frank?'

Her husband said, 'Doctor says there's not much hope.' As if he were tired of looking at and listening to his wife, he pushed open the window and made a noise to draw the baby's attention.

Sylvia May said, 'Very little hope he said to me, Mr. Powell. It's a blow to him as well. They were such big friends.'

I supposed to myself they were. They had whisky in

common. And Pennant Rangers. And billiards. And motor-cars. Especially buying and selling motor-cars.

'You would like me to see him, Mrs. Evans?'

She wiped her hands and nodded eagerly.

'Yes indeed if you would Mr. Powell. We're not much for going to church as you know. We're very tied here, the garage, the cafe, the children – seven days a week, Mr. Powell. But my father – I don't know whether you know – he was brought up in Bethania. Thought the world of Bethania he did when he was a boy. He changed to church because of Elis the Chemist. But he's Bethania at heart. He would never have left the chapel but for the old minister and Elis the Chemist. I've heard him say that myself...'

Frankie turned his head. 'Take Mr. Powell to see your father, Sylvia May.'

'I'm just going to, aren't I?'

Outside she stopped on the concrete path that led to the bungalow's back door.

'My sister-in-law's looking after him, Mr. Powell. He won't have anyone else.'

I tried to look as if I wasn't aware that Ada Evans was generally assumed to be Wally Francis' mistress.

'He's taken against Frank since he's been ill.'

She hesitated again, and then as if she felt she had explained as much as she felt able to, knocked the back door.

When Ada opened the door it struck me at once how much better-looking she was than most women in Pennant and how much better dressed. It seemed absurd to think that she was this old man's mistress. Her hair was tied back and I was immediately struck with the beauty of her small, firm, delicate, smooth ear – a charm against loneliness in shadowed rooms. In our first greetings I think now we must have appreciated each other's existence.

Later I compared her with Enid. Enid was a dark copy book beauty; neat, gentle, meditative, loving. Ada's looks were not gentle. Her chin was too large, and her grey blue eyes too watchful. She was taller than Enid, more ample-breasted. Her taste in clothes was more uncertain but her manner more confident and more questioning. It was easy to see that Sylvia May was rather afraid of her. But she did not seem aggressive to me. I recognised that she needed comfort and affection just as much as I did, if not more so, and I saw, too, that she responded to my appreciation of her person.

She put us to wait in the cold clean drawing room that smelled of wax polish. Sylvia May was not at ease in her father's house.

'Mr. Powell.'

'Yes, Mrs. Evans?'

'If you speak to my father that is if you get a chance to speak to him by himself like I was wondering if you'd mind reminding him of his duty to his family. I don't mean so much Bill my brother who's away. My father sent him away. They didn't get on; Father was jealous. I mean me and my children, Mr. Powell. I've got three children and it isn't easy these days...'

She stopped suddenly hearing Ada approach.

'How is he, Ada?' She might have been a sympathetic neighbour paying a polite call.

'The same.' Ada looked at me. 'He says he doesn't really want a minister.'

Sylvia May was staring appealingly at me.

'Do you think I ought to see him?' I said. I must have smiled as well, because Ada smiled back.

'Quite honestly no. He gets too excited.'

It was difficult to think of her as Frankie Cwm's sister. Either he had let himself go or she had deliberately improved herself. Perhaps her suffering had given her this command of herself. As we passed through the hall, the sick man's bedroom door was open and I caught a glimpse of him lying neat and rigid in his clean bed, his protruding eyes staring at me.

'Mr. Powell!' he called out suddenly.

I stood in the doorway of his room.

'Who asked you to call?'

'Your daughter, Mr. Francis.'

'You know what she wants, don't you? I'll tell you...'

Ada moved with exaggerated calmness to the head of the bed.

'Now don't excite yourself, Wally.'

'I'm not exciting myself, Ada. Do you know what I've always called you, Mr. Powell, Elis the Chemist's Flopper.'

He moved his thick lips slowly in his still face to indicate a smile.

'Don't excite yourself, Wally. You'd better go Mr. Powell.'

'If you knew half as much about Elis as I do Mr. Powell, you'd flop away. If God knows his business he'll keep that Bethania crew of yours out of heaven or they'll give him no peace...'

Stimulated by his own wit he had begun to sit up, but the effort was too great and he fell back on his pillows, unable to stop coughing, his face going redder and redder.

'Mr. Powell, please ring the Doctor.' She was calm, capable, but frightened. 'Quickly please. 653. 653.'

While I telephoned Sylvia May hesitated in the back doorway and then ran back to the cafe. Coming back into the bedroom I was shocked to see the red face turned yellowy white and the large combative eyes covered by heavy lids that looked as if they would never open again. Only faint irregular bubbles of air were passing through his slack lips.

Ada had changed too. Her composure was gone. Her arms hung useless and her face was crumpled and ugly with crying.

'He's gone into a coma. He's going to die.'

She looked at me helpless and bewildered.

'He's going to die. I don't want him to die. He needs me.'

I put my arms about her and she did not move. I watched her bowed shoulders shaking, and touching her hair with my lips I felt myself warmed with a tenderness I had not felt before. I felt as if I was coming to life again. I wanted to give her all the help I could. She moved away to wipe her face. She did not look at me and we did not speak.

III

I left when the doctor came. On my way home I was absorbed in attempting to epitomise what I, as a minister, had to offer. 'I have no sacraments and I'm not a doctor. I have only myself to give.' But indoors in the empty Manse it didn't seem so clever. No minister was worth having unless a living host to Christ. Wally Francis wouldn't listen to me talking about God and Jesus. He knew the facts already and what I had to add to them wasn't worth having. Presumably he needed me more than Ada; but I had easily taken her in my arms because I needed her.

Wally died in the early morning. When I called, Williams the Undertaker's man had finished taking measurements. When he met me in the doorway he gave me his patronising nod: a man who had been at the game a good deal longer than I, and moreover, a member of my congregation who was inclined to hold it against me that he had not yet been elected a deacon.

'Trouble about the will. You'll see. Keep clear of them, Powell bach. They're a rough lot.'

They were in the drawing-room. Sylvia May was trying her hardest to be dignified and correctly sorrowful. With a twinge of disappointment I saw that Ada had composed herself. She was standing by the window, smoking.

Sylvia May said, 'Bill ought to be sent for. He ought to come at once. Haven't you let him know, Ada?'

Sylvia May seemed much readier to speak in my presence.

'He's your brother, Sylvia May.'

'And what I want to know is, oh dear.' She paused to sob, 'is there a will? These things have to be faced. Is there a will, Ada? That's all I want to know.'

'No. As far as I know there isn't. And that's the second time I've told you.'

'You can see our point, Mr. Powell. There's the children to consider and the garage, and the cafe, and the Terrace and Bronllwyn. It's worrying me.'

Frankie spoke. 'Do you know, Mr. Powell, what happens if there's no will. Isn't it divided between the next of kin?'

'That's Bill and me.'

'Yes. That is so. Divided equally.'

Sylvia May said, 'Perhaps it's better this way,' and she lowered her head to conceal her relief.

'There could be a will Ada doesn't know about. We'd better ask Dr. Pritchard. We need to be careful. How soon can we find out? When is it usual, Mr. Powell, to settle these things?'

'Usually, after the funeral. Almost always after the funeral.'

IV

An unusually dismal funeral. In spite of his noise and bonhomie, Wally seemed to have few friends. There was a small bunch of relatives from Penygraig, where Wally was born. Silent hard-faced quarrymen and their women, who looked around the bungalow like strangers who had never been inside before. Winnie Evans, Frankie's mother – easier to think of her as Frankie's mother than Ada's – faded and bent as she was acted as their sprightly guide and hostess, with a lack of taste and restraint which I thought embarrassed Ada, although she was determined to show no signs of shame. Parry Castle Stores arrived to represent, he told me afterwards, the Town Council, and looked very surprised to see me. It was obviously his opinion that I should have left the whole occasion to the

Vicar. But for Ada, I would gladly have done so. Although it was Sylvia May's wish that I should pray before the coffin left the bungalow. It was her idea of rewarding me for responding so promptly to her call for help.

Dr. Pritchard was present, in black, immaculate as usual, silent, small, plump, grey haired, sunburnt, glowing with motionless impatience. I had seen him the same at a football match, standing throughout the game, on the touch-line, his hands in his overcoat pockets, without saying a word anyone could hear. As a doctor he was said to be reliable. His interest in his work, like all his interests: billiards, soccer, new cars, whisky, was something cold and secretive. Me he regarded as a harmless fool whose exact use would be difficult to determine.

Bill, the son whom Wally had sent away, arrived at the cemetery when the service was over and the coffin had been lowered, and the mourners were just beginning to move away. He stood at the edge of the grave gazing stupidly downwards, his thick mouth open with animal surprise. Then he turned his puzzled face towards the Vicar and myself, and the members of the family still standing about; he seemed eager to run away as breathlessly as he had arrived. The Vicar, large and cool (he always addressed me as 'My dear Powell.' He had been an army chaplain in Persia and the Vicarage was full of enormous Persian vases. His hobby was carpentry and nothing seemed to worry him. Not even a congregation of five or six on Sunday morning); the Vicar captured Bill's arm, murmured bass consolation and gave the arm a friendly squeeze before he let it go. I was more awkward and the podgy young man stared at me, clearly puzzled to know who I was and what I was doing.

Back in the bungalow, the Vicar made skilful excuses and got away quickly. I stayed because I wanted to talk to Ada again. It was a mute longing that rooted me to the spot, just to be near her. The doctor stayed too, when he could easily have got away.

Bill Francis was showing himself to be a foolish creature. He smiled now as if the company were celebrating his birthday. He listened to Frankie and with Frankie behind him he had acquired a new boisterous confidence.

'All right if I sleep here tonight, Syl,' he said loudly. 'All right by you, Ada?'

There was an uncomfortable silence.

Winnie Cwm, bent over her glass of sherry, seemed to thrust herself forward so that everyone could hear her.

'Ada can come home to her old mother. There's always a home for her, she knows that.'

The older women relatives from Penygraig murmured their choral approval. There was nothing for them as they had expected, but there was no reason why they could not pass their opinion or even mediate and judge.

'We'll manage somehow, won't we, Ada?' Winnie was watching her daughter anxiously: quite unable to predict her behaviour, and surprised to see her so cool.

Ada said, 'I've got a house of my own now. I'll sleep there.'

'A house of your own, my love? Where?'

'Bronllwyn. Bronllwyn is mine now Wally's dead.'

‘So *that’s* it!’ Frankie moved towards his sister. For a moment I feared he was going to hit her.

‘Yes. That’s it. Wally and I were joint owners. Now I am the sole owner. It’s mine.’

I admired her calmness. They were a family given to rows and they took up their positions against her with the hallucinated precision of sleep-walkers.

Sylvia May’s voice trembled with accusing and yet still nervous anger.

‘You made him buy it! Made him give four thousand five hundred for it! That’s what he gave for it, wasn’t it? And all for that broken down mansion. And you made him do it!’

‘Fair play,’ said Bill trying to sound wise. ‘What’s going to be left for us?’

‘All the rest, Bill,’ Ada said. ‘All the rest.’ She turned to ask the doctor who was standing by her, for a cigarette. He supplied her with one from his silver case and lit it, with clinical speed and efficiency.

‘How much did he owe the bank?’ Frankie said.

‘I don’t know,’ she said. ‘You’ll have to find out.’

‘You’re sitting nice and pretty, anyway. As usual. Why should you worry?’

‘I’m not worrying.’

Sylvia May screeched hysterically. ‘Listen to her! Just listen! Does she care if my children starve? She twisted my poor old father against his own flesh and blood. He was a decent man until she got hold of him. Just a common whore that’s what she is. Everybody knows about her. She ought to be under lock and key.’

The doctor gripped her firmly by the shoulders and

pushed her towards the settee by the window. Her breathing had become almost stertorous.

'Get her some water! This kind of scene doesn't do any good. These things must be settled calmly. I happen to know why Wally made Ada joint owner of Bronllwyn.'

'How do you know?' Frankie's anxiety made him less careful than usual.

'Income Tax,' the doctor said. 'Wally was worried about Income Tax. And I'm afraid that's going to be your big worry too. Now Wally's gone they'll be after the estate.'

Bill's mouth was open again. He didn't seem clear about what was happening.

'If you come home, Bill, and you and Frankie work the garage between you and work damn hard, you'll be all right,' the doctor said, 'You might have to sell the Terrace houses or even this bungalow.'

'What for?' Bill asked.

'To pay Income Tax. Your father has been dodging it for nearly ten years. This is when they catch you. This is when they catch everybody. When you're dead.' The doctor smiled grimly. It impressed me to see how they all accepted his authority. I noticed it was only Ada who was not listening to him with absorbed respectful attention. She was looking at me. I thought she was considering what I was thinking. I wanted to smile and show her how much I wanted to comfort her. I felt that I was the man who should hold her in his arms.

CHAPTER EIGHT

I

I think one of my faults as a minister is that I am only intermittently anxious about the lives of people around me. Not merely do I have absent-minded moments when I hurry past people, leaving them hurt and dissatisfied with me and not merely do I forget that I am a symbol of the gospel and that it is my duty at all times to demonstrate to people that the gospel is interested in them personally: my whole aim seems to be finding love and salvation for myself rather than dispensing these elements to others. (Yet how can I dispense to others something I do not possess myself?) And even though I am able to see the secret of my failure so clearly I am able to do nothing to change my ways. I was too weak to capture and hold the brief vision of Love revealed to me with Enid. I could compare myself to Sisyphus, but in my case the stone is pushing me gradually farther down the hill and as I grow older, in moments of laziness and despair, I foresee the day when the stone will finally roll over me and come to rest as my last monument.

I satisfy the Elises because I do not intrude too much and usually conform to their wishes. I sometimes fancy they are kindest because they need me least and therefore I disappoint them least. Even Hannah, much as she needs intelligent friendship, has seen me for what I am, and has found me wanting. This is the best use they have for me: letting me wait in the bottle-green gloom while they get on with their work. I may as well be sitting in the Manse; indeed this could well be a room in my own house. It gives me just the same degree of loneliness and unease.

I never liked the Manse. It still seems another man's house after my having inhabited it alone for almost three years. Because I was unmarried they didn't bother to redecorate it for me. The wallpaper of my bedroom seems impregnated with the stale breath and fragmentary dreams of my Edwardian-looking predecessor whose enlarged photograph lies face upwards on the floor of the back room. At first some thought I intended to marry soon, or that I was avoiding the choice of lodgings for the sake of church peace; but by now everyone attributes my living alone to my eccentricity. I am the cross they not only bear but also pay.

In two unfurnished bedrooms piles of my predecessor's

junk still lie, unmoved on the bare floor, accumulating dust: vases, pictures with worm-eaten frames, and a pile of buttoned denominational diaries. My predecessor was not a very exciting diarist. He recorded his visiting, his texts, his preaching engagements, funerals, weddings, baptisms, and occasional acts of God over a pastorate lasting thirty years. To read them for any length of time depresses me. I feel sorry for my predecessor. But why, when he was so faithful and conscientious a labourer in the Lord's vineyard? From what I hear his deacons were far worse than mine. Mannie's father-in-law, Uriah Roderick; Stephens the old schoolmaster, and Peter Tudno Williams, a lay preacher who travelled in Cattle and Poultry Food. Vavasor Elis was his most loyal friend. His wife, an invalid, died years before him. But he stuck it up to his death. That was his victory. It would be more appropriate for me to be sorry for myself.

I have a library, and most of the books were once his. There was nothing else to do with them, except leave them here. But I'm not a great reader. I'm not very interested in Theology, although I try to be. I read detective stories actually, to help me fall asleep. I can't read more than half a page of Theology at a time. I don't seem to have any definite point of view. I believe in love and all sorts of idealism. And the Truth. Telling the Truth to myself is the only real gift I've got. I think that was what Enid loved most in me. Or at least I hope it was.

I can sit in my chair for hours with an open book on my lap, going over and over and over some small event as if looking for a special revelation. One of my chief impulses in living is this persistent appetite for meaning in events: against all reason I am emotionally convinced that I am moving towards some daring revelation that will explain everything to me and justify the entire length of my existence. And I am convinced that this revelation need not necessarily be death, although, once it is made, it will make death an unobjectionable parting.

II

In these trances of contemplation I consolidated the conviction that Ada needed me. Excited by the idea of helping her, I felt warmer towards my congregation. People even remarked on the improvement in my praying and preaching. I wondered whether at last they were beginning to listen and whether I was reaching that turning point in his career at which every young minister is supposed to arrive. I lay in bed tingling with warm success, overhearing voices at the Presbytery saying 'Young Powell's done wonderful work at Bethania, Pennant. Put new life into the place...' And Lambert saying and Enid hearing: 'Idris has been terrific...'

The bright morning of the first Sunday in November, Robert Ifan Williams, roadman, stood by the yew tree leaning on his stick.

'I liked that idea in your sermon, Mr. Powell. Often thought of it myself.'

'Which idea, Robert Ifan Williams?'

'About the universe reflecting as much of God as a drop of dew reflects of clouds and hills. Often thought that myself in the early morning, going out to work. Best sermon you've ever given us.'

I wondered if I got the kind of revelations reserved for the simple, as I watched him stump off down the gravel path to the wrought-iron gate.

He was in chapel again in the evening. I watched him singing the second hymn. It was a favourite hymn and he was beating time quite inaccurately with his book. His aged exaltation brought tears to my eyes. Suddenly I saw each singing face as the face of a child, trusting, longing, innocent, united, Christ's family, God's children, who had the power to move the Father to Eternal Pity. When I preached I was moved to unusual eloquence and warmth and without my usual throat clearings, hesitations, recapitulations, qualifications, reservations. It was incredible that I could ever have imagined them as monsters: Parry Castle Stores, Mannie Elis Jones, Mrs. Emrys Wynne, Mrs. Felix Elis, Mrs. Dr. Bleese, Mrs. Mannie Jones: I could have circulated the chapel bowing before each one and begging them to forgive me for having even thought of them as my tormentors. These were the heirs of God's love in Christ.

It seemed as if in wanting to comfort and give affection to Ada I found the power to comfort and give affection to others. I began to enjoy my work and although I wondered even then why knowing Ada should make such a difference and whether it was a renewal of the vision I had first seen with Enid, I was too busy gathering up my destiny to stop and analyse its progress. All I knew was that Love of any kind made the world bigger.

III

At this time I finally found the strength to overcome the last objections to my Youth Club connected with the church. I wanted to show young people that religion was not just gloomy and old-fashioned and depressing. I wanted Pennant to come into line with changes in outlook that had taken place in the world outside. I wanted to be an energetic effective pastor. Emrys Wynne agreed to take a drama class. He was exceptionally pleased because he believed that I was inspired by his go-ahead spirit. Parry Castle Stores was pleased and flattered when I asked him to take charge of the Youth Choir. Elis the Chemist I persuaded, with the help of Miss Hannah Elis, by dwelling on the moral dangers of a generation left to itself on street-corners. It surprised me how moved he was by my arguments. When I was leaving he came with me to the door, his hand on my arm. 'I can tell you, Mr. Powell,' he said, 'something like this was what my son Dick needed. A blessing on it I say.' Miss Hannah promised to organise a library and to act as treasurer. She encouraged me all she could, a firm and loyal supporter. She was wonderful.

But the greatest diplomatic triumph was inviting Mrs. Emanuel Elis Jones to direct a class in country dancing. This completely overcame the opposition of Mannie Elis Jones, who adored his wife.

She wore clothes that were youthful twenty years ago. Her faded brown hair was coiled in 'ear-phones' on either side of her heavily powdered face. She contrived to be both very playful and very delicate. She had taught infants once, but her mother's death brought her home to keep house for her father, the bearded terror Uriah Roderick, of whom it was whispered even Vavasor Elis had been afraid. (Pennant is the sort of quiet Welsh small-town that cherishes such figures.) I played the piano while Mrs. Mannie pranced about with the young men and maidens teaching them 'Gathering Peascods', trilling out the tune in her high breathless soprano, and trying to conceal how much she was enjoying herself.

For these more important meetings the club hired the hall of the Assembly Rooms. Interest in our activities ran high, and for the first time I felt myself on the verge of becoming a public figure. If only I could give my congregation some good reasons for admiring me, they would not be unwilling to do so: and then my place in local life would be assured.

IV

It seemed a season of new hope, the beginning of last winter. There were moments when I felt myself possessed of a new power. In Sunday School I was beginning to make some impression on the unresponsive adolescents in my class and their occasional smiles lifted my heart like the call of a cuckoo in dull weather. The week-night meetings, although never attended by more than fifteen people suddenly acquired a more rapid spiritual pulse. I began to tolerate people I had found intolerable. I found virtues in Mannie Elis Jones' detailed Biblical knowledge and Parry Castle Stores' long prayers that I had never seen before. I found visiting easier. I lifted door-knockers without worrying about what kind of a reception I was going to get.

I do not know if I could have kept it up without the daily possibility of meeting Ada and my inward resolve to help her. A very vague resolve because I had no idea then what I could do.

She had moved to Bronllwyn. The terrace houses had been put up for sale. Frankie Cwm and Bill Francis were running the garage between them. It was said that they had quarrelled with Ada. Every day I resolved to visit Bronllwyn and every day something turned up to help me put the visit off. It was a long conspicuous walk out of the town. When was the best time to call? I was busier than I had ever been since coming to Pennant. And I had not been able out of my contemplation of Ada to transform my urge to cherish her into some considered and concrete line of action.

On an afternoon in November I paid my first visit. The fallen leaves of the beech trees sank into the soft earth under pressure of the season. With a beating heart I walked up the untidy drive towards the house. The grounds were unkept and the lawns rough and the square house overgrown with ivy. Behind the house and the outbuildings Bronllwyn Woods stretched up, wild, mossy, and romantic, covering some seventy acres. Along the wooded slope ran the overgrown drive that led to the West Lodge, now empty. There was no lodge at the entrance nearer Pennant. There the unhinged rusting gate stood always open.

The front door was open. In Pennant they said that Wally Francis had intended to convert the old mansion into a guest house. No doubt Ada was determined to carry out his intention. Sylvia May had accused Ada of persuading Wally to buy the place. From where I stood I could see that the hall was still unfurnished. The glass-roofed conservatory on the south side was in very bad condition. I was wondering how much it would cost to repair such things and to restore order in the gardens, when Mrs. Winnie Evans appeared in the doorway.

I had not expected to see her. I had not even prepared in my mind how I was going to explain my visit to Ada. It upset me rather to see that Mrs. Evans did not seem at all surprised to see me. She wore her customary ingratiating smile.

'Very, very glad to see you, Mr. Powell. Haven't seen you since the funeral. Do come in won't you? We're in a bit of a mess still as you might expect. Did you want to see our Ada?'

I tried desperately not to give myself away, not to blush, not to stutter. What was the woman doing there on the steps above me? Like some monstrous guarding witch, servile, ingratiating, ready to be familiar, ready to be injured, and ready in the last resort to screech and claw. She was something I wanted to forget, not to meet. An incarnation of all that was detestable in Ada's background, an omen to trouble a mind that was longing to dream.

'I was so glad to see you in the funeral, Mr. Powell. Old Wally wasn't such a bad fellow. He would have liked to think the minister of Bethania was there to see him off like. You know I think he had quite a soft spot for you. It was the old ones he didn't like. Wally liked to have young people around him. We were old old friends, Mr. Powell, Wally and me. It's sad to see our friends going before us, one by one.'

She heaved a pious sigh. I said I would really have to be going.

'Sorry our Ada isn't about, Mr. Powell. She would have been glad to see you. Both of us having taken a great liking to you at the funeral. Come here again soon won't you? Always glad to see you. Glad to make a welcome.'

V

My visit to Bronllwyn disappointed and worried me more than I cared to admit. For one thing, I had hoped that Ada had fled there for refuge from her odious family; I had been glad to hear that Frankie was his mother's favourite. I was ready to do anything to help her and defend her from the cormorants. But when I arrived there I found her mother in possession. Her ties with her family were deeper than I dared admit, and however much I needed her friendship or she needed mine, I had to remember that this was a notoriously pagan family and that I was a Christian minister. We weren't on the same side.

Before Christmas the drama class produced two one-act plays translated and produced by Emrys Wynne. Mrs. Wynne made my life difficult for days before the performance by an endless stream of odd-jobs she found for me to do in connection with the plays. She blamed me for every single thing that went wrong and her conversation degenerated into one long insinuation that I did not appreciate what her husband was doing for me, and that if the dramas should fail it would be due to my cowardly lack of enthusiastic support. At first Emrys himself pretended that his wife spoke for herself alone and implied that I was not to notice her, but the night of the performance, when the make-up man failed to arrive, he lost his head and started blaming me in exactly the same terms his wife had been using, so that it became obvious to me that he had been complaining to her all along. Then the actual performance in the Assembly Rooms was marred by Jonathan Adoniah Jones having a fit. We all saw his tall thin silhouette wavering slightly before the foot-lights like a tree in a storm (he was sitting in the front row) and the farmer's son who was playing the part of the dying Saul stopped speaking and shaded his eyes with an inquisitive hand. The climax of the play was ruined. The drama class was dead.

The choir had already petered out. After the first flush of interest Parry Castle Stores began to complain that 'the Youth' (by this time members of the Club had become known collectively as 'the Youth' in Pennant) hadn't any real interest in good music, and there weren't enough tenors, and he had been invited to conduct a small male voice choir in Penygraig.

The only success was the country dancing. But the real cause of the success was for a long time concealed from Mrs. Mannie herself. It was after she had gone home, glowing with yet another triumph and smiling at me in a way she had never smiled before, that the bolder spirits started ballroom dancing. I confess it was my notion at first, but I had started something that was stronger than I could stop. There was to have been a book-talk for half an hour after the country dancing, but Miss Hannah Elis gave way very graciously. She did not dance herself and after one or two meetings stopped coming unless I asked her to take my place at the piano. My piano-playing wasn't satisfactory for ballroom dancing and my place was taken by Norman Parry Castle Stores who had perverted the family gift (as his father put it) into knocking out the noise normally generated by two or three stout instruments. His pale spectacled face gleamed with the sweat of his exertions and since there was always a cluster of admiring girls around the piano he worked harder and harder. All I could do was stay with them, 'keeping an eye on things' until the caretaker of the Assembly Rooms shuffled in at a quarter to ten. Occasionally Miss Hannah Elis kept me company, but the noise rather got on her nerves and she didn't come often.

Before Christmas the problem of 'guests' had already become acute. Boys and girls, 'youths', who did not belong to Bethania Chapel asked to join the dancing class and to become members of the Club. In the first instance I was inclined to take this as a sign of success, and it distressed me when Miss Hannah Elis opposed my suggestion that each member be invited to bring one guest when our meetings were held in the Assembly Rooms. She was also opposed to a proposal from 'the Youth' which I rather favoured: that everybody should pay sixpence a week towards an Equipment Fund. I was anxious then not to damp their enthusiasm. They were all-out for a band: buying their own instruments and having classes to learn to play. I liked the idea, I must admit. I still believed that I was strong enough to remain at the head of what was after all a movement I had started. But I can see now that she was right. I am the stone that gives way to start an avalanche, not the giant dam that can convert torrent water to useful purposes.

Mrs. Mannie, who had been so elated by the success of her dancing classes, became annoyed at the unwieldy mass of red-faced unwilling youth that crowded the doorway and corners of the dancing floor, waiting for her to finish and refusing to join in 'Gathering Peascods'. They annoyed her particularly by wandering in and out from the billiard rooms and leaving the doors open so that older men came to grin and pass remarks in her hearing. She forgot to smile at me and became short-tempered and said that I would never earn a living as a doorkeeper and said that she was no longer in favour of the 'unofficial dancing' as she called it, and intended to bring this matter to the notice of the deacons.

VI

The deacons were uncertain how to proceed. For one thing Elis the Chemist, whom they all expected to be horrified at the whole notion of the church sponsoring dancing, was strangely silent. I myself imagined that he knew a great deal from what Miss Hannah had told him and had had more time to think about the problem than his colleagues. When Parry Castle Stores brought up the subject, Elis astonished everyone by pointing out that the Old Testament was full of praise for dancing and that there could be no doubt that under proper supervision it was quite a healthy habit. He was smiling in his blind way when he said it, but he usually smiled when speaking, so that people often forgot that he had a sense of humour. Mannie Elis Jones was inclined to take this as a compliment to his wife.

'The young people certainly need something...' he murmured wisely.

'Yes,' said Parry Castle Stores. 'They need something. Something good for them. In the right way.'

'It's quite right that we should think the whole thing over,' said Emrys Wynne, in his most statesmanlike voice. 'It's a big problem in a town like Pennant. I'm inclined to think it's a problem for a Town Committee myself, on a non-denominational basis. But I quite see that isn't the point we're discussing now.'

'What happened to the choir?' Elis asked suddenly.

'The young people of today have got no interest in music,' said Parry Castle Stores. 'Not a scrap. It's most disheartening.'

'When I was a young man,' Elis the Chemist said, 'we had an excellent Young Temperance Society attached to Bethania. It did enormous good. It was militant. It got things done. Forced the public houses in the district to close on Sundays. We had processions. Do you intend to have any processions, Mr. Powell?'

'I hadn't thought of it, Mr. Elis. But thank you for the suggestion.'

'But the question at issue is whether we as a church have to carry outsiders in these activities. Are we to allow them in?' Parry Castle Stores had a passion for deciding what was allowed and not allowed.

'There's only one solution,' Emrys Wynne said, 'as I see

it. And that is to broaden the basis of the whole business. It's a town affair as I said before.'

'But that isn't the point we are discussing.' Parry Castle Stores' voice was getting dangerously thin. 'Outsiders are being let in. I'm against that.'

'So am I,' said Mannie. 'And I would like to say on my wife's behalf that she is too.'

'What does the minister think?' Elis the Chemist blinked in my direction.

'Exactly,' said Emrys Wynne. 'The man on the spot of course.' He gave a smile that was all things to all men; jocular to me, critical and disparaging to the others who could see.

'I can only tell you what the club itself has decided...'

'Who gave them the right to decide?' Parry Castle Stores asked indignantly.

'Let the minister finish,' Elis the Chemist said. 'What have they decided, Mr. Powell?'

'They want to co-opt new members by a majority vote.'

'The question is,' said Parry Castle Stores, 'are young people that age to be allowed to do just what they like? I don't think so.'

It occurred to me then that Parry Castle Stores' indignation had its origin in some domestic crises. Norman was his mother's spoiled boy; the dancing had become a bone of contention in the living room behind Castle Stores. It was a place much given to cold meat and hot argument, both flavoured with shop sauce. And Norman, so his father said, wanted to enter the ministry. His father was keen on the idea and felt it was time Norman began to train for life-long respectability: but his mother, who called herself broad-minded, saw nothing improper in her dear son banging dance music out of a quivering piano.

Mannie said: 'I tell you frankly it's my wife I'm concerned about. She has enough to do as it is.'

'They're not old enough to decide such things,' said Parry Castle Stores, giving Mannie a quick nod, as if they were in perfect agreement, whereas in fact they were talking of different things.

'My view,' I said, 'is that the Youth Club should be as autonomous as possible but that the link with the church should be a strong one. They must learn to conduct their own affairs because that is in accordance with our ideas of church government; and they must remember at the same time what church it is their club belongs to. They must be taught to make decisions and abide by them...'

'Idealism!' Parry used the word as if it were a term of abuse.

Emrys Wynne was shaking his head doubtfully. 'We mustn't be too narrow and denominational,' he murmured. 'This is a universal problem.'

Elis the Chemist had had enough debate. 'Mr. Powell is right,' he said. 'But this club if it is a church activity is responsible to the Church Meeting. It's all quite simple. Our proper course of action is to put this question before the next Church Meeting.'

VII

A church meeting was held after evening service a fortnight later. After an additional hymn I came down from the pulpit to take the chair. There is always an air of expectancy about a church meeting; not I fear in our day for a descent of the Holy Spirit, but for some dramatic outburst on the part of a discontented member. But even this very rarely happens.

I myself had to put the Youth Club point of view: the young people, scattered apart and anchored in their family pews, were too intimidated by the occasion to speak. It was difficult in those sober quiet moments to recall the image of their power that had come to me as I watched their tireless dancing. I had asked Norman Parry to speak on behalf of the young people. He had been an eloquent advocate of complete self-government in the Youth Club. But he had also just confided in me his ambition to become a minister, and for some days he had been my most frequent visitor at the Manse. In my study he borrowed books and collected material for his first sermons. At the next church meeting he was sanctioned as a lay preacher on probation. All he did at this one was to state carefully in his odd over-adult fashion that I had put the point of view of the young people very fairly and that he had nothing to add. Passing his hand over his thick black wavy hair and glancing apprehensively at his father's narrow back in the big pew, he sat down.

The nearest thing to a dramatic outburst was an unexpected speech from Mrs. Mannie, who grasped the pew in front of her tightly as if that would stop her voice from trembling. 'I don't want to speak, but I feel I must speak. This dancing class was a good thing for the young, and it was a success and I don't feel outsiders should be allowed in to spoil it. I...' She paused, sniffed back a tear and sat down.

Members of the Youth Club were asked to inform their friends of the Church's decision to confine the Club to Church members only, in a kindly Christian spirit.

VIII

At the next meeting of the dancing class, Mrs. Mannie was in good form. She felt her speech in chapel had won her sympathy and renown and she did not notice that 'the Youth' about her was unusually subdued. It was after a modified version of the 'Llanover Reel' that a stone came crashing through a window. Fortunately, the dancers were moving from the centre of the room and no one was hurt.

Mrs. Mannie ran to and fro from the piano at which I was sitting to the empty centre of the room where the stone lay.

'Keep away from the glass! Mind your feet! Sit down everybody please! Keep calm!'

Everyone was calm except Mrs. Mannie: indeed it occurred to me that 'the Youth' were too silent and unsurprised.

'Call the caretaker, Mr. Powell! Glass must be swept up! Before anyone moves! Someone could have been killed by that stone! Fetch the police, Mr. Powell! Just think of it! Someone could have been killed! One of us could have been seriously injured!'

Vaughan the Caretaker came shuffling in with brush, bucket and shovel. He held his toothless mouth open for a pause in Mrs. Mannie's flow of speech to allow him to give off one of his gnomic utterances, and closed it again, going to sweep up the glass without having spoken.

'Keep the stone for the police!' Mrs. Mannie said. 'It might be a clue.'

The members were sent home without ballroom dancing and for once they seemed very eager to go. The policeman when he arrived said it was a pity they weren't there for him to ask them one or two questions.

'I can answer any questions you want to ask, can't I?' said Mrs. Mannie. 'And Mr. Powell is a witness that what I say is true.'

IX

Unlike the drama and the choir, the dancing class did not die quietly or easily. After the stone-throwing, the attendance fell off. But when the class met again after the Christmas holidays, early in the New Year, it became well attended once more. There were occasional interruptions but nothing serious until the third week in January. The doors were thrown open by bold young men who then stood in the doorway smoking and commenting on the country dancing. Mrs. Mannie confronted them boldly, took down their names in which, she told them, the police were sure to be interested, and shut the doors triumphantly in their faces.

The next interruptions came from small children. At first Norman and his friends chased them off, but one evening the doors opened while the dancers were resting and two small children were pushed in: Gerald and Violet

Whimsey. Their father, Jack Whimsey, was locally known as a gipsy although he himself claimed to be English. The children danced as they had been told to do and men crowded in the doorway to watch. I saw Frankie Cwm and Bill Francis among them. Gerald and Violet sang as they danced and it was easy to recognise the tune as 'Gathering Peascods'. I saw Frankie Cwm bend to speak to an elder Whimsey and point towards the piano, and lift his hands laughingly in imitation of me. But the older child was not so willing, and hung back, perhaps a little worried about the fate of his little brother and sister who were advancing more boldly into the centre of the room.

I tried to shoo them out but they evaded my capture only too easily. Some of the older members took hold of them and propelled them towards the door, but the men in the doorway, Frankie and Bill Francis among them, blocked their way, laughing among themselves.

'Selwyn!' I called out to one of the biggest members of the club. 'Selwyn. Will you go down to the Police Station and ask Sergeant Roberts to come here. Tell him what's happening.'

The young men in the doorway barred his way too. Most of them had been drinking.

'Let him pass!' I spoke as authoritatively as I could.

They didn't move. Bill Francis swayed slightly, pretending to be drunk. It seemed to amuse the others.

'I tell you, let him pass!' I reached out for Bill's shoulder and gripping it tried to pull him out of the way. With startled despair I felt the immoveable muscles solid under my weak plucking hand. Bill's pale stupid face somehow belied the unusual strength of his body.

'What's the matter with this bloody crow, say?' he muttered almost to himself, and then, brushing off my hand, hit me with all his strength so that I was knocked backwards off my balance to fall in a ridiculous heap on the floor.

When I sat up the intruders had fled out into the night. Only the caretaker stood on the front steps, as usual in his carpet slippers, peering out into the damp darkness. There was blood in my mouth, but I was more aware of humiliation than pain. I would be the first minister of the gospel in Pennant to be knocked down in public by a local ruffian – no, not even a ruffian, hard-working simple Bill Francis. That was the mark of respect due to me. In such esteem was I held. There was no anxious rush to my assistance. I picked myself up. The boys who were left stared at me with the cold curiosity the young take in the defeated. The girls were crowded around the piano, where Mrs. Mannie sat dabbing her eyes.

The young policeman was anxious to take particulars. Mrs. Mannie gave him a full account of the proceedings. She saw the whole affair as a calculated attempt to discredit Bethania and herself and even religion in general and she named Bill Francis as the ringleader. The policeman was sympathetic and eager.

'Battery and assault. Serious charges,' the policeman said hopefully. 'Would you make a definite charge, Mr. Powell?'

Mrs. Mannie couldn't wait for me to take my handkerchief from my mouth.

'Of course he will,' she cried. 'It's our duty to see that hooligans are punished.'

They still waited for me to speak. 'No,' I said. 'I don't

want to make this a legal matter. I don't wish to make a charge. Thank you.'

'But you must!' Mrs. Mannie lifted her angry heavily powdered face at me. The tear patches around her eyes had dried, giving her an extra ferocity. She didn't look like Mannie's 'little girl' now. 'It's your duty! People like that shouldn't go unpunished. They get away with it once and they go on doing it again and again.'

'I don't think they'll do it again. This will be enough to warn them.'

'I'm telling you that if they get away with this, they'll become local heroes. The young people will be looking up to them and not to us.'

What gave her the idea that the young people looked up to her? I had no such illusions myself. The success of 'Gathering Peascods' had gone to her head.

'I'll wash my hands of this class and this club if you don't prosecute those men! What is the law good for if people like that can get off, scot free? They'll go on doing it again and again.' I said I wanted time to think the matter over, and the policeman sighed and said he would call and see me again the next day.

It was Mannie Elis Jones that called first. From such persons, who are accustomed by nature and training to dispense tradesmanlike amiability, it is particularly difficult to endure ill-controlled and ill-tempered indignation.

'This is what she gets, Mr. Powell, for putting her talents selflessly at the service of the whole community! Without any regard to sectarian interests! The youth of the whole community! And this is the thanks she gets, this is her reward! I may as well tell you straight out, I'm not going to allow it any longer. I'm not going to stand by and see her ill-treated in this way.'

Did he expect me to believe that it was his wife who had been knocked down and not myself? Leave me alone! I wanted to shout at him as he prated on about his wife's honour, leave me alone, little man. Leave me alone.

Perhaps I should have prosecuted. Or at least insisted on an apology. A public apology. Instead I did nothing. It is difficult to decide exactly why. Partly as a form of graceful defeat. At least I could fail gracefully. But I know what my strongest motive was. I did not wish, by taking action against Bill Francis and Frankie Cwm, to widen even more the great gulf that seemed to lie then between myself and Ada.

CHAPTER NINE

I

I called at Bronllwyn in the morning. Ada was hanging clothes out on a line in the small green paddock between the kennels and the scullery. It was a windy day and I admired the way in which the well-built handsome girl battled determinedly to peg flapping sheets to the swaying line. When she saw me she waved. I offered to pull up the heavy line when she had finished. We both took hold of the rope and pulled together. Her hands were wet and cold. I took them in mine and rubbed them to warm them. For a while she stood still, awkward with unaccustomed patience; and then, as if resuming her habit of making up her mind quickly for herself, she withdrew them with a brief smile. When she invited me in for coffee I picked up the empty clothes basket and followed her in.

The kitchen was very large and wonderfully clean. I admired it while Ada poured the coffee. I said it combined the virtues of the old and the new. I was excited to be alone with her and I must have talked too much, an over-eager expert.

Ada laughed. 'What a lot you know about kitchens.'

'That's because I live by myself.'

'Why aren't you married?' As she asked this she sat down and I was thinking how pale she looked without her make up, and with her hair up under a scarf. Almost lemon yellow. Her eyes looked bigger and seemed to be more blue, light-filled and anxious. I noticed too that to be still for her was an effort of will. Her long fingers gripped with gleaming tightness the circumference of her coffee cup.

'I've often thought of asking you the same question.' I cursed the tactless jocularity of my unconsidered answer.

'Been listening to village gossip, Mr. Powell?' She lit a cigarette and inhaled vigorously in a way that jarred on my nerves. 'It's the chief industry of Pennant. Gossip. If they put as much energy into their work they'd all be millionaires, if they worked as hard with their hands as they did with their mouths.'

'If I listened to a quarter of the gossip in Pennant I would go off my head in less than a week.'

'Most gossip is true, Mr. Powell.'

'I don't think it is.'

She turned on me quite fiercely.

'Well it is. And if you've come here to criticise I can tell you I'm not ashamed of anything I've ever done. I do a harder day's work than most and I always have done...'

'I came because I like you.'

'That's very kind of you, I'm sure. I suppose I like you too. As a man anyway. But I don't like your job and I don't like the people you work for.'

'Who do you think I work for?'

'The Elises of course. And I may as well tell you I can't stand that lot. I hate that frozen old woman. She's done me more harm than anybody else on earth, your boss has. I hate her. I'd like to kill her and dance on her grave.'

She sat down again, defiant and uncertain.

'She'd like to see me dead too. She'd like to see me out of this house. She can't stand the idea of me in this house. She wants me to fail. She'd like to see the last of me. But she's not going to. I'm settling here. I'm going to make this place a success, right in front of her nose. If it's money that counts round here, Mr. Powell, I'm going to see that I get more than she's got. So there you are. That's me and that's my business. Put that along with the gossip and there isn't much change left for you is there?'

I could see she was trying to be as tough as she could and I was glad she was talking to me in this way. Each time she spoke I rejoiced in a new sense of my own power as I realised that nothing she could say could put me off.

'We're not on the same side, Mr. Powell.'

'I'm not on anybody's side.'

'You may like to think that, but you are. Everybody is on a lead. We can only run around the post we're tied to.'

'You're a theologian.' I tried to sound unclerical, but using the word 'theologian' wasn't the best way of going about it.

'I don't know anything about that. I only know about

life. And I'm sure I know a good deal more about that than you do, Mr. Powell.'

I stood above the kitchen chair on which she was sitting. I put my hand on her shoulder.

'Now you're going to tell me I'm a lonely little girl that needs protection. Well don't you believe it, Mr. Powell. And for God's sake don't think of kissing the top of my head again. That would make you the third man to try and kiss me against my will in twenty-four hours. And that's even more than I can stand. Especially coming from a minister.'

'Ada.'

She did not look up.

She shook her head slowly.

'Ada. I want you to marry me.'

She looked up at me, her mouth open with surprise. She drew her shoulder away from my hand, and bent her head in silence.

'Flopper.' She spoke quietly, almost to herself. 'That's what Wally used to call you. Flopper or Young Come-to-Jesus. I wonder what he'd say if he knew that Flopper had asked me to marry him.'

Because my coat was always open, because of my rapid strides, my big ears, my excitable manner, because of? My skin, which is so sensitive that a remark lighter than a fly can set it trembling all over, tingled now with embarrassed humiliation. I sat down before the stove and stared into the flames of the fire through the open fire-hole. We were alone in a desert of silence, but not together. I had believed we wanted to come together, that we both hungered for the same comfort; but instead we were two figures in an empty landscape, far apart. Why was it so difficult not to despair?

'Don't look so hurt.' She smiled at me and I smiled back. She got up and came to sit on the arm of my chair. 'Don't look so hurt, little boy. You can kiss me if that will do any good. Where did that ape Bill Francis hit you?'

I ignored her question. 'I mean it seriously, Ada. I know it's difficult. It may sound impractical to you.' I stood up to speak with greater emphasis. 'But I honestly mean it.'

She touched the bruise on my cheek.

'You'll have to make yourself tougher. Don't let them bully you.'

'I'm not as weak as I look,' I said. 'I can put up with a lot. I may look like a weakling, but I can put up with a lot.'

'You are nice,' Ada said. 'But you don't understand things. You haven't learnt to look after yourself.'

I took her in my arms and she sighed, and I felt her body relax against mine. At first I whispered my love into her ear, telling her we were no longer alone, that we had found each other and love and peace and understanding and happiness and then we clung desperately to one another in utter passionate silence.

Ada was crying. 'What do you see in me, darling? What do you see in me? I didn't know a man like you existed. You're a fool you know. And I'm a fool. It won't work. I told myself the day of the funeral "I'm not going to let myself fall in love again." It's a bad business. I'm a business woman. What's so wonderful about you, Flopper? I can't see it. I used to laugh at you. Hold me tightly, darling. Crush me to death, darling. I want to die.'

Later we went upstairs to her bedroom. If it was sin, I can remember thinking, it was a necessary sin and it would be forgiven in our suffering. There was no stopping such exaltation. There was no end to it except the end to which we were going. While we were apart for a few moments we kept our eyes fixed upon one another as if not to lose contact and also in some obscure kind of challenge. But when we came together there was no hindrance between us, and in our abandonment we found our triumph; and every moment was bright with a limitless timeless illumination.

II

I felt irrevocably committed and calm and certain in a way I had never felt before. I knew what I was doing and from now on I would know what I had to do, and this love, this commitment, would give me the power to do it. No problem would be too much for me any more. Not with this love, this commitment to love, inside me. Out of my very weakness, the strength that would carry me to a more than ordinary destiny would grow, and grow the more rapidly because of the advanced state of decay my weakness had reached.

Ada seemed to be sleeping. I looked at her without any wish to disturb her, brushing her pale cheek lightly with my lips. She had murmured that she never wanted to wake and that she wished this hour of peace and fulfilment could last to the end of time. I could tell by the light through the window that it was now late afternoon. For a moment I thought of the whole life of the district around us, the garage where Ada used to work, my empty Manse, Bethania chapel waiting in silence for Sunday, the Chemist's shop, Castle Stores, my congregation scattered about its week-day tasks from Glyn Farm shore to the road to the hills. Bronllwyn was an island in this sea of living, where Ada and I were alone. I laid my hand under her breast to hear her heart beating.

We were disturbed by the noisy ringing of the front door bell in the empty hall.

'God!' Ada sat up suddenly. 'Oh Lord! You've got to get out quickly. Be quick! Quick. I'll show you the way down the back stairs. What time is it? Nearly half past three! Oh be quick please.'

She ran out on to the landing in her dressing gown. I followed her as quickly as I could, carrying my shoes.

'What will you say?' I asked hurriedly.

'That I was resting of course.'

'We must talk, Ada. When?'

'I don't know. We'll see. Please hurry.'

She allowed me to kiss her hurriedly and then sent me speeding down the narrow servant's staircase. The front door bell was ringing again. I stepped out through the back door and round through the stable yard to a point behind the rhododendron bushes where I could see the front entrance. The doctor's car stood in the drive, but the doctor himself had already gone in and the front door was closed.

III

A day later, Mannie, who was alone in the shop and therefore felt entitled to raise his voice, asked me whether I had heard that Ada Evans – 'or Ada Cwm as we call her' – had dared to renew her application to the magistrates for a licence to sell liquor at Bronllwyn. Outside it was raining and Mannie thought it was my pastoral duty to help him while away his tedious mid-afternoon hours in the empty shop.

'Young madam,' he said, in a virulent way that made me hate his little envious toad-like being. 'She'll never get it. Not for many a long year. Mrs. Felix Elis will see to that. I could tell you some things about that Cwm lot, Mr. Powell.' I detested his face of mock-horror. But my heart beat with a self-disgusting curiosity. 'Winnie Cwm's children never knew their own father, Mr. Powell, and they never saw the inside of a Sunday School. I can remember Winnie Cwm when she was Mrs. Felix Elis' maid. When Felix Elis the MP was alive and they lived in that house across the road there. And this Ada no better than her mother. Those are women who've got no right to anything except to be ashamed of themselves. Oh, they've caused trouble, especially for us.

'Dick, poor boy, he got into trouble over that Ada, you see. Their only boy, Mr. Powell, and it's sad to think of it. She was two years older than him. But sly you see. She enticed him, as they say. They had secret meeting-places. The West Lodge of Bronllwyn was one of them. It's still empty, too, by the way. They used to meet there. I caught them once when I was walking that way on my afternoon stroll. Oh that was a nasty business.'

Mannie pushed his head further across the counter in an attitude of great secrecy and I listened in a horrified trance. I wanted to hear everything and I wanted him to stop. It poured over me, his hot scalding news. I said to myself, no, don't go. Listen. This is the Truth. Listen. You say you like Truth and that you can take it all. Well, swallow this, whether or not it does you good.

'Poor Dick had to clear out. Glad to get in the Army he was. Wally Francis it was helped Ada Cwm to get rid of the baby. Naturally Mrs. Elis denied absolutely that her son had anything to do with Ada having a baby. They say Wally took her to Liverpool by car. It was a shocking business. But they don't seem to mind. They hold their heads higher than anyone in Pennant. There isn't a haughtier girl, or woman I should say, in the whole of Pennant than Ada Evans. Looks so proud and innocent playing the lady at Bronllwyn if you please. And all the right she has is to be ashamed of herself. It's a public disgrace. But what can we do? They laugh in our faces. And they get on too. Although I can't see that waster Frankie doing much at the garage. He's not as hard-working as his sister. Give her her bit of due, she's a good worker. Her mother was too before her. I think sometimes that sort of people would be reasonable if they were put under proper iron control. Discipline, isn't it? Good for us all, Mr. Powell.

'And that Wally Francis had her under his thumb. After that Liverpool business I expect. Called her his cashier-secretary. Although come to think of it she must have had him under hers by the end. It was she that wanted that big house. Wally wouldn't have thought of that. Even if it was going cheap. Oh she's smart enough, Mr. Powell. Knows how to take care of number one. But it's hard to see the wicked flushed with success, don't you think?'

I realised I was smiling my agreement. With a sudden excuse I hurried out into the rain.

IV

What else could she have done? When I went out every face on the street had information about her that I did not know. Time was divided in two, not because I was haunted by a sense of guilt and sin. My sense of sin has never been strong enough. But because our act had committed me completely deeply, to another person in a way I had always longed for and always dreaded. In this almost casual encounter began the vocation for which I had been born, began my destiny, my task of devotion.

I only bore in mind the facts that made it my business to love her. The desperate girl without a father with a worthless mother and brother driven by her need of love into disaster, made pregnant by the heedless over-grown youth she clutched in her need, taken to an abortionist by that horribly gay old man who drove himself and his paunch in large cars to distant towns to dine and dance on the edge of his open grave, and left in her weakness to his senile power. How could I be jealous of him, or Dick Elis? How could I reproach her?

I was not concerned to judge her character although with other persons it pleased me so much to exercise my little gift of critical understanding. I longed to know her in order to know how best to employ my love which should be applied as a salve where old wounds still waited for the final cure. In some sense that I only partially understood, I believed that this love of mine was something essential towards her salvation.

Our marriage, I prepared to argue passionately, was the

first step we had to take, however unacceptable it would be to the neighbourhood. In life, I prepared this phrase of self-encouragement too, it was action that counted; the only good reasons were deeds, and every good reason deserved an immediate action.

V

It wasn't easy for us to meet. We needed secrecy. We needed complete privacy because we had so much to discuss that concerned only ourselves. Ada had her mother to avoid and everyone who had any claim upon her. I had to avoid all the people who felt entitled to direct or at least judge my own behaviour.

The West Lodge was empty, cold and unromantic. The afternoon we first met there snow fell. I thought of Dick. For me there was a heavy melancholy about the place. We sat on the empty kitchen window sill or walked up and down the room to keep warm. Ada often laughed and I asked her if she was enjoying the adventure.

'It's not that,' she said. 'It's just thinking that all that big house is mine. All those rooms and all those beds. And here we are shivering in this little hole.'

'See that cupboard,' she said. 'I'll leave messages for you there, darling. Telling you when to come. I'll give you the key. I've another key in the house.'

'I didn't want to be in love again. I told myself a long time ago I'd had enough,' she said, holding my hands. 'But you. You. A minister of all people. I'm in love with you. Excuse me.' She put her hand to her mouth and laughed again like a naughty girl. I stood watching her so seriously. She lifted her hand and pressed her fingers against my soft nose. 'Cold,' she said. 'Your little nose is cold, darling.' Then we would kiss, our lips warm and restless in the cold air.

'Ada,' I said.

'Don't talk, darling. Remember I'm an ignorant girl. Just kiss me. Just love me.'

We met as often as we could. I left it to Ada to decide when we should meet. Nearly always it was in the evening, after dark. When I called in West Lodge and found no message in the dusty kitchen drawer I felt miserable, alone, deserted, condemned and imprisoned in the small dank Lodge. If there was a message – usually written hastily on the back of an envelope '*Not till Friday after six*,' or '*Tuesday after eight*,' no signature, no endearment – life became immediately warm and exciting, unendingly hopeful. For a period of time that must have been about six weeks I lived under this regime, in a manner my conscience disapproved of, but condoned, on the grounds that it helped me to understand Ada better, and committed me more and more irrevocably to her and made me, my being with her, more indispensable to her. Lovers are often compelled to do things they completely disapprove of.

Come and see the Music Room, Idris. Come on. I want to have your opinion. You can help me choose the new paper... Will you help me move the wardrobe in the Rose Room?... I found these books in the attic yesterday. Thought you could tell me if they are worth anything. You know how ignorant I am. Thank God it's an advantage for a business woman to be half-educated...(She stood before the fireplace, smoking, trying to look like a receptionist at a fashionable hotel, her arm extended, wrist bent to allow her bracelet to pour over her upturned hand.) ... *I've advertised, Idris. Only the best people I want; that's why I'm charging top prices. I've got so many plans for this place, darling. I'm going to make it the most famous guest house in the country. I've got plenty of ideas. Plenty of plans. I know how to look after myself. And your friends the Elises won't stop me. Half a dozen enquiries this morning, Idris – for Easter and Whitsun! There's so much to do ... I must bore you talking about the house all the time. Did you find out by the way, about those sixteenth century Lloyds? I'll have a booklet printed, a history of the house. People are interested in that sort of thing, I mean the right sort of people. I've thought a lot about this kind of thing ... I can't tell you how much this place means to me... I want to move that corner cupboard...*

'We must marry, Ada. Please. We must marry. That's all I know.'

Does it hurt you so much to sin, darling?

'We must marry, Ada. That's the proper beginning.'

Does it make you miserable, darling, all this love? It doesn't worry me, darling. I'm under no obligation to be good.

'We must marry, Ada.'

You should have thought of that before, darling... We must be thankful for small mercies ... take what we can while we can. That's my motto, darling. And learn how to look after yourself. You've got to learn that...

'Marry me. Marry me.'

It is so impractical, darling. Especially now. Say in ten

years' time. This is the best we can do... Marrying would be a mess, do us both harm. I know more about life than you do... Marriage has got nothing to do with love... It's better this way. Don't be in such a hurry...

I tried to ask less often, but I never gave up asking. As I discussed it solemnly and slowly one evening as we sat before the fire in the Oak Room, Ada suddenly threw her cigarette into the fire, and switched on the radio. She stood listening to music from some foreign station with her head bent and her finger tips still on the knob.

I got up and said 'Living for the moment' and we both smiled as lovers do when they repeat their private catch-phrases.

'Can you dance, Reverend Powell? Come and dance with me.'

I pushed back some chairs and took her in my arms.

'But you dance beautifully!' she said. 'Darling, where did you learn?' I grinned at her, very self-satisfied, and thought of the college dances I had attended after laborious instructions from Ken, who liked boxing and dancing. How green and how absurd I was then. Hair in my eyes, panting with eagerness to please, ready to try anything. Idris Powell rushing hopefully down life's side streets – to this encounter.

'It comes to me naturally,' I said.

'Idris, the dancing minister.' She began to laugh, very amused by her joke.

'You find me very funny, don't you?'

She nodded, pressing her lips together, and then taking hold of my nose.

'Leave my nose alone,' I said.

'Now don't be cross, darling,' Ada said, letting her hand slide down my cheek.

'You don't take me very seriously, do you?'

'I love you,' she said. She took hold of my hand and put it to her lips. I was moved and tears stung my eyes.

'Come and sit down on the settee.'

'You must try and understand, Ada. I want to marry you. I want it more than anything.'

'Think of yourself, Idris. It's so impractical.'

'I don't want to think of myself.'

'That's foolish to say that. It gets you into trouble and other people too. People who like you.'

'If you'll be my wife I promise to think of both of us for ever after.'

'Can you see me as a minister's wife? Just think of that!'

'We needn't stay here. There are other churches. We could go to America. I've often thought of that lately.'

Ada was shaking her head. Impatiently, I got up and opened the French window.

'Hush!'

I heard a noise in the deserted conservatory.

'There's someone here!'

I stepped into the draughty conservatory without thinking, leaving the French window open. The lamp in the oak-room flared up and Ada rushed to turn it down.

'Wait a minute!' Ada called, 'I'll bring my flash-lamp. Here we are.'

The beam of light fell on the crouching figure of Norman Parry, Castle Stores. The collar of his coat turned up, he looked like a flat-faced ferret.

'Norman! What are you doing here?' I cried.

'It's quite obvious,' Ada said. 'Spying.'

The unhappy youth screwed up his eyes against the light.

'You're trespassing you know,' Ada said coldly. 'In fact you are doing more than that. It could be argued that you had broken in here.'

'The door wasn't locked,' Norman said.

'Just a moment, Ada, please. Did you follow me here, Norman?'

The youth did not answer.

'Who told you to follow me? Not your father?'

'More likely his mother,' Ada said. 'Isn't she the one that prays in public?'

'Yes. It was my mother,' Norman said. 'And she was right too. People have a right to know what their minister is doing. He should be above suspicion.'

'What a nasty little rat he is,' Ada said. 'Worse than his father.'

'Just a minute, Ada. He's very young. He doesn't know what he's doing.'

'Yes I do know what I'm doing,' Norman said. He was trying to wipe his glasses with his trembling hands. 'It may look bad, but it's right what I'm doing. I'm sure of it.'

'We won't argue about that now, Norman. Perhaps you are right. In any case you can have some news to take home. You can tell your mother and anyone else who is interested that Miss Evans and I are going to be married.'

VI

They must have heard of course. They are always the last to hear, but they always do hear eventually and from them comes the judgement that will count, the verdict that is effective and can influence the course of events. For Mrs. Elis the pronouncement of opinion is part of the exercise of power: and among my people an old majesty is attached to her word. What they decide is that which is put into effect. It is their word that can transform opinion into action. Their verdict on me. Their verdict on Norman.

I begin to wonder in my own slow way which breaks upon my euphoria like a stormy dawn breaking up the night, why they have kept me waiting so long in this middle parlour? The unconscious technique of those who are accustomed to exercise power, softening up their victims with the pestle of their own petrified nerves, keeping them waiting; letting them stew in their own apprehension until, when the summons comes, they have no resistance, are pliable, can be pushed or even poured into the knot-shaped moulds of new forms of servitude.

Hannah hasn't come to speak to me as she often does, in this room, when I am waiting. She has always been kind in her abrupt impatient way. She was my keenest supporter over the youth-club project. I have always thought of her as my friend, honest and loyal, tough and not easily offended. Always her criticisms have been useful suggestions and I admit that they were always for my own good, and often it would have been better if I had followed her advice and not my own intuitions.

But not in this matter.

After the week-night service in the vestry, very badly attended, when we were the last to leave, Miss Elis closed the harmonium slowly, and I said, making conversation more than anything else, my mind dwelling on Ada and the differences between us that I was going to overcome, 'Very few here this evening, Miss Elis.'

'Do you know why, Mr. Powell? It's quite a simple reason.'

'No. I don't think I do.'

'This story about you and Ada Evans. That's the reason.'

I tried to smile and look master of the situation. For some reason with Hannah Elis I always felt compelled to act the wise man whom nothing could surprise. Perhaps as a defence against the uneasy knowledge that in some way I could not understand, I was always disappointing her. I should have troubled more to think out what it was she expected of me.

'This is the kind of occasion which shows us what people are really worth, Miss Elis.'

'Is it true?'

'Yes. It is true. I want to marry Ada, if she'll have me. I don't know whether she'll have me.'

I waited to hear what she would say while she put away some hymn books, but she didn't say anything. I watched her drawing on her gloves.

'I don't much care what most people think, Miss Elis. But I'd like to know what you think.'

'I don't think you really would, Mr. Powell. Not at all.'

She began to walk towards the vestry door.

'I wouldn't mind anything you said, Miss Elis. I know you're my friend.'

She shook her head.

'You seem to have no idea who are your friends and who are your enemies. That's part of the trouble.'

She stood looking at me as if she had never properly looked at me before. Her white face was more strained than usual. She was trying not to cry.

'It hadn't occurred to me, I must admit, that you could do something quite so foolish.'

I could love you all, I wanted to say. All. But she had gone and I was alone.

VII

'Foolish' is a poor word to indicate a miracle. Our idyll.

My love, she said, *what are you teaching me? You make me better. Ah, you take me on such long journeys, away from myself. This belongs to us. No one else could ever understand. We can love wherever there is sunlight and wherever we love we light up with our sun.*

I am worshipful and do not know what I am saying.

One healing wholeness, I said. *One white communion of one man and one woman my love I worship you. I wander over one white landscape of love no yesterday and no tomorrow one golden world inside one wide moment. One...*

She puts her hand over my mouth.

Work, she said. *Now. Yes. Give me yourself blindly wildly. Yes. All. All. All. All. Never mind the world. No words. Yes. Yes. All.*

Praise or blame came from her without words. Touches that can burn or bless. *I do not use words* she said. *I attach no value to words. Love must be strong in action and powerful and masterful. If there is weakness in you it shows in love.*

Yes, she said. *Yes. I am beautiful. I am seventeen tonight. Yes. Yes. You make me young. You make the world smile again. You have great power.*

Yes, she said. *You can give me all you have to give and more. Be gentle tonight. Understand me. You must understand me. Love understands.*

I must understand her. Love understands.

She won't see me. But I must be patient and understand.

VIII

When Norman Parry had gone she lit a cigarette and smoked in the impatient unattractive way I did not like. We did not speak. I became apprehensive. The room around me, perhaps because the French windows had been opened, seemed cold and the fire seemed to have lost its brightness. All fires die out I remember thinking to myself, fatuously, unless they are kept alight. Pantycelyn will always be remembered – a roll of drums and comes the answer – because he will never be forgotten.

Who was to speak first? Would speaking first be an admission of fault? I could see she was angry. It was natural. I had taken the law into my own hands. Perhaps I had interfered with her plans in some way that I still had not understood.

Instead of speaking I moved to her side, but she shook off my arms when I attempted to embrace her.

'No!' she said. 'You're selfish. You're no better than all the rest of them. You must have your own way. You and your mouldy religion. You're worse than Wally. At least Wally wasn't a hypocrite.'

'Darling,' I said. 'I don't understand.'

'Darling. I don't understand.' She mimicked my voice childishly. 'You don't understand that you've spoiled everything. You don't understand that this is the end. That's all it's worth to you.'

'But darling, I want to marry you,' I said. 'Isn't that clear?'

'Oh stop saying that, you fool. Go home for God's sake, and don't come here again. It's finished. Finished.'

She burst into tears and when I tried to take her in my arms a second time she did not resist me. I put her to rest with her feet up on the settee. She would not speak and I had the sense to keep quiet, but there was no peace in the silence. Only a huge assembling of unease.

HANNAH ELIS

CHAPTER TEN

I

The two maids, chattering in the kitchen, were so absorbed in their own noise that they did not hear me come in. Katie and Doris, able, I know, to read and write, but both repulsively backward. Katie is thin and rodent: she scuttles about the house, always too fast to do anything properly, her small head carrying a flopping flappy cap, and when she speaks, her teeth seem very sharp as she makes her indistinct squeaks and noises. Doris is fat. She longs for promiscuous sexual adventures and her laughter is a high-pitched nerve-racking scream. They are a difficult pair. Most of the men dislike them, but they understand that we would not keep them if we could find any better.

'The old maid's just like them,' Doris was saying. 'Only worse. Cold as a corpse.'

'She needs a man.' Katie spat out her words so quickly, I could not have understood if it hadn't been repeated. 'She needs a man.'

'Powell the minister. He'll be here tonight. Mention it to him!'

'Or Morus the milkman! He's not particular!'

It was a huge joke. And then they saw me. But after the first moment I was the one that retreated after making a feeble pretence of looking for something I couldn't find. And after this I am the one who has to continue to treat them as if they treated me with respect.

I came straight upstairs. To my own room. This lonely room. The twilight fosters self-pity. I don't mind being a barren spinster. I know that sex has no delights for a sick and unlovely creature. I take pride in my mind, not my body: if I have no love for my own body I realise no one else can love it either. It wasn't my body I expected Idris to love.

But I am not cold. They have condemned me. There was truth in their chatter. *Just like them. Only worse. Cold as a corpse*. I am bound to my uncle and my mother in the blood-cement of likeness. I have their coldness, their calculation, their trained hypocrisy, their perpetual misery, their unexpiated guilt. When they die, the thin large-headed fragile man in his thick suit and the tall square-framed powerful woman whose jet-earrings fawn upon her pierced ears, I shall be left as their perishable monument, I shall perpetuate their habits and by exercising their power bear the tattered robes of their decaying sorrow to the day of my death.

That red-faced lump of concupiscence whom I caught once scrambling out of the straw with her cowman lover, blaspheming quietly in her anxiety to make her tears flow quickly, she is the only prophet God can spare to announce briefly in passing my unimportant fate. I have become like my uncle and my mother in the long effort I have made to live with them. I have accepted their rule and become their heir, ready to perpetuate to the end of my being all the chief features of their power. I have to thank them for making me a most pliant and efficient warden of my own prison.

If I wanted to save my soul I should have set out long ago in search of my lost brother. But I have acquiesced in everything; always I have allowed myself to be overwhelmed with my own excuses; and with this hot girl's words am I rewarded. *Just like them... As cold as a corpse. Only worse.*

II

Why should I be surprised that Idris Powell should prefer to marry Ada Cwm? Katie and Doris, the rat and the sow, they have given me the answer. I have no claim on anybody, cold as I am, colder than a corpse.

The question that throbs in my mind is why does he want Ada? Am I to believe that not only is he naïve, tactless, weak, incompetent, but also unable to resist his crude physical desires? How much does he know about Ada? How much does the foolish creature allow himself to know about her? And why have I myself not told him all I know about her before this? Pride? That he should not think that I am 'chasing him'? Or this coldness, the rat and the sow spoke of? This willingness to see people suffer for their folly that makes me more my mother's inexorable daughter than anything else?

I gave him all my sympathy and support. Uncle Vavasor believed me and listened to me when I said he was a young man of great promise, handicapped by a curious Christian innocence and inexperience. But he had nothing for me – I was only an undistinguished but sometimes useful female figure in the unimportant background. To be delighted with the reward of a quick smile.

Why, why, why, should he turn to her? Has some dark law appointed her to ruin him as she ruined Dick? Does the cold hostility towards this house give her the destroying power? I must tell him. But how do I know how much he already knows? All knowledge is transformed by the knower into some form of judgement. He has so many reasons to reject me.

III

Was I trapped into being on their side? Certainly I have seen their son punish them and I think it was after Dick's death my unwilling sympathy hardened and cooled, to imprison me in this posture of cold patience. Directed and encouraged by Ada his life was an untidy clawing at the great regulated folds of their protective padding.

On Sundays he sat in the back of the chapel among the roughest boys he could find, pulling faces that were meant to mimic his father's laboured and unmelodious method of singing, and his mother who stood in the big pew with the other deacons could not help seeing him; and worse, could not help seeing that others saw him.

She said nothing to his father about his misbehaviour in chapel. Perhaps she hoped it was some foolish phase that he would soon pass through and forget. But he did not change. She could see his contemptuous attitude, the companions he chose, she even saw him going into Wally Francis' garage. His excuse was buying a new inner tube for his bike. Dick was always very ready with excuses.

Now she held out a bran bucket of affectionate gifts in order to drop the halter over his wild head. They became guarded and restrained toward one another. I could not bear the uncomfortable pity the sight of their weakening bonds of affection seemed to thrust upon me, although I managed to appear indifferent, since neither would have attached any significance to my reactions. Cold as she was to me, I found no delight in the spectacle of her slow punishment.

Dick forced himself on to his father's notice by failing his exams. Special coaching was arranged and Uncle Vavasor began to organise Dick's work. On Saturday afternoons, and occasionally from five to seven of an evening, Richard Davies was asked into the middle parlour, in order to invigilate Dick's studies. At one end of the green plush table Dick, before his untidy pile of books, constantly running his fingers through his curly hair; and at the other, his cap over his knee, one great elbow on the table, the head carter, the mud dry on his leggings; Richard Davies watching every move of his opponent's head and eye; alert cat ready to pounce on the first flicker of inattention.

Previously Dick had had more than enough pocket money from his mother. In the breakfast room where she measured out bounty to Miss Aster, she would ask this faithful witness whether in her opinion Dick had been a good boy. Miss Aster would answer with a limited repertoire of winks and coughs and nods that on the whole he had. Then my mother would hand her the silver and she in turn would pass it to the smiling but impatient Dick. Many times I witnessed this ceremony. But just when money was beginning to be a thing he could not do without, the sums handed over were reduced, and an undercurrent of bitterness which Miss Aster never properly understood marred the ritual. A sudden attack of short temper from one side or the other would leave Miss Aster open-mouthed and bewildered.

It puzzled me in those days how my mother could have been so ignorant of what was going on. Perhaps when a boy is sixteen a mother is still reluctant to attribute to him more than childish appetites. She had become a county councillor about that time and very preoccupied with the Education Committee. This helped her to avoid seeing things she did not wish to see. Their routine was a highway that avoided contact with the side-street encounters that make up the everyday life of a community. They both tried and still try to be living figureheads. It is hard to tell when the tight masks hurt such tough faces.

Dick's wilfulness had become systematic. He had his friends at Derwen, especially Ossie Rowlands the butcher's son; he had Frankie Cwm, who worked at Wally Francis' garage, and he had Ada. Always he needed money; for cigarettes, for billiards, for the cinema, for unspecified vices, for Ada.

'Hann!' He would approach me, assuming a rough pose of winning friendliness; rough because it could be more easily thrown off, and because he resented having to use it. 'Hann! Lend me half a crown, Hann.'

'What do you want it for?'

'Ossie Rowlands. I owe Ossie two bob, Hann. For games of billiards.'

'Better ask mother for it.'

'Oh come on, Hann. Be a sport.'

'I shall want it back.'

'Of course you'll get it back. With interest.' A glance at the coin in his palm. 'Thanks. So long, Hann.'

And he pestered me to let him drive. When he was seventeen he said he could drive. We had had our Austin Ten two or three years, and it was always driven by either mother or myself. My uncle insisted that I should learn to drive in order to chauffeur him to and fro from the shop. Dick was wildly anxious to acquire a driving licence. He took out the car and practised in the farm lanes, until he broke the leg of a bullock reluctant to move out of his way, smashing the left side headlamp. When this was reported to Uncle Vavasor he was forbidden to touch the car under any circumstances; but he continued to practise his driving with Ossie Rowlands. I heard how they came driving wildly along the main road from Derwen to Pennant, Dick, Ossie Rowlands, Ada and Frankie and some others, in the oldest of Rowlands the Butcher's vans, shouting and singing at the top of their voices, and Dick at the wheel, rolling from one side of the road to the other and pondering, even as he shouted loudest, what new antic he could perform next to coax more admiration out of Ada Cwm.

It is curious to enumerate the disasters large and small that overtook Dick. At the time it seemed that he was fortunate among men; endowed not only with robust health, good looks and general popularity, but also with a special gift to make each moment flower with a pleasure native to itself; he seemed, like sunshine, an amoral elemental force that found complete satisfaction in merely existing. But, now, in retrospect, he appears doomed and his life a puny provincial tragedy, and it is difficult to reconcile the one view with the other, even though they co-exist in my mind, the event and the memory of the event, myself as I am and myself as I was.

IV

We had been without a qualified assistant in the shop for almost a week and Uncle and I were constantly in the shop. Fortunately the weather was good and we were both reasonably free from asthma: but Uncle wanted to be at the farm helping to push on the delayed hay harvest, so his temper was shorter than usual. If Mannie had been qualified our constant attendance would not have been so necessary: Uncle Vavasor did not trouble to conceal this fact, so that Mannie was daily reminded of the great grief of his life. The strong smile, made by the unusually large set of false teeth that pushed out his lips so far that he had difficulty in closing them, shone as brilliantly as ever; but, as he confided to me when Uncle Vavasor was out of earshot, his skin wasn't as thick as an elephant, and Cousin Vavasor could be very trying at times, worse than trying... (Mannie's career in the shop has been a thirty year old struggle to convince himself of his own indispensability in spite of his lack of qualification to dispense.)

Mannie kept the keys and he opened the shop at ten minutes to nine. He longed for the title of manager, but as my uncle would never hesitate to explain to him no qualified chemist would ever agree to work for any length of time under an unqualified man: and I picture to myself Mannie striding around the premises in a lordly manner during those ten minutes before nine. He had a grand manner with the woman who dusted and cleaned and scrubbed the floors; and with the part time errand boy, and, I fancy, with poor Idris Powell the minister. (I resent the pompous way Mannie addresses Idris: and I think Uncle Vavasor does too.) When we were children he exercised this manner towards Dick and myself. But Dick had declared war on him before reaching school age. I think it must have begun when my mother left Dick in the shop on wet days when on her way to some council meeting. Mannie accepted Uncle Vavasor's dominion with resignation; but he always resented the use my mother made of him. His restrained politeness towards her she treated as a token of the submission that would allow her to ignore his existence; whereas he meant it as a combination of self-defence and declaration of independence.

At midday Mannie went off home 'to that wife of his' as Uncle Vavasor called her. For lunch my uncle allowed him three quarters of an hour. I myself either lunched in a nearby cafe or shared sandwiches with Uncle in the back room. On this particular day, when the clouds were being driven towards the hills like sheep into the fold, walking back from lunch, I noticed a group of youths of Dick's age on the pavement opposite our shop. I noticed Dick's bicycle was there, with the drop-handle-bars like a ram's horns. And Frankie Cwm was there. I hurried towards the shop as if pursued to a sanctuary. I had time to notice that they were all looking towards the narrow shop door with unusually solemn faces, as if they were waiting for a coffin to emerge.

Mannie was standing in the doorway of the back room: even his back was restless with excitement. Uncle Vavasor stood by the small fireplace. The small heavy cash safe on its iron stand against the wall was open. One look at Dick's miserable face showed he had been caught red-handed.

'Asleep was I?' Uncle Vavasor talked to Mannie.

'Yes. You were asleep. I came in quietly I expect because of these rubber soles. I saw him actually opening the safe. With my own eyes.'

'Where did he get the key?'

'From its usual place.'

'Has he taken anything?'

'I don't know. Have you taken anything?' Mannie spoke to Dick, looking upwards accusingly. Dick was the tallest person in the room.

'No.' I wanted to sympathise with him, caught red-handed, probably the first time: he was evasive, elusive, but not sly enough, too self-assured, to make a thief: but he wouldn't want my sympathy.

Uncle Vavasor cleared his throat as if he were about to address the Presbytery Meeting.

'Look through his pockets, Emmanuel.'

Dick moved away.

'Won't you take my word? I said no.'

'No. Of course not. Emmanuel.'

'He's not going to touch me,' Dick said.

'No need for him to touch you,' Uncle said. 'Search his pockets, Emmanuel.'

The little man's plump hands plunged into the tall boy's jacket pockets.

'Four pound notes,' Emmanuel said. 'And another two here.'

'They're mine,' Dick said.

'I thought as much.' The bushy red eyebrows rose and fell twice. 'Emmanuel, send for the police!'

Mannie looked at me where I stood now in the doorway. I was shocked to see Dick's face begin to tremble, on the verge of tears.

'Telephone?' Mannie asked Uncle.

'Telephone,' Uncle Vavasor said.

'Uncle!' I said.

'Hannah! You here too. Did you see him at it?'

'Don't send for the police, Uncle. Do you want him to appear in court? In front of his own mother. Don't call the police in.'

Mannie had suppressed his first urge to hand over his young, well-born, disrespectful, fortunate enemy to the police, to an authority he would have to obey. Dick, realising that we were all being restrained by our concern for the good name of the family, began to recover. He put his hands in his pockets.

'Perhaps you are right,' Uncle Vavasor said at last. 'For the sake of our name.'

Dick tried to make me a wink.

'Can I go then?' he said, very coolly.

Uncle Vavasor thrust his head forward in his anger, staring wide of where Dick stood.

'Where do you think you're going, tell me that? And would you mind telling me why you were stealing this money and exactly what you intended to do with it? Would you explain exactly why you planned this theft like a criminal...'

Everything he said was a waste of breath. How could he hope now to influence his son? Dick did not listen. He turned his head about, smiled brazenly at Mannie, and kept winking at me as if his father's anger and his father's partial blindness were a great joke. Yet they went through the scene. The son had to listen and the father had to finish.

'Once you start on this road, my boy, you can't stop. It becomes part of you, and you end up in prison. Why do you do it? You've been given every advantage. You come from a good family. In the course of nature you will inherit an excellent position. You've had nothing all your life except love and care and every advantage. We've lavished everything we have on you and this, this is the way you repay us...'

Uncle Vavasor had become urgently aware now of a problem he had chosen to ignore for so many years.

'Don't think, my boy, I haven't a cure for you. You're

not going to get away with it. Work is the cure. Plenty of work. Take him up to the stock room, Emmanuel. Give him an overall. Give him cleaning materials. Plenty of work up there for several days to come. Nothing like work for keeping young fools out of mischief.'

In the course of the afternoon more of Dick's friends assembled on the pavement opposite. They seemed greatly amused by some kind of antics that were going on in the windows of the store room on the top floor. To me they seemed the enemy: and if the struggle was between the young and the old (I was twenty-five then) I was on the side of the old; if between Order and Licence, I was for Order. I had always yearned for a saviour and a reformation and a restoration which would restore me to my rightful place: but Dick's follies reformed nothing and his rebellion only threatened to destroy the parts of our edifice that I most wanted to preserve.

CHAPTER ELEVEN

I

Idris Powell doesn't seem to make any distinction between Licence and Order. He seems to regard it a virtue to ignore convention, to disrupt the settled order of things in our society and destroy our traditional way of living. His irresponsible actions show that he attaches no importance to the traditions which I have come to believe it is our family duty to preserve to the fullest extent of our authority, from the foot of the mountains to the sea. It is manifestly absurd now that I should ever have thought of him as the man who would give my life a new meaning, the saviour for whom I have always, it seems, been waiting. A man known, I thought when I first began to see admirable qualities behind his apparent weakness, is better than a man unknown who might only exist in order to come one day and extinguish my life-long dream. I saw idealism in his unacceptable plans, sincerity in his lack of tact and social sense, integrity in his determination to live alone, modesty in his stumbling sermons; and in his great dog-like eyes a barely concealed longing to exchange love and devotion.

It was my particular folly, in spite of my cold patience, my appetite for truth, to imagine for longer than I shall ever admit that the love and devotion were something meant for me. Here was my stout rescuer to carry me out of the house of solitude in the valley of despair; a maker of sunlight and laughter who would bring health and joy to my bent body and imprisoned soul and teach me to rejoice freely and without guilt in the act of living.

But throughout that time he was preparing to hand himself over to our enemies. And shall I tell him about Ada? In what way can I show him, without betraying myself, how she was responsible for my brother Dick's unprofitable destruction? And how I fear now she will somehow be responsible for his. How can he begin to listen to the deep waves of understanding that long to expand themselves from my soul to his?

II

Miss Aster's fall from her long held position of precarious power. One day the china statuette, a tough and ancient shepherdess gleamed on the high mantelpiece; the next it lies in pieces before the grate. Without knowing it Dick put it there and knocked it down. The day after

Dick's escapade, having spent the afternoon in the sewing-room upstairs, at four o'clock she came downstairs almost visibly licking her lips at the prospect of what she called a real good tea. That afternoon, by his father's decree Dick was cutting thistles and nettles in a distant field. Like everyone else, Miss Aster knew there had been trouble. But her information was hazy and inaccurate.

'Shall I get a cup for Dick, then, love?' She spoke to my mother who presided silently over the teapot, one hand resting on the cosy. Miss Aster made virtuous movements, shifting her chair, as if she herself could not bear to let a morsel pass her lips until the dear one had been provided for. 'Shall I lay a place for him?'

'Sit down!' Uncle Vavasor said.

'Dick's cutting thistles in Cae Llwyn.' I felt bound to explain. 'He'll be having tea in the field.'

'What!' Miss Aster screwed her head round to study the rain drops running down the window. 'In this weather! He'll catch his death. Boys of his age never think of their health. He's so reckless. I'll take him his tea first and then I'll come back for mine, and take him a mac as well. He's sure to be without one if I know him.'

Uncle Vavasor was trying to concentrate on knocking off the top of his lightly boiled egg. My mother was stirring her tea with a melancholy slowness that showed her mind was on other things. Miss Aster began to struggle up from her place a second time.

'I won't be a tick. Which field did you say it was, Hannah?'

Uncle Vavasor dropped his egg spoon.

'Sit down woman!' His voice cracked with restraint. 'You've done all you can to ruin the lad. Finish your tea! It's the last you'll get at my table.'

Miss Aster's mouth hung open and her head swayed a little on her broad shoulders. She glanced appealingly at my mother, but my mother continued to stir her tea and to stare at the white table cloth.

'You don't really mean that, Mr. Elis?' Miss Aster said at last.

'Of course I mean it. Have you ever heard me say anything I didn't mean?'

'He means it, my love.' She looked at my mother, lifted one hand as if she would like to touch her to attract her attention; but too uncertain any more to make any kind of positive action, she let it fall again. Her face began to crumple up. Creases appeared all over it. Great gulping noises were emitted as if she were choking after a mouthful of hot tea. Then she began to wail, sticking out her chin, her hands feeling shakily through her pockets for handkerchiefs. One small one wasn't enough.

'Finish your tea, Miss Aster,' Uncle Vavasor said. 'I'll have no more of this.'

His command was absolute. She did finish her tea. Sorrow had no effect on her appetite. And it was her last meal at Uncle Vavasor's table. Her status, lacking my mother's support, declined immediately. At first she made straight upstairs for the sewing room and took tea in the kitchen. But the sewing work seemed to decrease and her visits became infrequent. The maid said it was wonderful how Miss Aster could sometimes make half a pint of milk last three days.

For many days our meals were eaten in silence. Uncle Vavasor imposed his full authority on Dick and my mother appeared to have handed him over completely to his father. My uncle and my mother began to spend more time in each other's company. Ever since I can remember after Sunday lunch my mother had read the commentary on the appropriate passage to prepare Uncle Vavasor for Sunday School. But at this time every night before going to bed my mother read to him in her harsh monotonous voice.

'A thing like this,' I can remember my uncle saying to my mother (he was referring to Dick's attempted robbery) 'is a judgement, Mary. A judgement.'

She did not answer because I was present. But her tight-lipped silence suggested to me that she disagreed. He sat staring at the fire, sighing deeply from time to time: my mother sat upright on her hard chair staring at the book open on her knees. Their son had heralded the arrival of their old age and the doom of their arrogance. The legendary yearling toad had begun to gnaw the entrails of his progenitors.

III

Before the results of the Higher School Certificate announced his failure, Dick had begun to make a reputation for himself on the farm as a hard worker, and an early riser. He had always been a favourite with Thomas John, the husbandman, my mother's most devoted servant (just as Richard Davies was my father's and Sam Daniels wanted me to believe he was mine).

Thomas John, an honest hard-working soul who loved a simple joke and dreaded a long sermon, was delighted when Dick worked at his side on the great corn stacks and admired the husbandman's skill and speed in stack construction, and asked polite questions and made simple jokes. Dick was popular among most of our people, especially in the role of the cheerful-no-nonsense-son-and-heir, who could often make a joke at the old man's expense and no harm done and no disrespect meant. They allotted him such a place in their superficial but cherished and immutable order of things. The maids we had then might perhaps have enjoyed resisting his advances, but he gave them little more than an obligatory wink or a little token off-hand teasing. Y Glyn, they all agreed, would be a dull place without him.

It was decided without any discussion that I can remember that Dick would become 'a practical farmer'. It was obvious how the succession was fixed in my uncle's mind. I should inherit the shop and Dick the farm. Young and hopeful as I was then I only thought of such things as the inheritance in order to romanticise about my missing brother, he who had been given away so quickly after my father's death. I seem to have wished that everything should be his, as my father's heir and that I should help him to recover his lost inheritance.

Dick, I believe, took a more practical view of such matters. His egocentricity was much the same as my mother's. He had the same single-minded devotion to getting what he wanted and the same possessive domineering attitude to what he regarded as his. But his character was altogether weaker than hers. He was willing to grab small things as consolations in order to avoid the unbearable condition of being disappointed. In spite of his noise, his good-looking strong physique, and his charm too (he was the only one among us to have any charm I suppose) he was a weak boy.

Because he worked hard and showed an intelligent interest in the farm and because he appeared so willing to obey his father's orders, my mother's affection for her son began to show itself again, and she began to persuade her husband that things with Dick were taking a turn for the better. 'It's a subject for thanks, Vavasor,' she would say; and reluctantly he began to agree with her. They noticed with great pleasure that Dick had begun to read books on Agriculture and that he was showing a special interest in the possibilities of Market Gardening. Conversation at meals took on a new strength. Dick learnt to argue carefully with his father, who in turn tried to remain silent long enough for his son to be allowed to make his point.

'We have the labour,' Dick would say, 'and we have the market. In a thirty mile radius of this farm there is a population of nearly fifty thousand. None of the big farms have thought of trying it yet. Leaving it all to the nurserymen. All we need are a few greenhouses and a van for quick marketing – to begin with...'

Dick was quite obsessed with his new idea. He actually began to attempt to build a greenhouse himself. Uncle Vavasor was sceptical but my mother said he should be encouraged. Dick said a van would be useful for all sorts of things to do with the farm – not merely for marketing vegetables. My mother lent him twenty pounds to buy an old Morris. Calculations were made at meal-times and Dick proved that he could deliver carrots, cabbages and potatoes in Pennant and Derwen and even further afield in large quantities in the time it took Richard Davies to deliver one load in Pennant and still be back on the farm to do a couple of hours work while Richard was jogging slowly homeward sitting on an empty cart, doing nothing.

Dick's new commercial activities allowed him to make money for himself. He was never particularly honest: if he wanted money, he took it. And he was always wanting money. Thomas John, endlessly delighted that the missus' son should be so fond of him (Dick only had to put one arm around those stout shoulders for the white moustache to widen with delight) – Thomas John was only too willing to let Dick have his way with 'those old figures.' Thomas liked to philosophise – preferably reclining on one of his well-made ricks about midday, his old felt hat tipped over his eyes – in his deep bass voice about the behaviour of crops and animals and the strange passage of time; but he did not like 'those old sums' and he was glad to have Dick work them out so quickly.

Dick kept the van in the lean-to of the hay barn. This was a discreet spot for, unless the wind lay in the east, the arrival and departure of the van could barely be heard in the house even at night. With the van Dick was able to spend his evenings where he liked.

There wasn't much to keep him home. In the little parlour on winter evenings, his father and mother sat in silence on either side of the fire. Their evenings were devoted to melancholy silence, as if their spirits had left them and had gone, bound together, riding the cold currents of the wind that leaves this world. With my book sitting near the table lamp, I too was a comfortless figure. As for the company that assembled on such a night around the kitchen fire, sometimes he joined them; but they were too slow for him now, and too unwilling or perhaps too dense to follow the dictates of his humours.

He was assumed to visit Miss Aster quite frequently. When she called to collect her milk she expressed her pleasure. *'Oh the boy still likes his old Auntie. He's good to me he is and I won't hear a word said against him. He looks me up and cheers me up and that's a lot in this world I say.'*

IV

I had gone up the stone steps to the granary to get grain for the chickens. It was a cold February day and Sam Daniel was crushing corn. All afternoon the ancient tractor that only Sam understood, rattled and roared and smoked in its shed driving the pulley belt that worked the screaming corn crusher in the granary. For two hours Sam tended these two machines; walking down the stone steps with exaggerated fat-legged care to pour oil into the entrails of the tractor and to feed it with buckets of water at intervals, since the radiator leaked. That day he also had the *gwas bach* as his assistant, watching the long bags filling with the coarse meal, tying them up ready for loading through the granary side door into the cart backed up by the second carter against the wall beneath.

When I entered the granary Sam was bringing the afternoon's crushing to an end. He sent his small assistant to stop the tractor. Both Sam and his assistant were white with flour dust.

'Cold today, Miss Hannah.'

I agreed it was.

'Hens need plenty of corn in this cold or they'll use up their energy keeping warm instead of laying eggs.' Sam liked to tell me things which he believed I ought to know. He wanted me to learn to value his knowledge and advice.

'How are your hens doing, Sam?' Sam had a smallholding of his own.

'Can't grumble, Miss Hannah. Doing their best I should say.'

Richard Davies and the rest often murmured that Sam Daniel came to Y Glyn to rest all day so as to have strength to work at home in the evening. I liked Sam. He was big and friendly and even-tempered. He paid special attention to me and he was always a comfort if he could possibly manage it.

'Did you hear Winnie Cwm has got a house in Pennant, Miss Hannah? A very nice little house too they tell me. People are wondering how she managed it. But do you know what I think?'

Sam moved the quid of tobacco in his mouth and spat through the open side door without stirring from the sack of crushed corn on which he was sitting.

'That Frankie now. He's begun to work at Wally Francis' garage, hasn't he? I wouldn't be surprised to hear that that little house belongs to Wally Francis–'

Many years ago Wally Francis had sent my uncle a bill twice for repairs done to a plough. But the receipt of the first bill had got lost and Wally would not accept my uncle's assurance that the bill had been paid in cash even though Richard Davies said he had delivered the cash at the garage to Wally himself. Uncle Vavasor was compelled to pay a second time. He went to the garage in person and said: 'Allow me to tell you, Wally Francis, that no good will come to you of this. The Lord isn't sleeping.' Wally, stout even in those days, stood shaking with silent laughter, the cheque still between his greasy fingers, watching my step-father groping his way back to his shop with his usual staring cautious jerky speed.

But Wally Francis had prospered. His was the biggest garage in Pennant and at one time he ran a local bus service. He ceased to lie prone and fat under cars himself, became Mr. Francis and had a seat on the Council. In his early days he had attended our chapel, but unable to compete there with my uncle's influence, his ambitions became purely secular. He wanted very much to become Mayor of Pennant, but he had little hope of achieving this while my step-father and my mother were alive. He had turned his attention to the County Council but he had not been elected; and he blamed my parents for that too. It appeared indeed as if Wally had become the focus point of all opposition to our authority in this district; and it was with this concept in mind that Sam Daniel was giving me his information. Sam was as sensitive to the alterations in pressure of local power groups as any trained political commentator.

'Natural,' said Sam, 'isn't it for Wally to take to that

Cwm lot, knowing as he does how much your uncle and your mother don't like them.'

As he spoke his large brown eyes searched my face for every minute reaction. I did not mind this habit, since I assumed it arose out of his anxiety to please; and in any case I liked his eyes. They were a lively feature in a thick heavy face.

'I think that Wally would do anything to spite your uncle.'

Sam always referred to my step-father as 'your uncle.' Richard Davies always called him 'your father' and Thomas John 'the mister.' I wish I could tell someone how attached I am to this institution, where each of us takes his proper place and where each of us has his own staunch henchman, and where all are united in a common devotion to this estate, our little *patria*. I want this state of affairs to flourish forever, and not to wither as we die one by one without a generation to succeed us. I wish I could call my brother out of the great ocean of humanity, to come and claim his inheritance. Dick, even at his most industrious, never loved the place as I wanted him to. But what hope can there be that my missing brother will come fully armed with protective love for a patrimony he has never seen? Less even than Idris Powell beginning to understand what all this means to me.

'You'll want to watch your brother Dick, Miss Hannah.'

'Why?'

'People say he's visiting Winnie Cwm's new house in Pennant. I've seen the van parked outside the house once myself. People say he's being "included". I don't like to hear them say that. That could mean serious trouble, Miss Hannah.'

Dick was barely eighteen then and I had never before thought of his getting married. But when Sam Daniel said he was being included at Winnie Cwm's place, I was alarmed. His behaviour had become a matter which concerned me intimately. He was on the verge of adult status. His children would become my heirs. It was my duty to watch him and consult my parents.

It wasn't easy to break that melancholy evening trance before the fire. It was a part of their routine which they identified with wise resignation. After the consultation with Thomas John and Richard Davies, after the Bible reading, after the shop, the committees, the chapel meetings, after supper, this melancholy silence and the sighs that occasionally escaped. All this seemed a great shelter designed as proof to any shock, designed to allow in any circumstances and in spite of disaster the 'carrying-on-as-if-nothing-had-happened'; although they probably regarded it as 'waiting on the Lord'.

Sam had told me a lot about Winnie Cwm and her family. Ada was illegitimate, born after Winnie had been dismissed from my mother's service. Soon after, Winnie had married a farm labourer, a simple creature called Jacob Evans. Sam said that Jacob Evans wasn't Frankie's father either. In his opinion Frankie's father was a Mr. Mathers, a collector of bad debts, who had lived near Seth Cwm's cottage just after the first war, about the time Sam first got rheumatism in his back from carrying wet corn at Rhyd-y-Maes. This Mathers was a big man in the district for a while. Sam believed he was the first man to introduce Whist Drives into Pennant. It seemed that most of the bad debts he dealt with were his own and he vanished overnight – a moonlight flit. If anyone asked Sam he would be inclined to say that there was Frankie's true father.

Poor Jacob didn't last very long, Sam said. Went into the decline and something else and went soft in the head; dying to leave his wife all that she really needed from him, the title of Mrs. Evans. Now she was styled Mrs. Evans, Hyfrydle, in her new house. Winnie Cwm, or Winnie Seth Cwm, had become Mrs. Evans, Hyfrydle; a very respectable title.

V

When Dick was out late it had been my habit to leave the back door open so that he himself could lock it after coming in. When I realised where he was spending the evening I decided to wait up and speak to him. At a quarter to ten Uncle Vavasor departed armed with his candle, spittoon and asthma powders, moving fast along a familiar route. They assumed that I would be the last to go to bed and that it was my concern to turn out the lamp in the little parlour and see that the back door was bolted.

Sitting before a big fire, I dozed and when I looked at my watch I saw it was half past eleven. It was a windy night and as I walked down the passage the candle flame danced wildly in the draught. (We still have no electric power at Y Glyn. Although they have long declared how useful it would be, Uncle Vavasor and my mother, in spite of all their influence in local affairs, have never exerted themselves to get it.) I found the door locked and felt relieved that Dick had already gone to bed. It was a difficult interview that I was almost willing to postpone.

On my way to bed I heard a slight clattering sound in the dairy. Thinking that one of the cats had been left indoors and was getting at the cream pot on the slate slab, I turned back to put the cat out. I stood in the dairy holding my candle aloft when I became aware of someone behind me, but before I could move my candle was blown out and a large rough hand clapped over my mouth. Dick whispered cheerfully in my ear.

'It's only me, Hannah bach! Getting a glass of milk. Don't wake the baby.'

'You've been stealing cream again! I might have known it was you. And you've been with those Winnie Cwm people. You've got no pride or sense. You're dragging our name in the mud. Don't you know what kind of people they are?'

'There's a snob you are, Hannah.' He spoke calmly; I was nothing to be afraid of, however angry.

'I'm not a snob. I'd rather see you going out with one of the maids than that Ada. I mean that. They mean mischief. Can't you see that? They just want to make use of you. That's why they make you so welcome. To harm our family if they can. Both those children are illegitimate. Don't you know that?'

'I know a lot more than you do, Hannah. A lot more. And there are worse things than being illegitimate.'

He didn't even thank me for leaving the door open for him. He never recognised my sympathy. What could I do but inform my mother...?

VI

I looked up from my book as calmly as I could. Even before I spoke I felt more strongly than I ever felt before that it was better to leave things alone...

'I don't expect Dick will be in before midnight.'

My mother stared at me, her long solemn face illuminated by the candle in her hand.

'Why do you say that?'

'It happens rather often. But I'm not going to wait up tonight. And I'm going to lock up before I go to bed.'

'How will he get in?'

'Last night he got a short ladder from the barn and put it against the garden wall. From the top of that he climbed up the garden shed roof and from there through the bathroom window.'

She listened intently, distrustfully, as if there was a second meaning audible behind what I was saying.

'Where does he go – so late?'

I had planned that she and I should be near the bathroom window to receive him. I thought that would make a deeper impression upon her than any words of mine. From childhood she had silently impressed upon me the unimportance of my thoughts and words.

'Where is he? Where do you think he goes?'

'Hyfrydle.'

'Hyfrydle? What Hyfrydle?'

'Where the Cwm family live. He's friendly there. With Frankie and with Ada. They say he's being "included".'

'How long have you known? Why haven't you told me before?'

'I wasn't sure. He's very secretive. I thought you knew more about his activities than I did.'

She did not move, still staring at me.

'Have you said anything to your uncle?'

'Not yet.'

I was giving her the first chance she realised that: and that I wanted him dealt with.

'Will you come there with me now? You drive better at night than I do.'

She needed glasses but refused to wear any: a curious vanity in a woman who had never used cosmetics. I did not, for myself, like going out so late at night. It was bad for my chest.

'Go to their house? Now you mean...?'

'Yes. That's what I mean. Get your coat on.'

'If you think it's the best way...'

'It's the only way.'

I almost picked up a hymn book from the top of the bureau, because normally the only place we went to together in the evening was chapel. The car made too much noise as I started up and backed it out into the yard. I drove carefully down the farm lane, stopping to open and shut the gate by Beudy Mawr, where we could hear the rich breathing of the milking herd and the occasional rattle of chains.

We did not speed. Away from the farm it was always difficult to make conversation. Out of our basic landscape our figures lost their recognisable shape and we became foreign to one another.

There was a fire burning in the front room of the pleasant white-washed little house, but no light. It was about ten o'clock and the dimly lit street was quieter than a field in the country. We thought the family was assembled in the back kitchen. My mother murmured that we'd better go round the back. A dog kennelled in their back garden barked at our approach. Mother knocked the door. We heard someone shuffling and the door was opened by a woman younger than my mother, but more worn. She held up a lamp. She was smiling. Winnie Cwm always smiled.

'Who is there please? Who is there?' Her voice trembled, always ready to fall into sobbing or laughter.

'Dear me, Mrs. Elis, Y Glyn. Mrs. Felix Elis. Yes, of course. And Miss Elis. Wait a minute now. Just a moment. Wally. Mr. Francis! Frankie my boy. It's Mrs. Elis, Y Glyn; and Miss Elis.'

'Well damn it, Mrs. Evans, Hyfrydle, ask them in.'

I heard Wally Francis laughing in the kitchen.

'Well yes, indeed. Come in, both of you.'

We stepped inside. I could see Frankie combing his hair, lounging alongside the large fireplace in the narrow kitchen. Wally Francis sat in the corner farthest from the fire, grinning, his brushed back black hair so much younger than his face. There was a football pools form on the table, a bottle of ink and a cheap pen. Frankie had been filling it up. Wally Francis' green trilby hat with its grey pheasant feather stood on the sideboard. It did not seem he had been there long.

We did not move from the passage. I tried to avoid Frankie's eye just as hard as he tried to catch mine.

'Is my son Dick here, Winifred?'

'Don't laugh now, Wally Francis. Mrs. Elis always called me Winifred. It's a nice name after all.'

'Is my son Dick here?'

'Have you seen Dick this evening, Frankie?' Winnie Cwm's voice trembled more than usual. 'They're great friends, Mrs. Elis. Strange, isn't it? Your son and my son.' Wally looked at Frankie and pointed under the table.

'Tell me where he is Winifred. If you don't I shall call the police.'

Wally whistled dramatically.

'Is he in this house Winifred?'

In the silence the whole house seemed to breathe.

'Dick!' My mother did not shout, but her voice rang through the small house.

Everyone was silent. Perhaps Frankie hoped by now that Dick had made his escape, through some window. Then quite quietly the parlour door opened and Dick stood in the doorway, the firelight flickering behind him.

Wally's small eyes darted keenly from mother to son. He was already composing an anecdote for his boozing pals.

'Come home, Dick,' my mother said.

Ada, bare-footed, and therefore short and different and soft, appeared behind the tall Dick, who was calmer than his mother or I; appeared softly, bare-footed and long-haired and beautiful in the shadow; substance of vital beauty I could understand my half-brother Dick loving and desiring and never losing from his young mind.

'Come home. At once, I tell you. Home.'

'Why can't you leave me alone? Following me here. I want to be left alone. I come home when I want to.'

'You can do what you like, Dick. I know you're growing up. Naturally you want to be your own master. You've got a strong character, like me. But you mustn't come here. This place is a wicked place and this woman is bad. They're trying to entice you in order to harm your father and me. This woman worked for me once...'

'I know that,' Dick said.

My mother said, 'She told you. You can't believe what she tells you. She's dishonest and immoral.'

'Hold on,' Wally said.

'I can prove it, and she knows it. She stole my travelling clock. My gold travelling clock. A wedding present. But I forgave her. I let her go.'

'All that's long ago, Mother,' Dick said. 'I know more than you think. It's all old stuff. It doesn't make any difference to me.'

'Come home, Dick. I can't explain things here. Things I should have told you about long ago. You've grown up so quickly.'

'There isn't much you can tell me. I know more than you think. I don't want to know any more.'

'You can't believe what they tell you. This woman's a liar. I can prove it and she knows it. A liar and a thief and worse than that...'

'Hold on, hold on,' Wally said.

Winnie Cwm was applying her apron to her eyes.

'Stop it, Mother,' Dick said. 'There are names they could call you too. That sort of thing doesn't get us anywhere. It's time that old stuff was forgotten.'

'I can't forget it.' Ada's voice was determined and fierce, ready for fight. 'And I don't intend to forget it.'

Dick looked at her. She alarmed him. He couldn't be calm with her.

'You've got to live and let live. All of you. I'm sick of this hostility. Listen, Mother. I'm going to marry Ada. You don't like the idea but you've got to get used to it.'

My mother looked cold and horrified.

'Family matters,' Wally said, plonking his hat on the back of his head. 'I'd better leave you to it. 'Night all.'

Nobody answered. He strode down the passage and let himself out through the front door.

'Your father won't let you. Won't let you make a fool of yourself. You're a minor. You can't marry. That girl. You know what she is. You know what her mother is? You must be mad. This won't happen while I'm alive. Never. Never.'

'Go home, Dick,' Ada said quietly. 'Argue it out with your mother. Plenty more I can find that will marry me, if I need to marry.'

'Don't talk like that, Ada, please.' He heard every word she said. There was no need for her to raise her voice, every syllable struck him like a blow.

'She's right you know,' Winnie said. 'She's a beautiful girl. She can pick and choose.'

'Come home,' my mother said. 'This place makes me sick. Don't you know what they are? Can't you hear it in their voices?'

'I've got my faults,' Winnie Cwm said, 'but I've got no one's death on my hands. He liked me better than her, that's what she can't bear. She still can't bear it.'

For some reason she addressed me.

'Your father was Ada's father. You didn't know that, did you? Now you're here you may as well know.'

'Don't listen to her lies, Hannah. Everybody knows she

tells lies. Always has done,' my mother said. 'She was always a liar and a thief and worse than that.'

'But no one's death on my hands,' Winnie thrust her face forward. 'Like you.' My mother struck her face with hard force across the mouth. Her wedding ring cut Winnie's lip and the woman clasped both her hands to her mouth, rocking herself and wailing. Was it the face I had seen at the side of the open grave? Was there so much truth in what I heard and saw?

'Now will you come!'

'I've got the van. Why did you hit her?'

'Because she said the truth,' Ada said. She stared boldly at my mother, ignoring her own mother's wailing.

'They're liars. Harlots, liars and thieves.'

'It's time she was told the truth. It's time everyone knew the truth,' Ada said. 'Then everyone would be surprised at my marrying you.'

'Will you come, Dick? Now. At once.'

'I've got the van. Listen, Ada. This kind of quarrel mustn't go on and on. It's got to end with us.'

'I'll wait for you at home, Dick,' my mother said.

We went to the car. The engine did not start at once. I released the brake and the car began to move slowly. As we moved I heard the thud of something heavy and soft hit the back of the car. Frankie stood in the road. He was pelting the car with clods of earth from Hyfrydle front garden. In my nervousness I braked. They were against me as much as against my mother because I was on her side. And how much right, had I to admit, did they have to hate her? As much as I had?

My mother said looking straight ahead of her: 'What are you stopping for? You've caused all the trouble you wanted, haven't you?'

VII

I heard Dick's van coming down the lane before I had locked the garage. There was a light in Uncle Vavasor's bedroom. My mother had gone straight up to him. I waited for Dick. I wanted to help him I suppose. He wasn't quite eighteen. But when I faced him by the back door he seemed older and far more experienced than I. I was the sheltered one, who knew nothing.

'Dick,' I said. I tried to make my voice sound sympathetic, but it was a windy night and all he heard was a cold fragment of speech swept away by the gusty wind from my small wrapped figure standing in his way.

'Dick,' I said.

'What do you want?' he said. 'You've caused enough trouble, haven't you?'

He walked past me into the house. My mother heard him come in. She called him before he reached the stairs. I followed him.

'Your father wants you.'

'Not tonight, Mother. I'm tired. It's late. Haven't we had enough for one night?'

'Come here, boy,' Uncle Vavasor called from his bed. My mother had put pillows behind him; he was breathing heavily as if about to have an attack. My mother spilled some asthma powder into a tin and struck a match to start it smouldering. My uncle twitched nervously at the red flannel dressing gown my mother had thrown over his shoulders. In the pale lamplight he was a bed-ridden judge. He was knowing things that had been kept from him, I had believed, in fear of his wrath: but I myself at that moment knew that wrath was not the first reaction to knowledge of things long unknown.

'How much of a fool are you? Think you're clever no doubt deceiving your mother and me. Well, you're not clever. You're just a young fool. Did you say Wally Francis was in that house, Mary?'

'Yes. He was there.'

'He's behind this mischief too. They want to harm us. Are you too much of a fool to see that?'

Dick didn't speak.

'And you want to marry that chance-child! How are you going to keep her may I ask? Or is she going to keep you?'

'I can work,' Dick said.

'Maybe you can work,' his father said, 'but not here with that chance-child. You don't bring her here. In any case the Law says you're too young to marry. I'm telling you now, put it out of your mind. You've seen her for the last time.'

Dick didn't speak.

'Do you understand? The last time.'

He paused again but Dick still kept silent.

'The last time. What do you say to that?'

'This place doesn't belong to you,' Dick said, excited by the sound of his own voice.

'What!'

'Don't think I don't know. You got rid of Hannah's

father and her brother – to get this place. I know all about it. And did you know, Hannah, Ada Cwm is really your sister? They've kept you in the dark. But they couldn't keep me in the dark. She's only my second cousin but she's your half-sister.'

'They've stuffed you up with lies, you foolish boy,' my mother said. 'Lies. Lies. Lies.'

Uncle Vavasor lay back on his pillows, struggling for breath.

'Yes. Lies,' he said. 'Wicked lies. We settled it years ago. And now they're starting again. With you.'

He dismissed Dick with a weak wave of his hand. I waited in case they should need me.

'Lies,' he said. 'How can you stop them? God knows the truth, Mary. He's our judge.'

My mother turned to look at me.

'Hannah's listening,' she said. 'Go to bed, Hannah. I don't want to have to spend the next month nursing you. Go to bed.'

CHAPTER TWELVE

I

Spinsters, it is their function and their fate, are custodians of family history. They knit the temporal net with ropes of their heart's blood. I failed this boy Dick. When he was fully-grown and free I should have gone after his friendship. My friendship would have saved him from his worst follies and saved me from this cold island of loneliness. But I was hurt by his contempt. Awake in bed I would wonder whether I really was the repulsive being Dick seemed to see: weak, ugly, sanctimonious, unsympathetic, getting in his way and spoiling his appetite and getting on his nerves. I had got used to being ignored and taken for granted: it was new to be actively despised by this captive boy who could hate me more freely than his gaolers. It hurt me and drove me farther in on myself. And to think of it now renews not the pain of being disliked but the long tireless pain of failure.

My romantic imagination took comfort in figures of my father, Elis Felix Elis, so long revered and so long dead, and my missing brother, so long lost, so long unspoken of: the rightful heir to whom in due course I could hand over the whole estate, compact, thriving and in good order. I visited my father's grave in the old churchyard. I kept the grave neat. I fed my pride on his distinguished career. *Destined for high office. High Offices*. His fame was my legacy. I left the image of my father untouched and sat at his graveside on fine afternoons dreaming of my brother who would restore the happiness I lost even before my innocence. I could not believe Ada Cwm was part of the picture. I refused to accept her. If it was true, it was her mother's fault. But I saw no proof and I saw no need to accept her. My father and my brother belonged to me.

My mother exerted her power. She chose to consider she had rescued Dick. She forced my uncle out of his brooding moods. She pursued her committees with renewed force. She successfully blocked a strong effort to make Wally Francis Mayor of Pennant.

About this time, Frankie Cwm, we heard, married Wally Francis' daughter, Sylvia May. Sylvia May, like her father too fat, her little face set like a polished self-satisfied button in a harassed wig: it seemed credible that Frankie had married her to become son-in-law of his boss. They were a low family scheming to rise. Pennant is a small town and my movements through its streets were often dictated by an obsessive determination never to pass Britannia Garage on foot. On one occasion I could not avoid, Frankie and Bill Francis and a mechanic were standing by the petrol pumps. Frankie whistled after me and passed remarks that made the others laugh. How could I accept his sister as mine; or allow our family pride to be fouled by gutter people like Winnie Cwm and Frankie Cwm?

It would be terrible for Dick to marry Ada. I still believed that. I still helped to keep watch on him.

II

'Dick's still seeing that girl,' I said.

Showers. Low clouds. Uncle Vavasor in bed. A good year for blackberries. With the aid of a walking stick a quart gathered in a few minutes. The horses free of work galloped around the salt pools in the rough fields near the shore. Smoke from the chimney of Miss Aster's cottage blown about. Wet sheaves still out sticky to touch. A slow corn harvest.

'Where?' My mother's head shot up and the black earrings trembled. 'Who told you?'

'He may be seeing her this afternoon.'

'Where? Who told you?'

'She cycles along the shore road: sometimes to the old church. Sometimes to the Far Barns. Sometimes to Ty Porth. Depends where Dick is working.'

'Ty Porth? Does Miss Aster know?'

'I expect so.'

'Who told you?'

She asked this while we walked down the lane that led to Ty Porth.

'Sam Daniel.'

Sitting on a cart, leaning forward, his elbows on his knees, his cap low, the peak shading his eyes, chewing, his heavy body shaken by the rumbling passage of the cart, the horse's glossy black rump rising and falling between the shafts: and his dark eyes scanning all the green acres with tireless curiosity.

'If he worked harder he'd have less time to look around,' my mother said. (The words might have been Thomas John's.)

She knocked impatiently. In the small doorway Miss Aster leaned back in tall astonishment.

'Gracious. This is a surprise. Come in, my dear. It's nice to see you, my love. Indeed it is. A rare pleasure. How have you been keeping? Now take your coat off and sit ye down. Tell me all about yourself.'

My mother said, sitting on the edge of one of Miss Aster's horse-hair chairs, 'Does Dick come here often, Miss Aster?'

'He doesn't forget his old auntie, my dear. I'll say that for him. A fine hard-working lad he is, my dear. And the image of you like I always said, the living image. He'll be a credit to you one day he will.'

'How often, Miss Aster?'

'Quite often, my dear. He knows I'm a lonely old bird. He knows I like to see him...'

'What I want to know is, does he meet that girl here?'

'Which girl, my love?'

'Ada Evans. Ada Cwm as they call her.'

'Of course not, my dear. What would I be thinking of,

letting a thing like that happen? She's the pretty girl I see sometimes in church, isn't she? Very civil she is. I'll say that for her. Not a bit like that awful mother of hers.'

'Dick's not to see her, Miss Aster. If she comes here, you'll have to go.'

My mother got up. 'That's all I've got to say. Come along, Hannah.'

'I was going to ask you to join me for a cup of China tea. I know how much you like China, my love. I'll just see if I've got some...'

'Don't bother, Miss Aster. We're going.'

Somebody knocked at the door.

'Was that someone knocking? I'm having a lot of visitors in one afternoon. You wouldn't think I go days without seeing a soul, would you?'

'Better answer the door, Miss Aster,' my mother said.

'Alone for days I am. No use to anybody. Too old.' She opened the door.

Ada stood there, red and gold flowers lying along her arms, blue-eyed and neat in a grey belted mac. I stared at her. I wanted to see if there was any resemblance between us. How would she look if ill-health had made her thin? The bare features without the glow and bloom of youth? The arms thin and not carrying flowers?

'Chrysanths!' Miss Aster said. 'Have you brought them for me, child? You're not going, my love. Won't you stay and have a cup of tea? For old time's sake as they say...?'

Without speaking, my mother walked past Ada as she laid the flowers in Miss Aster's outstretched arms. Ada's bicycle leaned at an acute angle against Miss Aster's garden wall. To me, my chest tight and weak, it seemed an accessory of the girl's bright young strength. Was she my sister? She was beautiful and her mother had wept at my father's open grave.

III

'Who's there?' My uncle blinked into the gloom. Mannie had locked the shop door and I had switched out most of the lights. My uncle was working his arms into his loose overcoat.

'Me, Vavasor Elis,' Wally Francis said. He was smartly dressed as usual: the latest fashion overdone on a fat man far beyond fifty.

'I thought I told you never to set a foot inside this shop years ago, Cadwaladr Francis. Stand where I can see you.'

'I've come for your own good, Vavasor Elis,' Wally said. He stood under the naked electric lamp bulb in the centre of the back room and pushed back his trilby hat, so that the light glistened on his strawberry-coloured forehead.

'What do you want?'

'Your lad is in trouble again.'

'Is that any of your business?'

'Yes. It is. He's been helping himself to my petrol.'

Uncle Vavasor stretched his lips and blinked rapidly.

'Start the car, Hannah. It's getting cold in here. Is that all, Cadwaladr Francis?'

'Yes. That's all. Except the police.'

'What about the police?'

'He's been at it for a long time. Taking advantage of my friendship. Drives up to the side pump and helps himself.

We've seen him at it. We've got witnesses.'

'Hasn't he got an account with you then?'

'Yes. I'm talking about what he takes and doesn't tell us about.'

'How long do you say he's been doing it?'

'Four or five months. Maybe longer. Frankie said he saw him at it soon after you gave him that van.'

'I didn't give it to him. His mother lent him the money to buy it, more's the pity. Well, Cadwaladr Francis. How much do you want? What's your price? Out with it.'

'I don't want anything, Vavasor Elis. Nothing at all. Except for you to send him away.'

'Away?'

'Send him away. For not less than two years. I don't care where. If you don't send him away, I prosecute.'

It was a mistake to think of Wally Francis as jolly; his laughter was only part of the strain of all the things he had to conceal. I saw how tight and mean his mouth was under the electric light. He wanted the girl and he wanted to be a respectable public man, some day Mayor of Pennant. He was determined to have both.

On the way home Uncle Vavasor's head was sunk on his chest, his long nose breathing out of his brown muffler. Near the main gate we passed Miss Aster carrying her shopping home. From force of habit I began to slow down.

'Who is it?' Uncle Vavasor asked, without looking up.

'Miss Aster,' I said. 'Shall I give her a lift?'

'Drive on, Hannah,' my uncle said. 'That stupid woman caused most of this trouble. Ruined the boy. Brought this judgement on us.'

At tea and at supper I waited for him to speak. But he said nothing. I do not even know whether he had told my mother. The meals were eaten in complete silence. Dick finishing first and pushing back his chair hurried out as the men do when they wish to demonstrate their conscientious anxiety to get back to work.

After breakfast next morning Dick and Thomas John came running into the house from the direction of the barn. We ourselves sat at breakfast in the little parlour. Dick rushed in, followed by Thomas John.

'The van!' Dick shouted. 'Somebody's smashed the engine in!'

'Speak more calmly, boy,' Uncle Vavasor said. He was exploring the base of his boiled egg with his careful spoon. 'How do you expect anybody to understand you at that rate. Haven't you been taught to speak clearly?'

'Somebody's smashed the bonnet of the van in. With a sledge-hammer I should think,' Dick said.

'Quite right,' Thomas John said. 'It's a terrible mess. Never be able to mend it. Some madman did it I should think. Smashed to bits.'

'That's good,' Uncle Vavasor said. 'I'm glad to hear that.'

'What, Father?' Dick said.

'I said I'm glad to hear it. Because I did it.'

'But...'

'Words don't make much of an impression on you, Dick. I've found that out after long practice. So I've tried a little action. Understand what I've done. If thine eye offend thee, pluck it out. It's time you grew up, my lad. I'm sending you to an Agricultural College for a year or two.'

He pushed back his chair.

'Come into the middle parlour, and we'll have a little talk.'

IV

Where Idris is waiting. My minister. And what shall I tell Idris? *This Ada whom you love is my terrible sister, who wishes to destroy and will never leave us in peace*. But will he believe me? I want to help him. I have always wanted to help, but to no purpose. My life is sterile and ineffective; has always been.

Where do they meet? I worried and wondered. Why doesn't he tell me something? I could help him. I could carry messages. I could protect them, warn them, bring them together. I was not opposed to their meeting. I was ready to go over whole-heartedly to their side. If only they showed one sign of needing me. But Dick would tell me nothing. He was young and frightened. He was being sent away in order not to go to prison and he believed it. Everything was rushed and he acquiesced in everything. He seemed paralysed by nameless fears that I could not understand, and the only positive action of which he was capable was hating me and hurting me, whenever he found the energy to stir himself out of the huddled sulking and dazed despair into which his tall handsome but young and unprotected presence was sunk. He was convinced that his father was prepared to destroy him for any further disobedience as surely as he had driven the sledge-hammer into the engine of the van. There was no resistance left in him; hardly enough to conjure up a screen of plans to hide his own capitulation from himself. *He would come back*, the plan scribbled out like thin smoke a fresh wind could effortlessly dissolve, *he would come back, in a year or two. When he was stronger and they were older. Come back to Ada, when he was richer and they were weaker. In a year or two.*

The day he left, in the still autumn afternoon when the clouds seemed balanced in the low sky and mirrored in the water of the ditches as I walked to Ty Porth, and the tide was out and seemed in no hurry to return, I worried and wondered about her. Until I saw her bicycle leaning against the wall of the house. Did Miss Aster already know she was to be evicted and was this her last act of independence? Or was the girl still so desperate and so hopeful with her armful of flowers? I wanted to find her and give her some kind of comfort. I waited and decided she was not in Ty Porth. I would look in the Middle Barn, the kind of place in which they could have met while they were still unsuspected lovers. I walked there with hallucinated certainty. She was there now, I kept saying to myself, and I would go to her. I climbed the ladder that lay against the bay in the Barn and I saw her lying with her face on her arms and I was moved with a pity near love, and I would have liked to have kept that feeling a part of myself for ever. It was something weak in me that I was desperately anxious to foster.

'Ada!' I said.

Her face was red with sorrow, fury and surprise.

'He's gone, Ada,' I said.

She did not answer but stared at me as if she were

trying to remember something about me, something unpleasant.

'He's gone,' I said. 'I'd like to help you.'

'I'll never forgive you,' she said, glaring at me. 'He didn't want to go.'

'You're wrong to blame me,' I said.

'You told them about us in the first place,' she said. 'You started the mischief. You know how your mother hated me and my mother. You made the trouble.'

'I didn't know,' said I. 'I never dreamt you could be my sister.'

'Your mother knew,' she said. 'Anyone could see that. That's why she hates us so much. Because he preferred my mother to her. That's why she killed him.'

What was this tormented girl saying, what old secrets were being exhumed from the familiar ground before me? Was there no end to my ignorance and defeat?

'Don't believe it, do you?' she cried, sitting up. As if my horror was restoring to her some measure of contentment, momentary release from her own grief. 'He had pneumonia. But how did he get it? He was ill in bed. Miss Aster could tell you. And then he had pneumonia. She would nurse him herself she said. At the farm he was ill. Miss Aster saw her empty the water jug. He had no water to drink. She let him die. At the farm it was. Miss Aster can tell you. And he was around, your uncle. They were mad then. Praying together in the middle parlour. Asking for His will to be done. Asking for Pardon. Waiting for him to die. Your father and mine. You can ask Miss Aster. But you'd better hurry. She's had her notice to move. Oh why did hc go? Why has he left me?'

Her wailing was pitiful. I kneeled on the hay beside her waiting for her to stop, afraid to touch her, and trembling at what she had said about my father. It coiled itself as smoothly as a trained snake into the empty spaces in my knowledge of the past. It was familiar as soon as I heard it in the way that only Truth can be.

I watched her shoulders shaking and I wanted to lie down beside her and take her in my arms and comfort her. I wanted to share her sorrow and I wanted her to recognise me. Together we could know there was still love left in the world.

But she shook off my hand when I touched her.

'Leave me alone,' she said.

'I want to help you,' I said, forcing myself to speak even though I knew I sounded futile and foolish.

'You can't bring him back, can you?' she said.

I did not answer. It did not seem to me as it did to her the heart of the problem.

'Can you?' she said. 'Can you?'

I did not know what to say.

'You don't want me to have him any more than they do,' she said. 'You are on their side. You're just their little servant. So leave me alone. You go to them and tell them all about me. You go and tell them how I hate them. I'll kill them just as they killed my father, tell them. Go on! Get out of my sight! I can't bear to think of you as my sister. Go and tell them about me. Go on!'

I moved down the ladder afraid that she was going to hit me. She wanted to hurt me and I couldn't bear it. She had put her hands on a pitchfork and I was afraid she would hit me with it.

'It isn't your farm yet, is it?' she said. 'Any more than theirs. It's the boy who was sent away's farm, isn't it? His and Dick's. Not yours and theirs. You can go and tell them that too. Tell them I know everything about them. They can't treat me like dirt. And you can't either. I've got as much right to be here as you have.'

She kept talking after I had left her. Outside the barn I could hear her lonely crying in the still autumn afternoon. Each of us was alone. There was no love in our world.

I remember now how much I wanted to help her. It is distinct as the memory of pain. I put my hand on her shoulder. But she would not have me. I wanted to tell her that I would help her and to tell her about Wally Francis demanding that Dick should be sent away. I wanted to help her. Why should she hurt me so much?

V

A stranger was buying a toothbrush and Uncle Vavasor in the back room had his ear against the wireless set he had just installed there, to keep in touch with the Crisis. I never knew anyone so devoted to the news. Listening to the news was a ceremony in which he supported the existence of the universe by giving it his rapt attention. The customer stopped to listen, his hand outstretched still grasping his change. My mother came in. She stopped to listen too. The words from the wireless held us in a spell in which breathing became an intolerable roar that we could never prevent other people hearing.

'Put it off, Vavasor!' my mother said. 'Put it off!'

The customer looked at her in surprise and hurried out to his car in the street, muttering 'Well, it's come. This is it.'

She switched the wireless off herself. He seemed dazed with surprise that the solemn noise should stop so suddenly.

'Dick,' she said. 'A letter from Dick. He can't go. He's only a boy. He could come home. It would be safe here on the farm. Why won't he come home? He'd rather go out there and get killed.'

Uncle Vavasor didn't say anything. My mother lifted her arms. The letter was clutched tight in her left hand. 'I want him home,' she said. 'My boy.'

Uncle Vavasor shook his head. They couldn't even console each other.

VI

Once he came in uniform. To see Ada I believe not to see us. In uniform further from us than ever. Looking at our world with the eyes of a man longing to grow up as quickly as he can. He saw Ada once. She was cashier at Wally Francis' garage. They must have quarrelled. He left before his leave time had expired more distant than a stranger. He kissed his mother unsmilingly as if he were putting his lips to his own tombstone. He could not bear the house or the people that were in it. He was eager to get away. The men noticed how much he had changed. 'Doesn't laugh the same as he used to,' Thomas John said.

PHILIP ESMOR-ELIS

CHAPTER THIRTEEN

I

Think about it, I said to myself. I have thought about it I said. Practically and impractically. More than I wanted or want to think, I've thought of things not worth thinking and thinking of.

I dragged out the tin trunk under the roll-top desk. Before I opened it, I looked at my father's photograph again. Me with a wing-collar and walrus moustache. Me in disguise. Blast him. Nothing to do with me and yet still interfering.

'I kept it all,' she said, her hands clasped on her bosom like an Edwardian actress in a postcard posture of romantic love. 'For your twenty-fifth birthday, Philip. Now the key is yours, my dear. In more senses than one... You see, for me, he did not die. I kept his spirit alive, for you...'

I didn't want the damned key. Or any of her morbid psychopathic notions. I didn't want to write his biography or engage anyone else to write it. I was sick of her fantasies that continually resurrected the long dead to interfere in the glad process of living. I never wanted to open again whatever romantic hopes that the headmistress had locked in the tin trunk. *The unpublished papers of Elis Felix Elis* now presented to a breathless impatient public, thirty years after his death, by courtesy of his ever faithful mistress, Gwendoline Esmor (the Jones was dropped before she came to London), MA, Headmistress, the Archbishop Bancroft Grammar School for Girls, Surrey.

Dreary the scent of old lavender and brown photographs of secret smiles. *Dear Elis and I at Bournemouth, July 26th 1919. Dear Elis on Magdalen Bridge, November 16th 1918. Peace for us too!*

How her loyalty glittered and her longing for loving sacrifice. *Today began this Scrapbook. A record of Elis' progress for posterity!! He has seen this empty book which I said he must fill with a glorious record. He said he approves with reservations... Elis and Mr. Lloyd George on the Terrace... Elis receiving an honorary degree in Cardiff... Elis' fighting speech on Disestablishment at Holyhead. Elis addressing an open-air meeting at Oswestry. Elis at the Garden Fête, Bibby Manor... I shall be with you in spirit where ever you are, darling. I am not ashamed. I have nothing to be ashamed of. For my own release and comfort, not yours my beloved, I put together these fond records... Elis is agreed that I keep a journal which will be an honourable and intimate account of our relationship as it progresses from day to day. He does not grudge me the comfort, bless him, and I shall write as if he were always at my shoulder and his noble handsome figure will never be far from my eyes... Met Elis outside the Abbey. Quickly we were swept into the blessed freedom of London's millions. Gave him the memorandum I had prepared on Higher Education. Hope it will be of some use to him. Discussed the future. Elis nervous of Mr. Lloyd George. Is a combination of Radical and Labour the Party of the future? I enthusiastically argue for this. Elis more cautious, bless him. But I have thought a lot about it. That way his future lies.*

Problems. Problems. Problems. Elis' wife is being difficult. An absurdly jealous woman. As if she had anything to be jealous about! What can I give Elis except the spiritual comfort he has a right to expect? One cannot expect her to understand our kind of friendship. Not that she knows about it. What then has she got to be jealous about? Poor Elis, how much he has to suffer... absorbed in her provincial narrowness she sees nothing of the greatness of his soul.

Spent the holiday week at the Radcliffe preparing material for Elis' lectures. Joyful work. He must cultivate the academic side of his reputation... Elis in Wales. Life seems so empty. What can Wales offer him? I want to see him in the main stream of political life. Must press this more when he returns to London. The misfortune of being Welsh. Wales has nothing to offer him except narrow sectarian servitude... Exciting secrets from Elis. Trouble in the Cabinet. Sir M.T.F. and H.S. are certain to resign. Elis very hopeful and yet cautious. The Coalition is unnatural he says: can't last: so that when it comes apart everything will be in the melting pot. Anxious and trying times. On Elis' advice I have begun to apply for headships. Never too soon to start he says. But if I climb, I shall climb for his sake...

Wonderful project! A holiday together in Geneva next Easter. I am so excited. Elis says he is almost certain he will be free then. We have begun to make plans. I think of little else. I am determined that everything will be arranged to the last detail and all our meetings will appear either accidental or coincidental...

Elis in Wales for more than a week and no word from him. I hate that octopus country, that cannibal mother country. I am beginning to worry. What price is to pay for my small happiness? It seems so little that I ask...

No word... If nothing comes by tomorrow I shall go there myself...

And she found him dead? And has been romantic about Death ever since. And about my birth. Was she surprised to find the despised wife pregnant by her pure-souled hero? Can anything surprise a spinster in the grip of such an obsession? My vague abduction. What obscure deal did she and my blood mother clinch over me? I am sacred to the memory of... She doesn't know it (so few people know the cause of their own actions) but would like me to be an animated tombstone, turning west and bowing to his shade at sunset. My function was to keep alive her dreams – in which I have not been fool enough to favour her. Elis, Flower of Kings; and Philip Elis, Dauphin and devoted to the quiet Queen who cuts up history with slices of bread and honey.

So few people seem to accept the fact of death. If they saw as much as I do of the cold reality, the sad mortal ruin, they would not turn the brief gift of life into a feed-tank for the rank convolvuli of their illusions.

They think I am hard; but nothing picks up the Truth and handles it more tenderly than Science. The truthful have nothing to fear from me.

II

'Philip!' she said. 'How nice! But why?'

Behind her on the wall of her study in school that pair of blue hands praying. More piety. And all over the wall behind me, the time table, spread out like a battlefield. Miss Esmor, the organising genius. She takes off her glasses and gives me a toothy headmistressly smile. Her spotless blouse, chaste pearls and unringed hands folded on the blotting paper before her. My patron aunt.

'It's rather urgent,' I said. 'Hope I'm not disturbing you?'

'Of course not,' she said. 'Would you like to give a talk to my sixth form girls next period?'

'Sorry, Auntie,' I said. 'I'm in rather a hurry.'

'But sit down, Philip,' she said. 'You look like a head prefect.'

'Margaret's father...' I said.

'Sir Christopher?'

'He's being difficult. Some nonsense about my family. Finding out about my family.'

'Did you tell him Margaret had been here with you?' she said.

'Oh yes,' I said. 'All that. But he's got fascist ideas about stock. Heredity. All very unscientific. Wants me to find out all I can about my family. Aunt, I know it's a lot to ask, but can you lend me two hundred? I could manage with two hundred. Whether the old man likes it or not, we'd go to Switzerland!'

'What does Margaret say about that?' she said.

'She'll come. I haven't put it to her quite so bluntly yet,' I said. 'But she'll come.'

'Even if I could collect two hundred,' she said, 'I don't think I ought to encourage you to do that.'

'Two hundred,' I said. 'With interest. It's a loan. That's all I ask.'

'That's not a very pleasant way of putting it, Philip,' she said.

'Well it's true,' I said. 'I'm not asking for a gift.'

She looked at her hands sorrowfully.

'I think you owe me a little more consideration than this, Philip,' she said. 'Don't you?'

'I'm sorry,' I said. 'I can't help my manner. I'm grateful to you...'

'Are you?' she said, in her most long-suffering voice.

'Well,' I said. 'If you won't, you won't. Sorry to have bothered you.'

III

'Why don't you go and see for yourself,' John said. 'It sounds romantic but it might pay off. You could kill two birds with one stone.'

'Don't want to kill anybody,' I said. 'All I want is peace and quiet to get on with my job.'

'And Margaret,' he said.

'And Margaret,' I said. He seems to think more about Margaret than even I do.

'Don't want to charge in like a bull in a china shop,' I said.

'Quite,' he said. 'Quite so. On the other hand if there's money in it...'

'That's far-fetched,' I said.

'But you are the son,' he said. 'And therefore you are your father's heir. If there is anything to inherit – except bad habits?'

'There is a sister,' I said. 'Older than I.'

'That won't make any difference. You were born before 1926. You're still the heir. You are positive there isn't a brother older than you?'

'Not that I've ever heard of.'

'Your enthusiasm overwhelms me,' he said. 'Are you sure your mother's still alive?'

'As far as I know,' I said. 'Uncle, Mother, Sister. As far as I know they're all alive. But I'm not keen on meeting them.'

'Not very curious are you, old chap?' he said.

'I'm forward-looking,' I said. 'On to the next pint. I know all I want to know.'

'Except for the cash. And except for the Master,' he said.

'To hell with the Master,' I said.

'Tut! Tut!' John said. 'Can't you make discreet inquiries? Send a private detective or something? Why don't you nip down there yourself?'

'Can you see me doing anything discreetly?' I said. 'And who's going to pay a damned detective?'

'Hmm,' John said, thinking very hard. 'Here's an idea.

You're a sort of doctor. Why don't you get in touch with a local doctor?'

'On what excuse?' I said. 'I'm not good at excuses.'

'That's simple enough,' he said.

'Well, what?'

'Genealogy,' John said. 'Ancestor worship. Digging up the past. Anything like that. Have another one?'

'You're frightfully keen on pushing me into it,' I said. 'Anybody would think you were deeply interested.'

'Well I am,' he said. 'It is interesting legally. But seriously I'd like to help.'

I couldn't help feeling it was good of him.

IV

After too much to drink no doubt, a long vivid dream.

I wore my father's enlarged photograph like a mask and marched through the streets of a small town and up the Town Hall steps and into a chapel, like Annie's Welsh chapel, and into the pulpit. At first Annie sat there by herself and then all the people of the town filed silently in. In the big pew my mother and her second husband stood loaded with chains. My mother had the shape of Auntie Gwen and the face of a witch. Her second husband was fat and shook like a jelly in his fear of me, five sausage fingers trembled on his lips. In the corner stood a large parrot cage in which my winged and red-beaked sister squawked accusations I could not understand. 'Silence and sense!' I shouted, and my index finger shot out like a stick which I could no longer bend but only point at my mother, or my sister as I shouted 'Silence and sense! Silence and sense!'

But there was no silence. John Neade, turning somersaults down the aisle landed on the seat in front of the organ, and began to play cacophanously with the gestures of a narcissistic clown. To my horror, Margaret was bent behind the organ plying the bellows, her dark head turned from me and deaf to my cries. My finger caught in the bars of the parrot cage and the bird began to peck it, peevishly, regardless of my pain. The Master stumped in, cleared the chapel, thumping each pew with his heavy stick. Margaret ran out. My wing-collar burst open as I tried to release my finger and the paper mask fell off my face.

'Amputate!' the Master cried fiercely and brought his stick down on my finger, so that part was left in my sister's beak and the blood spurted over the chained figures of my mother and her second husband.

I was driven out, alone. In a dark house in a dark room my father sat in a white dressing gown, speechless, cold, also alone, a faceless heavily framed photograph as a glassy footstool for his naked blue praying feet. He lifted his white arm and I looked through the window. On a green hillside Auntie Gwen armed with a handbag was keeping at bay my witch-mother whose wood-carved body left bare withered breasts exposed. They held their pose without moving. The bag never struck the face it was aimed at and the streaming witch hair was still as the branches of a tree. My father appeared swaying on the verandah and beckoned me to follow him. He showed me money hidden in a loose stone wall. Without being told I know exactly how much is there. Then in the dark house my father lifted a floor board and I saw exposed a heap of banknotes and documents all nibbled to rubbish by the grinning mice which scuttled away.

My father fell back on a stretcher and waited with patience to be lifted. The P.M. technician came in and Sam the ambulance driver who always jokes respectfully with me. 'Another guinea, sir!' Sam said with a respectful smile. 'B.I.D.?' And outside around the waiting ambulance the people were whispering noisily 'The dead are nobody! A worthless corpse! The Council ought to collect the rubbish oftener.' 'Not so!' I said indignantly, 'Elis Felix Elis, Member of Parliament, His Majesty's Under-Secretary of State for Family Affairs! My one father and his sacred loins and you take damn good care of him! Treat him respectfully! Treat him well!' A last glimpse of a yellow face before the ambulance doors are shut and Sam touches his cap, nods, winks, and drives away into the dark.

CHAPTER FOURTEEN

I

As we walked up and down the station platform we seemed on the verge of a long and serious conversation. On the verge because Margaret didn't speak and I didn't speak. We held hands. My hand understood her hand. My body longed to embrace her. But we were troubled. We wanted each other's sympathy in words but they would not come. We are often silent together. But usually the silence unites us; we lie back in it together. But in this silence there was no repose. Margaret was uneasy and so was I; although I can't judge whether it was for the same reason. The possibility of fatal misunderstanding appeared so great it seemed dangerous to talk.

When the train came in, quite suddenly, she looked up

into my face with a frank longing for me that seemed to well up like unspilled tears in her great dark eyes. She touched my face with her small hand. 'Darling,' she said, 'You must not think...' There seemed to be something she was unable to say.

Then just as our endearments were beginning to flow freely, John Neade came galloping along the platform, waving his umbrella, wanting to say goodbye.

I tried to look friendly.

'Are you really going there, Philip?' he said. 'D'you know I've half a mind to come with you. Damned interesting.'

'Why don't you?' I said. 'You could help me make conversation.'

'Perhaps I'd better stay and look after Margaret,' he said. 'We'll talk about it all the time won't we, Margaret?'

Margaret didn't say anything. I thought she was cross that he had come and that cheered me a little.

I got into the compartment, slammed the door and leaned out.

'What fascinates me,' John said, looking up and screwing up his face rather stupidly, 'is this other sister the Doctor writes about. Your old man was quite a lad.'

'Could happen to anybody,' I said. I was staring gloomily at Margaret.

'This Doctor Pritchard could be a phoney,' John said grinning, 'Just the pseudonym of a poison-pen auntie. Be discreet, Philip, I beg of you.'

'Name was in the Medical Register,' I said. I wished he wouldn't be quite so jocular.

'Perhaps he was struck off after going to print,' John

said. I could have done without his sense of humour. I wanted Margaret. I didn't want to leave her. I felt that I was losing her. What, for some reason I was burbling to myself, what shall it profit a man if he gain his soul and lose his whole world?

I watched her as the slowly moving train severed us apart; it was three minutes past two on a dull afternoon and her figure was the pin point that kept the whole station in place: we gazed with all our longing at each other; and I tried to ignore the figure of John standing friendly, patient, ready with his comfort no doubt, at her side.

II

As a matter of fact I never much like travelling alone. Introspective rhythm of the wheels. Intrusive chatter of well-meaning fools. Oh all those houses, all those depressing swarming millions. Too many. Too many. Too many... Margaret does not cry easily. Her sadness is like mine, distilled and bitter. Her face was pale and I love her. Neade was too damned anxious to send me on this wild goose chase. But it's for our sakes. Our future together. She's done so much for me already mostly without knowing... I watched her dancing at that mid-winter party John Neade dragged me to...

'You're unsociable, old Philip,' he said.

And I was. I snuggled into a corner with my glass and watched the pretty young men and pretty young ladies dancing, Generation O Splendid Generation. Got up from time to time to fill my glass. Saw Margaret. A brown evening dress. A big smile. Big eyes. Very gay, very happy. I watched her all the time.

'Margaret,' he said. 'I want you to meet the most unsociable man in Cambridge, Philip Esmor. The man of blood. Philip, get up and meet Margaret Able.'

Up I bobbed. Quite bold after all my quiet drinking.

'May I have the pleasure?' I said. And we were dancing. I said nothing. Except at the end of the dance I said, 'Will you dance with me again? You're very beautiful.'

When she smiled and nodded I became confident and gay. Gay as anybody.

'Do you like red hair?' I said as we danced around.

She looked at my hair and said 'Yes. I think I do.'

After the third dance we were friends, and I was on the crest of a wave.

'Ichenor,' I said. 'Good Lord, I was stationed near there in 1945.'

'But I was in school then,' Margaret said. 'In pigtails!'

'Ichenor,' I said. 'Ichenor. To think I might have... well, well, well.'

'Yes,' I said. 'I am interested in blood. But I'm really a protozoologist... Science, Margaret. Wonderful. Truthful. Exact. Precise. It makes me happier than anything else.' She listened to me and I went on and on about the asexual cycle of malaria, and she listened. We stopped dancing and stood in a corner and she listened. She was interested in me, in my work. I began to boast without knowing it.

Then we danced again.

'I love you,' I said. Quite drunk, but quite certain and quite happy. It was so easy to say it. Unguarded. She could have shot bullets into me and I would have gone on smiling. 'I love you,' I said.

She shook her head laughing. 'Of course you do,' she said. 'You're wonderful. You are going to fill those big gaps in knowledge.'

'Yes,' I nodded. 'Yes. As a matter of fact I am.'

'I love you,' I said. And the music stopped.

It was a wonderful beginning. I can remember telling myself as I went to bed, 'Esmor, old chap. The tide has begun to turn for you at last. The tide has begun to turn...' Oh Margaret, what would I do without you?

Go on thinking too much about myself. Worrying whether people liked me. Afraid of being swindled by all the rogues and knaves and bitches and sluts that swarm in this irrational outside world. That's what it amounted to. My superficial coolness and caution. Margaret, Margaret. Our love keeps me, protects me. The magic in my heart...

'Would you come with me?' I said, half-heartedly.

'No, Philip,' she said. 'I couldn't come. In any case it's something you'll have to work out for yourself. I don't want you to go. This is a dream I don't want to end. But we've got to face reality.'

'I suppose so,' I said. But now I think of it I'm not sure what she meant. And I was silent. It would have been so undignified to say, *But promise you'll love me until I come back. And when I come back you'll come with me to Switzerland... You and my work. You and my work.* I was being sent on some kind of trial. 'Into darkest Wales' as John Neade said making one of his inevitables. They see more in this than I see myself. To me it's just a damned nuisance. A blasted inconvenience. If there's any money there of course I'll be glad to collect it, but all the rest of the stuff that Aunt Gwen and Margaret's father and Margaret and John Neade seemed anxious to expect doesn't really interest me; even if my mother turned out to be a negress and my sister a Chinee. But to know where I stand will be good; then I'll settle things with Margaret and her father.

III

'I only saw your mother once,' Aunt Gwen said. 'The day I went to collect you I took a taxi to the farm. A huge Topply Queen's Nurse (as she called herself) met me at the open kitchen door. I never found out where the front door was. "He's all ready," she said about you. And there you were in a wicker basket on the kitchen table. "Where's Mrs. Elis?" I said. "She'll be down in a jiffy," the nurse said. "She's not at all well, poor dear. Not at all well. I tell you confidentially I fear for her mind. I do indeed. Now where shall I put you? In the middle parlour. It's a bit damp in the front to tell you the truth." "Miss Aster! Miss Aster!" I heard a harsh voice from the top of the stairs. "Good Lord!" the nurse said, "O goodness me! She's out of bed by herself. Topple downstairs. Coming my love!" she shouted. "Don't move my love!" I followed her as she lurched hurriedly down the dark corridor.

'I saw your mother at the top of the stairs. She was in a white nightgown and her long black hair hung over her shoulders. A strong looking woman; but nothing beautiful about her. Miss Aster pulled herself cautiously upstairs with one hand on the bannister rail. "Who's this?" your mother said pointing at me. "This is Miss Esmor, love. From London. Mr. Elis' cousin. Come to fetch the child." Miss Aster looked up and down stairs as she spoke. She was half way up, a mediator. "You are taking the child?" your mother said to me. Her voice was harsh and rather deep for a woman. You couldn't help thinking how unattractive it was. "As we arranged," I said. "As Mr. Bromley told you, I shall adopt him legally." "You are taking the child," your mother said again. As if she had heard nothing. I said "I only ask one thing." She said, "I never want to see it. Never. You understand that?" Miss Aster looked down at me inquiringly. "If that is your wish," I said. "It will be better for all concerned that way," Miss Aster said. "I don't want to see it," she said. "Don't let it ever come here." "Not if that is your wish," I said.

'Then a tall red-haired man came groping along the wall behind me. "Good afternoon," he said, touching the light cap on the top of his head. "Miss Esmor isn't it? I'm Vavasor Elis. Cousin on the other side. Take Miss Esmor into the middle parlour, Miss Aster. What are you thinking about leaving her standing there? I'll put Mrs. Elis back into her room. Mary," he said to your mother, "back into your bed at once. You know what the doctor said. Rest. Continuous rest. That's the cure."

'Miss Aster took me back to the kitchen. "Expect you'd like to see the wee mite," she said. "He's a healthy child. I've reared him myself and got very fond of him. He's a good baby. No trouble at all. Bottle milk. Allenbury's he's used to.

I've a tin here half finished. Isn't he a beauty?" And I looked at you. You were a fine baby. It went straight to my heart.

'"Terrible isn't it," Miss Aster said, shaking her head. "She's never looked at him. Never set eyes on him. When he was delivered she turned her head into the pillows and wouldn't look. And she never has. And never fed him. Milk in her breasts, not much I know: flat chested you know, but in my opinion enough to turn her head. Terrible."

'"The taxi's waiting," I said. "I'll take him now."

'"But what about the grandparents," she said. "And the legal thing? Mr. Vavasor Elis was going to bring it."

'"Confidentially," I said, "I've had enough of this place. The atmosphere is downright unhealthy for the upbringing of any child." And off we went. Poor Elis, what he'd had to put up with.'

And off she marched, to grow plainer and powerful in middle-age with me as her captive. Off like a Roman general and my basket in the procession to lead chained timid female teachers and generations of uniformed girls... A moment's compassion and then a return to the servitude of her obsession. Bringing me up as his memory as if he were the Lord God himself. The woman was doomed to be disappointed: as are all who put their trust in illusions.

I resent this journey. A journey I have never wanted to make. It has been difficult enough for me to reach an equilibrium of living. If Margaret's father and Auntie Gwen were reasonable beings, and not neurotics feeding their whole life substance to gross illusions, this journey would not be necessary. Happiness is within my reach now as it has been before; and I have to go on this worthless pilgrimage...

Dear Mr. Esmor, Your family does indeed still flourish here. They still own the family property Y Glyn, the largest farm in the district. Mr. Vavasor Elis is also a chemist and owns a flourishing business here in Pennant. He lives with his wife, Mrs. Mary Felix Elis, widow of the late Elis Felix Elis, MP, and his step-daughter, Miss Hannah Felix Elis... Dear Mr. Esmor, If you intend to pay a visit to our district and pursue your family history further, I suggest you stay at the newly opened guest house called Bronllwyn. This was formerly the country seat of the Elis-Edwards family which became virtually extinct with the death of the late Sir Robert Elis Edwards. They will make you very comfortable there and I think I may tell you in confidence that the proprietress, Miss Ada Evans, is an Elis (a natural daughter of the late Elis Felix Elis, MP).

His having a natural daughter didn't, in fact, as I might have expected, endear him to me. He merely seemed a bigger old hypocrite than ever. And more to blame.

The main advantage of my solitude gone, I am descending into a swarming pit of relatives. Not merely sadistic Calvinists and hypocrites but fat and jolly guest-house proprietresses. God what other kin are lurking in those green hills...?

IV

The compartment was too full. Should have put another carriage on at the junction. Tried to read *The Times*. Then began to fill my pipe. There was a silly faced soldier opposite me already smoking. I was surprised how little the people talked. Not like Annie Lewis. But she came from the South. Taciturn mountain lot these. Might have been in the Balkans.

'Young man,' the woman said. 'You must not smoke in here.'

I happened to be striking a match as she said this to the soldier. She thrust her tough face forward as she spoke and the long black earrings she was wearing trembled.

'As for you, sir,' she said turning to me, 'put that out at once.'

I actually let the match drop because it was burning my fingers.

'It shows great lack of consideration for others,' she said, 'that you should have lit it in the first place, just when I was pointing out that this was a non-smoking compartment.'

My temper was roused.

'Such bad manners,' the woman said in Welsh to someone opposite. 'These English think they can just do what they like. They have no right...'

'Madam,' I said, leaning forward. 'If consideration for others is your criterion, may I point out that I understand what you are saying? And that in my opinion your manners are rather worse than mine.'

Rather pleased with my restraint I got up and stood outside enjoying my pipe and studying the scenery. It looked damp and misty which was no better than I had expected. It was a relief after the tension and restraint of the last few days to have asserted myself, even in this trivial way.

The soldier came out and asked me for a light.

'You understand Welsh then?' he said. His Welsh accent was heavy.

'Moderately.'

'She wasn't expecting that,' he said. 'It was lovely. Wouldn't have missed it for anything.'

It annoyed me that his praise should give me any pleasure. His face was vacant and unintelligent and I had no wish to talk.

'Going to Derwen?' the soldier said.

'No. Pennant.'

'Oh. That's where I live. I'm going home on leave.'

'Going to stay with relatives, are you?' he said.

'No.' I didn't see why I should give him a brief outline of my life history.

'She comes from Pennant, too.' The soldier nodded his head towards the compartment we had left. 'Tough old bird. Boss of the place. Boss of the Town Council. Boss of the chapel. And when you've said that you've said everything in Pennant. Things haven't changed there since the Flood. Mrs. Felix Elis. A big woman. A very big woman. Damn, it was worth a pension to see you tell her off.'

V

It amused him, the brainless ass. But I was upset. I had begun to regret coming. At the station my main preoccupation was to avoid her. Through the dirty window of the Waiting Room I watched her march out. (She greeted whom she chose and ignored whom she chose, although she must have known almost all of them. And it was a shock to have a mother so formidably ugly. Would that also happen to my so-called rugged good looks?)

The town's name was spelled out in pebbles on the station embankment. Around it were wet rocks. A small town in a drizzle. Terraces of grey stone for the working classes. Retiring brick villas behind fir trees. A chapel with a façade like a mosque. Slated on the windward side. The Town Hall above a market place which was locked in behind gates. Drab shops. All small somehow. Humped together, turned in upon itself, seeing the world in its own reflection, and my mother striding through it, her legs kicking her long skirts forward masterfully. Her town. She could keep it.

She had favoured my extinction. It would be poetically just for me to return, shake up their complacent order, claim my own and vanish as swiftly as I came, a scourge of the Lord. Not involved with her. I had a useful and happy life before me, important work to do and I wasn't going to be deprived of it. I was here on business and I wished Margaret was with me, as indeed she should have been, to keep me sensible and laugh with me and keep my morbid curiosity in check. She was the woman I had chosen, often with some difficulty nourishing myself and eliminating my youthful urge to go after women older than myself. I understood myself well enough and I knew what kind of love and help I needed. It was disquieting that she wouldn't come. If she loved me her first loyalty was to me...

A fair-haired thin-faced man tapped my arm.

'Mr. Esmor?'

'Yes.'

‘I’m Frank Evans. My sister asked me to drive you up to Bronllwyn.’

‘Oh, thank you. Thank you.’ I was at my most academic. It was my only form of protection. This was her brother and she was my half-sister. Good God, what a mess. I was entering a jungle unarmed.

‘That’s my garage,’ he said, when we had, it seemed in no time, driven through the town. He seemed proud of his property, so I nodded. He turned right into a drive bordered by beech trees, rhododendron and azalea shrubberies.

I didn’t expect to find my half-sister so young and so good-looking. She seemed to be on tip-toes, welcoming me. I knew that the slightest sign on my side and she would have indulged herself in an emotional scene, tears and embraces. I had to avoid her eyes because I didn’t want her to see my first impression of her. A touch of the bar-maid about her for all her smartness. I was miserably at my most academic, my most English. Anyone who knew me could easily read the signs of my intense discomfort. But nobody knew me here.

IDRIS POWELL

CHAPTER FIFTEEN

I

It is better to start with the worst of a person, I was thinking, and work towards the essential child-like core that never becomes so dead that it will not respond to the application of pure love. And what is pure love, I was thinking? Not my present longing for Ada. My heart beat louder than the ticking of the grandfather clock. I longed for her with an intense physical hunger, as if her body were the road I must take towards the realisation of pure love. The flames of our love would be purgatorial, my soul said with all this thumping dogmatism of desire, that also said that there was no limit to the pleasure of the person loved, in form or thought or feeling. The lover is lost in the landscape of love, lost in a field where Time cannot tread, exploring a face and a form that can never tire. Lovers may dare to love under the Yggdrasil Tree of Time, and the beasts Age and Death wait in the branches; they cannot fall upon lovers' backs while the golden moment lasts.

I was thinking of Ada with longing and fear. I longed and yet trembled that my longing too much would spoil the delicate balance of the act of love. Life that is love-shot, I formulated, depends upon the perfection of this centre. My failure would be a worm to nibble at my living heart; an agent of death that had wandered its way into the heart of living. To think of her with all the love she needed.

I was thinking such troubled heresies as Hannah knocked lightly and came in. She apologised for my being left so long on my own.

'I'm perfectly happy, Miss Elis,' I said, jumping to my feet and smiling and being all my silliest self. 'This is a restful room to sit in. Indeed it is! So don't worry. I've been perfectly happy.'

Like one who knew me well, barely bothering to listen, small, grey, thin, she sat herself on the edge of a green armchair, holding a screwed up handkerchief between her bony hands that lay coldly on her lap. There was a century between us as I stood up still burning with my thoughts while she sat primmer than a spinster of a time past before I was born. I felt so strongly the difference between us that kept us from any real depth of understanding.

But her silence and stillness forced me to become aware of her dignity. Solemn historical process could express itself in her poor thin face. She would never hurry in speaking. She was controlled in a way that I would never be. That was something I envied about her. And as soon as I began to envy, the distance between us diminished.

'You've offended the Parrys,' she said, smiling faintly.

I put on a ridiculously bold and carefree face.

'About time I think,' I said. 'A little bit of the truth won't harm them.'

'Not many people have got an appetite for truth, Mr. Powell. I know I haven't.'

'Why should they be so sensitive?' I said. 'Why should they consider their own feelings and pride so sacred?'

'Everybody does,' she said.

'But he was spying on me. And him a candidate for the ministry! It quite disgusts me. Doesn't it disgust you?'

'I'm not so easily disgusted, Mr. Powell,' she said. 'Young people always do foolish things.'

She was implying that I was still young and was still doing foolish things. Now my pride was hurt and I felt angry. What she said was just unless I modified it by explaining to her my unique position.

'What is it you've got against Ada?' I said. 'I'd like you to tell me, straight out. I'm not afraid of the truth.'

Hannah did not speak. She looked at me as if I were something to pity. I wanted her to understand that I knew fully what I was doing and that I had no illusions.

'I know all about her,' I said. 'Taking the worst view of her relations with Wally Francis I would still marry her, call her what you like.'

'She's my sister,' Hannah said. 'I'll call her that.'

I was too amazed to speak. It seemed incredible and yet there was no excuse for my ignorance.

'Your father...'

'My father,' she said. 'The late Elis Felix Elis, MP, got her mother with child. When Winnie Cwm was our maid-servant. You haven't heard the story?'

I shook my head.

'I was about your age when I heard it first,' Hannah said. 'I couldn't believe it either.'

'Is it really true?' I said.

'I think so. I believe it. That's the nearest one can get I suppose.'

'If it is true,' I said, 'I'm glad. I'm very glad. You two, you have been the only persons I felt happy with since I've been here. It is true and it's wonderful. It's like good news.'

I ran my fingers through my hair and glanced at my reflection in the dim mirror. I was prepared to be enthusiastic and to rejoice and even to campaign for the sacred concept of sisterhood. Fragments of oratorical phrases began to glow in my mind: about sisterhood and brotherhood. I would be a brother to Hannah.

'You haven't noticed,' Hannah said, 'that she hates me?'

'Why should she?' I said. 'I've never discussed you with her. It never occurred to me that there was any connection between you.'

'But you had noticed we were on opposite sides?' she said. 'You had realised that she hated the Elises?'

'I refuse to pander to these absurd feuds,' I said. 'I ignore them. I refuse to take them into account.'

'Didn't you know why she hated us so much?' Hannah said. 'She was in love with my half-brother Dick. Dick, my mother's Dick. Didn't you know that?'

'Yes. I had heard something,' I said. 'But what does it matter? The poor fellow's dead. We can all love the dead. That's easy enough.'

'He left her when she was pregnant. That's why she went to Wally Francis. He helped her to get rid of the baby. She blames us for all this. We sent him away from her, she says. We sent him to his death rather than let her have him.'

'But that's absurd. That's exaggerating,' I said.

'That's the way she looks at it. But she hasn't discussed all this with you?'

'No. No, she hasn't.'

Hannah wiped her thin lips with the tightly rolled handkerchief.

'Have you thought, Mr. Powell, about Ada as a minister's wife?'

I was ready for this. I had come prepared and I was quite eager to answer.

'"*He that is without sin among you, let him first cast a stone at her*,"' I said.

'I wish you were right, Mr. Powell. But in this case it is the woman who wants to throw stones at us.' She smiled briefly and it seemed a pity we could not go on all evening discussing the problem objectively. It was an activity that gave us both pleasure, it was a narrow gateway into each other's company. Something we both needed so urgently.

'You must see the thing clearly, Mr. Powell,' she said. 'I used to long to be friends with her. But Ada and her friends are not only against my family. They are against our chapel, our religion, our whole way of living.'

'That seems to me an over-simplification,' I said. 'Where human beings are concerned, you just can't reduce things to black and white like that.'

'That's not what I'm doing,' she said. 'It's just that everyone has to decide which side they are on sooner or later. I have had to do that against all my natural inclinations. You are refusing to do that. That will only bring you into worse trouble. How can I help you when you refuse to see anything clearly? You don't want to be helped. You prefer to cherish your own absurd illusions.'

I thought she was going to cry. I was upset by her unusual display of emotion. She was always so cool and so grey.

'What can I do?' I said, forgetting to defend myself. 'She needs me.'

'I don't believe she does,' Hannah said. 'Ada hasn't needed anybody since Dick died, except to make use of them.'

'I want her to make use of me,' I said. I wanted to ask how much Ada had loved Dick. Hannah spoke as if she knew. I wasn't jealous of a dead boy – just a longing nostalgic curiosity that yearned for satisfaction.

'That's it,' Hannah said. 'It's you. It's you that needs her. You want to give yourself. You invite punishment. It seems to satisfy you better than love. If you want to give yourself away, give yourself to someone that needs love – there are others who need it more than Ada. If you chose to look. Excuse me.'

Quite unexpectedly she left me alone in the room. I wondered whether I would go home. (Go home and compose a letter of resignation.) I still chose Ada. If necessary I would compose a letter of resignation that evening. But I had to stay. I owed this family something. They had helped me so much. Done so much to make my difficult pastorate less difficult. I didn't care about my position. I was a failure as a minister and I was prepared to admit it. But I wasn't going to fail my Ada.

II

I heard Vavasor Elis' voice in the passage before the door opened.

'Mr. Powell? Are you alone? I thought Hannah was entertaining you. It's dark in here. You must excuse us. My wife hasn't come home yet. She's been attending the Education Committee. Expected her home before this. Train must be late. Will you come through to the little parlour? There's a fire there. And the lamps are lit. Go on now please. You go first.'

In the little parlour there was a table laid for supper. A square mahogany table, covered with a starched white cloth and places laid for four. The house seemed full of grandfather clocks. One ticked also in this silence, where the fire and the lamp kept out the shadows. Against the wall was the locked roll-top desk dedicated to farm business. On the window table the wireless took its place. Before me on the wall hung an enlarged photograph of the deacons of Bethania of thirty years ago. A small minister in the middle folds his arms Napoleonically and strives not to appear like a ventriloquist's doll in a high collar. In my present mood I challenge those solemn self-important faces. Vavasor Elis is among them, the youngest deacon, standing at the end of the second row. Less of an ally then than now I think. The bearded seated giants with whom I should have done battle. The giants of old. Men who moulded this society. The great bully Uriah Roderick and the sea captain Beuno Edwards. And the lay preacher who travelled in Cattle Foods. More worthy opponents to my masterful courageous mood than those mice Mannie Elis Jones and Parry Castle Stores. Why should I resign? This situation wasn't too much for me. It was what I had long waited for: a tension on which to practise my powers of reconciliation. By this concept of Reconciliation I was greatly warmed. It gave me the sense of purpose and dedication without which I could never be happy for long. There was no need to give up. My authority would be the authority of Love. They should all listen to me because I loved them all.

'I'm glad we can have this chat by ourselves,' Vavasor Elis was saying, and I was nodding with vehement smiling goodwill. 'Very glad. I want to speak quite frankly, Mr. Powell. You know me well enough not to take offence if I speak too frankly.'

'Of course I do, Mr. Elis,' I cried.

'I have always admired your preaching, Mr. Powell,' Vavasor Elis said. 'As you know your theological standpoint is more liberal than mine, but I have had great blessing and comfort from your preaching. It has been thoughtful, personal, evangelical, sincere. You have preached redemption for sinners. And we all need that, Mr. Powell. We all need to be reminded of that.'

I was moved by his praise. What a glorious religion that can make men so different from each other indebted and bound to one another in an unceasing obligation to love! I could have embraced the blind man, blinking as he was, with a thin cap on his head, his long freckled hands spread out to warm before the fire.

'As I explained to Parry and my cousin Mannie, your own private life, Mr. Powell, is no concern of mine. It is true that a minister of the gospel is in a very special position; but I am not in favour of any attempts on the part of his congregation to curtail his liberty. He is a man, entitled to as much freedom as we demand for ourselves. Any gossip about a minister is something I have always refused to listen to. I hate gossip, Mr. Powell. It should be labelled poison. It's an agent of the devil: whispering mischief has always been his weapon. I have always minded my own business; I expect other people to mind theirs. That's what I told them, and they didn't like it. Now I'm afraid I must ask you, is there any truth in what they are saying?'

'What are they saying, Mr. Elis?' I said. 'That Norman Parry has been spying on me?'

'Ill-bred lot those Parrys,' Vavasor Elis said. 'I can remember his grandfather. Never tired of asking questions. Always leaning over his front gate down by Rhos cross-roads. "Where can I say you are off to?" he used to say. I can remember Richard Davies here, a young man passing with an empty cart. "Where can I say you are off to, Richard Davies?" the old man said. "Say you don't know," Richard said. I've always regarded that as an illustration of their family character. A breed of busy-bodies.'

He stared judicially into the heart of the fire and I wondered what red blurred shapes he saw.

'I may as well be blunt, Mr. Powell,' he said suddenly. 'They say you are carrying on with Ada Evans. That boy Norman says he's seen you visiting Bronllwyn several times. They are putting the worst possible construction upon everything. I'm tired of their nonsense. I want you to deny the whole thing. They want a Church Meeting. But I think it would be enough for you to meet the deacons and tell them the whole story is a gross exaggeration. An emphatic denial. That's what I recommend.'

To me he seemed to have become a different person: old, cold, calculating, unable to comprehend anything outside pounds and pence. Cursed with blindness for his cold calculating heart, ready to buy peace for himself at my expense.

'I don't want to,' I said.

'Don't want to what?'

'I don't want to deny it. I hope to marry Ada. Why should I deny it? I have a right to love her.' I was nervous and I found it difficult to control my voice and keep out a high-pitched trembling note. I was afraid of this old man and that was why I had begun to hate him. I struggled to prevent myself from becoming afraid.

'I'm very shocked to hear this,' he said. 'Very disappointed too. I thought better of you, Mr. Powell. It's foolish you know. Do you know what that girl is? You can't refuse to face the facts.'

'I know what she is,' I said. 'I know her better than most people. I'm going to marry her.'

'I'm sorry,' he said. 'I'm truly sorry about this. It's very distressing.'

'I'm sorry it should distress you,' I said.

'I don't know how to advise you,' he said. He was thinking hard and blinking oftener than usual. He was assuming that I wanted his advice. 'I don't want to suggest it, but I think it would be wisest for you to resign. We don't want unpleasantness. Whatever my personal feelings are towards you, for me the good name of the Church comes first. I don't want any unseemly scenes. I... Hannah, is that you?'

'Supper's ready,' she said. 'We won't wait any longer for Mother.'

He did not pursue the subject on our minds. He seemed to subscribe to a curious fiction that Hannah did not, and indeed should not know of the things we had been discussing. Was it his acute sense of privacy and seemliness? Or did he wish her to be a girl for ever, a dependent relative, a giver of devotion and service, not qualified to pass an independent judgement and expected never to do so? I began to think of her instead of myself. Of her position in this household, of her life, of her chances of happiness, and I found myself in that silence during which I was assumed to be meditating on my own distressing position, sympathising with her and understanding her as I had never been able to do so before.

Supper was cold ham and tomato salad. Plates of home baked bread and farm butter. An egg-custard and gooseberry tart. A red cheese. Good for a hungry minister. Blessed, I thought, are those that hunger and thirst, just hunger and thirst. I felt I was eating with irresponsible vigour and I wanted to joke about it. With Ada of course.

With Ada. Hannah was watching me across the table. Vavasor Elis was staring gloomily at the lamp and chewing rapidly, monotonously. The grandfather clock ticked loudly in the silence.

III

Mrs. Felix Elis bustled in, still wearing her coat, still carrying an umbrella and a large black handbag. She threw off the fur around her neck and drew out the hat pins that attached her hat to her hair. I stood up. She nodded and the jet earrings trembled.

'Kept, Mary?' Vavasor Elis said, without getting up. 'Train late?'

'No. It wasn't late. I called on Mrs. Parry Castle Stores. Has Doris gone out, Hannah? She asked if she could have the evening off?'

'Everything is all right, Mother,' Hannah said. 'Sit down. Shall I pour you a cup of tea now?'

'A cup would be good.' She sat down opposite her husband and allowed Hannah to pour her a cup of tea.

'A comfortable journey?' Vavasor said.

'Rather crowded. This tea is good. A rude young man in my compartment tried to smoke. It was a non-smoker. I soon put a stop to that.'

'Who got the headship at Llanrhos?' Vavasor said.

'An excellent young man. Haydn Glyndwr Jones. A South Walian. For once we've made a good appointment. An excellent speaker. Quite took everybody's fancy. And first-class qualifications. He's against gambling and drinking and an excellent Welshman.'

Was I being sensitive or was she ignoring me more than usual?

'And the surveyor's complaint?' Vavasor said.

'The grant is to be increased,' she said. 'Mr. Powell.' She turned her attention to me suddenly, as if she had just determined on a course of action. 'There are nasty rumours circulating Pennant about you. Have they told you?'

'Yes, Mary,' Vavasor Elis said. 'I've told him.'

'Are they true, Mr. Powell?' she said.

'It is true that I am going to marry Ada Evans,' I said. I put my finger on the handle of the clean knife that I had not used, alongside my plate. I was their guest I told myself and there was a limit to what they would say to me.

'I suppose it is left to me,' she said, 'to tell you that it's ridiculous.'

'Others have suggested that,' I said.

'It's more than ridiculous. It's outrageous. It can't be allowed.'

'Now, Mary,' Vavasor said. 'Moderation.'

'This is no time for moderation. This poor young man is being trapped into marrying that scheming immoral girl...'

'I asked her to marry me,' I said stubbornly. 'I want to marry her. She has refused me once, but I asked her again. It's my wish more than hers.'

'Then you must be an utter fool,' she said. 'An absolute utter fool. Ridiculously gullible and weak. I'm sorry to be so frank but you force me to it. What good do you think this will do the church? I'm astounded that you could behave so irresponsibly, dancing at that so-called guest house. Dancing with that lying immoral unwholesome girl.'

'I don't want you to talk about her like that,' I said.

'I'll talk about her as I like. What I'm saying is true and if you were a sensible man instead of a gullible fool you would know it. Where do you think she is going to get money to run that place as an hotel? Wally Francis died over his ears in debt. Have you even asked yourself where she gets the money from? Have I got to tell you?'

'I don't care...' I began to say.

'Well, it's time you did. You're a minister of the gospel. Remember that. She gets that money from Dr. Pritchard. Did you know that? If you don't you can easily make a few inquiries. And why do you think he gives it her?'

'He can invest his money as he chooses,' I said.

'But why?' she said, banging her fist on the table and glaring at me as if I were a criminal. 'Because she's that man's mistress. You know that man Pritchard has an invalid wife. And this is the way he treats her. And this is the way your precious Ada Evans makes use of him. And this is the woman you have the audacity to announce you are going to marry. Well it's not going to happen, Mr. Powell. If you're a sensible man and if you'll remember all we have done for you in this house, you won't let it happen. If you have any regard for religion...'

'I don't believe it,' I said. 'I refuse to believe it. It's disgusting gossip. Chatter of evil-minded hypocrites.'

I pushed back my chair. The scene seemed abnormal, unreal. Hannah's face was spinning before my eyes and her uncle's dessert spoon, suspended between his plate and his expectant mouth seemed to be trembling like a metronome.

‘Of course you don’t,’ she said. ‘Impossible to part a fool and his folly. But I suggest you ask her, Mr. Powell. Ask her. Ask her. Find out for yourself.’

‘Mary,’ Vavasor Elis said. ‘Mary. You are going rather far. You are being rather rough you know.’

‘For his own good,’ I heard her say, before I left the room. ‘Somebody had to open his eyes. What is the world coming to? Or are we to condone everything? For his own good. For everybody’s good...’

CHAPTER SIXTEEN

I

The woman was fierce and unkind, but I felt no hatred towards her. It was her duty she imagined she was doing. I was concerned with Ada: my Ada. The intolerable wrongs. The cruel misunderstandings. The doom in which every hand seemed turned against her.

I hurried home through the evening mist that spread inland from the sea. My heart burned with anger and pity. I leaned against a wet gate and pressed my hot cheek against its wet wooden surface. The green mould came off on my face and hands.

I could take her away from this terrible trap, this forest of calumny where lethal weapons lay about her feet like fallen leaves for any hand to pick up and use against her, where her own family gave her no refuge but led the attack against her. O brave girl, hard with impossible courage, fighting a battle you must lose, let me take you away!

Was it true about Dr. Pritchard? In the most disarmed and innocent moment, life trembles on the edge of disaster. Imagine the unhappiness of the girl. Her lover killed. Everyone against her. Her protector dead. Where can she turn for comfort? There could have been some lapse of the moment, a secret wrapped in time like a grain of seed in great folds of cotton wool. Why should I begin to believe it? Because I had seen the doctor going into Bronllwyn: seen his car there more than once. Taking help where it was offered. As she had taken me. Anyone can suspect. Anyone can deceive. Anyone can betray.

If it were true, what was I to do? I, who find it so fantastically difficult to be a Christian, but unbearable to be anything else. Not to forget nor ignore, and then call ignorance forgiveness. To examine all to the last horrible details and begin to love again. The love where Christ comes?

Let it be true and then let me see if I still have the power to love. I must ask her. Why had she been so unwilling to see me this last week? Why had I acquiesced when she said *You must leave me alone for a week or two, Idris. Leave me alone. I want to think about the whole thing as clearly as I can*. How willing and gallant and masterful I had felt when I said *Of course. Of course*! How certain of my position. Making my love into a love that lets be; that gracefully accepts. In command of everything; ready to perform miracles.

I dreamed a great dream of reconciliation. *Brothers and sisters*, I dreamed, *come together in peace and harmony through me, for I love all of you, and you must all love me. And if you love me, love this woman whom I love, this most beloved woman whose gentle heart will bring you joy. Ada,* I dreamed, *do not be afraid. These are my people, my flock who follow me and are not driven. Take them all to your heart and love them because they love me.*

Heretical dreams an excuse for my inaction. I had waited too long and dreamed too long, believing that in some obscure way I was waiting upon the Lord. An excuse for the endless poverty of my inaction. I must see Ada at once, without waiting any longer. It was imperative to act at once, to save a rapidly deteriorating situation. The first step was to see her and put an end to this period of ambiguous abstinence. To come to a working understanding. I should not hesitate: I had enough experience in the politics of the heart.

II

'I want to see you,' I said.

Her mother was in the kitchen, listening, grinning. I didn't care anymore who listened or who grinned. I didn't feel well. I had a temperature and my throat was hurting. I was worried about my whole being and an answer of some kind from Ada was immediately curatively necessary.

'We're busy,' Ada said. 'Very busy. I can't even ask you in. We've got people in.'

'I see the doctor's car's here,' I said.

'He's here on business,' Ada said. She closed the kitchen door behind her. 'What is it you want?' We stood in the empty carriage house. My feet were cold and curiously tender so that I felt the hard cobbles under the damp soles of my shoes.

'I wanted to see you, Ada. There were things I wanted to ask you. I don't feel very well.'

'You'd better get home quickly. Get into bed. I'll tell the doctor to call. Your head is hot.'

'I don't want to see the doctor,' I said. 'I want to see you. When can I see you again? When are we going to decide what to do?'

'Give me time to think,' Ada said. 'I'll work something out.'

'Is it because of the doctor?' I said. 'Is that why you won't marry me?'

'What do you mean?'

I found it difficult to speak. The words seemed to choke me before I could get them out.

'You know what they say, about you and Pritchard. Is it true?'

'What do they say?'

'That it's his money behind you.'

'Yes. He has lent me money.'

'How much?'

'Two thousand pounds. He's really a partner in this business. He doesn't want it generally known. That's why I haven't told you.'

'Is that all?'

'I'm cold. I want to go in. Why have you called now, disturbing everything? If you're unwell you ought to be in bed.'

'Is it true that he's, that he, that he's your lover?'

It was dark and she didn't answer and I couldn't see exactly where she was.

'Is it true? Why don't you answer. Is it true? Have you let him make love to you? Answer me.'

'Yes.' That was all she said. I groped for the wall, lifted my arms and pressed my head against them to stop myself from sobbing. I cannot tell how long we were silent. She stood quite still in the darkness and did not mention going in any more.

'When?' My voice was an absurd croak. 'When?'

'The week after Wally's funeral. Here in Bronllwyn.'

'And afterwards.'

'Once or twice. I had to keep my part of the bargain.'

'He bought you. Is that it? Took advantage of your position.'

'You could put it that way. That's what everybody does in this world, only you don't seem to have noticed. Will you go home now?'

'Give him up,' I said. 'Give the whole thing up. This whole place. Come away with me. You love me, don't you? I love you. I'll live for you.'

'That's out of the question,' she said. 'It's better this way, Idris. For you too. You don't belong in this place. I've no claim on you. You're lucky. You're free. You go away alone.'

'I love you,' I said.

'You'll find somebody else,' she said. 'It isn't so difficult.'

'Can't you see what it means? I love you. In spite of everything. Because of everything. You've got to listen.'

'You'll get over it,' she said. 'Everybody does.'

'It didn't mean anything to you?'

'Don't spoil it,' she said. 'Don't quarrel.'

But that was exactly what I wanted. My eyes were filled with bitter tears and I wanted to hit her.

'Go home,' she said. 'You're not well.'

'You whore,' I said. 'You...'

'All right,' she said. 'All right.'

She hurried back to the kitchen. I didn't go home down the drive. I went up through Bronllwyn Woods, weeping. What right had I to reproach her and cut myself off from her when I needed her most?

ADA EVANS

CHAPTER SEVENTEEN

I

I've cried too much. It's time other people cried. Weeping is no good. He was sweet to me. He appreciated me. He was hard and soft and young and hairless and pleasing and in his innocence and inexperience gave more pleasure and promise of pleasure than he imagined himself capable of. He was a loving child whom I loved to stroke. But I'll say no more and regret no more. He was like all men, wanting his own way.

He softened me too much. Opened old wounds with his gentle hands when I needed to be strong and whole and powerful with my work to do. His niceness was a danger to my purposes. His youthful trust was impractical like Dick's beautiful young brown-eyed arrogance. Like Dick he was a child who could make me foolishly neglect my own interests. To go on being a child is to go on being defeated and hurt. I've had too much defeat and too much hurt.

Oh Dick how you hurt me and how I liked being hurt. Oh Dick why did you die and crush my last lingering foolish hope? How I loved you. How I loved you, and how long this love lingers and how easily it reappears, even though everything ends and nothing happens twice.

II

'Such a nice boy,' my mother said so that he could hear her. 'Come again soon,' she said, treating him like a grown up – always the flattering welcome, importunate farewell. 'Don't be a stranger now. You cheer us up so.'

'I want my children to be happy,' my mother said. 'I've had a terrible life as anyone could tell you. But I want you two to get on. I'll do my best for you. I'll work my fingers to the bone. Then you won't forget your mother in her old age. When you've got a big motor car, Frankie, you'll take me out for rides in the country. Won't that be nice?'

'He's not our father,' Frankie said. The poor bent man I wish I had done more for, had just wearily climbed the narrow wooden stairs to the small bed chamber where my mother made him sleep alone. The smallest poorest room in the cottage with a tiny window overlooking the river. It smelled always of his working clothes, saturated as they always were with his sweat and farm smells. 'God! How this man sweats,' my mother said, as she pummelled his clothes among the soapsuds in the tin tub. 'This man,' she always called him. Among the many, the one Fate had compelled her to stick to. Wearily he went to his narrow bed, the odd man in the house, whom neither Frankie nor I called Father. Due to rise at five and walk three miles to work. A most reliable and conscientious worker, they called him. Simple and even stupid, but a hard hard worker and kind too in his abstract distant way, and fond of me, always fond of me. I wish he were alive now for me to give him some comfort. He would have been happy looking after the gardens at Bronllwyn: would have made a good job of it.

But Frankie never liked him. Never forgave him for being stupid. 'He's not our father,' Frankie said. 'Thank God. Not yours or mine.'

'How do you know?' I said.

'Never mind how I know. I use my ears and my brains. I've heard things. He's not our father.'

'We'll have a picnic,' Frankie said. 'You're coming, Ada.'

'Indeed I'm not,' I said. 'I don't play with little children.'

'Dick's coming,' Frankie said.

'I don't care if he is,' I said. 'He's only your age. Why should I care?'

'He wants you to come,' Frankie said, smiling and nodding. Making me smile, making Mother laugh because she is listening. She has a gift for working hard and listening. Doesn't miss anything that goes on. Frankie always makes us laugh. That is our great bond and makes us feel one, laughing, usually mocking at other people, before they get a chance to look down on us.

'Good God,' Frankie says standing at the window. 'Ada,

Mam. Come and look at this. Emanuel and his little cowslip taking an evening stroll.'

And it was funny. The small man with his important grey hat, cuffs, heavy watch chain, silver-topped cane and highly polished brown boots: and the thin woman, taller, with short skirts white powdered face and yellow hair poking out of her cloche hat and her pointed feet turned out. We laughed together. Frank knew he could always make us laugh. Hate the Elises and laugh at their dependents.

Jubilee week it was. Extra holidays.

'You go, Ada,' my mother said. 'Mustn't disappoint the gentlemen.'

Somebody's car. Ossie's I expect. Somebody old enough to drive. It wasn't very far. Dick was noisy. Looked much older than fifteen. Tall, curly brown hair. A few pimples, strong teeth, impudent smile. Deep brown eyes. Already he knew how to use them.

June, and the river full, the water bright, the mill-wheel damp and mossy and our seclusion perfect. A dragon-fly, the snake's servant, flew steadily above the gnats that swarmed closer to the stiller patches of the surface of the river. Look up and there is the blue sky in fragments between the ascending certainty of a million leaves.

'Under the trees,' I heard Dick say.

I shook my head. 'The gnats will bite you,' I said. 'They don't bite me but they'll bite you.'

'That's because I'm sweet,' he said. 'Under the trees. Come on.'

I wanted him to kiss me. I wanted to feel him lying on

me. Feel the length of him on me. From that day I was in love, and mad as love makes a foolish girl.

III

Two years' difference was nothing when the moment was everything. At different places I waited for him as often as he waited for me. The sea shore, the Hen Eglwys, the Middle Barn, the Lime Kiln near Miss Aster's cottage, the waiting room of the railway station at Derwen, and most exciting of all, Bronllwyn Wood, and the West Lodge and when Bronllwyn became empty sometimes even inside the house itself.

Inarticulate and always hungry for each other.

'I've been here an hour,' he said. 'Where have you been?'

'Wally Francis came.'

'He's got his eye on you. I've been watching him.'

'We're moving, Dick,' I said. 'Moving house. We'll be in Pennant living and then you can come and see us, easily.'

'So will Wally Francis.'

'Dick!' I said laughing in the way I would laugh with Frankie. 'You're not jealous of that fat old thing! Do you think I'd let him touch me?'

'I'd kill you before I'd let anyone else touch you,' Dick said.

'Yes.'

'Kill you. Do you understand?'

'Yes. Yes. Yes.'

He could do anything to me. I was his slave and being his slave was the only happiness in my heart. A happiness I had the sense to cover. I tried to appear a quiet sensible girl, anxious to get on, studious, polite, inoffensive, hard-working, so as to hide the laughter in my heart that shouted my love and my enslavement through the moments when I gazed with silent concentration at Trallwm, the Maths Master, in the decorous sixth-form room.

I learned to guard against my mother too slowly, but I learned.

'He's a nice boy,' she said thoughtfully. 'He's a very nice boy. But you be careful now, my sweet? We must be careful you know. Where did you go tonight?'

At first I told her. At first I let her feed on the flushed excitement in my open face. But when her temper was bad she used it against me; or when she wanted to amuse Frankie and herself.

'Don't answer me back,' she screamed. 'You take care of yourself, my girl, or you'll be in trouble, for all my taking care of you. I can see you're ready to make a fool of yourself. He'll be all right. He's an Elis. They're always all right...'

'Don't disturb her, Frankie bach.' My mother grinned at me. 'She's dreaming of love in the churchyard. Nice place for loving!'

Then both laughed at me. They were always ready to join up against me. Always expecting the best from me, always greedy, clamouring for my attention; always giving me their worst, congenitally ungrateful. Ready to laugh secretly and quietly even when poor old Jacob died, who never harmed anybody. 'He was a good man,' my mother said in public. 'There were a lot of good in poor Jacob. And I looked after him well. Terrible to lose him. I've been thunderstruck by his death.' But after the quick funeral when the door was shut on the last mourner she went to the cupboard and brought down a bottle of rum. 'Feeling a cold coming on,' she said. 'Drinking to old Jacob's health, Mrs. Evans?' Frankie said in his whispering humorous way. 'Oh you wicked boy! How could you say such a thing?' She began to giggle. 'Oh dear I'm giggling. Ada, what can I do? I can't stop.' She can look dignified sometimes. She has a fine nose and when she holds her mouth still you might think she was an aged aristocratic beauty. But giggling, she let her loose mouth go and she looked lewd and obscene. It frightens me because I can remember thinking, if you die, Ada, she'll laugh just like this after your funeral. I saw how terrible it was to love nobody except yourself. And yet she loved Frankie and she claimed that she was fond of me: she loved as much of us as would conform to the pattern woven for her own benefit; the images of a daughter and a son filled, she hoped, with the same love and pity for her that she felt for herself.

IV

If I knew things then that I know now: but that's just it. The learning has taken away the taste for innocent love; for all forms of innocence. It's important not to be young more than once and to be young for as short a time as possible.

'You ought to know more than you do, Ada fach, and I'm your mother and I'm the woman to teach you.' At some celebration Wally Francis had bought her too much gin. 'Better not be too serious with that boy. Never let a man have it all his own way or you'll land in trouble the same as I did. You had a fine father. A Member of

Parliament he was. But he didn't live to do anything for you or your poor old mother. Died and left me in the lurch. And I can't swear he would have done even if he had lived. He was a slippery customer when you come to think about it. Just remember, my girl, that Dick's the same breed. As a matter of fact, you're second cousins. That's nice for you to know.'

I hated to see her in a fuddled condition. In those days she was worse; always after the drink and always dirty. At least in those days she looked worst; clean clothes and calculated sobriety are something to be grateful for and she's anxious to help, but I still have to remember I can't trust her. She is Frankie's spy inside my own house.

What a mother. What a childhood. Something to numb a little girl with perpetual shame. I carried bottles home for her in a long leather bag. They clinked against each other as I hurried down the road.

'*What you got there, Ada Cwm? Mother's milk? Give us a swig, Ada Cwm. Penny on the bottle. Penny on the bottle.*'

I pulled long grass out of the ditch and wrapped it around the dark repulsive bottles to deaden the sound. I told Dick about it. We were lying in Bronllwyn Wood. A red sunset and the dry smell of old pine needles. I was sad. I was telling him about it. Hiding bottles in the hedges and going back to collect them after dark. Melancholy I was, watching the red sunset, and the last long shadows of the trees.

'Squeeze this one,' he said. 'This one on my chin. Come on. Never mind about the bottles. That was a long time ago.'

I didn't move. I was so oppressed with my own

loneliness I wanted to cry. He wasn't interested in my old meaningful sadness.

'Ada,' he said. 'What's the matter? Get on with your job. Thought you liked squeezing my pimples.'

He laughed and picked up my hands and used them like unwilling tweezers on his chin. He pulled silly faces and put out his tongue. I couldn't keep up my sadness. I threw myself on him, ruffled his hair and we had a fight until I lay helpless under him panting, laughing, and saying, 'You wait, you wait,' over and over again until he began to kiss me. To remember it is still an intolerable sweetness.

V

There was never anybody I could trust. Not even the preacher boy, because he's so innocent and foolish, a religious fanatic with ideas that would give me no peace. And yet when I first let him kiss me I thought, Yes let him do it. Let him take you. He's not only attractive, he's sincere and honest and you can trust him completely. Relax. Let him take you. Trust him. Trust him! There doesn't seem to be an end to the new ways in which you can make a fool of yourself.

'Dick,' I said. 'Dick. Didn't they tell you? I'm pregnant. I'm going to have a baby.' He pulled a piece of dry grass and looked at his feet like a naughty boy. It was autumn and the falling of the leaves. I never like autumn. It fills me with sadness to see the falling of the leaves. 'Can't you understand? I'm going to have a baby. You can't go away. Not now. You can't leave me now. Not now when I need you.' He didn't answer. 'Why don't you answer?'

'I've got to go, Ada. There's nothing else for it. I've got to go.'

'What about me?'

'I'll come back to you. We'll have to wait. Have to be patient. God, they can't live for ever.'

'What about the baby? What if I have a baby?'

'Wally said he'd help us about that. He knows what to do. He says he'll take care of you. Take you to Liverpool. It's only a small operation. Nothing serious. You'll be all right.'

I forgot my bike. I started walking home along the shore without my bike. I lay down on the smooth grass by the lime kiln and I cried my heart out. I saw the clouds gathering over the dark mountains and the shadow of the night creeping over the sea.

I still shudder if I go near the place. I believe the ground where I lay was wasted for all time by the convulsions of my unhappy body and the bitterness of my tears.

VI

I was sick before we got to Chester. I got out of the car and I was sick. I was cold and trembling. I couldn't stop trembling. Wally went into a pub and got me some whisky.

'Here, Ada,' he said. 'Drink this. Down with it. Cheer up now. You're not going to your execution. Have another one.'

I nodded. Yes I would. I would have another and another.

'No. No. Not too much now, girlie.' Wally said.

I began to cry. He put his arm around me. I put my

head on his shoulder.

'Wally look after... Wally look after you... Wally... Wally...' I could hear him repeat his own name in a soothing voice.

'It's a place for animals,' I said. 'Look. That woman with a dog.'

There was a tall woman with a hairy dog under her arm. Its eyes were yellow and it kept whimpering.

'It's through the entry,' Wally said. 'Don't take any notice. Just walk through. Go on.'

The streets were wet, and damp seeped into the entry. The stairs were dry, dirty and dusty.

'Next floor up,' Wally said.

'The doctor,' Wally kept calling him. He was from Vienna. A very clever doctor Wally said. He was young and clean. I was surprised. His hands were cool. He had an enormous mouth. I wanted to see how far it would stretch if he smiled. But he didn't. He was very very serious. 'You know my fee,' I heard him say to Wally. 'You will wait here,' he said to Wally. 'Come this way please.' I lay there trembling while he put on a white overall and scrubbed his hands in a wash basin. He talked to me with his back turned.

'Now this is a simple operation. You have nothing to fear. No pain. Perhaps a little discomfort. I shall explain it to you now so that you can co-operate intelligently. Do you understand?'

'Yes,' I said.

'Take hold of this,' he said. 'Relax. Forget about me. Breathe this as you need it; keep it on your face. Analgesia. Do you understand?'

He kept on asking me if I understood.

'You will bleed,' he said, 'of course. That is necessary. Don't be frightened. It is perfectly normal.' Bleeding. Bleeding. Bleeding. 'I shall ring up the hospital,' he said. 'They will take care of you for a few days. For safety's sake. A moment please.'

I heard him telephone. 'Ah, doctor. Good morning. I have a woman here. She is bleeding rather badly... Never mind. Never mind.' I heard him ring up again. 'Hello. Carriston Hospital. The house surgeon. I want to speak to the house surgeon... Ah, good morning, doctor. I have a woman here. She is bleeding rather badly...'

He rang up four times before he turned to Wally.

'All right, Mr. Francis. Take her to Breadfather Street Hospital. Thank you. She will be admitted. She might have to stay a few days. It's a good hospital. No, don't say anything. Just take her in. Routine. Very simple.'

I was sick and sick of myself. Bleeding. Bleeding. Bleeding. Weak. Tired. Glad to be where someone didn't know me. Glad Wally had gone. Sick of him asking 'Has it stopped?' Sick of his anxiety. Why should he worry. In bed alone and silent I didn't speak. Not even to the nurses. I wanted to be alone for ever.

CHAPTER EIGHTEEN

I

People behave better when you have some sort of power over them. It doesn't pay to be helpless. The whole purpose of living is to become independent and put yourself in a position where you can have power as you need it: to strike down the hostile or reward the friendly. Had I been independent I could have kept Dick alive, I could have hit back at the Elises, I could have kept my mother and my brother in their places, I could have done without Wally and I could be doing without Matt Pritchard and I could have rewarded this preacher boy and kept him and the balm of his soft loving, had I been independent.

But we are only independent in dreams. Living is a struggle for power, but when does the power come? When you are too old to make use of it? But you must struggle to keep what you have won. And you can only keep what you have won by acquiring more. And all living is learning this; to go on struggling, as a housewife battles with dust day after day and keeps the trophies shining and tracks down and annihilates the sources of dirt and smells.

'I could have,' 'I could have' is nothing; like nostalgia, of no value. You remember in order to learn lessons, to know what never to do again, to acquire sagacity, to become expert in the craft of living. So that the hardened housewife may sing as she polishes her brasses, her duster free to flick at every corner of her own proud house.

II

Wally made use of me. I wasn't blind. But it took me some time to learn not to hate him, to learn to let him touch me when he wanted to and to learn how to get around him, how to handle him. I only liked him when I'd learnt to handle him and it took a long time and by then he had changed and I had changed.

'College is out of the question, isn't it?' he said.

I had to agree. At that time I had to agree to everything. My mother stood at the foot of my bed and every time her head nodded I said yes. His excellent false teeth blocked his mouth whitely. 'Work for me, Ada,' he said and he twisted his red neck towards my mother for her approval.

'Of course, she'd be delighted,' my mother said. And I nodded. I had to do what was the only thing to be done. Wally was always certain what ought to be done. He always knew which way the traffic should go.

Bill still in school, Sylvia May with her ponies. Both completely dull; but at that time Wally hadn't seen it. He thought Bill was backward because he played about. And because Wynne the School was chapel. Hadn't realised that Bill was backward because he was backward. 'I spoil that girl,' he said as Sylvia May flounced out of the garage in her riding breeches carrying the pound note he had given her from the cash box. 'Better stay late tonight, Miss Evans. No use letting these accounts accumulate. Get them off before the end of the month. That's my policy.'

'You grasped it all pretty quick, Ada, fair play to you,' he said. His breath smelled very strongly of whisky. 'Don't know what we'd do without you.'

'Frankie want to work here?' he said. 'Can he work as hard as you, Ada?'

'Yes,' I said. 'He can work hard.'

'We'll give him a try,' Wally said.

'What about Edwin?' I said.

'This is my garage,' Wally said. 'Edwin will do what I say.'

Surly, greasy, with blood-shot eyes Edwin Pendaler came into the office to enter a petrol sale and swear at the boss.

'Four gallons to Jones Gwynfryn,' he said. 'Where's Wally Francis, the lazy devil?'

'In The Goat,' I said. 'He'll be back in half an hour.'

'Lazy pig,' Edwin said. 'Leaves everything to me. Look at that damned girl. Bottom like a pancake. Your brother going to work here?'

'Yes,' I said.

'Time I had a bit of help. Carried this place on my back

I have for the last three years. One day I'll be opening a place of my own and then Wally Francis will laugh on the other side of his face.'

Sylvia May began to hang around the garage more. She liked to watch Frankie working. She would stand in the office wasting my time and getting on my nerves.

'Can you tell me where we can find a new maid, Ada? This girl we've got is terribly sloppy and she can't do anything except break dishes. It's not fair you know really. I mean I'm too young to have the responsibility of running a home... Going to the dance next Friday? Would you like to come with me? I'll lend you a dress. Dad'll fetch us home in the Rover. Aw come on. Soldiers there you know. Airmen mostly. Frankie better come with us to look after us.'

Sylvia May and her nice boys. Sylvia May and her ponies.

III

Was that what I loved and dreamed about so much I wondered, as I watched the tall boy in uniform sulk as he waited for me to finish my work. I kept on working to the last minute in the effort to preserve my self-possession. He had left me in trouble and now he came back suspicious and jealous and resentful that I had accepted Wally's help.

'Come on,' he said. 'Hurry up, Ada. How much leave do you think I've got? Come on. Never mind those damned files. Let Wally Francis look after his own files.'

'Where shall we go?' I said, when I was ready.

'Miss Aster's been chucked out,' he said. 'Poor old

girl's in the Almshouses. Must go and see her before I leave. She thinks the world of me.'

'Do you want to go there now?' I said. 'There'll be a bus in twenty minutes.'

'Let's go down to the shore,' Dick said.

'No,' I said. 'I never want to go there again.'

'Bronllwyn, then,' Dick said. 'Bronllwyn Woods. Like old times.'

For a while we were excited. After wet weather the ferns had grown tall and smelled strongly like an inducement to loving. I suppose we both hoped to forget everything that had happened and to reclaim those early impulses of love that the woods of itself seemed still to treasure; its green silence, the owl that disengaged its grey self from one dark branch and flew at tree top level to a darker place, the brambles catching at our feet, and higher up the wild abundant and luxurious ferns calling us back to our former abandon.

I trembled when he kissed me as if I had been in a sleep of death and he was awakening me. I wanted him to go on kissing me for ever, just holding me and kissing me, while I wept inwardly for all my sorrows, holding me and kissing me until the last inward sob had dissolved and I was encased in peace, moored in a haven like a small boat that still sways to the gentle rhythm of the long glittering lake.

'No,' I said. 'Dick. No. Just kiss me. That's all.'

'No,' I said. 'I mean it. No. How can you be so selfish?'

'I don't care what you learnt,' I said. 'Or who you've learnt it with.'

We were sitting up and quarrelling, bitterly and foolishly.

'I'm just something for you to play around with while you're on leave,' I said.

'You don't make it very easy,' he said. 'And what have you been doing while I've been away. Been a good girl for Wally?'

'What do you mean?' I said.

'You know what I mean,' he said. 'Haven't you seen through his game all along? Didn't you know he got me sent away?'

'You were so willing to go. So ready to jump out of trouble.'

'I'm not to blame,' Dick said. 'Blame that dirty old man you work for.'

'You never cared how much I suffered,' I said. 'It was nothing to you. You went off to learn more about it from other girls...'

'Don't talk like that, Ada,' Dick said. 'Are you so good yourself?'

It was misery. Black suicidal misery. He was there by me, alive. I could stretch out my hand and touch his face. The next day he would be gone. And I couldn't get through to him. I barely knew who he was and I wanted to spend all my life finding out who he was and he was leaving the next day and we couldn't speak to each other. We left each other without saying a word. It was the end and I wanted it to be a new beginning. It was the end and I couldn't call him back. He went and I was left. I went home alone. I pretended not to see my mother's inquiring face and went up straight to bed. Lying awake, cold with my misery. I heard Wally Francis come in through the back door. 'Are the lovers still out?' I heard him say to my mother. 'Hush!

She's upstairs,' I heard my mother say, and then a lower voice, speaking rapidly giving some welcome news and advice. Later I wondered was she selling me that night. Me in exchange for the house or the mortgage on the house. Later I wondered whether at the same time Wally had been my mother's lover: there was a curious intimacy about the way they spoke to each other. But that night I thought only of Dick. He had brought me back to life. Made me aware of the joy that belonged to just being alive. First he had shown me the existence of delight and glory. Then of misery, abasement, and despair. Had he done all this utterly unaware of what he was doing, pursuing his own childish ends ignorant of his own power and my enchantment? That was what I wondered most and whether he knew how much I loved him and how I could get hold of the Dick I loved and win his attention and tell him how I loved him. But who was he? Who was my Dick? Did he exist at all? If he didn't what was the good of my continuing to exist?

I had my plan – I had learnt that much. It was a step away from helplessness. And it gave me some comfort. Fanny Lloyd and Maisie Lewis with whom I had shared a vapid sort of friendship in school had joined the women's A.T.S. I met them together one Saturday afternoon in the crowded streets of Derwen, where talking groups move unwillingly when an impatient motorist hoots them out of the way. They made noises of delight on seeing me, but I was puzzled for a moment to remember who they were. They were too anxious to tell me their own stories to ask too many questions about mine. They wanted me to realise how far they had travelled from the lunch time clinging to radiators and whispered talk about boys. Fanny, I remembered well enough, had been the first to explore the possibilities of soldiers. She was the quieter one but she was the one who had surprised and excited me by quietly boasting that she had done it, twice.

'What are *you* doing now, Ada?' they said, perking their capped heads.

'I'm a clerk,' I said. 'Clerk in a garage.'

'Do you like it?'

'Not bad,' I said. 'Not very exciting. A bit dull sometimes. A bit lonely.'

'Why don't you join up?' they said brightly. 'We're ever so glad we did, aren't we?'

That was the solution, the attractive way out, with all the advantages. Away from my mother, from Wally's garage, from Sylvia May, from Pennant parish, from the Elises, away from all these perhaps to somewhere near Dick, perhaps to some form of independence where I could meet Dick on equal terms. Make my own life where my origins would be no handicap to me; where my ability would be appreciated and recognised. Gain promotion, work hard, learn, get on. Always nearer the independence that I wanted.

'What's this I hear from your mother?' Wally said, bossy and annoyed that morning. Frank was home, being nursed by my mother – too tenderly in Wally's view – so that we were short at the garage and he had to work himself. 'This nonsense. Don't you know what the A.T.S. is for? Hasn't anybody told you?'

I was a little afraid of him then, but not as much as he thought I was. That was his big mistake.

'I'm going to join,' I said. 'Lots of girls I knew at School have joined. They all say it's good.'

'What's going to happen here?' Wally said, spreading his fat red hands towards my empty chair. 'Who d'you think I'll get to replace you these days? You don't give a damn about me do you? I'm nobody. After all I've done to help you. Here's a fine way to repay me. Walking out on me when I need you most.'

'I'm sorry,' I said. 'But I'm going.'

When he saw I meant it, his tone changed. He began to plead and he sat down in my chair as if he hadn't the strength any more to stand on his own feet.

'Look here, Ada,' he said. 'This place wouldn't go on without you. You know the ropes as well as I do now. I need your help. There's that damned cafe on my hands. How was I to know a war was going to start? It was a good idea you said so yourself. A row of shops would have made all the difference to this end of the town. You said yourself. How was I to know a bloody war would break out? And there's the bungalow to pay for still. Don't go, Ada. Look. I'll put up your wages.'

'I want to go,' I said. 'I'm young. I want to live my own life.'

'The world's a nasty place,' Wally said. 'You can easily jump from the frying pan into the fire. I know. I've seen the world, not like most of the people in this dump. I've seen the world and I know. You've got to have money first, Ada. That's the only thing people respect, wherever you go. Cash, Ada. Cash.'

'I can look after myself,' I said. 'I want to go.'

'No you can't, Ada. You can't. But listen,' he said. 'I need you. It makes life worth living for me to have you around. To come in here and know that you'll be here. I'll marry you if you like. But you wouldn't want to marry an old man like me. I'll make it worth your while, Ada. You'll never regret it. I swear to you now, I'll see to it you'll be all right. You'll see the world. I guarantee that. In a few years' time. When this damned war's over. But now, just now, I need you here. Don't rush into anything, Ada. Think it over will you? Don't rush into anything. It's a big step.'

'You're not going and that's that,' my mother said that evening. She had had some gin, which was unusual. Since we had moved to Hyfrydle she had begun to go in for respectability. She was Mrs. Evans, Hyfrydle, the quiet widow who had done so well for her children, whose language was restrained, who did not drink and could be, when the occasion arose, taken by her daughter into the best hotels of Wales and England and no disgrace to her at all and could be a model mother-in-law to her son Frankie's wife, however rich she turned out to be. 'Whoring about soldiers' camps, as if you haven't given me enough trouble already. I'll have none of it. Don't you know a good thing when you're on one? No thought for your poor old mother. And what about Frankie? Do you want to spoil his chances? Selfish stuck up madam. All right, go on to bed and sulk. What do I care!'

'Ada,' Frankie said.

'Yes.' He stood in the doorway of the office, looking

over his shoulder to make sure there was no one around.

'Ada,' he said, watching my face closely, as he always did to try and anticipate my reactions. 'Ada. Want to know something? Don't laugh. I'm going to get married. To the beauty queen of Pennant.'

I wasn't going to laugh. He was after something and I could guess what it was.

'I'm going to marry Sylvia May,' he said.

'Yes.'

'I know what you're thinking,' Frankie said, smiling. 'You may be right you may be wrong. It's all the same in the dark. She isn't so bad. I'll soon knock that pony nonsense out of her. Couple of kids will set her right.'

'What does her father say?' I said.

'Exactly,' Frankie said. 'Good old Ada. Always straight to the point. He says she's too young.'

'So she is,' I said. 'And so are you. And you'll be in the army soon.'

'War's not going to last for ever, Ada. I'll be back. And I want something to come back to. You follow my meaning.'

'I usually do,' I said.

'Look here, Ada,' he said. 'This is the point. If you go off to the A.T.S. Wally won't have me as his son-in-law.'

'Couldn't you elope?' I said. 'Gallop away on one of Sylvia May's ponies.'

He laughed too much. Frankie never realised it didn't pay to put it on too much with me.

'I want to be son-in-law,' Frankie said. 'Not son outlaw. I'm not marrying Sylvia May for the pure pleasure of her pretty face. Stay on a bit longer, Ada. Stay on until the wedding's fixed. Stay on until I'm safely married.'

'I'll think about it,' I said.

'There's my old sister talking,' Frankie said. 'All for one and one for all. We'll show 'em, Ada. We'll show this one-eyed town what's what and who's who.'

He often went on like that in those days, believing that it was the kind of talk I wanted to hear. For his sake I stayed, much as I longed to escape. Force of habit I suppose to put my family first. They find a weak spot and they play on it. That's how they get away with so much.

IV

But would I ever have escaped, just by going away? In me I carried my father and my mother's blood. Blood does not speak, you may say. So why be afraid? But there was their history inside me, grown from the wounding accident that made me, all the darkness of it; and there was Dick, related to me through my father's blood, the mirror in my heart in which I watched the whole world move. Go away was possible, but not get away. I am glad now that at that time I failed, and I do not even regret those months of lonely misery, because they helped to make me understand that it was here in Pennant, in the face of the old opposition, my battle was to be fought and won.

V

I was surprised to see her, because whenever she came down the street she always crossed the road to avoid passing the garage and hurried past on the opposite side of the road with her head down. I used to think of her inheriting the Elis property, not Dick. She seemed the natural heir; the patient and faithful daughter who would carry on all the family traditions with blind fidelity.

She stepped in the office nervously, stared at me for a moment as if she wished to speak, but had no words and then dropped the folded piece of paper on my desk, and hurried out. That was how I got to know that Dick had been killed.

I didn't rave or scream. I went on working all day. I knew it was something I would have to live with all my life. I almost felt the burden being placed on my back, and my shoulders becoming heavier. I never cried, not even when I was in bed alone. I just felt myself hardening. I knew I had grown older. I put my fingers to my cheeks and I knew my skin was harder, coarser. I accepted losing my youth prematurely as an expression of sorrow.

I felt drawn towards the farm by his death. It was not merely the pleasure of being where we had lived so joyously and of the whole place still being stained with the colour of his childhood and our love. I began to realise that I liked the land, each field each lane each hedge, each group of outbuildings, not only because of Dick and the memories of childhood and youth; but for itself and its own virtues. I realised what an excellent farmer's wife I would have made: hard working and loving the land. The idea of property came into my mind then. To have my own place, my own castle, my own plough and pasture, woods, gardens, hills, rivers, my own domain.

I spent much of my time walking quite boldly the length

and breadth of the land. Some spots I avoided; the shore didn't interest me; I kept my eyes averted from Miss Aster's cottage, the lime kiln, and the Middle Barn. But I often walked almost up to the house. This became a game. When Dick was alive we avoided the house with elaborate care: alone I felt challenged to go as near as possible to it; as near as possible to the house until even the hens that stalked daintily over the cobbles, their feathers blown out by the breeze, could not fail to see me.

That summer I watched them hay harvesting from the public footpath that led to the old church. There was a young man among them tall and strong, a new farm hand, and from the distance he looked like Dick. I watched him and daydreamed: his arms seemed beautifully bare and strong as he held the cart horse's bridle and turned its unwilling head while Thomas John, whom Dick had liked, leaned forward on his hay-fork on top of the load to keep his balance and chewed calmly at his tobacco quid. The old man was in the field as well, looking more like a chemist than a farmer, and relying I suppose more on his sense of smell than on his sight to take in what was going on about him. He seemed to be smiling. It was a heavy crop and the weather was perfect.

Something made me go towards the house. Perhaps now I could actually pass it and even look inside, because there would be no one about, the hay was being taken to the Middle Barn. Peer through the very back door which I had only once been up to in my life. When I was very small and my mother had sent me to buy some eggs. I remember the blind man in the door and my great fright. '*Mother says have you got a few eggs to give her. She's ill and she's got no money.*' I can remember now the speech I had been taught. He gave me some eggs. *But never come here again girl! Do you understand? Or you'll be sent to an institution. Do you understand*? I fled. Two of the eggs were broken. I can remember my mother cursing the Elises for their meanness. *Bad devils they are. Bad wicked devils. But one day they'll see what will happen. They'll see.*

I passed the north side outbuildings and walked on until I stood in the yard looking about like a tourist. After all it was interesting to me. It had belonged to my father. Part of it somehow belonged to me. If Dick and I had been married, it would have been ours: I was deeply connected with the whole place.

There was a water pump in the centre of the yard and a horse trough. Everywhere was strangely silent in the warm afternoon sun. The hens were clucking away in the paddock and on the hedges of the lanes that led into the yard from the south and the west there were wisps of hay. There were geese in the orchard: the garage door was open and the cars were out. On the slab outside the scullery, upturned newly washed milk churns and buckets stood. The kitchen door was closed. I wanted to look through the lace curtains on the windows. I wanted to recognise the different rooms that Dick used to mention. The little parlour, which was the little parlour window?

Alongside one wall of the house there were three stone steps to a small stone platform, used for mounting horses in the old days. I climbed those steps to get a closer glimpse of the interior. How dark and depressing it looked.

Dressers, grandfather clocks, oil-clothed table, stone floor. Which room was it? I was trying to look closer my hands pressed against the grey wall of the house, when I heard the back door open. It was Dick's mother. Before I could get down she had seen me.

'Well?' she said. She had a basket over her left arm and carried a heavy walking stick in her right hand. Her flat black straw hat was kept in place by two long hat pins. I remembered her visit to our house, late at night, to fetch Dick home and I realised once more what a formidable woman she was.

'What do you want?' she said.

'I wanted to see where Dick lived.' Then I realised she had not immediately recognised me.

'You,' she said. 'You dare to come here. You bring your wickedness here, you little harlot. You killed my boy. He would be out there in the fields working happily today, but for you. It's you that ought to be dead, not Dick.'

She was walking slowly towards where I stood on the stone platform. I was afraid of her and uncertain of what she would do. Her anger was so powerful she longed to destroy me.

'Aren't you afraid God will strike you down?'

She lifted her stick at me.

'Get down! Get down, you brazen whore!'

She swung the stick at me and it struck me across the legs. I cried out with pain. She lifted the stick a second time, but this time, too angry to be afraid any more, I wrenched the stick from her hands and threw it as hard as I could into the orchard where the startled geese hissed and scattered.

'I'm not! I'm not! I'm not!' I shouted. 'You sent him to his death. You killed him. And you killed my father before him. I know. Don't think we don't know. It's you woman!' I shouted. 'Aren't you afraid God will strike *you* down!'

She ran to the stone staircase that led to the men servants' sleeping quarters above the stables, calling some of their names, but no one answered. Like the house, all the buildings were empty; all the animals and all the human beings were out in the fields.

'The police!' she cried. 'I'm going to call the police. They'll deal with you. I'll telephone now. I'm a magistrate. You won't get away with this kind of thing. Loitering about an empty house. Peeping inside. I'll summons you. I'll get you into prison.'

She rushed into the house. I went up to the door and shouted in after her.

'Send me a summons!' I said. 'Carry on. Call the police, Mrs. Elis. I'd like to appear in court. I've got lots of things I'd like to say.'

I walked away ready to sing for joy: I felt I had won a great victory, even though there was no one to witness it except those grey walls. Perhaps the walls were the witnesses I most wanted. It still gives me pleasure to remember the occasion. I felt as if for the first time I had asserted my own strength. I had entered the heart of the enemy citadel, won a skirmish with the she-devil herself, and retired unharmed and in good order.

CHAPTER NINETEEN

I

'We're related now,' Wally said. Sylvia May and Frankie had gone off on their honeymoon. Wally didn't know yet that Sylvia May was three months gone. He seemed very pleased with everything. More pleased than he ought to have been because Edwin Pendalar had given his notice. He had got a better job, 'Better pay,' Edwin said, 'in a better garage in a better town. Lazy devil will have to set to himself now. Mechanics are hard to get. Let me know when he puts on a pair of overalls. I'll take a day off to come to see him at it.'

'Work of national importance,' Wally said. 'I'll see the next man that comes here doesn't move so easily. I'll get a deferment for Frankie. Put him on this ploughing business.

He'll be safe enough there. We'll all be one happy family.'

He took to stroking my hair while I was working. And then fondling me. I didn't say anything. I hardly took any notice. To tell the truth the appearance of him used to embarrass me. He seemed quite happy so long as I sat still. If I'd pushed his hands away he would have been upset. I wanted a quiet life.

It was easier to bear with Wally's fumblings than my mother's talk.

'He's the best friend we've got,' she said. 'A good sort old Wally. He's done his best for us, and we must do our best for him. Be nice to him, Ada. A little kindness goes a long way. He's always done his best for you, you know. Mustn't be ungrateful.'

I began to understand that in his own dumb way Wally was infatuated with me. I laughed at myself for being so slow to see it. To think I had even been afraid of him. At first I thought he was a tough businessman, very determined, aggressive, ruthless, and very rich. Perhaps that was what he imagined himself to be: he may even have been shaping that way in his younger days. But when I first went to work at the garage he was already resting on his oars. Edwin was right. He was lazy and work-shy and used his loud-mouthed talking to cover it all. Apart from buying and selling second-hand cars, his chief interests were billiards, the football club and whisky. Even before the war broke out he had begun to lose his grip on the business: he was too slow, too negligent, too careless, and the change in the business after the outbreak of war was too much for him.

But I was sorry for him in a way. I couldn't leave him because I knew he would go to pieces if I did. And apart from joining up, what else could I do? Slowly I made up my mind to make the best of the situation. I was beginning to learn to take care of myself.

When Sylvia May's first baby was born six months after the wedding Wally got angry. He cursed and swore at the girl and at Frankie.

'Get out of my house!' he yelled at Sylvia May. He seemed mortally disappointed in her. It was funny to me but he seemed to have imagined that there was something wonderful about his daughter and the disillusionment was more than he could bear. 'What would your poor mother say if she was alive! Get out of here. And as for that deceitful good-for-nothing so-called husband of yours the quicker he gets into the army the better it'll be for him. He'll be safer there than here. You deceitful little swine.'

I calmed him down. I made the peace. Sylvia May didn't like that, but Frankie managed to keep her mouth shut. They were to move into the rooms at the back of the cafe. Wally would sell the house which was much too big for him and the shop underneath, and move into the bungalow between the garage and the cafe. We pulled a lot of strings to get the bungalow completed inside. Wally liked the idea because I said I would look after him there. He seemed to imagine the place would be a little love nest and I didn't say anything to spoil his dream. I had gained control of the man almost unconsciously. Occasionally I slept with him. It wasn't pleasant but I felt I owed it to him and it made him more obliged to me and more enslaved than ever. Besides there was something touching in his love. It was the only gentle thing I had left in my life. And he put himself so completely in my power. 'I've got perfect trust in you, Ada,' he would say, breathing deeply. 'Perfect trust. I don't know what I'd do without you. It's wonderful you know to trust any other person the way I trust you. It's like a peace if you know what I mean. Peace inside. Peace in the heart. May I kiss you?' His childishness touched me more than anything.

Touching, pathetic, irritating sometimes, but in my power. And I did him good. He drank less. I kept him out of the bankruptcy court. I handled his affairs when he would have made a complete mess of them himself. I looked after his health. He became absolutely dependent on me and I liked it. It wasn't like the explosive emotion of love: it was something of a low temperature that would last.

II

Frankie tried to upset things. He didn't like having to go out with the tractor and the ploughs in all weathers and he didn't like having to take orders from me. So he tried to upset things. Always a mischief-maker. He hadn't got any influence with Wally. Ever since the birth of the eldest child Wally had disliked him intensely. They hoped to soften him by making the children play up to him. But Wally didn't care much for the children either: they were too much like Sylvia May or too much like Frankie and he didn't know which was the worse. Also they called him Taid which made him feel old: just at a time when he imagined himself to be my gallant lover.

So Frankie tried to influence me against Wally. He took advantage of his old brotherly intimacy with me to pour poison in my ear.

'You had a rough deal, Ada. You haven't had fair play at all. Wally's treated you very badly. I wish I could tell you all I knew.'

'What's stopping you,' I said. 'Go on, tell me.'

'It's too late now,' Frankie said. 'No use opening up old sores.'

'Why do you start doing it then?' I said.

'He wasn't any friend of Dick's. You know how he got him sent away? More or less told him to help himself to petrol, and then went to Elis the Chemist and said he'd prosecute Dick for stealing petrol if Elis didn't send him away at once. He didn't want you to marry Dick. He wanted you himself so he did the dirty on Dick to get rid of him.'

I was angry for a few days. Angry and depressed. Wally couldn't understand. He came into the office and bent over me putting his hand on my breast. I knocked it away.

'What's the matter, girlie?' he said. 'Anything wrong?'

I shook my head.

'What have I done then?' he said. 'Don't be nasty with me. I'm not feeling too good today.'

'Leave me alone, Wally,' I said. 'I'm not feeling well either.'

He went off like a fat dog with his tail between his legs.

But in the end it was Frankie I was angry with for trying to make mischief, and not Wally. Maybe it was dirty of Wally. But he wanted me and that was something.

There was no certainty that Dick wanted me. He was only too ready to run away. He was at the mercy of his mother. He hadn't the strength. He would always have let me down, and I suppose I would have clung to him as I've clung to the dream of him, becoming more and more miserable. I was wild at first, but in the end I didn't hold it against Wally. I could make excuses for him. I preferred to use my hate on that Elis woman. But I knew I needed to watch Frankie. He was up to no good. I thought I'd give him one little warning.

One morning as he was starting out on the red tractor, I put my coat on and a scarf over my head and I went to speak to him.

'Frankie,' I said, 'I thought I'd just tell you. Don't try any more mischief making.'

'What do you mean, Ada?' he said. 'That's no way to talk.'

'You know what I mean,' I said. 'Don't make any more mischief. If you do, you'll be in khaki before you can say knife.'

'I'd rather be in khaki than on this damned tractor in all weathers,' he said.

'That's all right. Any time, Frankie. Just say the word. It can easily be arranged.'

III

I got the idea in a woman's magazine. Some retired naval captain and his wife had bought an old mansion, restored it, and opened it as a private hotel. There were pictures of a lounge, and a dining room and a conservatory and of outbuildings, stable lofts and so on converted into flats. While I was daydreaming over the story and the pictures the idea of buying Bronllwyn came to me. As soon as it entered my head it excited me so much that I jumped up and held on to the edge of the table to try and control my trembling. It was an inspiration, a kind of call that my whole being immediately responded to. This was it.

'Wally,' I said. We were alone in the bungalow. 'Wally, how much do you think Bronllwyn is worth?'

'No idea, Ada. Why?'

'Can't you guess? How much is it worth? Five thousand?'

'Less than that. Why are you so interested? Thinking of buying it?'

'Is it for sale?'

'Has been for the last twelve months. Army looked it over before the war ended and then decided they didn't want it. Probably be on sale for the next twelve months too. The day of the Big House is over. Isn't worth much more than this bungalow: less without the land. Nobody wants those things any more.'

'I do,' I said.

He laughed. His trouser-belt, resting on his stomach, shook up and down. 'Frankie thinking of setting himself up as Lord Cwm?' he said.

'Listen.' I explained my idea to him. There wasn't a decent residential hotel in Pennant. And there wasn't a licensed club. There wasn't a posh guest house that would attract the richer kind of visitor. Bronllwyn was going cheap. The costs of conversion would be reasonable. There were woods and gardens and lakes and a fishing river. It could be made marvellously attractive. I was wild for my idea. I was going to get my own way in this at all costs. But Wally didn't like it.

'I haven't got the capital, Ada,' Wally said. 'You know that as well as I do. I'm in no position to launch out on a new adventure.'

'I'm getting on, Ada,' he said. 'I'm too old for new responsibilities and worries. I want a bit of peace.'

'You'll get your peace,' I said. 'I'll do the work. You don't need to do a thing except sign cheques.'

'And carry an overdraft bigger than my backside,' Wally said. 'No, Ada. I'm sorry. I'm not having any of it.'

'Think it over first, Wally,' I said. 'Don't just condemn it out of hand.'

'Put it out of your mind, girlie,' he said. 'Those ideas have got to be nipped in the bud or they'll grow on you. Crawl into your ear and nibble at your brain like an earwig. Shall we go for a run? Three or four gallons in the car we can use.'

'No thanks,' I said. 'I'm going home.'

'But you said you'd stay tonight. I've been looking forward to it all week. Don't be cross, girlie. Come on, let's go out. Make a night of it.'

'No thanks, Wally,' I said. 'I'm going home.'

Then he showed his temper to me for the last time.

'Go on home then,' he said. 'Keep your mother company. Don't think I can't get on without you. Don't get too big for your boots. Don't give me this Frankie business. I won't stand for it. Go on home.'

I went. I was glad he'd lost his temper. It had to come. I was confident that next day he would be after me begging forgiveness. I decided to rub his nose in it. Early in the morning I took a train to Chester. I told my mother I was going to do a day's shopping. I decided when I got there to spend the night in a large hotel. I wanted to watch how they did things, from the professional point of view. I took a notebook and made notes. The staff were puzzled that I should ask so many questions. They couldn't make me out.

When I got back to Pennant, my mother decided to be in a state of desperate anxiety.

'In God's name, girl, where have you been? Wally's nearly mad with worry and so am I. We began to imagine all sorts of things. Poor man's nearly out of his mind...'

'Stop fussing and make me a cup of tea.'

The tone of my voice was something new to her. It was high time I got her organised too.

IV

'You've got to stay in bed,' the doctor said. 'And lie still. As still as you can.'

'God, Matt, I feel all right. I feel fine. I can't afford it, man.' Wally was getting childishly proud of his black brushed-back hair. '*Look at it, Ada*,' he would say, '*black as a raven's wing. Good enough for a young man of thirty. Leave the top button open*,' he said. '*I look better with an open neck*.' And he asked me to move the dressing table so that he could see himself in bed. It surprised me that a sick man could be so vain. He didn't see the puffy coarse face: the bags under his eyes, the granite-like blackheads in his cheek that I never wanted to squeeze. He only saw the shining brushed-back hair.

'I can't afford it you know.' It delighted him to talk familiarly with Dr. Pritchard. He used the 'ti' as if it were a privilege.

'You can't afford to be dead either,' the doctor said. He used the second person singular as if he were talking to a child or a fool. 'Keep him in bed,' he said to me. 'He's not to get up on any account. Not even to go to The Goat.'

Wally laughed delightedly. He loved to be teased by Matt Pritchard. He seemed to think that was a privilege too. As for me, I didn't see why I had to kow-tow to the man. His bills were big enough. And in any case I didn't like him.

'You've got a good nurse, Wally,' he said. 'Lucky man aren't you?'

Wally grinned and nodded like an idiot.

'Nice to have something pretty to look at when you wake up in the morning,' the doctor said, as he took Wally's pulse. Wally began to choke with laughter. 'Look out man, damn it. I know the world's a funny place but you don't want to kill yourself with laughing.'

'Nice chap,' Wally said. 'One of the best old Matt is. And a first rate doctor. Best in the country.'

'It's nice to have a doctor who's your personal friend,' Wally said. 'It's a great comfort. Look at old Matt now. Comes to see me every day. And there's absolutely nothing wrong with me.'

'Follow these instructions carefully,' the doctor said to

me. We were in the drawing room of the bungalow. He was giving me two boxes of tablets. 'Correct timing is quite important. The man's seriously ill and I think you ought to know it.'

'You look tired,' he said. 'Let's have a look at you.'

He put his hands on my shoulders and drew me towards him. He was staring boldly at me and I didn't like it. He put his hand on my cheek as if he had a right to, and taking his time he drew down my lower eyelid.

'You're anaemic,' he said, 'I'll give you some iron.'

'Don't be so unfriendly with Matt, Ada,' Wally said. 'After all he's not only my doctor. He's my friend.'

'I notice you tell him everything,' I said.

'There you are,' Wally said. 'That's just your attitude. He's a good business man, Ada. He understands the law too. His advice is worth having.'

'We'll see,' I said.

'Wally's telling me,' the doctor said, 'you've persuaded him to buy Bronllwyn. What are you thinking of doing with it? Setting up as Lady of the Manor?'

'That's my business,' I said. I was always longing to give him the rough side of my tongue, but I was afraid, because he was attending Wally. And he was the best doctor in the district.

He didn't take offence. He laughed and tapped a cigarette on his silver cigarette case. He was always neat and elegant. I liked that about him.

'Don't misunderstand me, Ada,' he said. 'I like you. And I like your idea too, about Bronllwyn. I'd like to help you. In fact I think I have done that already. I've suggested to Wally that he buys the place in your name as well as his own. Joint ownership. You'll find that a great help. He likes the idea.'

'I don't quite understand it,' I said.

'You will,' he said. He picked up his black case. 'What I like about you,' he said, smiling at me, 'is, you make life interesting.'

'He's cute,' Wally said. 'It's a smart idea, Ada. Income Tax will be catching up on me. It's a way out you see. Fair play to old Matt, he's always been a good friend. We've had a lot of fun together. Did I tell you about the time we drove to London in the Daimler he had then to see the Cup Final? My God, we had a good time I can tell you. He's a lad he is.'

'His condition is, as they say, deteriorating,' the doctor said. 'Of course he can linger on for some time.'

I didn't like his matter of fact tone. Anyone would think he was in business with death and he knew all about it. I didn't want Wally to die.

'You don't sound very sorry,' I said.

'Oh I am,' he said. 'I like old Wally. But we've all got to go some time. That's how it is.'

I didn't answer. He liked this sitting in the drawing room alone with me on the excuse of smoking a cigarette before going on with his visits.

'Don't misunderstand me, Ada,' he said. 'I'm not as cold-blooded and hard-hearted as I sound. But I can't bear pretence. I always say just what I feel.'

I wanted to reply that it didn't seem he ever felt much.

'Don't worry,' he said. 'I'm doing my best for him. I don't like being beaten. I always fight through to the end.

Not that many of my patients are worth the trouble. But it's my job to fight disease and I like doing it. Had any more ideas about Bronllwyn?'

I couldn't make out whether he really was interested in Bronllwyn or whether it was a way of drawing himself closer to me. I thought perhaps both. He said he was interested in his work but outside that there wasn't much comfort. His wife was a faded sort of invalid. She worshipped him. (It amazed me, the complacent way he said this.) Their only son was studying medicine in London. He was nice to her of course, but he didn't get much out of her company. There was football. He enjoyed watching football. He liked being President of the local club. But he wanted me to understand there was nothing for miles around that interested him, outside his work, as much as me. I laughed when he said this; and he laughed too. I liked him better when he laughed. His teeth were so clean and his whole person such a healthy cool and excellently preserved fifty. He was much more lively than he allowed himself to appear in public. He wasn't only a cold and calculating efficient medical man; he had an intense humorous curiosity about people that appealed to me. We were becoming friendly because he wished it so much, and since he was determined to make himself so useful to me, and because I could see nothing against it. I had begun to learn that it always paid to be nice to people who could be useful to you. And there weren't all that many of those in Pennant for me. I began to enjoy his company. He had a way of talking that suggested that he and I were superior beings of greater power and intelligence, who could rightly enjoy looking down on the rest of the community. I enjoyed doing this. I'd been looked down upon by the rest of the community long enough. He made me feel my turn had come.

'It's surprising how much we've got in common, Ada,' he said. 'I'm wondering whether it would extend to another sphere of activity.'

'I don't understand,' I said.

'Never mind,' he said. 'How's the patient today?' We went into Wally's bedroom. 'Well, old Wally, my lad? We've got to get you out of here. What's the football team going to do without their centre forward?'

Wally smiled broadly, like a delighted child. He was neatly shaved and his hair was brushed smartly back. He was still most particular about his appearance. I bought him two new pairs of silk pyjamas, one red one blue. He liked it when the doctor teased him about them. He only wore the blue one once. The doctor explained to me he was in a state of euphoria. 'He's perfectly happy, Ada,' he said. 'So don't worry about him.' But the idea of euphoria was no comfort to me. That the last illusion should be the biggest of all depressed me terribly and not even thinking of Bronllwyn could take my mind off it.

V

One of the last things Wally and the doctor talked about was getting a licence for Bronllwyn. Matt had told Wally that he was seriously considering becoming a partner in the venture and that he was taking a personal interest in the club side of the project. 'Think of it, Wally, buying a drink and putting the money in your own pocket,' he said. 'It's like eating your cake and having it. The kind of business I've been looking for all my life!'

'It's those bloody Elises,' Wally said. 'They've always been in my way. Everything I've ever tried to do to improve this place they've always blocked. Miserable lot of snivelling hypocrites.'

'I'm thinking of going on the Council myself,' the doctor said.

'Just the kind of man we need,' Wally said. 'I'll hold you to that Matt. Damn it all, we could fight the lot of them you and I. Sweep the Elises and their minions out of power. That's the truth of the matter you know. All very quiet and respectable, but they've had this town and district on the palms of their hands for the last forty years and nobody's doing a thing about it.'

'Maybe we'll have a try,' the doctor said. 'Makes life a bit more interesting.'

'You're just the man for the job,' Wally said. The doctor had to tell him to curb his enthusiasm. It was two days before his death.

VI

I wanted to talk to Matt Pritchard alone and I thought the young minister would never go. I liked him. I liked the friendly way he looked at me but I wished he would get up and go. He was an ornament, not part of practical living. He was a long time moving.

'How are you going to manage?' Matt said. He was

concerned about me and I would need his help. But I wanted to keep my independence. I'd been tied down by other people's arrangements once too often.

'I'll manage that,' I said.

'Look, Ada,' he said. 'Come off it. I'm not trying to get something for nothing. I want to help you now just for the fun of it. When I want anything else you won't find me slow in asking.'

'I'd like to get away,' I said. 'Away from the whole bunch of them. I think I'll move in to Bronllwyn as soon as I can.'

'That's a sound plan,' he said. 'I approve of it. You won't mind being there alone?'

'I shall love it. It's something I've never had. Being alone in my own house.'

'Look,' he said. 'As soon as you've settled yourself in, make an estimate of the money you'll need for renovations and running costs. When you're ready I'll come over and we'll talk business.'

Bill Francis tried to see me by myself before I left the bungalow. He wanted to talk business too. I was packing my own clothes and he just walked in.

'Hello, Ada!' he said. I disliked him intensely because he fancied he had a right to be familiar with me because I had been intimate with his father. I found something repulsive in him and the way he used to pester me before Wally got jealous and sent him away.

'Don't you knock on people's doors before coming in any more?' I said.

'Well, after all, it's my own home, Ada,' he said. 'You

look nice, Ada. Honestly, you're even more beautiful now than you used to be.'

'Ada,' he said, 'there's no need for you to move. You don't need to take any notice of Sylvia May. You know what she's like. Always giving trouble.'

'I want to move,' I said.

'Listen,' he said. 'I haven't got much of a head for the paper work. I don't think Frankie's all that good at it either, although he says he is. Listen, Ada. Sell that white elephant and come into partnership with us. Listen. I'll tell you. There'd be you and me then against Frankie and Sylvia. Two shares against one. I've nothing against old Frankie, but I'd rather have you in as well. I may as well tell you, Ada, I've always liked you and I like you now more than ever.'

'No thanks, Bill,' I said.

'No ill feelings?' he said. 'Shake?'

'No ill feelings,' I said.

'Tell me, Ada. Can I keep hoping?' The silly young idiot gaped at me with what he imagined was an attractive look. I wondered what cheap dance-hall he had used to develop his technique.

'It depends what you are hoping for,' I said.

VII

My mother annoyed me. She'd been helping me, working hard in the kitchen all day and there was a great deal to be done, but she kept on chattering about the doctor in a way that got on my nerves. I hadn't realised that she'd already noticed his interest in me.

'Humour him, Ada,' she said. 'Don't treat him unkindly and you'll find it will repay you.'

Having her putting in her own crude way what I suppose I had already decided to do got on my nerves unbearably.

'Sheep's-eyes was here this afternoon,' she said.

'Who?'

'Sheep's-eyes. The minister. Wanted to see you. Said he'd call again. Might be a good thing to humour him too.'

'What on earth are you chattering about?'

'All right, don't lose your temper now. That's no way to talk to your poor old mother. The fact is, Ada, that poor boy's in love with you.'

She took a great pride in my conquests. She imagined most men wanted me and took it as as a direct compliment to herself.

'It's really quite a joke,' my mother said. 'D'you know who they say is very keen on him, Hannah Elis. Hannah's sick for a lover. Those ugly sort always are. Never wanted one myself. It was all I could manage to keep them off me. Do you know there was a time when she was after our Frankie. When he was only a boy too. Oh you don't know everything. And if you keep yourself to yourself up here you'll get to a state so as you won't know nothing. It's a good job you've got your old mam to keep an eye on you.'

'You know what would be funny,' she said, giggling in a way that made me wish I could stop listening to her. 'For you to pinch him from her, eh? Duwch, that would be one in the eye for those Elises. And haven't they been asking for it. Haven't they just. You humour him, Ada fach, and it will pay you. Humouring a man never did anybody any harm and often did him a lot of good. You listen to me. I know what I'm talking about.'

'I don't doubt that you do,' I said.

VIII

'Two thousand,' I said.

The doctor lifted his eyebrows and pulled a face.

'As much as that?' he said.

'That's a full estimate,' I said. 'It's got to be done properly. It's got to be a smart place or it won't attract the right people. Then there's advertising and so on in the best papers. Do you want the details?'

'No. No, Ada. I rely absolutely on you. You can have the two thousand. And I won't expect any form of profit for the next two years!'

He was holding out his hand to me and smiling.

'Just an occasional favour, Ada, to keep me patient,' he said.

He was suddenly nervous and unhappy. If it was necessary I would do it but the whole idea of another attack on my freedom made me feel tired and ill.

'You don't love me, Matt. Why do you want me?'

He took hold of both my hands.

'Why do we live, Ada, except to want? What do people mean by love, anyway? I've often wondered. I want to be honest. I desire you. I can hardly go beyond that. To me you are the most beautiful, attractive and desirable woman in the world. But I want to be honest about this love business. If it means I'm completely infatuated with you and can think of nothing else but you, that isn't true. Wanting you doesn't disturb my work. It doesn't make me any less patient with my wife. But I do want you. And apart from that again I want to be your friend and I want to help you.'

'Let's put it on an absolutely business-like footing,' he said. 'I'm getting something I want very much. You're giving it me. It's up to you to state terms. You can see how far I'm willing to go.'

He waited for me to answer. It was a wet afternoon and the rain was leaking through the glass verandah outside the oak-room in which we were sitting. It was one of the innumerable things about the place that wanted seeing to. The woodwork was rotten. I needed that two thousand pounds. This was my chance, the only chance, and I had to take it. 'Humour him' my wise experienced mother said.

'All right,' I said.

I thought afterwards that my willingness was what he wanted most. He was paying for me to become a new department of his life and he liked the idea of it more than the reality. He was paying to have his own way with a toy he had fancied: a rich child who wanted the brightest in the window. He wasn't impotent – but his interest in love-making was very slight. What he paid for, I decided, was the notion that I had become his mistress and that he was a man who lived a very full and very interesting life.

That was as near as I could get to understanding him. I took some trouble to cultivate the aspects of our relationship that pleased him. It pleased him very much that I should take him into my confidence. He liked nothing better than that. My ways of thinking seemed to interest and amuse him. Intimacy with me was a prized possession and demonstration of his power.

IX

'That long necked preacher's keen on you,' Matt said. 'Have you noticed? Queer type. A bit of a fool I should say, flopping all over the place like a wet duck with a broken wing.'

I tried to avoid discussing Idris. It wasn't easy because Matt liked talking. Funny that I used to think he never talked. If a subject took his fancy he wouldn't leave it alone until he'd shaken it to bits and it lay still under his feet.

One afternoon I found him in my bedroom: he was in the wardrobe looking through my coat pockets. He wasn't a bit put out when I said, 'Looking for something, Matt?'

'Hope you don't mind,' he said. 'Came across this in your handwriting and wondered if you had any more.'

He opened his neat carefully manicured hand, and I took the piece of crushed paper on it and unfolded it. *Not till Friday after six* I read, in my own writing.

'Where did you get this, Matt?' I said. 'What is it anyway?'

'Found it,' he said. 'Found it on the floor of the kitchen in West Lodge.'

'How did you get in there?' I said. 'What on earth were you doing there?'

'That's what I wanted to find out, Ada: what you were

doing there.' He laughed at me quite cheerfully. 'Meeting the preacher perhaps?'

'Who told you?'

'Never mind. And don't worry. Lie down on this nice bed and tell me all about it.'

'Was it my mother?' She could have found out and told him for some purpose of her own. Or was it Frankie, or Sylvia May? Damn the lot of them. Always quietly spying and good for nothing else: the unbearable burden I have to carry. 'Frankie I expect.'

'Never mind. Never mind. Come and lie down here Ada, and tell your old uncle all about it.'

I wasn't willing to speak. My mind was confused. What did I want? What would I have to give up? How could I hope to control the course of events when everybody around me was so untrustworthy, unreliable, capricious and unpredictable? I was oppressed with a sense of defeat. I wanted Matt to go, and all the rest of them. I wanted to be left alone. To lock myself up inside myself and never let anyone in anymore. Life seemed designed to prevent me having anything I wanted.

'Don't worry, Ada.' Matt was laughing. 'I'm not jealous. I'm a calm middle-aged man who never expects too much and never gets disappointed. I don't mind about this boy. You're young and he's young. I'm not as selfish as I look. All I ask is you tell me a bit about it. You know, from time to time I value your friendship. That's something I haven't paid for. And I want you to value mine. Tell me about him. He's obviously not as daft as he looks or you wouldn't fancy him.'

'He wants to marry me,' I said.

'Does he now?' Matt folded his arms, frowned and nodded and bit his lip as if he had just been given an unaccountable piece of medical history. 'That's very interesting. He's quite a lad then, isn't he?'

Then Matt laughed, looking at me in his most friendly way; and I couldn't help laughing too.

'You must admit,' he said, shaking with laughter still, 'there is a funny side to it.'

I began to feel relieved. It was a shock to me that he had found out what I imagined to be a closely guarded secret. I thought it would upset everything. But all he did was laugh.

'Do you know, Ada, I wish you would marry him! I really do. It would make life in Pennant so much more interesting.'

'He's nice,' I said. 'He's very sweet.'

'Brings out the motherly instincts!' Matt said.

We laughed again.

'Seriously it might not be a bad idea to marry him. Become a respectable woman at one fell swoop.'

'I don't want to be respectable. Not that way.'

'But just think of the fun you could have at the expense of the Elises. I like the idea.'

X

Matt was furious when the licence was refused. Even more than I was. He seemed to take it as a direct attack upon himself, although his connection with Bronllwyn was still undefined. I hadn't realised how interested he had really been in that side of the project. I thought it had been just a manly joke with Wally about owning your own bar and drinking your own liquor at your own profit and all that sort of stuff. But Matt really meant it. Bronllwyn was another toy to him and having a bar there, and a drinking club of which he would be the power behind the scenes where he could bring his friends and where they would see me and quietly realise that I was another of his toys as well.

'Damn their hypocritical hides,' he said. 'It's lucky for them that they're not patients of mine or I'd give them some special medicine. Ignorant swine, don't even know a good doctor when they see me. That horse doctor Bartholomew they've been bolstering up for God knows how many years. Doesn't know a damn thing. Comes running over to me when he's made a mess of his patients, begging me to patch them up. He's a worm too. All this temperance business because he's scared of old Elis and swigging brandy on the sly. They make me sick. This place needs cleaning up, Ada. Somebody's got to start.'

'You'll have to get rid of the Elises first,' I said.

And only a day or two after I'd said that he came driving up to the door and running up the steps with most unusual speed.

'Ada! Come here! Come here.' He led the way to the oak-room. He came and went in Bronllwyn now as if it were his own place although the terms of our agreement were still incomplete. There was nothing I could do about it. 'Got anything to drink? Been wanting to come here all morning. Today of all days half the damn population of Pennant decide to call the doctor. Anybody'd think the damned Health Scheme had already started.'

It was unusual to see him so excited.

'Sit down,' he said. 'I've got a surprise for you. A big surprise. Did you know you had a brother?'

'Don't remind me,' I said. 'I'm trying to forget it.'

'I don't mean Frankie. I mean another brother. Your father's son, not your mother's.'

'No. I didn't,' I said. 'It sounds very complicated.'

'Well, you have,' Matt said. 'He's risen from the dead. I've been talking to your mother about him. She knew about him all right. And about him being sent away as a baby. But she was under the impression he was dead.'

'I remember the story vaguely now. Remember my mother telling me. The old dragon sent him away because she hated his father. Some story of that sort.'

'Well, he's alive,' Matt said. He was grinning at me.

'What's so wonderful about that?' I said.

'He is a medical research student. A pathologist in Cambridge. Sounds very English. I've had a letter from him. He wants to know all about his family.'

'He's in for a few shocks, isn't he?' I said.

'Why this sudden interest? Put yourself in his place. Talks about investigating his family history. Well why write to me? He says he found my name and address in the Medical Register. But he only had to make a few inquiries and he would have got into direct touch with the Elises themselves. What's he after?'

'Money,' I said. 'Property?'

'Exactly. That's what I thought. Do you know what; if he's the eldest son of Elis Felix Elis, it's not impossible that Y Glyn belongs to him.'

It's Dick's, I thought. It's Dick's and mine. But I didn't say anything. What was the use? I didn't want another brother turning up. Not really. I wanted Dick or something like Dick.

'It's going to be interesting,' Matt said. 'Very interesting. Are the Elises going to like it? I think not. This might be something. We might be on the verge of getting the Elises just where we want them.' He screwed the heel of his highly polished shoe into the carpet. 'Just there.'

He laughed and I laughed too, because he was beginning to infect me with enthusiasm. It was exciting to plan something against the old enemy. Something that might really upset them. I looked forward eagerly to his arrival and prepared to rejoice.

XI

Seeing him was an anti-climax. Not his appearance. He was good-looking enough in his pale red-haired way. Pipe-smoking, English, cold; impossible to believe he was as much my brother as Frankie who stood grinning behind him. He was tall and long faced and he seemed to have difficulty in smiling. He listened like a judge. You felt all the time he was weighing everything in the balance. I tried to be as friendly as I could, but it isn't easy to speak freely to a man who seemed to hold up every word you say to the light to examine the water-mark. He appeared to have worked everything out in his own mind beforehand; and having endorsed his own integrity was now carefully examining everyone else's. When I joked he barely smiled, so that, suddenly embarrassed, I began to suspect he considered me common.

In the kitchen Frankie and my mother were waiting for me.

'I was telling Frankie,' my mother said excitedly. 'There's no mistaking him. Just like his father.'

'And his mother,' Frankie said. He was longing to run him down. He lounged in a kitchen chair in a way that annoyed me. No wonder the stranger suspected me of being common. Look at these two I was tied to: as if they had a right to be in the place. For them Philip Esmor Elis was something passing in the street, to look through the window and laugh at. But I wasn't going to give them a chance. I didn't want any of their interference. He was my brother and I would be patient.

'The same kind of hair,' my mother said. 'A reddish tint in it. What's he like, Ada?'

'He's all right,' I said. 'Very English.'

Frankie jumped up suddenly, pulled a long face, gave a frosty smile and extended a limp hand, just as Philip had done. I couldn't help laughing although I was furious with myself for doing so. We laughed together until the tears began to run down our cheeks. I laughed, knowing I would be miserable after. Bound by this intimate cruel mocking laughter to these two whom I had always lived with and would never escape from to something better.

PHILIP ESMOR-ELIS

CHAPTER TWENTY

I

Wondered where I was when I woke up and what I was up to. The dream had been about de Veina Grooves and Swades. They had locked Margaret in the lab cupboard but wouldn't admit it. I was ridiculously furious. But John Neade said, 'They're right you know, Philip. Her father's got the key.' And he offered to fetch it for me. 'The old man's dangerous, John,' I said. 'Don't you worry,' John was smiling confidently. 'I can handle him.'

Through the windows I could see bare trees rooted in the stony slope behind the lawn and at the bottom of the window the top of an almond tree. I wanted to fix my gaze on the almond blossom and think about Margaret. Margaret and my work. The two things that really mattered. I had no taste for resuming contact with the people of the house. The sooner the better I got back to Margaret and my work.

II

A doctor called Pritchard and a woman called Ada Evans who claimed to be my half-sister. We sat in the lounge as they called it and I really felt the whole situation was absurd. I had made an error of judgement, a mistake. I was therefore uneasy and very much on my guard.

'I'm Pritchard,' he said in his clipped self-satisfied voice. 'We corresponded. Have you had a good journey? Do you smoke? Let's sit down shall we? I don't think Ada will be long. Well, what does it feel like to find you have a grown-up sister?'

He was ready to chuckle but I wasn't giving him any encouragement. I was on my guard right from the start. I hate making errors of judgement.

'I understand we are in the same line of business,' he said. 'Do you practise?'

'No. I don't practise. I'm really a protozoologist.'

'Really. How interesting. I always wanted to do research myself. What work are you on now?'

'I'm at present doing research,' I said, 'on the asexual cycle of malaria by liver biopsis on human beings, and also producing new strains...'

'Ah, here's the lady of the house herself,' he said. I felt a fool. He hadn't been listening and his declaration of interest was a complete fake. I could see he wasn't genuine and was more on my guard than ever.

What business was it of his? It was my family mess, not his.

'You explain, Matt,' Ada said. 'You can put it all in fewer words. An objective view would you call it?'

And he laughed as if the girl was madly clever. They were worse than provincial. So damned smug. The man was lacking I felt in correctness, in professional etiquette. Things I don't hold great store by myself but he was a country GP and it was his business to act like a good one. I was getting an edited version of the facts, a second-hand affair, after coming all this way: I felt I should be handling the investigation myself.

'So you have two sisters alive,' he said, 'and a half brother dead. And of course your mother too. She's very much alive too, isn't she, Ada?'

The girl nodded and pulled a face. She was holding her right elbow in her left hand and smoking affectedly with a cigarette holder.

'Now it's your turn to tell us your story,' the doctor said. 'We're getting curious aren't we, Ada?'

'There's very little to tell,' I said. 'Brought up by my father's cousin whom I call my aunt. An academic career. A few years in the Army. Very little to tell.'

'We were wondering,' Pritchard said, 'why you'd never investigated before.'

'My aunt discouraged me when I was young.' I had prepared myself for this question. 'Afterwards I was too busy. My work interested me too much I expect. The war. Abroad and all that.'

There was an awkward pause which I was determined not to break. I was quite prepared to be pompous.

'Anyway you're here now,' Ada said.

The doctor stayed to dinner. The food was adequate and we had beer to drink. There were long pauses while Ada went into the kitchen to get the food. The doctor and I sat facing each other without speaking. I had said all I wanted to say to him. The dining-room was chilly and over-crowded with sidetables. In the kitchen we heard voices being raised. When Ada came back she was flushed and her polite smile didn't conceal her discomfort. I couldn't make conversation.

'Who's there?' The doctor raised his eyebrows and nodded towards the kitchen.

'It's Bill Francis,' Ada said. 'He's had rather too much to drink.'

'Is Frankie there?' the doctor said. 'Can't he cope with him?'

Ada nodded, then she asked me would I have some more beer.

'As a matter of fact,' Ada said, 'we're having trouble with your mother about a licence. We want a licence to sell drink on the premises. Mrs. Elis and the magistrates in general won't let us have one.'

'Are they temperance people?' I asked politely.

'Fanatics,' the doctor said. 'Narrow-minded fanatics. Enjoyment of any kind is a sin you see. *Pechod. Pechod.* That's what they call it. I am afraid your mother is the worst of the lot.'

There was a scuffle outside the door and a drunken

young man with a cap over his eyes lurched in, pale-faced and powerfully built. Behind him was Ada's brother, Frankie, and the old woman who had turned away shyly when we were introduced. I had been touched by her shyness. I imagined the years of pain and shame she must have endured and the sacrifices she had made for her illegitimate daughter.

'What did I tell you!' The drunk pointed a thick finger at me. 'Bloody little liar you are, Frankie Evans, always was and always will be. There he is. A new fancy man, Ada? Hooked another one? Listen mate...'

The doctor wiped his mouth with his napkin and pushed back his chair.

'Now, look here Bill,' he said in his most business-like voice. 'This won't do. Take him out, Frankie.'

'You bloody little devil doctor,' Bill said with great drunken deliberation. 'You put your finger on me, fat boy, and I'll knock your teeth out.'

Frankie touched his arm: nervous, pale and smiling. Frankie was, I thought, rather enjoying the occasion.

'I'll say my say, doctor boy, and you listen. I know a thing or two. Now listen mate,' he pointed at me again. 'This bitch was my father's fancy bit, see. Understand? My dirty old man's bit of goods. And now she's his.' He pointed at the doctor. 'His. Fancy pants' fancy goods. They got rid of my old man and bought this place with my old man's money. My money. Look at it!' He waved his hands towards the ceiling. 'Wages of sin. Dirty sin and done me in. And what do I get? A bankrupt bloody garage that this little runt' – he pointed at Frankie, 'goes about saying 'tis his. Lying little rat. That's what they all are. Thieves. Thick as fornicating thieves. That's what they are. So you look out. Now.' He walked unsteadily towards my chair. 'Keep clear of her, mate.' He winked at me and whispered hoarsely, 'She tried to get me too.'

Ada pulled at his coat frantically.

'Get out of here, Bill Francis! Get out you drunken swine! Frankie, why did you let him in? You let him in on purpose! Get him out!'

'One little kiss, Ada, and I'm off.' Bill Francis turned to face her.

'That's enough,' the doctor said. 'Get out of here.'

'Come on, if it's a fight you're after.' Bill Francis lifted his fists.

'You had better go,' I said. I was trembling with the effort of keeping calm.

'You want to try,' he said. 'You. Funny face. Come on then.'

I got up quickly. He came plunging towards me and I dropped him with a right hook that hurt my knuckles. I was pleased with the blow. It was something done.

'Take him out,' I said, and Frankie helped him up. There wasn't any more fight left in him.

'That was a beautiful blow,' the doctor said. 'Beautifully timed.'

'You brought him here, Frankie.' Ada was almost screaming before I noticed how angry she was. 'And you let them in,' she said to her mother. 'Well this time you've gone too far. Think you can do what you like in my house! Well you're mistaken. I've had enough of it. I can't trust either of you. Well you can clear out now. Right out. I never want to see either of you here again. Go on! Get out!'

'Now, Ada,' Frankie said. 'Don't get excited. Jumping to conclusions you are, you know. I never brought him here. He followed me. I came here to take mother home.'

The mother was crying, and crooning to herself, 'What's to become of us! What's to become of us? I can't stand their quarrelling. Brother and sister they are. My own flesh and blood. I can't stand it. I can't stand it.'

I was sorry for the old woman. She hugged her sorrow in the dim light of the hall and no one seemed to take much notice of her, son or daughter.

'I'd be inclined to accept Frankie's explanation, Ada,' the doctor said. 'No sense in quarrelling over this drunken idiot.'

Bill Francis had nothing more to say. He sat on an oak chair in the hall like a casualty in a waiting room, nursing his chin.

'If you'll all excuse me,' I said. 'I think I'll go to bed. I've had rather a long day.'

Their voices broke out again as soon as I was up the stairs, but I refused to let myself become interested in their sordid quarrels. The drunken lout raised his fists at me and it's one of my principles to attack if threatened. That had impressed them. Showed them who they'd got to deal with. I mind my own business unless threatened: then I hit out. I needed a long think about my business here. It was too confused and complicated and it was up to me to straighten it out.

III

Breakfasted alone. Why should I feel lonely being alone now? Used to being alone, preferring to be alone. In John's rooms, after a late night, a late breakfast; before the gasfire; through the leaded windows gowned figures hurrying across the quad on a wet morning. Here my solitude oppresses. Should have left it to the lawyers. No use getting involved, unarmed and defenceless as I am in this kind of warfare, personally involved with people I have no wish to meet or be obliged to encounter. The future seemed mined with unexploded anger. I had come the wrong way and I had better retrace my steps. Catch the next train back. Back to my work. Back to Margaret. Blast her father. Although even he, compared with this and these, seemed civilised, open to reason, not vulgar, illiterate swayed by incalculable primitive passions.

It was their vulgarity, oddly enough, I found most difficult to bear. The indiscriminate collection of pewter and brass bits and pieces here, there and everywhere, the flourished cigarette holder, the knowing ill-bred nods and winks, the inability to keep their mouths shut, the cheap music on the piano, the unrestrained quarrelling, the unrestrained abuse. This wasn't my family. The girl was only accidentally my half-sister.

There was my mother: narrow, puritanical, fierce, long skirt-kicking masculine strides. A natural persecutor of smokers and people trying to get some fun out of life. Also repellent. Repellent in a different way and with a closer claim on my interest and attention.

But best to avoid the lot. Half-sister now known and unknown sister, unknown uncle. Best to observe uninvolved from a convenient distance not like this, breakfasting in the middle of one armed camp. Their wars were not mine. I had my own campaign to follow.

Ada came in. Friendly. Trying to look as if last night hadn't happened. But she looked worried and she was smoking all the time.

'I'm very sorry about that drunkard,' she said. 'Did you sleep well? Have you had enough to eat?'

She rang a bell and a young girl dressed up as a maid came in and cleared away clumsily. Ada was watching her, ready to correct her next time in the kitchen. What the drunk said could have been true of her; good looking, but defiant. It could well be true.

'I had an idea in bed last night,' Ada said. 'There's a woman who lives in the Almshouses near here. She was a Queen's nurse and she came to Pennant thirty-five years ago. Retired at fifty having been left something she says. She's rather sweet really. Remarkable considering her age. Tall and holds herself straight still. She told me once she nursed your father during his last illness. She probably attended your birth as well.'

'Miss Aster,' I said.

'That's right,' Ada said. 'You've heard of her then?'

'My aunt mentioned her name,' I said. 'Yes, I can say I've heard of her.'

'Well I thought we could go, I thought I could take you to see her this morning.'

I didn't say yes or no. I wanted to get away, but it would be interesting to see the old lady who brought me into the world. But not get involved. Interesting to hear her story; but to get away afterwards. Afternoon train perhaps. What would I say to Ada or that doctor chap? 'I've decided to go back' or 'My plans have changed,' or 'I've been called back.' No need to give any explanations. Just say 'I'm going' and go.

'As a matter of fact,' Ada said, 'I've always wanted to ask her about it. What exactly happened. But she's so cautious, she really never has made up her mind whether I want to acknowledge my father or not.'

She laughed and I laughed. It seemed the most attractive thing she had said since my arrival. Made her more attractive. Warmed me towards her; honesty and a kind of courage.

'All right,' I said. 'I'll come. But Ada...'

I had used her first name at last. We were on the verge of becoming friendly. One more spurt of emotion and I would be over the edge.

'...I'm thinking of going back this afternoon.'

'No. Don't...' she said, and then stopped suddenly. I could see she was bitterly disappointed. More than I could understand. What did it all mean to her? Had last night's scene upset any of her plans? I could not afford the expense of personal feeling it would cost to investigate.

'As you wish,' she said. She was biting her lower lip and blinking as though to keep back tears. 'I'll go and put my coat on.'

IV

An early Victoria building. A miniature barracks set oddly in the middle of the fields west of Bronllwyn Park. There was a small lodge and a narrow lane that led to the building itself. There were lambs in the field and the sun came out. You could see the sticky black buds on the pale ash tree in the hedge where the lane turned and flowed under the bridge-like entrance into the cracked concrete courtyard of the Almshouses.

Ada knocked Miss Aster's small door. We heard a bolt being shot open and the door opened a few inches. I saw a wrinkled greasy pale face that hadn't been washed for some time.

'Who is it?' She spoke with a North Country accent and a voice of surprising strength and authority.

'Miss Aster, it's me, Ada Evans. Brought you some things.'

'Ada, my love! I didn't see you. Haven't my glasses on. Now come in my love. And bring the young man with you.'

The room was small, crowded with old furniture and smelled of cats and poverty. The numerous framed pictures on the wall kept the wallpaper up: it had begun to peel off and hang down in the corners. The dirty lace curtains over the two tiny windows made the light very dim. But the longer one remained in the room the dirtier it seemed. A heap of cold ash filled the hearth and would soon overflow the fender.

Miss Aster had placed the bag Ada had brought on the table. The remains of her breakfast were spread over half the greasy and tea-stained cloth.

'Oh how nice of you, my love! A tin of bully! Oh how sweet of you – tomato sauce! And eggs. Fresh eggs. I've been near starving I can tell you. Locked up in this dreadful place. I can't get out you know. That woman upstairs. She's waiting for me to go out. Watching everything too. Wants to steal you see. She's that kind. I've told the Vicar about her. She's not a gentlewoman. Not even a church woman. Just a wretched nonconformist turn-coat, that's what she is. Absolutely no right to be here. And I don't like to say this in front of a gentleman but the truth's the truth: she's been using my privy. Oh dear I don't know. I really don't. But don't listen to my tale of woe my lovely. Tell me, how's yourself? Young and beautiful that she is, and the kindest heart in Pennant.'

'Miss Aster, this gentleman is Mr. Esmor-Elis.'

'Very pleased to meet you, Mr. Esmor-Elis.'

We shook hands. Her large hand was dirty and sticky, although a gold ring gleamed on one finger.

'His full name should be Philip Esmor Felix Elis, Miss Aster.'

'I'm a bit slow. Old Age you know. Eighty-five next birthday. What do you think of that? Say it again, my lovely.'

'Philip Esmor Felix Elis. You realise who he is? He's come back.'

'I don't have anything to do with the Elises now, Ada. You know how they treated me. Turned me out of a cottage twenty years my home. That was the thanks I got. I haven't met this gentleman before. What relation is he?'

'He's the baby she sent away. The baby that went to London.'

She frowned and turned her mouth down, looking at me disapprovingly.

'You are Miss Aster,' I said. 'My aunt told me that you were the midwife that delivered me.'

'That doesn't prove anything,' she said. 'I've delivered hundreds of babies.'

'I'm not trying to prove anything,' I said. She was beginning to annoy me. A cunning old woman. Trying to judge the value of whatever we were after. I would have said more but Ada frowned at me.

'I always said to myself he'll come back,' Miss Aster said. 'It was a sin to send him away. But that woman was so difficult and wild.' She was silent again. 'Listen!' she said suddenly. 'Listen! That woman's throwing her slops out of her window again. One day I'll catch her at it. Throwing her slops into my piece of garden, the dirty old witch.' She peeped out through the window, then suddenly she turned her head and stared at me.

'Got a strawberry mark on the small of your back?' she said.

'As a matter of fact I have,' I said. I wished there had been someone civilised there for me to laugh with.

'Then I'd better see it,' she said. Suddenly she became the brisk nursing sister exercising hospital authority. 'Come on my fine lad. Don't be shy. I've seen hundreds in their birthday suits besides yourself.'

'Good God I'm not shy!' I said. I took off my jacket and pulled out my shirt so that she could peer at the mark on the small of my back.

'That's it!' I tucked my shirt back in again. 'It's him all right. Ada, my lovely, it *is* him. I'll swear to it in court on earth or in heaven. I brought him into the world. This great fine strapping lad. Nine pounder he was. And look at him now! So Philip she called you. A nice name Philip. And you've had it for thirty years.'

She sat down on a chair and leaning an arm on the table began to shake her head. It seemed to shake of its own aged volition and I was afraid it might not stop.

'Be sure your sins will find you out,' she muttered. 'There never was a truer word and if you ask mc they've been waiting for it every day of these thirty years past. As true as Gertrude Aster is a sad witness. They've been afraid of this for thirty years. It's like a thing to be!'

'I was telling Philip,' Ada said, 'that you were nursing his father when he died.'

Miss Aster's eyes swivelled up loosely in their gummy sockets. 'He was your father too you know. I heard him admit it.'

'What did he die of?' I said.

'Pneumonia it was on the death certificate.' Miss Aster nodded her head.

'That's what my aunt always said.'

'But there was much more to it than that, wasn't there, Miss Aster?' Ada bent forward. 'Tell him, Miss Aster. It's right he should know.'

I nodded. I felt the excitement that belongs to the

approach of truth.

'It's true he had pneumonia. But he needn't have died. Old Doctor Probert had the case well in hand. What happened was you see I had to go to Liverpool for two days: and that was when it happened.'

'I told her before I left,' Miss Aster said. 'It was vital for someone to be with him and give him a little water and medicine at regular intervals. When I came back he was dead. Now I found that bottle in the wardrobe. Hardly any of it had been used.'

'You are saying,' I said, 'that my mother deliberately killed him.'

Miss Aster threw up her hands.

'That's a terrible thing to say and I'd be the last to say it. He'd been cruel to her mind, very cruel. Just think of him carrying on with her own maid, right under her nose. That sort of thing. And he had lady friends in London. This aunt of yours, his cousin Gwen he called her. She was one of them.'

'I didn't know there were others,' I said.

'Oh he was a ladies' man all right. And daring. I know all about him, don't you worry. And very strong-willed. He wasn't going to be bossed about by her.'

'And so she killed him,' I said.

'I'm not saying that. And you mustn't say I'm saying that. It isn't what she did so much as what she didn't do. I'm wishing nobody any harm. But she wasn't sorry he died. She was glad he died, you could put it like that. And what's unusual about that, after all?'

Ada and I found ourselves looking at each other.

She said, 'Our lives would have been something very different if he had lived, Philip.'

But that wasn't at all what I was thinking. I was thinking about truth. How difficult it was to get at the truth. And how maddening to realise the difficulties when by instinct you felt that somewhere absolute truth existed, waiting for your arrival however long you delayed on the journey. There lie waiting your life's meaning and the secret of your unrest.

'But I'll tell you something cheerful,' Miss Aster said. Her face cracked into a thousand wrinkles with her smile. Her gaze shifted coyly from Ada to me. 'That place belongs to you, Philip. You mustn't mind me calling you Philip. What else can I call you and me having changed your nappies! It belongs to you. You're the son and heir and that place really belonged to your pa. He took over your granddad's mortgages and paid them off. Now not everybody knows that, but I do. He put the place financially on its feet. He was great at business. Now your granddad wasn't. I've heard people say he would stop the harvest and take all his men to the weekly prayer meeting. That's your mother's pa. A dear old man he was, though I don't recall him myself. Your mother's ma now I knew. Very straight she was and always a little worried. Your mother had too much of her own way as a girl I reckon. She was spoiled by her pa. Gave in to her over everything he did. He didn't want her to marry Elis Felix. But she wanted it so much, so he gave in. Yes, my lad, it's all yours, lock stock and barrel. And I'd like to see that Vavasor's face the day you roll up to claim it. There's a wicked man if you like. Enticed your ma he did and I'd say it to his face, the uncouth fellow. He's a regular villain. Not worth your father's little finger. And not much of a chemist either if you ask me. He never did any good to my sciatica, him and his six-penny oils.'

As we were leaving the old woman suddenly gripped my arm. She twisted her head to make her smile look coy and persuasive.

'You won't forget your old nurse will you, Philip?' she said. 'I must get out of this dreadful place and there's the wish of my heart to end my days in that sweet little cottage. Happy memories, eh Ada? That's all I have left you know. My memories. If I could be there for the summer. It would be the last wish of my heart.'

V

The lodge-keeper's wife peered around the corner of her tiny house as we passed by.

'There are witnesses,' Ada said. 'Plenty of witnesses. It's easy to prove. I'm getting carried away. Really it's such a romantic thing, I mean your coming back.'

I wanted her to stop chattering. The more friendly she tried to be the more I withdrew into myself. A daring woman that mother. To kill him so openly. A cold crime of thirty years' decease and thirty years, my life's length, unpunished. To send me away so coolly. To calculate and possess my inheritance. I had a fight on my hands. The responsibility for justice moved in my blood. I was ready to accept the challenge. It was no use the small cautious voice in my head telling me to keep calm anymore and to make for limited objectives and to remember Margaret and our need for money. I couldn't ignore the influence of the place because the whole occasion seemed an unworded powerful direct challenge to my manhood. I was not too small or too afraid to play my part. For me all this had been waiting for all the seasons since the day I was born and for all the history that culminated in my birth.

'I want to see the place first,' I said.

'It's a fine farm. The best in the country.'

'I didn't mean the farm. I meant my father's grave.'

'That's right in the middle of the farm,' Ada said, laughing. 'The old church. We'll cross these fields. I know the way. You see those roofs over the trees? That's the little village where I was brought up. I played in these fields as a child.'

The sun shone more strongly and became warmer than the south-west breeze that was blowing. I became conscious of the beauty of the land for the first time. I tried to catalogue the wild flowers that grew in the hedgerows and the different voices of nesting birds. A young lad sat on the red frame of a roller drawn by a large black horse. He was singing to himself unaware that we were on the footpath. The roller drew the surface of flattened brown earth after it like a smooth carpet. We saw him stop the horses and walk in front to remove the eggs of a peewit. There were many peewits about. Their plumes trembled as they stepped daintily on the crushed earth.

We crossed a narrow lane and passed through a rusty wicket into a field of young hay where the sunlight gleamed metallically on the surface of the clean untrodden grass. Power would come to me with the occasion; my pulse raced with this wild conviction. If this was compulsive there was an elated freedom inside the compulsion. I wanted to sing and I wished Ada had not been with me so that I could have done so. Instead I suddenly broke into a run and vaulted the stile ahead. One foot landed on a concealed stone and I tumbled to the ground. I was made conscious of my whole body by the impact of the fall, pleasurably. I felt more fully alive than at any time since embarking on this journey. When I sat up Ada was looking over the stile and laughing at me.

'Dick!' she said. 'You are just like him. That's just the kind of thing he used to do!'

'Dick? Oh yes.'

'There's the church. Down there.'

'Come on then. Let's run.'

'No! Philip. Wait. Philip! Please wait for me.'

Rude or not I ran ahead of her. I wanted to be alone. I wanted to find the grave for myself. As if there were something hidden there. My key. I was a schoolboy again, worrying about his work, having a serious talk with my housemaster about my work. *These English marks are poor Esmor-Elis. Languages, not good. This History result is poor... Your aunt wants you to have extra coaching in Latin, Esmor-Elis.* They were all pestered by Aunt Gwen. All gave in to her, thinking of fees, etc. Except Pitt-Hooker. That man saved my career. Long nosed and unfriendly looking, with sparse ginger hair parted in the middle and cold green eyes. And a house full of babies and a fat fuzzy-haired wife. Going there to tea I stumbled over play-pens, blocks, prams, feeding-chairs and pots. But he saved my bacon. *Look here, Esmor-Elis*, he said in his deep chokey voice. *If it's science that interests you, you damn well do science. Take a firm line about it. I'll back you up*. Between play-pens and pots I met my turning point. It gave me the strength to stick in my heels. From then on, now that I look back, I began to know exactly what I was going to do. Pity I never thanked Pitt-Hooker enough. Too young to realise that a schoolmaster needs thanks. Pity we never got closer. I could have gained so much from him. I was bursting to talk to him, bursting to let it all out, about my aunt, my dead father, my who-was-my-mother, my loneliness, my confusion, and ask in what way it mattered and what was I to do. And he would have listened and his advice would have had the healing touch. But I never spoke and he never spoke. The spark just failed to bridge the gap. Some coldness in him, some lost rage of reticence and pride in me or lack of faith and trust. How could I go to a man and say, 'Will you be my father?' Might have brought this moment so much nearer. Would he have said, *Look here, Esmor, you damn well find out if you want to*? I would find the grave for myself.

The more recent graves were almost all tidy and decked with the season's flowers. It was the week before Easter. The older tombs were rectangular boxes of slate and the oldest of all lichen-blotched time-coloured grey and green stone. The church, low, ancient, unused, stood imperishably in the centre, and seemed to my hurried glance the last human building before the wild sand dunes and the immemorial sea. I was among my ancestors. They were buried all around, dead, humble and undemanding. And somewhere among them my father. The father I never had and always needed I had found, when it was too late. He lay waiting for my understanding and judgement, well beyond my young need for help and disinterested love.

A woman was kneeling at a graveside in the west corner of the churchyard. She was tidying the gravel of a modest white marble tomb. The metal vase for flowers was empty. I knew before I read the thick black lettering that it was my father's grave. His name and age. *Elis Felix Elis, Member of Parliament for the county*. And as a motto... *Gone to his reward*. A thin grey-haired mousy creature. She rose to her feet at my approach. Before I could ask her who she was, she folded her arms as if to warm herself and stepped carefully between the graves towards the path that ran alongside the church.

I had found my father. The spot where he lay from which he could never get away. A fixed point. Ada came up alongside me.

'You soon found it,' she said. I did not answer. But she did not keep silent for long.

'This place has so many memories for me,' she said. 'Sweet and bitter.'

I did not answer because it would have been cruel to say her memories meant nothing to me. I had no interest in whatever sentimental illusions she was preoccupied with.

'He caused a lot of trouble,' Ada said, staring at my father's tombstone. 'There must have been a streak of weakness in him. I mean he let her win, so easily in the end. She had everything her own way. He should have dealt with her in the beginning.'

'He had other things to think about,' I said. 'One must remember that he was a statesman. Some people think he would have become Prime Minister.'

I knew it was the gaff Gwen used to try and stuff in my head that I was repeating. But I didn't want this girl to think of him as just a local libertine.

'I don't suppose things would have been any better for me,' Ada said.

'Did you notice a small woman passing the church when you came in?' I said. 'Small, grey-haired. She was tending this grave when I arrived. Look! Over there! Crossing the field in a black coat, that's her.'

'I'm not sure,' Ada said, 'but it looks like Hannah Elis. Your sister.'

Allowing for the fact that she meant well I didn't like the knowing way she smiled. 'It seems a disgrace,' she said. 'This is the only grave in the place almost without flowers. *Sul y Blodau*. It's an old custom.'

'The house is that way,' I said, pointing.

'Yes.' Even the way she said 'Yes' seemed to attach her to me more than I wanted. All the morning I had the impression that she was trying to attach herself to me. Since I mentioned leaving she had become desperately winningly friendly.

'I'm going there,' I said. 'I'm going there now.'

'Doctor Pritchard said he'd bring the lawyer this evening, to Bronllwyn. Don't you think... I mean he's being so helpful.'

'It's really none of his business. I'm going to see the place for myself.'

'Of course it isn't,' Ada said quickly. 'He does rather...' She stopped and looked up quickly in the direction of the farm. 'It's a fine farm. Strong, sound buildings. The house is too much in a hollow, though. Too gloomy. I'll come with you as a guide, shall I?'

'No,' I said, awkward but determined. 'No, thank you. I want to go alone.'

Without looking at her, I left her where she stood in the churchyard and walked in the direction of the house.

VI

I found a lane leading to the house. As I passed the stable midden I heard the noise of a car backing out of a garage and it reversed across my view through the passage way between the stables, through which I could see a right-angled corner of the house and a partial view of the open kitchen door. It was my mother driving. Slumped in the seat alongside her, wearing a flat cap and swathed in mufflers and travelling rugs, sat the man I took to be her husband. Hardened and aged in their attitudes of respectable triumph. Two old idols it was my duty to cast down. For thirty years they had enjoyed undisputed possession of my kingdom. For thirty years they had drawn profit from my property, using it for their own ends, to consolidate their pre-eminence in the whole district. A pair of ageing power addicts, megalomaniac parasites sucking the life-blood of the whole community, terrorising that tired-looking second-rate town, immovable obstacles to any form of progress. An old dog and an old bitch in my manger. I wasn't going to tolerate it much longer. I was the agent of justice and I would be faithful to my task. I was standing at the heart of my own land and I was glad I had come. If there were regrets about not having come sooner they were extinguished by the knowledge that I came a full man, strong and capable, most properly equipped. I was strong enough to tread the winepress alone.

From the outer yard I watched the car, an old model, proceed jerkily up the lane. My mother was an aggressive erratic driver and smoke billowed out of the exhaust.

I knocked at the door and the small thin woman I had seen tidying my father's grave came quietly from the gloom of the interior. She was still wearing her coat. Two maids appeared in the open doorway of the outdoor scullery, their red hands clouded with soap suds, their mouths open with primitive curiosity.

'Good morning,' I said. 'My name is Esmor-Elis – Philip Esmor-Elis. I believe we are related.'

She saw the maids watching and she invited me inside. Her voice surprised me, a warm contralto, so different from her tiny worn appearance. Not the kind of voice I expected. I was pleasantly surprised. Through the window of the room she showed me into I could see the sunlight in the garden but it did not come near the room itself. A white-moustached man in stiff corduroy was painting the base of the apple trees with lime wash. I doubted whether it did any good. I noticed a microscope box under the window table. The books in the glass book-case were mostly Welsh and theological.

'I'm afraid those two girls are incurably curious,' she said as she closed the door. 'Did you say we were related?'

'I believe I'm your brother.'

Her head began to shake quite suddenly. She grasped the back of an armchair and bent forward in the effort to breathe. I could see it was a severe asthma attack. She pointed to a box on the sideboard. I pulled out the inhaler and gave it to her. She plunged it greedily into her mouth and pressing the rubber-bulb with desperate agitation, struggled for her breath. When it was a little easier she sat down in a chair. I sat down in the chair opposite her and waited for her to recover. As I waited I saw her eyes fill with tears.

The first thing she said was: 'What is your name?'

'Philip. Philip Esmor-Elis.'

'I'm sorry. Forgive me. It wasn't like this I used to think of welcoming you.'

I felt the emotional power of the room and the occasion closing in upon me. Her tears were too much for me.

'Is that your microscope?' I said, pointing to the box under the window table.

She nodded. 'Yes.'

'You're interested in science?'

'I used to be. I wanted to be a doctor. But my health wasn't good enough they said, so I've ended up as a pharmacist.'

'We've got something in common,' I said. 'I'm doing medical research. Pathology. Protozoology to be precise. Are you still interested?'

She nodded. She was staring at me quite openly.

'Excuse me.' She dabbed her eyes with a small handkerchief. 'You're like him. Aren't you. I'm not but you are. Anybody can see you are his son.'

She went on staring at me as if she would go on staring for ever, and I wasn't embarrassed or annoyed. I seemed to have lost my usual gaucherie. She was vulnerable, unprotected, weak after her asthma attack and one cold word would bruise her like a stone.

'You've come,' she said.

I nodded. 'Yes. I've come.'

'I always knew you would. I can remember now the day they took you away. The maid took me to the far outhouses to watch mangolds being covered with layers of straw, seaweed and bracken. October it must have been. They say the salt keeps out the frost. You were about a fortnight old. I said, "Where's the baby?" And my mother said, "There was no baby, Hannah." "But there was," I said. "I saw it myself." And Miss Aster said, "Come child. Come away now. Don't pester your mother. She's ill."'

She stopped speaking and stared at me again. 'It was you,' she said. 'You were alive all the time.'

'Did you think I was dead?' I said. She took the question seriously.

'There was a rumour. She must have started it. As far as she is concerned you are dead. But I never believed it. You were never dead to me. However long I would have to wait. If I had had more courage I would have come to look for you. I always told myself that. But now I think it was better I stayed here. Keeping watch for you. Waiting and watching.'

I got up from my chair and looked at some of the

portraits on the walls. Ugly varnished unskilled portraits they were.

'Who are these?' I said.

'Ancestors,' Hannah said. 'As a family we tend to stick together, the living and the dead.'

'That was your father sitting in the car with your mother?'

'My uncle. Uncle Vavasor. My mother's husband.'

'When will they be back?'

'They've gone to a Presbytery Meeting at Derwen. They'll be back in late afternoon. There's trouble in our church. Some of the congregation are trying to get rid of the minister.'

'Can I stay here?' I said.

'It's your home,' Hannah said. 'It's all yours. You don't need to ask.'

'Can I see the house?'

'This is the middle parlour... This we call the breakfast room but I've never seen anybody sit down in it. It's just a hall. The husbandman and the shepherd and the head carter come here to discuss the morning's work... This is our real living room, the little parlour we call it. These are the dairies. I don't know why there are two. This is the study as they call it. Father used it. Your father and mine, I mean. Now it's just a box-room as you can see. It's been a box-room for thirty years. Maids keep the cleaning things here even. There's nothing in the desk. Mother burnt everything. The books are mostly rubbish. This is the music room. It's the most pleasant room in the house and that's why we don't use it. Biggest windows. Best views. But my mother says it is damp. The piano is always out of tune. And of course it is damp because there are never any fires here. I think the room reminded her of my father. Miss Aster told me he used to do most of his entertaining in here. She remembers Lloyd George spending a weekend here. Others too, whose names are not so easy to remember, although they were important in their time.'

'It's a long time ago,' I said.

'Yes it is a long time ago. But it doesn't seem so long ago somehow now you've come back.'

We went upstairs.

'This is where they sleep. My uncle has asthma, and bouts of bronchitis. All the other bedrooms are empty, except mine. Herc's my room. I ought to move but this is where they put me when I was a girl and this is where I've stayed. It's a room I hate and yet I felt compelled to stay in it. Perhaps now you've come, I can move. This we call the minister's room. It used to be where our father and mother slept when they first came here to live from the house in Pennant, just after I was born. It seems to have rather an Edwardian red plush gaiety about it don't you think? This could have been the bed in which you were born. Dick was born in the other room. The guest room we call it, but we hardly ever have guests except ministers. Where would you like to sleep?'

'It all has an atmosphere of long-ago,' I said. 'Can I sleep in the bed in which I was born?'

'I'll have it aired by tonight. This narrow passage leads to the maids' rooms. I'm afraid we're not lucky with maids just now.'

'I must go and collect my things,' I said when we came downstairs again.

'Can I make you a cup of tea first? I'm sorry I haven't offered you one before. Where are you staying?'

'Bronllwyn,' I said. I felt a little uncomfortable in saying it. 'But I've already told them there I'm leaving.'

'I see.' She appeared to become more reserved. Was she wondering why I had not come to her first, and what Ada and the doctor and I said about her? I wanted to reassure her in some way, that I always formed my own judgements and that I attached no importance to second-hand opinions. 'You have come to claim what belongs to you?'

We stood facing each other in the dim corridor.

'Yes, I have,' I said. 'That is why I came. To claim what is legally mine.'

She nodded.

'You still think it would be wise for me to stay here tonight?'

'I think so,' she said. 'But this *is* your house. It is for you to decide.'

I was wondering whether to shake hands. She stood quite still in front of me, a small grey figure. Always as if she wanted to say more.

'Wait a moment,' she said. 'I'll get you the key. The master of the house should come in when he likes.'

She handed me the key. It was large and old-fashioned. I slipped it into my coat pocket.

'I'll be back soon,' I said. 'We have a lot to talk about.'

She nodded, smiling. 'You have the key. It's your key now.'

VII

At the post office I got Margaret's letter.

I can't marry you, Philip. It would never work. I must tell you at once. I tried to tell you at the station... Physical attraction isn't enough, Philip... and it isn't as if I don't admire your work, I honestly do, as much as I admire you, but I don't understand it any more than I understand you... My father's right basically. Marriage is something between families. It's got to be, in order to be a success... Romantic love is one of the things that's gone wrong with the world... Your kind of anarchistic rationalism is out of date, Philip. Much as I like you, I couldn't live with it... You see I'm too conservative for you... but you'll say I've just talked myself into doing what Daddy wants. He didn't tell you it was John Neade he wanted me to marry. I haven't thought about that yet. I wanted to get things straight between you and me Philip... And I know by writing like this, I'm writing my way out of your heart.

It was the *writing my way out of your heart* that stuck in my throat. It was all so bloody obvious, I can't see how I couldn't have seen through it all along. No wonder Neade was so anxious to dispatch me to Wales. And Margaret, to whom I had entrusted everything, she wasn't any better. She was on their side. One of the effete, daughter of a jack-in-office wire-puller, a degenerate imitation of an old English aristocrat, shoring up the ruins of another class to protect themselves from the remorseless forces of history that would dash the lot of them into splinters like a doll's house under a steam roller.

Margaret. Margaret. I walked back to Bronllwyn through the woods, angry and determined not to give way to weeping. But lonely, under a leafless tree, and sorry for myself as if I had reached the end of the world.

VIII

I had no lunch. In the house there was no one about and I wondered what to do. I could pack, but I wasn't in a hurry any more. I had come to this place for nothing. A wild goose chase while friend Neade was dazzling Margaret out of her five-minute misery. A nice clean English girl she was who wrote poems and kept her dark eye fixed on the main chance. Neade and publishing, of course. I swore at her to try and dull the terrible ache and emptiness inside me.

That it should happen like this when I was seeing myself on the verge of becoming a new man; returning to Cambridge, mature, tolerant, ready to tolerate her father because I had some wealth of my own, because I knew all there was to know and there were no more family secrets left; ready to deal wisely with people – my aunt, de Veina Grooves, Swades, John Neade. Damn the lot of them. Wisdom and Power and Mastery out of this solved Mystery, that would make her love me more. I must have known all along she didn't love me enough. I wanted to deceive myself, and this was the end of the deception.

The house was big and still among its untidy lawns and gardens. I walked aimlessly about. Golden yews needed trimming. There were pools and statuary hidden among the overgrown bushes. Whole place needed tidying up. There was a stone summer house at the top of the front garden. With holes in the roof. From there Ada had told me there was a view of the village and the estuary. And across the estuary low hills. The tide was coming in, and the shadows of the morning clouds were longer than the patches of sunlight on the water.

I saw Ada in the stable yard. She was leaning against a wall, her arms lifted above her head and she was crying. There were two buckets of poultry-meal on the ground beside her. I wanted to pass unseen. But a dog barked and she turned her head and saw me.

'Philip!' she said. 'It's all right. I'm not going to ask you for anything. When are you going?'

'Can I have something to eat?' I said. 'I'm rather hungry.'

She made tea for us in the kitchen.

'Nobody's given me a bill,' I said, trying to be jovial. 'I'm the first guest. It would be unlucky to forget.'

'You're probably the last as well,' she said.

'Why?'

'We'll be closing soon,' she said. 'Lack of support, financial and moral. I shall have to make a sale. Care to buy?'

'No thanks,' I said. 'What will you do?'

'Do?'

'Yes.' I tried to show remote but kindly interest.

'Sell and clear out. It was impractical. A stupid dream. Impractical. That's what I used to say to Idris.'

I didn't ask her who Idris was.

'The doctor,' she said. 'He had the money. Well now he's

backing out. Afraid of scandal. That scene last night, you know. And the chapel business. Doctor Pritchard has scuttled back to his respectable burrow. Very complicated, Philip. Local stuff. You wouldn't want me to explain it. "I've decided to postpone certain ambitions," was the way he put it.'

'Will you look for a job?' I said.

'Should have cleared out of this hole years ago,' she said. 'That's been my big mistake. Now I'm thirty and I'll get a job at six pounds a week typing, and lodgings in some deadly back street. I don't know how I'll face it. I was so confident everything would work out here. It was a fine idea. All I needed was a little more capital. It was bound to succeed. Only another thousand.'

She was looking at me with frank mercenary hope in her eyes that were still red from crying. I thought quickly of something to stop her from hoping.

'I'm in the same boat myself,' I said. 'I want to go on with my research. There's never enough money.'

I wasn't going to tell her about Margaret. I didn't want to get involved with her more than was absolutely necessary to be polite. My life was sufficiently complicated already. And she was the 'having' type. I could see that. I felt that was why she was being so nice to me. It was quite obvious that she hoped to get money out of me right from the beginning.

When I was going I said, 'Our meeting has been strange. I'm sorry you've had this patch of bad luck. But I wish you all the best. The sun will soon be shining again.'

She looked at me with unhappy objectivity.

'You didn't bring me luck, did you?' She appeared to be

staring beyond me. 'I expected your coming would set everything right. It hasn't turned out like that at all and the joke is I still don't really know what went wrong.'

'Well, cheer up!' I said. 'Let me know how you get on.'

She didn't say anything more so I put my bag in the taxi (it wasn't Frankie this time) and we drove into the town. I left my stuff in the station and went in search of a drink.

HANNAH ELIS

CHAPTER TWENTY-ONE

I

The sea was so calm that morning, level to an horizon of thirty years; still, undisturbable. How could it swell up so suddenly and how long did the shudder from its depths take to thrust upwards and throw me into this elation? He's here. He's here!

Knowing as I do what to do I did in normal simplicity, my heart beating too loudly in the empty house. Two hot water bottles in the minister's bed. Tidying the room. Preparing his place. The room empty, the house empty, waiting. The three trees at the top of Cae Boncan point north-eastward as they have always done and vast clouds sail the same way, and their shadows pass silently over our fields where the seeds last sown still wait in the dark soil.

Should I gather primroses under the little hill for his room?

He is coming. He is coming. He said he was coming. As for Ada he had seen straight through her. I could see that. He was like me; over-suspicious, not gullible. Not gullible like Idris Powell. He was cool and wise and stern and fit to judge and scrupulously fair and strong in his righteousness. He was fairer than my father had ever been; his feet were beautiful upon the mountains because he brought honest tidings, sincere, unbending, correct, undefeatable. His carriage was noble and bright his golden hair. My own brother come back, and here, within reach of my service and devotion.

Understand me quickly. Not like the others. See me at once and test at once the measure of my devotion. When I gave you-him the key did you-he understand? It came to my mind instead of what my poor lips could not utter. See through my unbearable skin of shyness, frightened, sterile, old maidish pride. I have deep in my heart here what I am, inviolable, kept in this, wrapped in this, let me not be too much punished for hiding it in a napkin. I shall act now with certitude and without fear.

I shall escape now. This is the end of my captivity. He will come to judge and I shall take my special place beside him. He will listen to me, and when he is weary I shall wash his feet with my store of unspilled tears and dry them with my grey hair.

The doors of this house shall fly open. The shadows that have stood in frozen stillness since the day of my father's death, shall all vanish. Philip the stranger from the south, brings all the birds of hope all the flowers of joy; and the old house becomes a new house, accustomed to laughter and free voices and the future heavy with the long memories of cloudless childhood.

Nothing they do can keep him out. He must come and they must go. Evil, guilt, remorse, when broken and buried become harmless as sheep's bones rotting gently in the purifying earth, the long darkness. They must accept the darkness, go out to meet it.

II

Tea was ready. The bread and butter was cut. I laid four places. The grandfather clock ticked so loudly in my solitude my waiting heart could barely stand it. In the kitchen I heard the maids march in, their clogs striking the stone floors. I heard their absurd chatter as they carried milk churns down the corridor to the dairy, with Morus the Milkman, their favourite who delighted them with bawdry. I heard their stupid cackle above the hum of the separator. Morus started it in the stiff first stages and then the maids took it in turns and the speed-bell clanged rhythmically to tell them how fast to go. They chattered and laughed and screamed loudly because they knew my uncle and my mother had not come back.

'Auntie, auntie, auntie oh!' Morus chanted and the maids screamed with laughter. 'Oh! OH! Auntie Oh! Auntie, auntie, auntie. OH!'

But today I was not concerned with life moving at that level, and therefore patient with it. Whatever they might say about me was of no consequence. My brother had come and I had acquired power and strength and indifference. My mother came in first, walking faster than usual, I thought, although she always moved quickly. Nothing for her between complete stillness and rapid movement. Victim of her own obscure pain.

Divesting herself of her fur, she stopped and looked at the table.

'You've laid for four, Hannah,' she said. It annoyed her.

'Hannah's laid tea for four,' she said to Uncle Vavasor as he came in, breathing heavily, and groping towards his armchair, into which he slumped with a struggling sigh, switching his cap, and then stretching his hands to the fire.

'It gets cold towards evening,' he said.

I made tea. My mother watched me make it. I remembered how fanatically she used to make me adhere to her formula. *Heat the pot, Hannah!* she said. *Get it hot!* she said. *Let the water boil. Two and a half, no more, no less. Pour to soak and let it stand. Keep the kettle on the boil. In a minute add the rest.* That's the way I was doing it now and she was watching me critically even as she spoke.

'A weak man, that's his trouble,' she said. 'I was against giving him a call, right at the beginning. I never took to him.'

Uncle Vavasor sighed and shook his head.

'A weakling,' she said. 'Doesn't know how to behave and doesn't know what to think. Never made a stand on any issue worth while. Peace. Or Patriotism. Never heard him say a word against gambling or drinking. Never a word against that hussy at Bronllwyn. And now he creates this fuss out of nothing except his slobbering infatuation. What right has he to oppose Norman Parry's candidature for the ministry? What right has he to point a finger at anybody? Dragging our church in the mud, before the whole Presbytery.'

'I liked his sermons,' Uncle Vavasor said.

'I never did,' my mother said. 'He never made a stand over anything. Academic sermons I would call them. But think of it. A Presbytery Commission coming to Bethania, as if we were a pack of illiterate heretics or religious hooligans. And it's all his fault. If he had the slightest sense of decency he would resign. This will do the church terrible harm. He's worse than weak: he's irresponsible.'

I was sorry for Idris but what could I do? So much of what my mother said was still right, although it was she that said it. Unpleasant truth; but there was no getting away from it. Perhaps afterwards, Philip, when I explain it to him, will help see justice done. Often the stranger brings the clarity that the near-sighted and involved cannot use. When Philip came I would be Idris' advocate before him. A place would be found for him under the new regime because he was faithful to many things that mattered.

I listened for his footsteps. He would come in half an hour. It would take him so much time to collect his things, so much time to do this or that and he could be here any minute. But I gave him half an hour.

'Hannah,' my mother said. 'You're not listening to anything I say. Do you want to come with me?'

'Where?'

'I've just been telling you. I said we ought to visit the Parrys. They ought to know that we support them. Do you wish to come?'

'No, thank you.'

'Do you still sympathise with this man Powell?'

'I don't agree with him, Mother. But I'm sorry for him.'

'Don't waste your pity. Sentimentality. Won't help matters. You should come with me.'

'My asthma has been very troublesome today...'

'Fine excuse,' she said, preparing to go and not expecting me to answer.

'It's not an excuse.' It burst out of me angrily. 'It's the truth. I'm not afraid of the truth. And not afraid of saying it.'

She stood by the door, adjusting her fur and eyeing me coldly.

'What are you talking about?'

'Don't be long, Mary,' Uncle Vavasor said. He wasn't aware of our hostility. He did seem to be left alone in his partial blindness with his own thoughts. How close they were to one another; tied close by old secrets they would not share aloud even with each other. And he, being older and weaker, more closely tied, more aware of ultimate helplessness. He was more ready to submit than she would ever be. If she knew what was coming, would she be less confident, hurrying out to the car, the arbiter of local affairs, going to settle one more disturbance of the status quo?

I could not leave the house. He might come any moment and I should be there to receive him. It was my duty, my function, my purpose. Unless I had it my life would lose its meaning. It was my right and I could not risk losing it, even though I wanted to leave Uncle Vavasor. His presence depressed me. He was something that should be put out of sight. He disturbed me; his helplessness pulled at the strings of my old pity for him, just as I was trying to assemble myself to play my part worthily when Philip should come.

It was too cold to sit in the middle parlour. I stood for some time in the breakfast room, watching through the window the men washing on the stone steps of the stable loft. Owen Owens was shaving as usual without a mirror. I shave better, I heard him say once, in a hurry without a mirror. Afterwards he would polish his big brown boots and leggings, and pump his bike. He was going to visit his family. Nor could I sit in the kitchen and listen to the chatter of those two half-witted sisters.

'You are restless, Hannah,' Uncle Vavasor said. 'Why don't you sit down and read to me?'

'What shall I read?' I said, sitting down despairingly. The lamp was lit. It was growing dark. Would he never come? My uncle handed me the Bible.

'Isaiah,' he said. 'Something from Isaiah.'

My hands seemed too weak to hold the Bible. It was like lead on my knees.

'Behold my servant, whom I uphold: mine elect, in whom my soul delighteth; I have put my spirit upon him: he shall bring forth judgement to the Gentiles.

He shall not fail nor be discouraged, till he have set judgement in the earth and the isles shall wait for his law.

I the Lord have called thee in righteousness; to open the blind eyes, to bring out the prisoners from the prison, and them that sit in darkness out of the prison house...

I read as my heart demanded, dreaming wildly among my own purposes. My uncle's eyes were closed, his hands lay in his lap and I knew he was dozing. He heard and did not hear. And I heard music over and above the words.

Who is this that cometh from Edom, with dyed garments from Bozrah? This that is glorious in his apparel, travelling in the greatness of his strength? ... for I will tread them in mine anger and trample them in my fury ... for the day of vengeance is in my heart and the year of my redeemed is come...

Someone was coming. Was it him at last? At last? As I wondered, Uncle Vavasor sat up with a start.

'Your mother's coming back,' he said. And still he had not come. And still I was waiting in my life-long posture, between patience and despair. She came in so pleased with herself.

'I'm glad I went,' she said. 'The Parrys were very grateful. It's good to see people appreciate what one does for them. They're very loyal to us you know. They were saying that Doctor Pritchard has taken his wife on a holiday to the south of England. It looks as if he has backed out of that Bronllwyn business, I'm glad to say.'

Why hadn't he come? Should I tell them now of his coming? Stop her vainglorious eulogy of her own wisdom. Just say: '*A young man called today*. Oh yes. *Said he was a relative.* Oh yes. *Said he was my brother.* Oh yes. What? What? *My brother. My father's son come back – come back to claim his inheritance*. With what terrified shrieks would she rush out into the night, into the woods above Bronllwyn to become the slave of an owl?

'Aren't you coming to bed, Hannah?' My mother held her candle high.

'Good night,' Uncle Vavasor said. 'Good night. Leave

her alone, Mary. She wants to read.'

I would wait. As I used to wait for Dick. In the same darkness, the same uncertainty. I would wait later than that. Up to midnight, up to the last hour. For him perhaps, with his foreign habits, it was still early. But where was he and what could he be doing? I had waited so long so patiently all these long years, but these last hours were intolerable. I would commit any folly to get hold of my brother, but find him, bring him at once to me, to where he should be. He had to come. He had to. He was a scientist, a serious person, kind to me, fair, not like Dick. He would not disappoint me.

III

'No. I won't come in,' he said. 'I'm sorry. I mean I shall only come in for a moment.'

He followed me through the cold breakfast room to the little parlour where I had kept food warm for him on the hob.

'But I've prepared your bed. Where will you sleep tonight?'

'I shall be all right,' he said.

'I've kept this hot for you,' I said. 'A boiled chop. And you can put butter on it. Farm butter. I'm rather fond of it. I'm not a very good cook, but I don't do this badly. You put spices in the water. It's so easy. Do have some.'

'I'm not hungry,' he said. He didn't seem to hear much that I was saying. 'I'm leaving it to my lawyers,' he said. 'I shan't stay here. I must go back.'

'But we agreed this afternoon you would spend the

night here. I've prepared your room. This is your house. Why shouldn't you stay here? Where will you sleep?'

'Things have changed,' he said. 'I've had bad news.'

I looked at him in the lamplight. I was slow seeing that he had been upset.

'I don't want to see them,' he said. 'The fewer people I see the better. I don't understand people. I never did and it doesn't look as if I ever will. I'm a scientist. I understand dead tissues. Nothing else.'

'I was engaged to be married,' he said.

I held out a cup of warm milk and he took it.

'What has happened?' I said. 'Is she ill?'

'Margaret? No. Nothing like that. No. She's fine. It's just that she's written me a letter.'

He unclenched his fist so that I could see the crumpled paper. Then he tossed it into the fire.

'Bad news?' I said.

'Exactly,' he said. 'Breaking it off. That's the technical term.'

'You want to go back and reason with her?' I said.

'No,' he said. 'No. I don't want to do that. Ten years ago I might have run back. Not now. I'm too old for that sort of thing.'

'Stay here then,' I said. 'Why don't you stay here?'

He shook his head.

'I can't pretend this place means anything to me. I'm a stranger here. I didn't come here looking for roots, if that's what you think. I came for practical reasons. I wanted money to get married. I wanted to realise my invisible assets. I was in a hurry. Well I'm not in a hurry any more. I fancy Margaret will marry my old friend John. Just to please her father, of course. That's the other reason why I came here. Just to please her father. Now I can see he was working against me all the time. They were all against me. Stop me getting a fellowship. Stop me getting on. Stop me getting Margaret. I don't fit in there. And I don't fit in here.'

I made him sit down by the table. I made him eat.

'That's life for you,' he said. 'People you like, you admire, people you love, you can't trust them. You can't trust anybody. From now on I'm going to mind my own business. Mind my work. I know where I am with that. I can get results there. I'm happy there. In the lab. From now on I'm going to stay there.'

'This morning you weren't like this,' I said.

'This morning I was a different person,' he said. 'Different motives. Different purposes. This morning I believed I was on the edge of a great discovery. I was a different person. Then or now, what does it matter who I am? I'm pretty useless outside a laboratory.'

'Please stay tonight,' I said.

He looked at me as if he was beginning to understand how urgently I asked him, but did not intend to allow himself to be persuaded.

'She didn't want to be my mother,' he said. 'I don't want to be her son. That's all there is to it.'

'Except that she got rid of your father,' I said.

'Do you believe that? Do you believe she killed him?'

'She was glad he died. I'm certain of that.'

'But depriving him of water, killing him in effect. A man

in that condition. Do you believe that story? I heard it this morning.'

'It's difficult to know exactly what to believe. When she sees you we shall know.'

'And how much better will we be for knowing?'

'There are things we must know in order to go on living.'

'I don't see it like that at all,' he said.

'If you're afraid of course,' I said, 'you had better go. I suppose she is rather formidable...'

'Good God, I'm not afraid of her,' he said. He looked at me again. I must have been crying because I tasted salt suddenly on the corner of my lip. 'If it means so much to you, I'll stay the night.'

IV

I could not sleep. It was as it should be. I had done nothing wrong. He was no guest or intruder. He slept in his own house. He was my brother and I had a right to persuade him. Would his presence work upon her soul even in sleep and force her to get up and find him? I wished that. I willed that. In the night I wanted her to wake up and walk to the minister's room with the candle high above her head, so that the light would fall upon his sleeping face and she should witness the resurrected image of my murdered father and the guilt inside her would drive her with open arms to embrace her punishment. It was what I willed and wished, but the house was dark and silent and everyone slept. I even got up and walked in the darkness to his bedroom door, and from there to the door of the room where my mother and my uncle slept. I burned for their encounter with a passion that frightened me, and sent me scurrying back to my own bed, bewildered and afraid of myself as if I had discovered in myself for the first time a power of evil I never knew to be there. In my own mind, without dreaming, had I not seen her standing alongside his bed, and the hot grease loosened by her trembling hand, falling upon his face, and he instantly drawing his knife from under the clothes and plunging it into her breast?

I tried to wash my fear away in prayer. When the dawn broke, green and luminous above the dark mountains, I was still asking for forgiveness.

V

'Hannah!' It was mother knocking. I had slept after all. 'Hannah!'

'Who is sleeping in the minister's room?'

I did not answer. I sat up in bed my heart beating. *Go and look* I wanted to say. *Go and look*.

'There are shoes outside the door. Who is it?'

She rattled my door-knob impatiently.

'Go and look,' I said softly.

'What are you saying? Speak up!'

'Go and look!' I said again, still quietly. 'You will know him when you see him.'

I heard her footsteps march away impatiently. I dressed as quickly as I could, glancing out of the windows, observing the signs of a fine day. It was late. The men were coming in for breakfast. I could hear their boots striking the rough surface of the lane. Philip should see them eat, I thought. It was a fine sight. Steaming bowls of bread and milk before fresh weathered hungry faces and Thomas John casting great slices of bread to each man in turn. The odour of dung on their boots to stimulate their hunger. Then I opened my door and I heard their voices. My mother's voice was loudest. 'You have no right to come here whoever you are,' she kept saying, loudly. I could not hear Philip's voice; it was lower; it sounded as if he were in bed. Then I heard my mother hurry downstairs.

VI

I found my Uncle Vavasor alone in the little parlour. He was groping about the table for a spoon to knock off the top of his lightly boiled egg.

'Hannah? Who is this man? Did you bring him here? Where's your mother? She went out very suddenly. I'm worried about her. She's very upset. Can you get me a spoon?'

His hands were shaking and a drizzle of sweat covered his pale forehead. I gave him a spoon. Clumsily he attacked the top of his egg. The egg toppled over and broke on his plate. The yolk spread out. He dipped his spoon in it and popped it nervously in his mouth, then turned it over, and sucked it clean.

'Did you bring him here, Hannah?' he said.

'No. He came here himself.'

'He had no right to come. Absolutely no right. That

woman promised he should never be allowed here. She would bring him up as her own son she said. She's betrayed her trust. Go and see where your mother is.'

'I'll boil you another egg,' I said. I put my hand on his plate to remove it.

'Never mind it. I'm perfectly able to look after myself. I'm not blind. Go and see where your mother is.'

Philip knocked the open door lightly and walked in.

'Good morning,' he said. 'Ought I to introduce myself?'

Vavasor stared at him, blinking furiously, his face twitching.

'You had no business to come here,' he said. 'There was a definite agreement. You have no claims of any kind. Gwendoline Esmor should have told you. Your – my wife – is very upset.'

'She was my mother before she was your wife,' Philip said. He smiled at me as if to show that not only was he not afraid, but that he intended to enjoy the occasion. 'Haven't you been expecting this? You knew I would come sooner or later.'

'It was a legal agreement,' Uncle Vavasor said. 'It should be adhered to. You don't understand the unfortunate circumstances. It was very wrong of that woman to send you here.'

'I came of my own free will,' Philip said. 'I always intended to come.'

'You'll gain nothing by it,' Vavasor said. 'Only unpleasantness.'

'It's natural for a son to be interested in his father's death,' Philip said. His voice seemed to dare the very existence of the walls around us. The trumpets of Israel around the walls of Jericho, mentioning the unmentionable, disrupting the cold false peace; cold chisels cracking the sarcophagus around the forbidden tomb.

'Be careful what you say, young man.' Uncle Vavasor trembled with anxiety. 'Just be very careful. This is a serious matter.'

'I know it is,' Philip said,

I heard my mother coming in through the kitchen.

'Get them all in, Thomas John, and lock them up!' I heard her hard voice giving clear orders. 'We'll do away with the lot of them. They only cause trouble. Better without them.'

When she came in I saw her sleeves were rolled up above the elbows. In one hand she held a bill-hook and in the other she grasped tightly by the neck a decapitated cockerel. The blood had spread over her hand and splashed up her naked arm. There was a spot on her cheek and another on one of her black earrings. These cockerels were her own buying and special care. Every evening she went to great trouble to shepherd them into their hut with unusual patience, determined to preserve them from a fox she was convinced was haunting the neighbourhood.

'Mary!' Uncle Vavasor said. 'Is that you? I'm trying to tell this young man it wasn't our fault that his father died. He had every care. He had no business to come here upsetting us like this. His father had every care and no expense was spared...'

'Trouble with these bastards!' my mother said, holding up the dead cockerel. Blood was still dripping on the carpet. I realised then that my uncle hadn't seen what she was carrying. 'Cut their heads off! That's the way to deal with the little bastards.'

Uncle Vavasor's mouth fell open.

'Mary! What's the matter with you, woman? This young man I'm telling you, says he's Elis' son. He's trying to insinuate serious charges about his father's death. I'm telling him it wasn't our responsibility. It wasn't our fault. What have you got there in your hands?'

'Felix?' My mother cocked her head to one side and stared myopically at Philip through her bifocal glasses. 'His own wicked fault of course. Everyone knows he deserved what he got. To hell with him they said and that's where he went. And they made me a justice of the peace. He was a traitor. He betrayed me. He betrayed Wales. He betrayed God! Only one medicine for treason.'

'Mary!' Uncle Vavasor was frightened and fighting for breath. 'What are you saying? Pull yourself together! You're going out of your senses. She's not well, Hannah... Hannah... Your mother's ill.'

'Come to find out about your father?' My mother was looking all the time at Philip. 'I sent you away to save you from knowing. I saved this girl from knowing. Wicked. Abominable. Wicked. Too wicked to live. I put a stop to his tricks. A woman here, a woman there. Lies. Lies. Lies. "Mary," he said, "would you like to read my diary for last week? Take a look."' She thrust out the bill-hook towards Philip. '"Interesting reading. You've been in my desk again. Reading my letters. I hate people to read my letters. I hate you to read my letters, Mary," he said, twisting my arm. "If there's anything you want to know I'll tell you.

Just ask me," he said. "Where's the water," he said. "Give me some water," he said. "There isn't any," I said. "It's finished. It's finished." He watched me lift the jug and pour the last drops on the floor. "Mary," he said. "Mary." "No," I said. "Justice," I said. Firm. You've got to be firm. I was firm with him. Cruel to be kind. What's the matter?'

Uncle Vavasor had sat down suddenly and buried his old head in tweed-sleeved arms.

'Want a burning powder, Vavasor? Get him a powder, Hannah. Don't stand there doing nothing...'

'Be courageous, never stumble, brother
Onward through the dark...'

She stopped her unmelodious singing and turned suddenly to face Philip. 'Who are you?' she said. 'You look like him, but you're not him. But he sent you. He can't get out himself. He's stuck there safe and sound. He'll never torture me again.'

She lifted the bill-hook menacingly.

'Better give me that.' Philip held out his hand.

'Don't you try,' she said, backing away from him. 'Don't touch me young man. Don't dare...'

He snatched it from her hand so quickly I barely saw it happen.

'Don't send me to him. He's waiting for me. Don't send me to him...'

They were both old and pitiable and both broken. In one brief moment their reign had ended and I was sorry for them again as I used to be when Dick died. When she was in bed, quite pale and exhausted, I stood by the door waiting for the doctor to come. I had hated her with varying degrees of intensity all my life; but now I didn't hate her anymore.

IDRIS POWELL

CHAPTER TWENTY-TWO

I

Was I going to ruin the church? That was the question. You have to define your terms, I said. I don't know where I got the strength from but I said it and I'm glad I said it even though Lambert was against me. They were all against me of course, but I didn't mind that. In a sense I didn't blame them. My whole actions were an implicit criticism of them and people criticised have a right to hit back. But Lambert. I thought Lambert would have understood. I was so glad when he came to see me, alone as I was in that miserable Manse. Buried alive I was and choking with my own private misery when he knocked the door. I opened the door, and there he was, my old friend. Strong and leonine as ever. Tears stung my eyes. I wanted to throw my arms around his neck.

'The Presbytery has asked me to make a few discreet inquiries,' he said. 'They know we are old friends. I said I would.'

I told him about Ada. I told him so that he would understand.

'Wait a minute,' he said. 'Stop a minute, Idris. You've quarrelled. You just said you've quarrelled.'

'I know. I haven't been happy for a second since, Lambert. Not for one second. When she needed me most I turned my back on her... What right have I got to be offended?'

'Are you telling me everything, Idris? About this doctor now. You're sure it isn't more than a business arrangement between them...?'

'But it's fallen through. I know it has. He's taken his wife away for a holiday. But even if she was his mistress, it's still my duty to help her. Because I love her I want to marry her. Oh God, how can I explain? It's all I'm good for. It is what we must do. It's a duty of love. Never mind about saving her. I need to be saved more than she does and loving her is my way of salvation. You live your way to salvation, don't you, and loving is living.'

'You're making a dogma of desire,' Lambert said.

'No. No, Lambert,' I said. 'You're wrong. It's funny you should say that. I said it myself. But it's wrong. I know what it is to give up a woman's love. No, I want Ada in order to save both of us. It's what I'm for. I don't imagine it will be a pleasure. I shall get on her nerves. She'll make me miserable often. It's making a dogma of my destiny. I want to put my blood into words. There's love in my blood. I want to use it. This is the way. It's a way of living. Not because I want her. Not because she wants me. But because there's love in my blood.'

'You could still use it on other people,' Lambert said.

'I'm not a strong type like you, Lambert. I'm weak. I've only got just enough strength to sustain my weakness, to accept it. And my weakness says Ada. The little happiness I get with her is the jumping off point into real suffering. It's an excuse for taking what I want. But it's also a trap I fall into voluntarily. That's the way I've got to take advantage of. Can you see that?'

'But she won't have you.'

'Maybe not. But I must keep on trying. I can't give up so easily. She's bound to need me sooner or later.'

'You'll make a fool of yourself.'

I laughed at him. 'I've been doing that for years.'

'Well let's get down to this Norman Parry problem. You've written to the Presbytery opposing his candidature for the ministry?'

Then I told him the story of Norman spying on me. I told him how the boy had shadowed me in the streets of Derwen, like a ridiculous amateur detective, finding out what I was doing and where I was going. And how we'd caught him red-handed at Bronllwyn.

'They thought I would collapse under the first whiff of grape shot,' I said. 'Well they were wrong there. I'm not as weak as I look. You're sitting there listening to me but I don't mind saying it. I asked myself then, how would old Lambert handle this? Anyway I decided to get in first. I gave them a sermon first. I got the idea of it from you; you know, your sermon on Luke 18, X. I attacked self-righteousness and spiritual pride. Modern Pharisees appealed to conventions of respectability and claimed these as the Law of the Prophets. Not on man's ability to do good or bad did his salvation depend, I said. You know the line. I said the Pharisee's prayer was the prayer of the regular chapel-goer, the respectable and successful man. Feeling better than other people, pride, self-satisfaction, were his sins. Respectability and religiosity were no substitute for loving kindness, mercy, and humility. All the Publican asked for was for mercy and that's all any of us have got a right to ask God for, I said.'

'What effect did it have?' Lambert said.

'They were quiet, dead quiet. I don't mind saying it was the best sermon I ever preached becausc it was really yours not mine. Never preached better in my life and I think it affected them. Some were sullen and some uneasy, but I thought a lot of them were moved as well.'

'What happened then?'

'I came down from the pulpit and I said that I had an announcement to make. They were all very quiet. None of the Elises were there, that made a difference. Nobody quite knew what to do next. A ship without a rudder. I expect they thought I was going to announce my resignation. They had rather a shock. "Dear brothers and sisters," I said, "as you know we have as a church passed on to the Presbytery the name of our young brother Norman Harris Parry as a worthy and suitable candidate for the ministry. It is now my distasteful duty to inform you that Norman Harris Parry's conduct has not been what I would consider worthy of a person who wishes to become a minister of the Gospel of our Lord Jesus Christ, and I must now ask you to reconsider our recommendation of his candidature in the light of what I have to tell you. For the past few weeks Norman Harris Parry has devoted a great deal of his time to following my movements and spying upon my private affairs." At this point, Parry Castle Stores jumped up from his seat and shouted angrily, "How much am I supposed to stand from this adulterer!" Then the uproar broke out. It was the kind of scene I never imagined could happen in a chapel and I never want to see it again. Norman Harris ran to the Big Pew without anyone's permission or invitation and stood there pointing at me. "Yes I followed him, and I can tell you who he was with and what he was doing and I'm not ashamed of what I did. I did it for the sake of the church. Is he ashamed? Ask him that. Consorting with the scum of the town and turning his back on the people who support him. What right has he to do that?" Emrys Wynne stood up. "Dear Friends," he said, "without taking part in this quarrel, may I ask those concerned not to raise their voices in the House of God?" "The lad's got a perfect right to defend himself!" Parry Castle Stores said. "His career's at stake. His whole future. It's no light matter." "I only wish to point out..." Emrys Wynne said. "Sit down! You're not in school now!" one of Parry's relatives said. It was Ned Kiff I think. A butcher's mate in the slaughterhouse. I decided my last chance to assert my authority was to go back into the pulpit. I walked up the wide carpeted steps as dignified as I knew how to be. Before I reached the top hands grabbed me from behind. "He shan't go there again!" someone said. I lifted my hand to clutch the pulpit rail and draw myself up out of their reach. But this allowed them to pull me when I was off balance. I fell backwards down the pulpit steps.

'I can't say exactly who pulled me down. But Ned Kiff was there and he had no business to be in the Big Pew. Seeing me on the ground seemed to sober everyone up. Most of the congregation began to leave. I didn't move. I could smell the dust on the red carpet. My nose was on it. Some members came up to me and held out their hands. That comforted me, Lambert.'

Lambert had let his pipe go out. Every time I paused for his comment he said nothing. Now I stopped speaking. I was rather hurt because I felt I had tried to give an objective account of what had happened and Lambert wasn't appreciating my objectivity. I remember giggling to myself when I thought of saying that it wasn't every day a minister got dragged out of his pulpit and told the tale without trying to deny his own culpability; but I didn't try the remark out on Lambert, because he looked so serious and worried. To him, obviously, I was a great problem. It was odd now that the worst had happened, I wasn't worried at all anymore.

'Well,' I said. 'What are you thinking?'

Lambert eyed me but didn't answer.

'Go on,' I said. 'Say what you think!'

'You must resign,' Lambert said.

'I'm not sure that I should,' I said. 'Maybe this is a chance to start afresh. The best people in the congregation have said they'll back me up. I never had so much support before.'

'That's why I say you must resign, and resign quickly,' Lambert said. 'You are on the verge of founding two warring factions, if you haven't founded them already. Once you've done that it will take the church twice as long to recover from this mess.'

'You call it a mess,' I said. 'Perhaps you are right. It is a mess. Worse than any I've ever heard of. Nobody can be thinking worse of me than I think of myself. But remember Jeremiah's parable about the potter's vessel.'

'Do you see yourself as the potter who can remould it?' Lambert said.

'I don't know,' I said. 'I'm not sure.'

'I'm sorry,' Lambert said. 'I'm sure you couldn't. You should never have come here, Idris. You're not tough enough to crack this kind of nut. But it's too late to talk about that now. There is one thing you can do; clear out quickly.'

'And admit I'm wrong. I'll admit I've been foolish...'

'That's the worst sin of all, Idris.'

'Not the kind you're likely to be troubled with, of course,' I said. I was thinking of Enid and the sacrifice I'd made, as it seemed at that moment, for his very sake. Hadn't I rushed here, into this trap, in order to save his marriage? It was his problem as much as mine.

'Let's keep to the point,' Lambert said.

'Very well. I thought a minister's business was to teach his congregation the way of loving-kindness, humility, mercy, reconciliation. Well there are some people who can't see these things because they're petrified in their own sanctity, embalmed in their own respectability, in love with the image of their own importance. Only an explosion like this can make such people see a glimmer of any light other than the glow of their own self-satisfaction.

Is it my job to lull them to sleep in their absurd cradles of self love? Or to wake them up?'

'All right,' Lambert said. 'You've done your demolition work very thoroughly. Now let the rebuilders move in. The technique is different.'

'But I've got a foundation of goodwill towards me here that I can quickly build on.'

'Fifty per cent goodwill; fifty per cent ill-will. They cancel out. The answer is nothing. Look here, Idris. Here's a test. Will you write a letter to the Presbytery withdrawing your objections to Norman Harris Parry?'

'Certainly,' I said. 'The moment he comes to me and apologises.'

'Oh no!' Lambert said. 'Oh no. Without waiting for that. Right away now. Withdraw your objection. Write the letter now.'

'But the fellow's behaviour was contemptible. First he spies and then he insists on justifying this spying. That's the part I can't stomach.'

'You can leave that to the Presbytery.'

'But no one in the Presbytery knows the facts of the case as well as I do.'

'I do, now,' Lambert said.

Suddenly I felt exhausted.

'I've had enough,' I said. 'You must give me time to think it over for myself.'

He nodded. He jumped to his feet briskly and began to draw on the driving gloves he affected. I hated the cheerful way he was looking at me. If he had won it was tactless of him to show it. If only he knew that he wasn't better than I at everything. 'How's Enid?' I wanted to say. Wasn't there a way in which I could damage his self-esteem as thoroughly as he had damaged mine? Just one hint at the great sacrifice I had made for his sake.

'You can't start back now,' I said. 'It's late. Better stay the night.'

'I've got a lecture at nine tomorrow morning,' he said.

'But it will take you two hours to get back,' I said.

He grinned and slapped me on the back.

'You know what, Idris,' he said. 'The children of this world are in their generation wiser than the children of light. The trouble with you is you're too good to be a minister.'

II

I talked endlessly to the man I could not throw off my back.

It doesn't count, what you say, how you argue: it's what you do that counts. (Quoting whose sermon? How much later picking up the word that fell at your feet?) And you do not know what you have done until you see yourself reflected in the judgement of another man's eyes.

'Stay' and 'Go' are rival breezes and you are thistledown and the breezes answer not to you but to the air that envelops God's favourite spinning planet. Stay and fight it out to the point of martyrdom. Resist passively until their own shame overwhelms them and brings them begging for your forgiveness. Go, as Lambert who knows better says. Go, and make way for a wiser man to rebuild the fallen temple.

Alone, an unwanted tenant in an unfriendly house, I can see the follies of which I have been guilty press against every window pane. They are purple ecclesiastical flowers that grow about my slate faced walls and squeeze through the window tops and open their hanging greedy mouths indoors to give off their stale and poisonous odour. Such strong flowers growing rankly out of the midden of piled up mistakes. Had I at the outset set out to show – what? Spiritual strength and inward balance which I have not. They would have responded to such authority, which I have not got. All wavering untidy giggling weakness, I was the push-over asking to be pushed: tempting the arms of people who never dreamt of lifting them before. Lambert was right of course.

You cannot argue neatly with the man on your back. Every answer is a question that answers back. You have only one voice between you and you never know which self of you is yourself talking. Resign. Resign. And 'Resign' can still mean 'Stay' or 'Go'.

III

It was a damp drizzly evening and one could not expect many church members for Fellowship Meeting. But one was the minister, engaged in the minutiae of one's duties, in the vestry, preparing for seiat, the society, the fellowship, the heart, as one has said on numerous occasions, of the church's spiritual life. One placed books on the seats that were usually filled places. One opened the harmonium. Opened the large reading Bible, opened the hymn-book, opened one's heart a little, sitting in the minister's oak chair on the dais in the empty vestry.

Ho, every one that thirsteth, come ye to the waters

etcetera. Come ye to the vestry where the water is displaced by me. I am bitter to taste and I burn the tongue and no one comes near. The heart of the church's spiritual life is empty, bitter and empty. It was time for me to go.

But I did not move from my chair, waiting for strength to perform some Act of Contrition. To turn again having turned again so many times could I ever turn again? A public fool, a well-known failure. Sit there the appropriate length of the service alone. Kneel there twice the length of the service alone. And at the end not know what to do?

Somebody came. I heard the outside door creak; an umbrella being folded and stood upside down on the cold tiles of the vestibule. My heart lifted. One, only one, and yet it would be enough. He pushed open the door and sat down on the nearest seat exhausted, slowly removing the black hat he always wore to come to chapel. It was too big for him and almost rested on his large ears. He nodded at me, a token greeting while he fought for his breath. Having regained his breath, he grasped the back of the bench in front of him and pulled himself to his feet. He placed his hat in its usual place on the window-sill and came forward to shake hands with me as was his custom.

'Wife won't be coming tonight,' he said. 'She isn't well.'

'I'm sorry to hear that, Mr. Elis,' I said. We were both anxious to talk as if nothing much had happened. 'What about yourself. You look rather tired, I must say.'

'Tired? Never mind about me. I'm all right. She's not at all well, Powell. I'm very worried about her.'

He sat down on the front bench and stroked his chin with the tips of his fingers, sniffing rapidly and then gasping for a longer breath than his tight chest allowed him. He took out his large watch and held it close to his face in a way that he had by which he could read the time and then turning round, seemed to realise for the first time that the vestry was empty. But there were others I had not seen enter. Two children had settled down quietly in their place by the radiator. They had already begun on their sweets. This evening I had not heard the tiny rustle of paper. They made their sweets last for an hour, allowing a minute each for standing up and cawing out their verses. They followed my movements with milky blue eyes and open mouths.

'It's time to start, Mr. Powell.'

He meant it. Where two or three I thought are gathered together by force of habit in Thy Name.

'Shall we sing, Mr. Elis?'

'Of course.'

'Then will you choose a hymn?' I said.

He did not open a book. He knew most of the contents by heart. Tonight there was no one but myself to admire his feat and he himself seemed too tired to take his normal pleasure in the exercise of his memory.

'Hymn number sixty-three. The sixty-third hymn.'

My soul, towards Thy God
The fountain of all Grace
Through bitter sorrow, shame,
And all temptation, race....

I read Hebrews, chapter twelve. Then we sang again. Elis' unmelodious croaking dragged behind my untutored tenor.

The children's mouths opened but made no sound. And then I said: 'Will you lead us further in prayer now, Mr. Elis?'

He stood up as he always did in the seiat. He never hurried when praying and he was not afraid of silence like Parry Castle Stores who shot from one sentence to another as if a full stop was an abyss that had to be taken in full flight, to avoid falling into eternal silence.

Elis' lips trembled as they always did before he began. His eyebrows twitched rapidly. But tonight I noticed his head moving slowly from side to side as if he were rocking some crying sleepless grief within himself.

'Almighty and... Almighty... O Lord in the words of Cain, my punishment is greater than I can bear... year after year... from the day my eyes grew dim to this thou hast visited me with these afflictions... Must I speak O Lord... Must I confess as a criminal still when I have accepted each affliction as a just punishment? ...I did withhold aid from a dying man... I was an aider and abettor in his untimely death: the waters of succour trickled away between my opening fingers as they approached his mouth. Thou knowest O Lord how I loved him and how he laughed at my love and how he took her from me, knowing she should have been mine... Thou gavest unto us a son to be the hammer of our peace and I bowed my head and murmured, so be it... Thou...'

He stretched out his arms and suddenly opened his eyes which he had screwed up with the effort of letting his heart speak aloud.

'He doesn't hear me,' he said dully, and sat down.

The small children were making cups out of their sweet

papers and trying to make them stand on the bench shelf in front of them. I often wondered if they had perfected some soundless mode of communication with each other. They were absorbed now in their wordless game.

'God doesn't want me,' Vavasor said. 'He's given me a lifetime to find out that the world would have been better if I had never existed.'

'God is Love,' I said. 'God can forgive everything.'

'He hasn't forgiven me,' Vavasor said. 'Old William Matthers used to talk about the kiss of grace touching our grey cheeks. He won't kiss my cheek.'

He leaned forward to stare at me more closely.

'Think how the Devil has tricked me, Mr. Powell. I worshipped the ground Felix trod on. I'm not saying that now to make out what he did to me worse than it was. I believed in him. He was a genius in his way. I believed he would save the best things of our tradition. I believed he was called to lead. I believed he would be a great man. But he took Mary and laughed in my face about it. Knew where we were to meet. In the lane near the gate. He jumped out of the shadow of the hedge and she thought it was me. She was unwilling but he was irresistible. She wanted me to forgive her and I did. But he only laughed. She was young and she was dazzled by him. She believed everything he said, about her being beautiful and innocent and wise. But after they were married it was another story. She came to me in her unhappiness. I did my best to comfort her. He was cruel. She had a right to complain. He was cruel and immoral. She said he wasn't fit to live and I said the same. A case could be made out for me. I did nothing legally wrong. But I wanted him to die. I longed for him to die. That illness of his was a blessing from heaven. Every day of my life the Devil has misled me and I have taken his lead. Repent you say to me. Repent. I have repented. I have been punished. I have tortured myself believing that I sent my son to his death. And now God has shown his hand. It's the same hand as the Devil's.'

'You're wrong,' I said.

'Of course I'm wrong. My mind tells me I'm wrong. All my theology tells me I'm wrong. But that's what I believe in my heart. That's what I feel. It grips me like a disease. I feel it like a cancer inside me eating me up. I've dreamt about it myself, sitting up in bed looking at my open belly watching the cancer at work. It's bigger than me. It weighs more than me. I'm only skin and bones around it. Waiting to be eaten up.'

'Pray as you used to,' I said. 'Pray...'

'My prayers can't get outside my skull,' he said. 'They rub themselves out against the bone of my skull. They can't get out. God can't get in. He doesn't want to. What can he want with me? I'm a burden no one wants. A blind man condemned, marked, turned out.'

He got up as if the service was over and shuffled towards his black hat. He was older. He looked frail and finished.

'Wait,' I said. 'Wait, Mr. Elis. I haven't said anything to...'

'Can you tell me anything I don't know already? The commandments are engraved on me like an epitaph on a tombstone.'

I told him it wasn't too late. That even now God's grace could reach him. I told him it was wrong for a man to despise himself. I spoke too quickly perhaps. He didn't seem to hear me. I felt as if I were telling a dying man that he would not die.

'I don't hear anything,' he said. 'I hear your voice and I can follow what you are saying but it doesn't mean anything. I know how to make out a case for myself. I've been doing it for thirty years. It doesn't make any difference any more. Everything's settled.'

'Nothing is impossible,' I said. 'Nothing is ever settled.'

'With me it is, Mr. Powell.' He hurried off towards the door as he always did as if he had endless business affairs waiting for his attention. 'Good night now then,' he said, as he always did leaving chapel.

IV

I was preparing my own supper when they knocked at the front door.

'Is my uncle here?' Hannah said.

'No. He went home after seiat,' I said.

'He's been in chapel then,' she said.

'Of course. Just as usual.'

'When did he leave? Did you see which way he went?'

'About twenty minutes ago. Surely you must have passed him on the way?' I was staring at the tall sandy-haired young man standing behind her.

'I'm sorry. This is my brother; Philip, this is Mr. Powell, our minister.'

He bowed coldly so I did not hold out my hand.

'Is there anything I can do? What is the matter exactly?

He told me your mother was ill.'

'Her mind,' Hannah said, her thin lips even tighter than usual. 'Her mind is sick.'

I was thinking of what the old man had told me when I heard her say:

'We must find him, Philip. He's not fit to be out alone. I'm sorry we've disturbed you, Mr. Powell. If you'll excuse us, we must go now.'

I ran after them to the car.

'I'll come with you,' I said. Philip was already seated in the front. I put my head in and he seemed to find it distasteful to have my face close to his. 'If you don't mind.'

I heard him speak for the first time.

'It's hardly necessary,' he said. 'It's purely a family worry.'

'He said things to me in chapel,' I said. 'We were alone together. I'm sorry I let him out of my sight. He needed me.'

I got in the back. Philip did not turn round to speak to me. I knew he disliked me at sight. It hurt me that so many men should take against me at sight. What he would hear of me he would not like. Good sound rational steady men so dislike a fool.

How blindly I had been locked in my own predicament not to have perceived long ago the old man's agony. Proof, if I needed any more proof, that I was a failure as a minister. Sitting in the darkness in back of the car I longed for a fresh start. I thought about Vavasor Elis and I wondered what I could have done to help him. What guidance could I have given him, what solace, what remedy? I should have spent my wasted years in this place preparing myself to be a fit vessel through which God's grace could have operated upon the teeming inward hell-bent miseries racking so many of the souls entrusted to my care. I was unprepared for anything. My lamp untrimmed even for this search in the wide unfriendly night. If I found him what would I say?

The search went on far into the night. The drizzle stopped and the moon came sailing above the clouds. It was a poor search. No one took much notice of me. Perhaps the family were unwilling to declare a general hue and cry, although all the men in the farm were out. I made for the old church in the field near the shore. Vavasor's cousin, the man whom he had loved and allowed to die, was buried there. If his ghost was not at rest on such a night he should walk abroad and I should be the one to meet him. I even imagined rescuing the old man from some paroxysm of fear before his cousin's grave. But the churchyard was utterly silent and deserted. I saw only the immense unconcern of the windy night sky. Perplexed which way to turn next, I stood on top of a wall near the foreshore. I saw a single lantern bobbing as some searcher crossed the potato field, swinging and bobbing helplessly as the man who carried it struggled across the wet furrows. No one seemed to shout as I did at first. The men seemed to feel that Vavasor would not have liked it. They still saw only the man who had filled his position with dignity and assurance along the years.

Returning to the house, I saw a light burning in his bedroom. I imagined he had been found and I broke into an agitated run; until I realised it was his wife there. They had preferred me not to see her. 'What can you do?' Philip snapped. 'She's insane. What can you do?'

There was one more place I wanted to search.

'The shop,' I said when I came in. 'Has anyone been to the shop?'

'We went there first,' Philip said, 'before coming to your house.'

He made me feel every suggestion I made was unwelcome.

'He may have gone there afterwards,' I said. 'He may have turned back from wherever he thought of going and gone there instead of coming home. He may have felt this wasn't his home any longer.'

Somehow the place had already changed. A reign had ended. Philip sat in the chair Vavasor had always occupied and the old man's indoor cap lay unheeded on the floor. It was I who picked it up. But when I held it in my hands I didn't know where to put it. I wanted to put it back on the odd shelf which seemed truly odd now on the top of the high backed chair. But not while Philip sat in it, his long legs stretched out, gloomily sucking his knuckles. When we were in the car again (Hannah politely insisted on taking me home, although I said I could easily walk) the cap was still in my hands. I let it drop on the floor there. No one spoke during the journey, until driving down the street Hannah said quite suddenly, 'There's a light in the back of the shop. He must be there.'

She pulled up the car with a jerk. We found that the shop door was locked and no one had the keys. Leaving me there in their haste, Hannah and Philip drove off to

Emmanuel Elis Jones' house for the keys. I stayed there until they returned. Mannie was with them and they seemed surprised to see me still waiting. Mannie nodded stiffly. He had been got out of bed, but in his overcoat, scarf and hat he was at his most important. No hands but his should turn the keys that opened the shop door.

We found Vavasor Elis at the sink in the dispensing room. He had knocked over several bottles in some blind effort to reach the water tap. It dripped now over his motionless head, soaking part of his hair and running down into his tweed coat.

Mannie broke down. He was unable to phone the police. Philip had to do that. Hannah sat on a chair with a broken back, staring at her uncle as if the secret of the change in his condition could be brought to light. Mannie turned to me. He was weeping and longing for someone to speak to. His jaw trembled. The scarf had slipped out of place and I could see the pyjama jacket beneath. I could make out what he was trying to say.

'Such a good man ... why did he ... I never had so much respect for anybody. What can I...'

I wanted to pray. Pray for the soul of. Beginning the last rites for. Exercise my proper office, kneel there in that room. It could have been effective, efficacious. Very sweet, right, and proper so to do. Instead I comforted Mannie.

HANNAH FELIX-ELIS

CHAPTER TWENTY-THREE

I

When I was ill I remembered Uncle Vavasor's head under the tap and the patch of water soaking his faded hair and immobile tweed shoulder. It used to be a habit of his to stretch out and tighten taps to stop them dripping. He hated waste.

Philip was good. I saw Dr. Bartholemew was afraid of him. But Bartholemew was afraid of his shadow. Philip said he wasn't much of a doctor. He said he made suggestions so that Bartholemew believed the diagnoses were his own. It was one of Philip's endearing misconceptions, this notion of himself being tactful. He stayed with me all that terrible week, and he was wonderful. I was still alive.

II

'There it is, Hannah,' he said. 'That's the difference between us. You've got Roots. I haven't.'

'Anybody can have roots if they want them,' I said. 'Human beings are like strawberry plants.'

'Maybe.'

'But you don't want them perhaps,' I said. We were sitting on either side of the little parlour fire a few days after Uncle Vavasor's funeral. Just as he and my mother used to. The same and yet absolutely different, not different and absolutely the same. Philip sat in his chair, I sat in hers. He had arranged for me to have all the nursing I needed. It was wonderful to have him behind me.

'I can't stay here. I'll just have to take "here" with me.' He smiled at me. 'Sorry, Hannah. All this Welsh stuff, chapel, traditions, language, family, it's too much for me to swallow at one go. Are you sure you won't come with me to Switzerland? You ought to see Europe, Hannah. And I could arrange the most up-to-date treatment for you there. You'd like it very much.'

'The farm needs me,' I said.

'I'm not sure you're well enough...'

'It does need me, Philip. It's good to be needed.'

We fell silent. He stood up and peered through the window at Thomas John crossing the yard with a sack on his back.

'What's he carrying? Never mind, he's gone now.' He came back to his seat and stretched out his legs to the fire. 'Hannah, I shall have to be getting back to my job.'

'I've been waiting for you to say that.'

'Hannah, I've got a grudge against this place.'

'I've been waiting for you to say that. It's keeping you from your job.'

'No, it's more complicated than that,' he said. 'It makes me feel guilty for something I've never done. It's like being punished for an offence before having committed it, if you know what I mean, and being forced to spend the rest of your life finding out what you did wrong. It's this place...'

'I hadn't realised,' I said, rather stiffly, 'you were so anxious to get away.'

He looked at me with unusual calm and patience.

'You see, Hannah. Your reaction proves it.'

'Proves what?'

'It's something I can't explain. A virus that you cannot isolate.'

'You want to sell the farm?' I leaned forward, trembling, waiting for his answer.

He stirred impatiently in his chair as if I had brought up a subject that did not concern him.

'I've told you, Hannah, the place is yours.'

I ventured to joke.

'I know,' I said. 'To hell with property.'

He looked up and smiled. And I suppose that was enough for me.

He said it would be all right for me to drive him to the station, and warned me to take the tablets regularly. I was afraid of being alone after he had gone. I was afraid his company was an artificial stimulus and that when it was removed I would be in a worse case than ever before: that our ripening understanding was just my one-sided, wish-fulfilling dream. After all I was my mother's daughter. When I said I felt it was my duty to be at hand in her case, he nodded gravely and seemed to understand. My health was supposed to bring sighs and tears to the surface of the hardest Pennant faces. But looking out through the window before going to bed early I could have shouted out to the whole world that my brother was a hero who had given me all these sweet acres and that at last I had realised that I had what I most wanted in the world.

'Write,' I said, when he was in his compartment.

'Yes, I'll write,' he said. 'I've got a lot to sort out in me, haven't I?' I wanted to say something: that a communication of this kind, once begun would never end. But I felt it was the noise of the train that was spurring me on too fast to declarations of intimacy. Between such as Philip and myself, intimacy grows very slowly I was thinking; so I just nodded.

Suddenly before the train began to move he bent out and kissed me. He kissed me!

I waved so happily I might have been watching my own wedding; and I had to remember in Pennant to look as solemn as I could and remember all the bereavement that everyone imagined I was suffering from. Wherever Philip wandered, I knew he would come back. I was something he wanted to need, and not to forget.

III

I called at the Manse. Idris Powell had announced his resignation in chapel last Sunday. I had not been present but Sam Daniel had given me his eye-witness account.

Everything had gone very decently, he said. It was as if, he said, my uncle's death and my mother's illness had brought them all to their senses. They all spoke reverently and quietly. No voices were raised. Reconciliations were made. Idris Powell formally withdrew his objections to Norman Parry and Parry Castle Stores went so far as to ask Idris to reconsider his resignation. Sam Daniel said that the minister paused a long time before replying; and, Sam said, Parry got really restless in his seat in case Idris accepted the offer. But the resignation was a firm one. And I was glad. Because in every way, everywhere, it was time for a fresh start.

I wondered if I could help him. He showed me into his shabby study, running his hand as he always did through his unruly hair. Was I, out of my new sense of well-being, detecting a pitiful shabby unsuccess about him? And had I realised how difficult it would be for him to start again, how absolute was his failure? His very jocularity seemed to depress me more than the drab little room. It seems incredible to me that I had ever looked – even I as I was in all my loneliness – to this so obvious failure for any kind of salvation.

'What will you do?' I asked him. His collar was unclean and his shirt was worn into a tear at the neck. I was genuinely troubled about him. I had not seen him before in so clear a light; so absolute and pathetic a failure. Ready for a shabby protracted martyrdom.

'Oh I'll be all right,' he laughed – but I couldn't. His smile made me uneasy. I did not want to trouble about him any more. 'I'll see the world.'

'How are you?' he said. 'Are you feeling stronger?'

His manner was still ministerial.

'You must take great care,' he said seriously. 'Dr. Bartholemew has been telling me it would be good for you to take a holiday. Why don't you, Hannah?'

It would shock him too much. I decided not to tell him I never felt better in my life. 'I'm quite all right,' I said. 'But it's you I came to talk about. What are you going to do?'

'Oh, I'll manage.'

'But what?'

He didn't answer.

'I suppose it depends on that girl. Does it still?'

He nodded. I could have wept with pity for him. Couldn't I make him pull himself together? Even now.

'She doesn't want you to marry her?'

'No. She doesn't want to see me really. Nor anyone else from Pennant she says. She's been terribly hurt, Hannah. Just think...'

'I'm sorry,' I said. 'Don't think me hard, Idris. But I can't see her as you do. As a sort of special case. Everybody gets hurt. She can look after herself. I wish I could say as much for you.'

He didn't answer.

'So you'll follow her? Wherever she goes?'

'Yes.'

'"Thy people shall be my people"...'

He looked up. 'Yes! That's it exactly. That's...' Then he stopped when he realised that I hadn't been speaking seriously.

Driving home, I passed a notice of Bronllwyn Sale – *For Sale – with Vacant Possession. Delightful Country Mansion Suitable for Conversion to Guest House...* She wasn't wasting any time. Should one buy it to prevent strangers coming and upsetting our way of life? That was exactly what Uncle Vavasor would have said.

IV

As for me, I have a function. If I cease now to complain and moan it is far more than passive resignation: and it is more than a case of the labour of others being beautiful from a discreet distance. When I stop the car in the farm lane because Richard Davies and Idwal are driving a herd of bullocks in front of me, I am very conscious of a certain bucolic charm in the scene, and when I walk into the hay meadow to wait for them to clear, a lark rising out of the half-grown grass in a clear blue sky confirms this impression.

This is far more than a romantic illusion. I can sit alone in the little parlour eating my boiled egg for breakfast and quietly rejoice at the benign complexities of our little world. Things are the same and yet they have changed forever. Doris and Katie have somehow acquired the ability to smile and even sparkle as they wait on me. I am not to wonder how long it will last. Has my change of status effected a change in their natures? Hardly. It is for the time being that our four hundred acres impose their own rituals, and it is my privilege to observe them while I can. A new style has established itself inside the framework of the old. The sisters feel it. They have taken to showing me a respect that borders on affection so I must return it in kind. Their genuine concern for my health encourages me to exercise the gentler forms of authority.

The day's work begins when Richard Davies takes up his stance just outside the open door of the little parlour, the same old cap in his hand, his voice deep and benevolent as ever, my very present help in trouble.

'Good morning to you, Miss Elis. And a fairly good morning it is too.'

My response echoes my uncle's. The voice is different but the formula must be the same.

'Good morning, Richard Davies. How is it to be today?'

'If I were in your place Miss Elis, I would move the stores to Cae 'Refail. It is high time it be done. And Wil bach with his cousin Ned should start thinning the swedes in Cae Ponciau. Idwal has already gone to help Owen Owens with the sheep and they've got a heavy day ahead.'

'And what should I be doing Richard Davies?'

This was an innocent question I knew made him smile even though I couldn't see him.

'Well now,' he said. 'John Jones Tan Graig called after me in the road to tell me the gable end of Beudy Mawr is bulging. As you know he is one for exaggeration, but perhaps you had better see for yourself.'

'Will you come with me, Richard Davies?'

And so we went out. Doris and Katie are invited to walk behind us to make sure I don't fall over and to look for stray hen's nests. Doris carries an extra cardigan in case I feel cold. They are enjoying the walk so much it begins to look like an outing.

Foreword by M. Wynn Thomas

M. Wynn Thomas is Professor of English and Director of CREW, the Centre for Research into the English Literature and Language of Wales at the University of Wales Swansea. He is author/editor of more than twenty critical works on literature, including *The Lunar Light of Whitman's Poetry*; *Internal Difference*, *Twentieth Century Writing in Wales*; *Corresponding Cultures*, *The Two Literatures of Modern Wales*; and *Transatlantic Connections*, *Whitman US/Whitman UK*. His Welsh-language monograph *Emyr Humphreys* appeared in 1989, and in 2002 he edited *Emyr Humphreys: Conversations and Reflections*.

Cover image by Brian Gaylor

Brian Gaylor is a photographer who finds his inspiration in the written word. He has published a book based on the writing of Dylan Thomas and has just completed an exhibition of photography responding to the poetry of Idris Davies.

LIBRARY OF WALES

The Library of Wales is a Welsh Assembly Government project designed to ensure that all of the rich and extensive literature of Wales which has been written in English will now be made available to readers in and beyond Wales. Sustaining this wider literary heritage is understood by the Welsh Assembly Government to be a key component in creating and disseminating an ongoing sense of modern Welsh culture and history for the future Wales which is now emerging from contemporary society. Through these texts, until now unavailable or out-of-print or merely forgotten, the Library of Wales will bring back into play the voices and actions of the human experience that has made us, in all our complexity, a Welsh people.

The Library of Wales will include prose as well as poetry, essays as well as fiction, anthologies as well as memoirs, drama as well as journalism. It will complement the names and texts that are already in the public domain and seek to include the best of Welsh writing in English, as well as to showcase what has been unjustly neglected. No boundaries will limit the ambition of the Library of Wales to open up the borders that have denied some of our best writers a presence in a future Wales. The Library of Wales has been created with that Wales in mind: a young country not afraid to remember what it might yet become.

Dai Smith
Raymond Williams Chair in the Cultural History of Wales
University of Wales, Swansea

LIBRARY OF WALES
FUNDED BY

Llywodraeth Cynulliad Cymru
Welsh Assembly Government